Matt Lynn has ghost-written several successful action adventure novels. As a journalist, he has worked for *The Sunday Times* for many years and now writes a column for Bloomberg in the US and is a regular contributor to the *Spectator*.

By Matt Lynn and available from Headline

Death Force
Fire Force
Shadow Force
Ice Force

MATT LYNN

ICE FORCE

headline

First published in 2012 by
HEADLINE PUBLISHING GROUP

First published in paperback in 2012 by
HEADLINE PUBLISHING GROUP

1

Cataloguing in Publication Data is available from the British Library

ISBN 978 0 7553 7174 7

Typeset in Hoefler by Avon DataSet Ltd,
Bidford-on-Avon, Warwickshire

Printed and bound by CPI Group (UK) Ltd, Croydon, CR0 4YY

HEADLINE PUBLISHING GROUP
An Hachette UK Company
338 Euston Road
London NW1 3BH

www.headline.co.uk
www.hachette.co.uk

To Isabella

Acknowledgements

Without the advice and encouragement of men who know far more about military matters than I do, the Death Force books would never be able to achieve any level of realism or accuracy. Thanks to Rob who taught me some of the basics of both surviving and fighting in the extreme cold of the Arctic. Thanks also to Yuval, who introduced me to the structures of the Israeli Defence Forces, and its relationship with the Mossad. Martin Fletcher and all his team at Headline and Bill Hamilton at A.M. Heath were constantly helpful. And, of course, most of all thanks to my wife Angharad, and my three daughters, Isabella – to whom this volume of the series is dedicated – Leonora and Claudia, who brighten up every day simply by being there.

Matt Lynn, Goudhurst, Kent, March 2011

The Unit

Steve West A South Londoner, Steve served in the SAS for five years, fighting in Bosnia and behind the lines in the second Iraq War. After leaving the Army, Steve started freelancing for Bruce Dudley's private military corporation, Dudley Emergency Forces – an outfit known in the trade as Death Inc. for the high-risk, high-stakes jobs it is willing to take on. With the money he made in Afghanistan – a mission described in *Death Force* – Steve has bought out his uncle Ken's half-share in a vintage car dealership in Leicestershire. At the end of *Shadow Force* Steve discovered that he had a son called Archie, but he has never met him.

Ollie Hall Once an officer in the Household Cavalry, the most blue-blooded of British regiments, Ollie was trained at Sandhurst, and was, for a time, one of the fastest rising young stars in the armed forces. But he had a problem with drinking and gambling, and eventually left the Army to make a career in the City. When that failed as well, he started trying to form his own PMC, before joining up with Steve for the mission in

Matt Lynn

Afghanistan. At the end of *Fire Force*, he breaks off his engagement to Katie, a London PR girl.

David Mallet With twenty years' experience as an officer in the Irish Guards behind him, David is an experienced, battle-hardened soldier, an expert in logistics and military strategy and planning. He is divorced from his first wife, with two children at private schools to pay for. With his second wife, Sandy, he has twins. In *Shadow Force*, David suffers from post-traumatic stress disorder but eventually manages to overcome it.

Nick Thomas From Swansea, Nick spent two years in the Territorial Army before joining Steve on the Afghanistan mission. An only child, he was bought up by his mother Sandra, now working as a lap dancer, and never knew who his father was. He is the man with the least military experience on the team. But he is also the best marksman any of them have ever met, with an uncanny ability to hit a target with any kind of weapon.

Ian 'The Bomber' Murphy A Catholic Ulsterman, Ian grew up in Belfast, and spent ten years working as a bomb-maker for the IRA. He was responsible for several explosions that killed both soldiers and civilians, and was sentenced to life imprisonment. After spending years in the Maze prison, he was released as part of the Good Friday Agreement. He is no longer a member of the IRA, and has severed his connections with his old life. But he is still an expert bomb-maker, able to fashion an explosion out of the most basic components.

Dan Coleman A former member of the Australian Special Air Service Regiment (SASR), a unit closely modelled on the British SAS, Dan fought in Afghanistan as part of an SASR unit deployed against the Taliban. He accidentally killed two children, and spent a year in a military jail, although he always maintained his innocence. Haunted by the incident, he has left the Australian Army, and has taken up freelancing for PMCs. Dan is an expert on weaponry, always aware of the latest military technology, and desperate to try it out.

Maksim Prerova A former member of the Russian Special Forces, the Spetsnaz, Maksim is a suicidally brave soldier. His father was killed in Afghanistan in the early 1980s, and he has a bad vodka habit. During the mission in Afghanistan described in *Death Force* he was tricked into betraying the unit, but was forgiven because he proved himself the most ferocious fighter any of the men had ever seen. Fit, strong and courageous, Maksim is always ready for a fight.

Henri Colbert A sailor with the French Navy, Henri qualified for Commando Hubert, that country's formidable unit of underwater combat specialists. After five years in Hubert taking part in missions around the world, Henri left the French forces and became a freelance consultant specialising in marine security. Brave and resourceful, Henri is a tough soldier, but he is also proud and argumentative, and finds it hard to fit into a team. He joined the unit in the mission against Somali pirates described in *Shadow Force*.

Bruce Dudley A gruff Scotsman, Dudley is the founder and chief shareholder in Dudley Emergency Forces. A former SAS sergeant, he left the Regiment ten years ago, and soon realised there was money to be made from running a private army. He was a legendarily tough soldier himself, and doesn't see why anyone else should complain about terrifying conditions. He has an acute understanding of what makes his soldiers tick, and knows how to manipulate them into fighting every battle as ferociously as he did when he was younger.

Maya Howowitz Maya comes from an Israeli military family. Of Ukrainian origins, her grandmother and much of her family were killed at Auschwitz. Her grandfather escaped to what became modern Israel, and both he and Maya's father were soldiers in the Israeli Defence Forces. Her father went on to become a Kidon, a licensed Mossad assassin. Maya served in the Caracal Battalion, the mixed-sex combat unit created by the Israeli Army. Unofficially, she is also an informer for the Mossad. She is fiercely loyal to the Israeli state. But she has started working in protection for a Russian billionaire because she wants to raise money for a kibbutz that is being converted from agriculture to manufacturing pharmaceuticals. Maya is tough and sexy and confident, and insists she is as skilled a military operator as any of the men – and, on seeing her in action, they are quick to concede that she is right.

Deceased

Ganju Rai A former Gurkha, Ganju served for eight years, in C Company, in the 2nd Battalion of the Parachute Regiment, primarily staffed by Gurkhas. He came from a small Nepalese village, and was fiercely loyal to the traditions of the Gurkha Regiments. Rai's brother, also a Gurkha, was killed in Kosovo, and his wife and children were not getting a pension. Ganju became a mercenary to earn enough money to help support his extended family back home. He was an expert in stealth warfare. He died in the mission described in *Shadow Force*.

Chris Reynolds A veteran of South Africa's Special Forces Brigade, known as the 'Recce' unit, Chris spent fifteen years in the South African Defence Force, and regarded the Recces as the finest fighting unit in the world. But he left the armed forces after he became disillusioned with the post-apartheid regime. He bought himself a farm in South Africa, but when that went bust he was forced to work as a mercenary to pay off his debts, even though it is illegal for South Africans to work for PMCs. He was brutally crucified in Batota, a mission described in *Fire Force*.

Jeff Campbell A former soldier, Campbell came from South London, and grew up with Steve. The two men were best mates. He was the man in the unit with the greatest sense of camaraderie, always organising a party, and making sure everyone had enough to drink. He died from wounds on the mission in Afghanistan described in *Death Force* despite the best efforts of the rest of the men to save him.

One

IT'S HARD TO KEEP YOUR make-up in place when a SIG Saur P220 pistol is pressed into the side of your face, reflected Steve West. Even when you are the third most beautiful woman in the world. Still, he noted with a grudging respect, Aletta Sansome was giving it a bloody good go. If anyone could get out of this scrap without smudging her blusher, then this was the girl for the job.

'What do you reckon, boys?' he asked tersely.

'I'd say third most beautiful woman in the world was pushing it,' said Ollie. 'I mean top ten, fair enough, but there's Keira Knightly to consider, and Angelina Jolie—'

'And Catherine Zeta-Jones,' interrupted David.

'Or Alicia Silverstone,' said Dan.

'Or Kristen Stewart,' said Ian. 'The babe from the Twilight movies.'

'Jesus, pal, that's vampires. Steer well clear . . .'

'I'd shag her,' said Nick.

'Yeah, but you'd shag a tin of frankfurters, so that doesn't really count, does it, mate,' said Ollie. 'Now, we haven't even started to consider Penelope Cruz or Cheryl Cole.'

'For Christ's sake, boys, can you sodding well leave it out,' snapped Steve. 'I *meant* how the hell are we going to save her life?'

The men fell silent, and looked through the pale, early evening light. Aletta Sansome was being held at gunpoint, a hundred yards in front of them, across a deserted stretch of wasteland alongside the District Line as it ran down from Fulham Broadway to Putney Bridge. One of the most famous models in the world, she was dating Chelsea's Argentinian striker Luis Fessi. But she'd been kidnapped, and was being held at gunpoint down by the tube tracks by a group of Thai gangsters intent on making sure Chelsea lost the match and cleaning up on the Far Eastern betting markets.

And it was their job to rescue her.

Steve glanced at his watch. There were only ten minutes left until the second half kicked off. Ten minutes to rescue Aletta and get her back to the ground. Christ, he reflected. When you work in close protection, there are impossible jobs, completely sodding impossible jobs, and then this.

How the hell did we ever get into this mess?

And how the hell are we going to get out of it?

The evening hadn't been planned this way. Half an hour earlier, the unit had been sitting in an executive box at Stamford Bridge, enjoying the first leg of a quarter-final Champion's League game against Barcelona. Steve had been enjoying himself immensely. It was a year since Dudley Emergency Forces, the elite private military corporation for which he'd worked after leaving the SAS, had completed its last job, taking on the pirates in Somalia, and it was great to see all the boys from the unit again. In the twelve months since they'd got back with their lives more or less intact, Steve had been concentrating on building up the vintage car dealership he'd bought from his uncle Ken up in Leicestershire, and although he kept in touch with the rest of the lads via the occasional text message, and some round-robin emails on the latest guns that Dan sent out, he hadn't seen much of the gang since then. He'd missed them, no question about that. They were the finest group of men he'd ever fought alongside. But any contact with the unit usually involved getting shot at, blown up, thrown out of a chopper and forced into a long march under brutal fire though a jungle, or a desert, or a mountain range. And he wasn't going to miss that. Not one bit.

The reunion had been Maksim's idea. The Russian former Spetsnaz soldier was the hardest, maddest warrior Steve had ever met but, like many ferociously fierce men, he was also a loyal friend. In the last few months he'd started working as a security guard for the Russian oil tycoon Alecsei Kolodin. A man who rarely travelled without a platoon of Red Army and Israeli special forces operatives surrounding him, Kolodin was also friends with the Chelsea owner, and Maksim was part of the team arranging security for the oligarch's travelling circus of bodyguards, businessmen, bankers and model girls. Maksim had managed to get an extra ten seats for the unit, and a text had gathered them all together at short notice. Ollie Hall, the ex-Household Cavalry officer who'd been a certainty for general at Sandhurst before drinking and gambling his way out of the Army; Ian 'The Bomber' Murphy, the former IRA man who'd done years in the Maze before being released as part of the Good Friday Agreement; Nick Thomas, the lad from Swansea who'd done a couple of years in the Territorials before lying about his age to join them on the job in Afghanistan; Dan Coleman, the Australian SASR man who now ran a beer bar in Majorca; David Mallet, the former Irish Guards officer; Bruce Dudley, the former SAS sergeant who'd made himself a small fortune from setting up DEF just as private military corporations turned into a boom industry; and Henri Colbert, the French Commando Hubert operative who'd joined them on the piracy mission, and was now as loyal a member of the unit as any of them. They might not see each other that often, reflected Steve, but they were bound together in the way that only a group of men who have been to hell and back several times over, and who have left good mates in graves along the way, can be.

'Maksie's arranging the footie, and I'm in charge of the beer,' Dan had announced, laying down a crate of Toohey's New, his favourite Australian lager, and one of hundreds he stocked at 'Dan's Beer Bar' out in Majorca. He slammed a fist down on Steve's shoulder, half knocking him over with the massive strength in his right hand. 'And maybe this bloke can find us some totty.'

'I'm on holiday, mate,' said Steve. 'And for an ugly bastard like you, that sounds like hard work.'

Steve had settled back in the box to enjoy the football. He'd supported Chelsea since he was a boy; most of the kids around Bromley, where he grew up, were either Chelsea or Charlton fans, and he'd been devoted to the Blues ever since. A ball signed by Kerry Dixon in the season he'd scored as many goals as Gary Lineker was one of his prized possessions. That, and some gold taps from a bathroom in Saddam Hussein's palace he captured during an SAS raid he'd led on the centre of Baghdad during the second Gulf War, were about the only two ornaments he had to decorate the small cottage he'd bought close to the dealership. Like every other fan, he had his doubts about what had happened to the club since the Russians had taken over, but he enjoyed their success, and anyway they didn't look like big spenders compared to Man City, so no one could say they were buying success any more.

It was a cracking game right from the kick-off, and there was nowhere better to enjoy it from than an executive box. Barcelona were playing with the swagger and verve the world had come to expect from them, but Chelsea had dug in for a hard slog, defending valiantly. The game plan was clear enough from the start. Defend, defend, and defend some more, then try to nick a goal on the break, and hope that would be enough to see them through at the Nou Camp for the return leg in a fortnight's time. It wasn't the prettiest football Steve had ever witnessed, not from the home team, and the chilly wind and gusts of rain sweeping through West London that evening weren't making it any more elegant. But the sport wasn't that different from soldiering, he reflected as he admired the way the Chelsea captain lunged in for a tackle that, for all its aggression, was also skilful enough to remain just on the right side of red card territory. Everything started with the right kind of defence. And guts, doggedness and determination were qualities that could overcome any opposition; without those, superiority of numbers, or skill, or equipment, counted for very little.

'This is the life, lads,' boomed Dan, opening up another round of beers, and putting a bottle down for each man.

Indeed it was, thought Steve. Kolodin travelled in some style. The man himself sat at one side of the box. He was short, with dark hair, slicked back over his head, and an air of brooding mystery about him. Only just over forty, how he'd managed to amass a fortune of many billions in the Siberian oil industry was a mystery to the business pages of the papers. No one really knew how much money he actually had, or how it had been acquired. There was some violence along the way, Steve reckoned. You could tell that just from one glance at the man. Steve had seen it before, in the SAS and even more among the men who ran the private military corporations out in Afghanistan and Iraq. There was a coldness to the eyes and a cruelty to the lips that told you this was someone who could send a man to his death without a moment of hesitation or regret. It was a rare quality, but one which, in the right circumstances, could win a man a war or make him a fortune.

Around the Russian was a close protection unit of six special forces men, big, heavy guys, commanded by a slender, fierce woman called Maya Horowitz, who sat next to the oligarch all through the first half, hardly moving a muscle, and rising just once to rearrange the two bodyguards who sat next to Kolodin at all times. Behind them was a retinue of bankers, some associates from the oil industry, and a collection of icy Russian beauties who pretended to be models but Steve reckoned were probably there to entertain any guys with at least seven figures on their bank balance. One of them had just brushed past Nick, leaving the Welsh lad open-mouthed, and lost, Steve decided, somewhere between lust and bewilderment.

'It's hard to know whether there's more talent up here or on the pitch,' said Steve, giving Nick a wry half-grin.

'It's sodding Chelsea, isn't it?' said Nick. 'Just a bunch of overpaid ponces. Not a real team like Liverpool.'

Steve grinned, and nodded towards the blonde who'd

brushed past Nick a second earlier, and was now talking with an equally stunning brunette. 'I tell you what, lad, there's more chance of our left-back scoring than you.'

'I do all right,' muttered Nick grumpily.

Steve just laughed, and nudged Ian in the ribs, and soon both men were smirking. But Nick walked up to the two women and began chatting away to both of them, though it was the blonde who had most of his attention.

'Jesus Christ,' muttered Ian. 'I'm jealous of Nick. I really have touched a new low in life.'

Steve focused on the football. Chelsea were still hanging on, but the Spanish striker had just had a diving header saved and it was going to be tough to get to half-time with the scores level.

I've made the right decision, he thought to himself during a quiet moment in the game. It's great to see the boys again, but I've hung up my AK-47 for the final time. He could remember the moment when the Gurkha Ganju Rai had died alongside them out in Somalia, and it stayed with him, a vivid reminder that in the mercenary trade every job you took was also another step closer to the grave. He'd seen death close up too many times now, felt its clingy, cold embrace, and decided he didn't want any more of it.

There's just one thing I miss. Samantha and, of course, Archie. My boy.

Down below in the stands, Steve could see a couple of dads next to their kids, and he felt a pang of jealousy. It wasn't something he'd ever experienced before. Plenty of his mates from the Army had got married and knocked out a couple of sprogs and he never felt anything but bemused sympathy. The nappies, the noise, and the way that a tasty young girl you fancied across the bar suddenly turned into someone who looked more like your mum on a bad day, were more than enough to put him off. But a year ago, he'd found out that Sam, the girl he'd slept with on the African job, had a son, his son, called Archie. She'd wanted him to know, but hadn't wanted to see him enough to let him know where she was. And although he'd tried to locate her a few times, looking on the web, or scouting the phone book, he hadn't been able to track her down.

Not that I'm kidding myself I'd make a great dad, he reminded himself. I'd probably be as rubbish as my own father. But it would be nice to meet the little guy. Maybe bring him to a game.

Down below, the ref was blowing for half-time, and the players were trooping back towards the dressing room.

Behind them, Bruce clapped his hands together.

'Playtime is over, boys,' he said briskly. 'There's some trouble brewing.'

TWO

THE BEAD OF COLD SWEAT on Bruce's neck revealed precisely how worried he was right now. A hard, strongly built man, Bruce had been one of the toughest sergeants in the SAS before founding Dudley Emergency Forces, a private military corporation with a reputation for taking on jobs so difficult and so dangerous that the men on the Circuit referred to it not by its formal name of DEF but as Death Inc.

Bruce doesn't do rattled, thought Steve. No matter what kind of fire they were under, or how intense the pressure, he always remained completely composed.

Steve wasn't sure he'd ever even seen him sweat before.

Until today, that is.

'We've got fifteen minutes, lads,' he said crisply.

They'd retreated into a back room across the passageway from the executive boxes, a square, concrete space used by the caterers who served the champagne and smoked salmon sandwiches to the people watching the game. There were six crates of Dom Perignon stacked against the wall, glasses next to them, and beside that an industrial-sized tub of caviar. 'What the hell's up?' asked Steve.

Maksim held up a picture.

Steve recognised it at once. Just about anyone would. Aletta Sansome was one of the most photographed women in the world. A supermodel who appeared on dozens of magazine covers, she had her own range of perfume and lingerie and, as if that weren't enough, she was also dating one of the world's most talented footballers – Luis Fessi, who'd just signed for Chelsea, and who'd probably been the best player they had on the pitch during the first half.

With tumbling, auburn hair, high cheekbones, and rich grey-brown eyes, Steve could see exactly why she was regularly voted one of the world's most beautiful women. She put the peroxide blondes he met up in the wine bars around Leicestershire to shame.

'She's been kidnapped,' said Bruce.

'I'd take her,' chortled Dan. 'I'd bring her back in one piece, though, even if her hair might be a bit messed up.'

'This is serious, boys,' snapped Bruce. 'Aletta has vanished from the box she normally sits in. She comes to every game, and she always gives her boyfriend a kiss before he goes back on to the pitch for the second half. Kind of a good luck thing. If she's not back in fifteen minutes, Luis will know something's happened to her.'

'What did I tell you?' said Nick. 'A bunch of overpaid ponces. Stevie Gerrard doesn't need a kiss from the missus before he gets out on the pitch.'

'Can't we just text her?' said Ian. 'She's probably getting her nails done.'

Bruce shook his head. 'She's been kidnapped to destabilise the team. The gaffer round here reckons it's one of the Thai betting syndicates. There's a fortune in Far Eastern money riding on Barcelona winning this game, and by taking Aletta they reckon they've as good as sewn up the result for the Spanish. Unless we can bring her back . . .'

Maksim had opened up a laptop. 'We've traced her mobile,' he said. His finger pointed to a Google Maps page displayed on the screen. 'She's right here. On the railway track that runs down to Putney Bridge.'

'Isn't this a job for the police?' questioned Ian.

'There isn't enough time to mess around with the Bill,' snapped Bruce. 'They'll call in a specialist hostage unit, cordon off the whole area, and spread the whole thing out for hours. We need to get cracking.'

'Then we're wasting time,' said Steve decisively. 'Let's move.'

There were two cars parked at the hotel adjacent to the stadium: Bruce's powerful Jaguar XJS and a Range Rover that Maksim was using to ferry the security team into the ground. The unit ran as fast as they could, hurtling down the stairs and leaving a pair of bemused ground stewards in their wake. Bruce took the wheel of the Jag, with Steve up front, and Dan and Nick in the back. Maksim took the Range Rover with Ollie, Ian, and Henri riding alongside him. Steve was about to slot the seat belt into place as the car screeched out of the car park, but Bruce told him not to bother. He'd taught himself how to disable the irritating voice on all modern cars that kept telling you to fasten your belt. 'You're safer without it,' he said crisply. 'So long as you know how to drive.'

'You need to teach me that one.'

'You don't exactly need it for the Aston DB5s and the Jag Mark IIs up at your garage,' answered Bruce with a rough grin.

'They knew how to make proper cars in those days without some snooty bird who sounds like your maths teacher telling you to get the bloody seat belt on.'

The XJS was already hitting fifty as Bruce steered it up on to Fulham Road. The streets were quiet by the standards of central London right now. Anyone with any sense avoided the Chelsea ground on a match night, and the crowd who'd come for the game was still inside the stadium. There were plenty of police cars, however, and Bruce had no option but to tap on the brakes, slowing the Jag as they cruised down past the junction with North End Road. There was no point in getting into an argument with the coppers. 'She's just down by the junction with Munster Road,' said Steve, looking at the map he'd called up on his mobile. 'Go, bloody go.'

With the police safely behind then, Bruce plunged his foot on to the accelerator, and took the XJS up to sixty-five. The smart shops and cafes along the stretch of Fulham Road that ran down to the river passed in a blur. The District Line snaked down from Fulham Broadway to Parsons Green, then headed around again, passing directly over the stretch of Munster Road that ran down from Fulham Road to New King's Road before ending up at Putney Bridge. Just before the old metal bridge that crossed the main road there was a strip of wasteland, with a pair of corrugated iron engineering sheds that had long since been abandoned next to a half-acre of scrub and weeds.

Bruce pulled the XJS up to a screeching halt. Five seconds later, Maksim braked the Range Rover behind them. Steve had already bailed out of the car, followed by Dan and Nick. There was a high metal gate with a strip of barbed wire across it, and a

Transport for London sign threatening prosecution for anyone who trespassed on to the railway lines.

'Give us a bunk up, mate,' Steve barked at Dan.

'Wait,' growled Bruce.

He'd already opened the boot of the Jag, taken out the spare tyre, and slotted his hand inside. He pulled out a Browning Hi-Power, the rugged reliable 9mm handgun that was standard issue for the SAS. 'Here,' he said, handing it across to Steve.

'That registered?' asked Steve.

'Let's put it this way, it's about as legal as the mileage I saw on the red Austin Healey 3000 in your garage.'

'We'll keep this between ourselves then.'

Steve tucked the handgun into the pocket of his leather jacket, and glanced up towards the fence. It was seven foot high. Dan had already crouched down, and cupped his hands into a rough ladder. Steve jogged forward, caught his foot in Dan's hand, then let the massive strength of the Australian lever him upwards. He slammed his fists into place on the strip of metal that held the spikes in place, then pulled himself upwards. It took all his strength just to get his body up, and once he was in position, there was no choice but to fling himself straight down, and hope there was something soft to land on down below. He flew though the air, his legs swivelling in front of him to carry himself forward. A spike snagged his shirt, but stopped short of cutting his skin. Steve ignored it, concentrating on getting his fall right. He'd practised coming down for a hard landing into Christ knows what plenty of times in the Regiment but this wasn't something you could really train for. Coming down from seven feet would take a toll on even the fittest man. He straightened himself out ready to absorb the impact of the landing in his knees, before hitting the ground with a thud. He could feel brambles and nettles all around him, and he must have taken at least fifty stings. But the ground was soft enough; it had been raining steadily for the past few days, and there was plenty of water in the earth. He rolled once, taking the rest of the impact on his side, where it wouldn't do anything worse than leave a couple of bruises, then looked back upwards just in time to get out of the way as Maksim narrowly avoided landing on top of him. 'Steady, pal,' he said, looking up at the Russian. 'We've got enough problems without trying to kill each other.'

While the rest of the unit levered themselves over the fence, Steve and Maksim started to advance across the strip of wasteland. They had no torches, and only the one pistol between them. Maksim had picked up a length of rusty old steel from the ground, and was holding it in his right fist like a mallet. Steve reckoned the Russian was probably as dangerous with that as a unit with a machine gun, but they still had no idea what kind of firepower they were likely to be facing in the next few minutes. He was struggling to see what was ahead of them. It was never completely dark in this part of London. The soft electric glow of the houses and the cars kept it illuminated twenty-four hours a day, but it was only when a train rattled along the tracks to their right, its headlamps flashing across the wasteland as it trundled towards the station, that Steve could get a clear sense of the lie of the land. The two sheds were fifty yards ahead of them. As the light swept across the brambles and thistles, there was no sign of her. It could only mean one thing. She was being held in one of the buildings.

'Stop,' he hissed. 'There's something in the second shed.'

Maksim paused. Steve was peering forward, his eyes straining through the murky darkness. He was listening, his ears alert to see if could catch some sign of her. But all he could hear was the crunching of feet behind him.

'Found her yet, chaps?' said Ollie.

Steve glanced around. The rest of the unit – Nick, Ian, Henri, David and Dan – were all lined up behind him. Each man had equipped himself with some kind of weapon. Ian always carried a knife in his boot, a legacy of his time in the Maze, where a man never had any idea when a scrap was about to kick off. The rest had picked up weapons from the ground: bits of metal or wood twisted into spears or clubs.

'She's in one of the sheds,' muttered Steve. 'And if you keep talking, they'll soon know we're here.'

'We've only got another six minutes,' said Ian. 'And we need at least three of those to get her back to the ground.'

He was right. There was no time for cleverness or planning. Brutal and sudden aggression was the only tactic that stood a chance of working.

'The second shed, I'm sure of it,' said Steve. 'I saw a light.'

'Then we storm it,' said Ian simply. 'Four men at each end, rush them, and hope to hell they don't feel like shooting anyone.'

Steve nodded. He handed the Browning across to Nick. The Welsh boy was the best shot among them, and if they needed some firepower, he was the man they'd most want with his finger on the trigger. 'If the firecrackers kick off, then you're in charge of disabling them.' He looked around at the rest of the men. 'Now run like hell,' he muttered.

They took off, splitting into two units. The corrugated iron shed was twenty yards in length, ten high, with no windows, and at this distance it was impossible to see where the door might be. Steve, Ollie and Ian hurtled towards one end, with Nick holding back slightly, the gun at the ready. Dan, David, Henri and Maksim ran towards the back. It took a matter of seconds to cover the strip of ground, and they were making enough noise to wake the dead, but there was no time to worry about that now. The door was held in place with a bar and rusty padlock. Steve crashed hard into it, but there was a surprising amount of strength left in the old metal, and he bounced right off it, leaving scarcely a dent. Behind him, Ollie had levered a steel bar into the lock, and was pulling hard at it. Sweat was starting to trickle down the side of his face as he pushed on to the metal. 'Bugger it,' he growled, slamming his fists down hard. The lock broke with a sudden snap, and Ollie reeled backwards. Ian moved swiftly into the breach, throwing his right leg upwards, giving the unlocked doorway a savage kick and sending it clattering to the ground.

Steve ran inside. The light was dark, soupy, and the interior of the shed was filled with the decaying remains of two 1950s milk floats. Four men were up ahead. Steve started to lunge towards them, until he realised who they were.

'There's no sodding sign of her,' snapped Maksim.

Jesus, muttered Steve to himself. The wrong shed. And another precious minute wasted.

'Stand back, stand back,' shouted a man.

There was a heavy accent to the voice, but Steve couldn't place it at first. Mid-Pacific, he realised quickly enough. The kind of Americanised Far Eastern accent you heard in Hong Kong action moves.

Steve spun round.

Three men were advancing out of the second shed. A train was rattling past, this time heading up to town, and in its beam of light, Steve could see them clearly enough. They were short and stocky, dressed in jeans and leather jackets, and with black hair. Chinese, maybe. Or Thai. Maksim must have been right. It was one of the Thai betting syndicates that had snatched the model girl, hoping it would be enough to make Chelsea lose the game.

Tens of millions would have been staked on the game in the Far East. More than enough motive to kidnap a woman. And to kill her if necessary.

The second man was holding her tight, his right arm gripped across her breasts, while his two mates were flanking him, cordoning her off from attack. They were moving slowly towards the railway line.

Steve and the rest of the unit had formed up in a solid line. It was eight men against three, and usually those were odds that Steve would stake any kind of money on, particularly when the eight men in question were the hardest bunch of warriors he'd ever encountered in his life. But she had a gun to her head. And if they attempted to rush the men, they could empty the contents of her brain on to the wasteland in a fraction of a second.

'Stop right there,' shouted the first man. 'We mean her no harm. At nine she'll be released, and you can take her back to the stadium.'

Nine, thought Steve.

After the second half has kicked off.

They advanced another ten yards, before the man yelled at them to stop.

Steve could see her quite clearly now. The men were just twenty yards in front of him. She was wearing a pair of designer jeans, so tight they could have been welded to her skin, and a loose-fitting shirt that revealed just enough cleavage to keep you interested. But her eyes were clear, and defiant; there was an anger to the way she was glancing between her three captors that suggested there weren't many photographers who'd dare to turn up late to one of her shoots.

And there wasn't a smudge on her make-up. Despite the Sig Saur pressed to her head.

'What do you reckon, boys?' asked Steve.

He listened in mounting frustration as they ran through an inane discussion about whether she was really the third most beautiful woman in the world. The clock was ticking down relentlessly, and there was no time to waste. Not with a semi-final place in the Champion's League at stake. Not to mention a woman's life.

'We'll release her at nine,' repeated one of the Thai gangsters across the open wasteland. 'But you make any move before then, and she dies right here, right now.'

'Maybe we should just leave it,' said Ian. 'I mean, they'll let her go in a few minutes.'

'Then we've sodding failed,' snapped Steve.

'But she could die,' muttered Ollie. 'It's only a football game. It's hardly worth a woman's life.'

'We said we'd get her, so we'll bloody well get her,' Steve told him.

Nick had raised the Browning. He was holding it in his right hand, level with his eye. The Hi-Power was the service weapon for the SAS, and a high-quality pistol, but it was mainly favoured because its thirteen-round magazine gave you a lot more firepower than standard handguns, rather than for any exceptional accuracy. The Mark III, introduced in the 1990s, was a distinct improvement on the 1930s original, but it was a battlefield pistol, not a precision weapon.

'Can you take him?' asked Dan.

Nick's eyes furrowed. He concentrated, locking on to the target, his expression calming as he relaxed into the kill. Steve had seen it plenty of times before. The Welsh boy just had to let his instincts take control of him and he could shoot the legs of a fly at a hundred yards.

Then his face screwed up. 'No,' he said quietly. 'Not without running a fifty-fifty chance of the girl getting killed. It's not worth it, not for a sodding Chelsea game.'

Steve looked at his watch. The moment was slipping away from them. Another minute, and they'd have blown it.

I've bottled out of plenty of things in my life, he reflected to himself. Taking exams. Settling down. Making a relationship work. But a fight? I've never bottled out of one of those, no matter how heavily the odds might be stacked against me. And I'm not ready to start now.

He looked into Aletta's eyes. He could see something, and not just beauty, although there was plenty of that. An invitation. It was the same as when a woman wanted you to go to bed with her, except now there was nothing sexual about it. She wants me to rescue her. Whatever the risks.

It's right there. *In her eyes*.

'Give me the gun,' he snapped at Nick.

Nick remained rock steady. 'If I can't make the shot, you certainly bloody can't.'

'I'll make it.'

'Sodding leave it, pal,' growled Ollie, touching the edge of Steve's jacket. 'It's not worth it.'

'I'll be the judge of that.'

Nick handed across the gun.

Steve started to walk, closing the space between himself and the three hard men. The Browning was gripped tight in his right hand, held close to his hip, cowboy-style. If he needed to shoot these blokes, the bullet was going into their bellies or their balls, places where 9mm of steel could do a lot of damage to a man.

'Drop her,' he barked.

'Fuck off,' shouted one of the Thais.

Steve kept walking forward. He glanced again into Aletta's eyes. She was still willing him on. Twenty yards melted into fifteen, then ten. He was close enough now to smell the cheap aftershave on the men's sweaty skin, and the expensive perfume on hers. And to catch the unmistakable scent of fear on all of them.

This wasn't what they reckoned on when they took the bird, he realised. They were just thugs, tooled-up muscle, but they were in a fight now in which they could easily die, and it takes a certain type of man to handle one of those.

'Back off, or she dies right now,' barked the Thai.

'And you'll die a second later,' growled Steve.

Seven yards, six . . .

Aletta moved like an alley cat.

Her teeth were among her most celebrated features. Fashion editors drooled over their whiteness, their immaculate curve, their fullness. But they never mentioned their sharpness. Her head snapped downwards, biting hard on the forearm of the man holding the gun to her head. They sank neatly into the flesh, like a set of surgical knives, instantly drawing blood. His head bucked upwards in pain. Steve had known the moment was coming. He'd seen it in her eyes, and was ready for the chance, waiting for it, tooled up, ready to strike. He fired once, then twice on the Browning, slotting two bullets into the man's belly. He shrieked in pain, and the Sig Saur clattered to the ground. One of the remaining two men grabbed Aletta by the hair, dragging her backwards, while the second rushed for the gun, but Steve placed another bullet into his foot, sending him crumbling to the ground. Nick pounced on the weapon with a skidding lunge across the ground. Behind him, the rest of the unit was charging with the fury and aggression of a band of Viking warriors. Dan, Henri and Ollie were setting about the man holding on to Aletta, assaulting him with a rainstorm of fists and knees. He was strong and determined, but the shed couldn't have survived the vicious storm of kicks and punches, never mind the man. He released his grip on the girl, reeling back on his heels, until a blow from Dan straight into his jaw sent him collapsing back on to the ground, blood pouring from a nose that had been cracked apart.

The fight was over.

Two men had nasty gunshot wounds. Not fatal, Steve judged. He'd seen a lot of blokes get shot over the years, and he could tell the goners from the ones who were going to pull through as expertly as any battlefield surgeon. These guys had plenty of blood pouring out of them, but if they got themselves patched up in the next hour or so, they'd recover fast enough.

Steve leant down into the man with a shot through his belly.

He was whimpering in pain, but still conscious, holding on to his stomach to staunch the flow of blood. Steve fished inside the man's jacket pocket and pulled out a Nokia mobile, checking it had some charge on it.

'I reckon you boys know a doctor in Chinatown who can come round and patch you up,' he said. 'Give them a ring. If you call the NHS, there's going to be all sorts of questions from the coppers about what just happened, and I think we'd all rather avoid that, wouldn't we?' He smiled softly, giving the man a prod in the belly that made him wince with pain. 'We'll call it evens, eh.'

A couple of yards ahead of him, Ollie and Dan had already helped Aletta to her feet.

Still not so much as a bead of sweat, noted Steve. And hardly a hair out of place.

'I don't suppose anyone has any lip gloss,' she said, glancing around at the men. 'I can't go back looking like this.'

'I'm fresh out,' said Steve. 'Meant to pick some up in Tesco this morning, but it clean slipped my mind.'

'I've got some balm,' said Ian. He fished it out of his pocket and handed it across to Aletta with a bashful smile. 'It's the weather,' he said, looking around at the rest of the men, his face reddening slightly. 'Been playing havoc with my skin.'

Aletta took the balm, applied it to her lips, then leant across to Ian, giving him a light kiss on his cheek. 'You're sweet,' she said.

'I'll never wash again,' said Ian.

'I don't think anyone will notice the difference, mate,' said Dan.

'She's out of your league,' said David.

Ian sighed. 'I know, I know,' he said. 'In fact, I'm not sure we're even the same species.'

Ollie pointed towards the gate. 'Shall we get the hell out of here?' he said. 'We've got three minutes left to get this lady back to the ground.'

Three

'BLOODY HELL,' MUTTERED NICK, AS he grabbed another bottle of beer, and a smoked salmon sandwich. 'I never thought I'd be helping out sodding Chelsea.'

'First decent cause we've ever fought for,' said Steve.

The men had just taken their seats, and the second half of the game was already underway. They'd made it back to the stadium with less than a minute to spare, but they'd just managed to rush Aletta to the player's tunnel with a few seconds left on the clock, and she'd been able to give Luis Fessi a kiss to send him out for the second half the same way she always did.

I hope he's worth it, thought Steve. We need something to liven up the second half.

On sixty minutes, Steve's worries were put to rest. Fessi scored from a free kick; from twenty-five yards out, it was a scorching shot that twisted round the wall and rocked the back of the net. After that, Chelsea shut down the game effectively enough, blocking the Spanish from playing, keeping plenty of men behind the ball, and as the clock ticked past eighty minutes, Steve was feeling increasingly confident they could nick a one-nil result to take back to the Nou Camp in a fortnight's time.

Every time Chelsea got hold of the ball, and played a few more minutes of possession football, running down the clock with determined aggression, Steve was cheering them on, and so was the rest of the unit.

'That was a sodding good job, and one well done,' said Bruce, slapping each man on the back in turn. 'The fact that Fessi scored makes it twice as good. That goal is probably worth ten million to this place.'

'We didn't even get paid for it,' said Ollie. 'And some of us aren't even Chelsea fans.'

'I think there will be a few monkeys for us in it, lads,' said Bruce, a broad grin flashing across his face. 'Kolodin owes the gaffer of this place a few favours, and there are more deals they'd like to do together in the oil industry. That job hasn't done any harm at all. There's a lot of money to be made in the Russian security market, and with Iraq wound down, and Afghanistan turning too rough for the PMCs, that's an important market for us to be in. We've got ourselves a foot in the door this evening, and that could be worth a lot one day.'

Steve glanced across at Bruce, dragging his eyes away from the pitch momentarily. He liked Bruce, and respected him as well. The man was the finest judge of soldiers he'd ever met. He knew what made them tick, how to keep them fighting, and could assess their strengths and weaknesses the way a carpenter could read the grain in a piece of wood. But he wasn't going to work for him any more. On that, his mind was made up.

'Some of us are just vintage car dealers these days,' he said sharply. 'It doesn't make any difference to us whether we have a foot in the Russian market for mercenaries or not.'

'So you keep saying,' said Ollie. 'But it's been a year now since we finished the last job, and some of us are running a bit low on cash.'

Steve shook his head in disbelief. 'We came away with a million in gold bars from the piracy operation.'

'Yeah, but we gave half of it to Ganju's family to make sure they were looked after,' said Ian. 'That left half a million split between eight of us. It's hardly a fortune.'

It was true they hadn't made much out in Somalia, but they'd hit decent paydays out in Afghanistan and Africa in the years before that. 'You've run out already?' asked Steve.

Ollie was looking slightly sheepish. He'd taken up with Nick's mum, a lapdancer called Sandra, a year ago, and now it turned out the pair of them had bought a lease on a property in Swansea and were planning on opening the city's finest lap-dancing club. That had consumed a large chunk of his money. 'And then there was a trip we took together to Vegas . . .' he added.

Ah, Vegas, thought Steve. Ollie had been considered a certainty for general when he'd gone from Sandhurst to the Household Cavalry, but the man had a weakness for drink and gambling, and had ended up being busted out of the British Army, too drunk and too broke to remain an officer. Those were his two vices. And Vegas was hardly a cure for either of them.

'So you see, a few roubles might be quite handy for some of us, old sausage.'

'I don't know why you're sodding well investing in a club,' interrupted Nick angrily. 'I've already told you, me mum's giving up the lap-dancing.'

'Of course she is,' answered Ollie cheerfully. 'She's going to be management.'

'Like an officer,' added Ian. 'They don't go near any actual shooting, and she doesn't get her tits out any more.'

Steve was distracted by a sweeping Barcelona counter-attack that drew a fabulous save from the Chelsea keeper, but by the time he tuned back into the conversation, it turned out all the men in the unit were talking about how short of money they were.

Henri hadn't been with them in Afghanistan or Africa, so had never made much in the first place. A marine specialist, and once a member of France's elite squad of marine special forces, Commando Hubert, he was hoping to take part in a transatlantic solo sailing race. But unless he could find a sponsor, that was going to take some serious cash.

Dan had sunk his money into the imaginatively titled Dan's Beer Bar out in Majorca, but the place had been expensively fitted out, and the tourist season last summer hadn't been as busy as usual, and the bar still wasn't quite breaking even. A bit like my car dealership, thought Steve. It was a good business, and one he loved, but the bit about making money had never quite happened.

Ian had sunk a fortune into a charity he'd set up for ex-IRA men, guys who'd been locked up in the Maze or one of the other high-security jails for years, and had struggled to make any kind of transition back to civilian life when they'd been released. They had one hostel to maintain in Belfast, and another in Kilburn in North London, places where the blokes could drop in, get a bed for the night and a hot meal if necessary, and some advice on how to find work, or a place to live, or just a referral to a counsellor who knew something about post-traumatic stress disorder, and wasn't too squeamish about helping men who'd blown up innocent women and children back in the old days. 'Sort of like Help for Heroes,' Ian had quipped when he'd told the rest of the guys about it. 'Except, possibly, without quite so much mainstream support.' The trouble was, it was draining all his spare cash. And outside of a few places in Boston and Dublin, none of their attempts to raise funds had been very successful so far. 'So, you see, I'm as skint as the rest of you.'

'And how about you, David?' asked Steve. 'Surely you've got a few quid left?'

Even as he asked the question, Steve knew the answer was almost certainly not. David had legendarily crippling expenses. There were the two teenage children from his first marriage, both of them at private boarding schools, and that alone didn't leave any change from sixty grand a year. His ex-wife consumed more alimony than most women did Sophie Kinsella novels. Her life, as David liked to complain, was one long luxury spa day, and all of that was on his tab. There were the twins from his second marriage to Sandy to pay for, and Sandy as well, of course, and the way she and the first wife Laura fought, David had to make sure both of them were receiving just as much money, otherwise his life would scarcely be worth living. He'd sunk a whole pile of cash into a Skoda dealership his brother-in-law ran down in Woking, close to where he lived, but with the recession, cars hadn't been shifting as well as they once did, and it was going to be a long time before he saw any kind of a profit on that investment.

'If there was some work going, I might well be interested,' said David.

'We could all use some new contracts,' said Bruce.

'I thought you were always loaded,' said Steve.

His attention was drawn back to the pitch. Four minutes had just been added in extra time, and the crowd was jeering, anxious to hold on to the one-nil score. Barcelona were surging forward in a last, lethal attack, but as they won a corner, he noticed the Spanish weren't throwing everything into it. They'd be happy enough to take a one goal deficit back to their own ground, he reckoned. The ball was skilfully caught by the keeper, and as it was thrown back into play, Steve glanced at Bruce.

'DEF doesn't run on hot air,' he was explaining. 'There are expenses, overheads, contracts to maintain, relationships to be supported. It takes cash flow. And right now, there's less of it coming in than going out. That's why it would be good for us to find a way into the Russian market. That's where the growth is.'

Steve looked at Nick. 'And how about you?' he asked.

'I'm fine for dosh,' muttered Nick. 'No worries.'

'There's a limit to how much a man can spend on Big Macs and Stella,' said Ian. 'Even Nick.'

'Actually I'm more of a TGI Friday's man these days,' snorted Nick.

'You see, money goes to everyone's head eventually,' said David. 'At this rate, you'll be a clubman in St James's in a few more years.'

'Well, not me,' said Steve. 'I'm just fine the way I am. I mean the garage isn't making much money. But the turnover is good enough, and the stock is all there, and I should be able to make a living at it. Without anyone trying to shoot my balls off either.'

Ollie rested a hand on Steve shoulder. 'So you keep saying, mate. And maybe one day you'll actually mean it.'

'I sodding mean it right now,' said Steve.

'Of course you do,' said Bruce.

All around them, the crowd was starting to drift away from the stadium. The mood was cheerful; it had been a strong performance, even if the second leg would require even more disciplined defending.

Kolodin was walking towards them, with Maksim at his side, plus the slender woman Steve had noticed sitting next to him earlier.

Kolodin patted Bruce on the shoulders, then shook each man by the hand in turn. There was a broad grin on his face, the smile of a man who cares only about money, and reckons he's just found a way to make some more.

'There's a celebration at a nightclub in town,' he said. 'I hope you can all join us. After the work you did for me at half-time, it's the least I can do for you.'

Four

A S STEVE WATCHED HER CHECK out the nightclub, he couldn't help but be impressed by the professionalism of the woman. Maya Horowitz commanded the unit of six bodyguards with the kind of natural authority that he'd rarely seen even in the Regiment, and certainly not in the regular Army. Every instruction was clipped and precise. Each check was made once, then twice, then a third time. Every man knew precisely what he was doing, and would carry out his task with enthusiasm and yet with a sense of the consequences should he fail in any way. It might only be a close protection squad for a Russian oil tycoon, but it acquitted itself with a discipline that could match any presidential or prime ministerial unit.

Steve had known plenty of women over the years. But none of them were soldiers. Not proper ones, anyway.

Sure, there were women in all the armed forces. Political correctness demanded that they had to be given their place alongside the blokes. There weren't any in the Regiment, not yet anyway, but the Special Reconnaissance Regiment, the special forces unit charged with military intelligence and surveillance, now had plenty of female members. The way Steve saw it, the women were just a distraction. I'm as much in favour of a bit of extra totty knocking about the place as the next bloke, he'd reflect to himself. But when it came to any actual fighting, they were about as much use as a bucket and spade in Birmingham. It just wasn't in their genes. When the fireworks started going off, they couldn't find the necessary aggression to get stuck into the fighting. They couldn't lose themselves in the battle the way a man could, and nor could they commit themselves so completely to victory.

Not Maya, though. She was a whole special forces unit wrapped up in a woman's body.

'She's something different, isn't she?' he said, glancing towards Maksim.

The Russian chuckled. 'You bet,' he said. 'I worked for some tough bastards in the Spetsnaz, but she's in a league of her own.'

The nightclub, Cancun Ice, just off Berkeley Square in London's West End, was a swank, upmarket place, favoured by footballers, models, celebrities, and the mega-rich, mostly Russians, but a few Middle Easterners and hedge fund managers as well. Steve had read about it plenty of times in the gossip columns, but he had never been here before. He'd never been much of a man for clubs. The last one he'd been to was the Liquid Heat down in Bromley more than a decade ago, when both he and his mate Jeff had been trying to get off with Alison who worked as a personal trainer at the Fitness First club. But this place was nothing like a Bromley disco. For starters, the décor was completely different. There were none of the overdone neon strips, the tin masquerading as chrome, or the huge beer adverts you found at the Liquid Heat; this place was all chandeliers and gilt and chairs so luxuriously upholstered you could have fitted them into a top-of-the-range Bentley, never mind a nightclub. The drinks as well: none of the cut-price Stella, no sign of a happy hour, and none of the names of the cocktails used the word 'screw' once, which Steve reckoned was a first for any drinks list he'd ever seen. And then, of course, there were the people. They, too, were from a different league, and possibly a different planet. Steve had seen five Premier League footballers, two actors he sort of recognised from EastEnders, a guy who'd been on *The X Factor* last year, a girl who was famous for something he couldn't put his finger on, and enough models to start an agency.

'Lot of footballers,' said Steve, looking around. 'Not surprised some of them can only play one game a week if this is where they hang out.'

'But two of them are from Spurs,' said Dan. 'So they don't count.'

Kolodin had reserved a private VIP area for his entourage. Maya, Maksim and the rest of the security unit had scoured the area before anyone else was allowed inside. They checked it thoroughly for bombs, then quickly but efficiently frisked the waiting staff to make sure they weren't carrying any weapons. The oil tycoon had obviously made a few enemies over the years and wasn't taking any chances. Once Maya was happy that the place was clean, the rest of them were allowed in. They had a raised section of the club to themselves, complete with three waitresses who kept them generously supplied with beer, cocktails and champagne. Kolodin took a place at the best table, looking down at the dance floor, accompanied by three icily beautiful women: two blondes and a brunette. There were another six guys with him, and another half-dozen girls, followed by Bruce, Steve, and the rest of the boys. As they sat down, a couple of bottles of champagne appeared on the table in front of them, followed by a selection of beers, and an unlimited supply of cocktails.

'A bit different to the clubs in Swansea, I reckon,' said Ollie, spilling some champagne as he attempted to pour glasses for both himself and Nick.

'The birds are better looking, that's for sodding sure,' said Nick.

'I think I'd stand more chance in Swansea,' said Ian morosely.

Nick stood up. 'Olga's here,' he said, walking away to join the blonde he'd been chatting to back at the ground. 'I'll see if she's got a mate for you.'

'It's getting worse,' said Ian. 'First I was jealous of Nick. Now I'm hoping for some of his cast-offs. I might just pop out and throw myself under a train any moment now.'

'Can I have your beer then, if you're topping yourself?' said Dan. 'No point wasting it.'

Steve grabbed himself a drink, and spent a few moments just checking the place out. It was getting close to eleven, and the place was filling up. The dance floor was getting crowded and, despite the number of celebrities, there was an easy-going, gentle vibe to the place, a groove that Steve could imagine himself easily getting into. Aletta Sansome made her way up from the dance floor and walked towards him. 'I owe you a dance,' she said, sitting down next to him.

'I'm bloody terrible,' said Steve.

She smiled. The moment her lips opened up, Steve was already wondering if 'third most beautiful woman' wasn't an injustice. Close up, she had a natural radiance which the pictures didn't capture; there was a perfection to her skin and a brightness to her eyes that Steve didn't reckon he'd ever seen before.

'You move OK when you fight.'

Steve laughed. 'That's different,' he replied. 'If there's a ruck on, I do all right. It's moving to the music I'm not so good at.'

She took his hand. 'Come on. You can't be that bad.'

Kylie Minogue's 'All the Lovers' had just kicked off. Steve followed her reluctantly down the twisting staircase that led towards the dance floor. Normally, he kept well away from them. Throwing up on a girl was more likely to get you somewhere than the kind of dancing he specialised in. But then, he reflected, how many times in my life am I going to get asked to dance by one of the world's best-looking girls? Probably never again.

He glanced around anxiously. When you went to a teenage nightclub in Bromley, you could usually count on some really manky dancers. Stay close to them and you wouldn't look so bad. Nick was already swaying close to Olga, and Steve was hoping that he'd be even worse than he was. But actually Nick was surprisingly good. Just relax, he told himself as the music kicked into a higher gear. Try and keep some kind of time with the beat.

Aletta leant up close to him. 'You're right, you're terrible,' she whispered in his ear.

Steve laughed nervously.

'It's OK,' she said, as the music stopped. 'Again?'

'I think once is enough for me.'

They started to walk back upstairs. 'You've got guts,' said Steve.

'That's not a part of my anatomy that men usually comment on.'

'Somehow I can believe that.'

He made way for her to climb the stairs. 'I meant out there on the wasteland,' he continued. 'A lot of women would have gone to pieces.'

'It's not just soldiering that breeds toughness, you know.'

'You do that all the time on the catwalk?'

'Every day,' said Aletta. She leant across and gave Steve a kiss on both cheeks. 'You're sweet. Gotta run . . .'

As he stepped back toward the VIP lounge, Ollie and David were knocking back the beers and chortling. 'Steve sodding West dancing with a supermodel,' said Ollie. 'Who'd have thought it?'

'I'd rather be back in those mountains in Afghanistan than have to watch that again,' said David.

'Jealous, boys,' said Steve, grinning.

'You've never seen Sandy with a toddler in one hand, a nappy in the other, and a bottle of expressed milk to put in the fridge,' said David. 'Why the hell should I be jealous?'

'Or Nick's mum first thing in the morning, before she's had a chance to put any make-up on,' laughed Ollie drunkenly. 'Now, there's a real woman.'

Steve looked around. Maya was standing right next to him, a bottle of Bitburger, one of his favourite German beers, in one hand, a mineral water in the other. 'I heard you were Regiment,' she said, handing Steve the bottle.

He paused before replying.

Most people referred to it as the SAS. Only the men them-selves referred to it as the Regiment. And maybe a few special forces specialists as well. She wasn't smiling, nor was she looking straight at him, but there was still a flirtatious manner to the way she posed the question. She was dressed in simple black slacks, with a white blouse, and round her neck was a gold chain, with a diamond at its centre. There was hardly a trace of make-up on her face. But she wasn't outshone by any of the model girls crowding around the club. Her black hair had a touch of auburn to it that lent it a slight glow, like the fading embers of the sunlight, and her eyes were deep brown, with shades of different colour in them, like looking into a forest made up of a dozen different woods.

'Off duty?' he said, taking the beer, and deliberately ignoring her question.

Maya shrugged. 'It's not the kind of job where you're ever off duty.'

'Then why do it?'

'You should see what I get paid.'

'I can imagine.'

Steve walked across to one of the booths and sat down. Without being invited, Maya followed him. A few yards away, one of Kolodin's mates had got out a line of coke and was snorting it using a fifty pound note. The billionaire hadn't joined in yet, noted Steve, but didn't seem to mind, and neither did any of the waitresses.

'You didn't answer my question,' said Maya.

'The Regiment? Five years. Before that I was in the Paras.'

'So why did you leave? You're not so old.'

'You obviously didn't see me on the dance floor.'

'Seriously. Why?'

Steve had thought about that plenty of times in the years

since he'd been out of the SAS. To say he regretted the decision would be an exaggeration. But there were moments when he missed the camaraderie, the discipline, and the purpose he'd enjoyed within the Regiment. The SAS was the finest fighting force in the world, and there weren't many moments in a man's life when he could confidently say he was part of a team that could beat any force on the planet.

'I didn't want to get killed without earning something for myself,' he replied. 'You'd see these old boys up in Hereford and they didn't have much more than memories to keep them going.'

'Sometimes memories are enough.'

'Not for me.' He glanced sharply into her eyes, and caught a sense of the steeliness within her. 'Not for you either, I reckon.'

'Meaning?'

'Which special forces unit were you in?'

She laughed. 'Finishing school in Switzerland.'

'No, really, I'm interested. I watched you scan this place. You know what you're doing.'

Now it was her turn to pause. Weighing up her reply, judged Steve. Wondering whether she trusts me. Or whether she can be bothered to tell me anything that matters. A few yards away, Nick was sitting with Olga, and she'd persuaded a few of her friends to come and join Dan, Ollie and the rest of the guys. Even Ian had a girl sitting next to him, although she probably hadn't graduated with the top honours out of whatever model school Olga had come out of. Bruce and David were talking to Kolodin and some of his pals, drinking Scotch, and getting out the cigars.

'The Caracal,' said Maya finally.

Steve had heard of it of course. The SAS had close links with the Israeli Defence Force, even if they were usually unofficial. Most of the IRA weapons had come from the Middle East, paid for with American money, and there were regular swaps of information and kit between Republican and Palestinian terror groups. The British and the Israelis had a shared interest in keeping tabs on them and, at an operational level, if there was any rough work to be done, the task fell to the Regiment. They'd swapped tactics plenty of times; there were few more accomplished masters of anti-terror warfare than the IDF, and everyone in the SAS was familiar with their structure. There had always been women in the Israeli Army. It was the only country in the world where they were conscripted into the armed forces along with the men. But they'd largely been kept away from combat roles. Until 2000, that is. The Caracal Battalion was formed under political pressure to increase the women's front-line responsibilities. Named after a type of cat that appeared identical in both sexes, it was a mixed battalion assigned to direct combat roles. Initially it had been tasked with policing Israel's borders with Jordan and Egypt. But it had taken part in plenty of other operations since then, and had, by all accounts, acquitted itself well. Like everything the IDF did, it was professional and dedicated, and didn't stop until its enemy was completely defeated.

'How many years?'

'Five?'

'Contacts?'

'Dozens.'

'Anything else?'

'Like what?'

From what Steve knew about the IDF, he was aware that their best soldiers were plucked from the regular combat units for special forces training. The Israelis were involved in so many wars simultaneously, and had so many enemies, the military structure had evolved a complex hierarchy of units and specialities. The Sayeret Matkal, translated as the General Staff Reconnaissance Unit, was the closest it had to the SAS; indeed, so closely was it modelled on the British force that it even had the same motto, 'Who Dares Wins'. It was still best known for Operation Thunderbolt, the audacious raid on Entebbe when more than a hundred hostages were rescued from an Air France plane, but it had been involved in countless operations since then. But there was also the Maglan, a unit specialising in operating behind enemy lines, and using advanced weaponry; the Yehidat Shldag, the special forces arm of the Air Force; the Sayeret Yael, a unit specialising in combat engineering, mainly demolitions and explosives; Shayetet 13, the naval special forces unit; and the Duvdevan Unit, which concentrated on undercover operations in militant Palestinian territories, usually disguised as Arabs. With her black hair, and dark, olive skin, Maya could easily pass for an Arab if she wanted to, decided Steve. She could have been seconded into any one of those units. And whichever one it was, she would have received some of the most punishing, brutal training in the world.

'The Sayeret Matkal?'

Her face tightened up. Maybe I've stepped too far, thought Steve. The Israeli special forces were not only famously aggressive, they were famously discreet as well.

'Let's put it this way,' she said. 'A woman has secrets.'

'Fair enough,' said Steve. He nodded towards the billionaire's table. Kolodin was leaning over the table snorting a line of coke, and pawing one of the two blondes. 'But how come you're working for this animal?'

'Every woman is looking for a big payday,' Maya answered. 'A dream, an ambition, something she can call her own. The Army is fine, and Israel is a cause worth fighting for, but you don't make any money at it. Not a payday.'

'That's my line,' said Steve. 'The payday, I meant.'

'And for you? What is it?'

'I bought my uncle out of the vintage car business he owned up in Leicestershire. It took a bloody dangerous mission in Afghanistan to get the money together, and another one in Africa to keep it afloat, but I've made it work.'

'Old cars? *That's* your dream?'

Steve had noticed that it didn't sound much of a dream when you spelt it out. Particularly not to women. Only Sam had ever really seemed to understand. 'Not old. *Vintage* cars. British ones from the fifties and sixties, a golden era. Austin Healeys, Aston Martins, Jaguars.'

Her eyes scanned the room, and for a moment Steve wondered if she was looking for someone else to talk to. Then he realised she was doing it every few minutes: a silent visual sweep of the place that checked and double-checked whether there where any threats close by. Professionalism, noted Steve. Her guard is never down, even at close to midnight.

'You need to see them to get the idea,' continued Steve.

'Maybe you can show me one day.'

'It's a deal,' said Steve with a grin. 'I'll take you for a spin in an Austin Healey 3000. A red one, with tan leather seats. Then you'll see what's so special about them.'

She laughed. 'I'm already looking forward to it.'

'And what's your payday?'

'A kibbutz,' said Maya.

Steve knew what they were. The kibbutzim – from the Hebrew word for gathering – were idealistic communities in Israel, where everyone worked and lived together. They'd started out mainly in agriculture but had branched out into crafts and industries; there were kibbutzim specialising in producing just about everything.

'My best friend from the Battalion has been working on turning an old fruit kibbutz into a pharmaceuticals collective, but it takes a lot of money. So I do this. For a few years anyway, until it can stand on its own feet, and we run it together.'

Steve nodded towards Kolodin. 'But working for this bloke? It's hardly idealistic.'

Maya laughed. 'He's not so bad. He's Jewish, you know. Like most of the Russian oligarchs. And he's a good friend of the state of Israel, whatever his personal qualities. A big investor. So, you know, we look after our friends. It's a small country, with a lot of enemies, and that is how we survive. My people are good at that.'

Steve nodded. There were a few Israeli special forces characters on the Circuit. They were some of the best operators in the world. But they were usually working for Mossad, or the Bureau as they always referred to it, as well. They'd only take jobs the Israeli government approved of. And they always put loyalty to their country above their client.

'He's got clearance from the Bureau?'

'You ask too many questions. Tell me more about the old cars.'

'*Vintage* cars,' insisted Steve.

A few yards away, Kolodin was standing up, clapping his hands together, and pointing towards the door. Time to go? wondered Steve. It's only midnight. Early for this gaff.

'This way,' said Maksim, rounding up the entire group. 'The big man wants to talk to us.'

Bruce and David were already following him briskly to the back of the club. Maksim had broken up Nick and the group of girls, pointing Ollie, Ian, and Dan towards the door, before finding Henri down on the dance floor and steering him back upstairs.

'Maybe it's payday,' said Ollie. 'A couple of grand in used twenties would be quite handy.'

'These kind of blokes never carry cash,' said Ian. 'A small oil field somewhere might be worth asking for though.'

Steve followed behind, watching Maya as she walked. There was no swagger to her. She was too slender. But there was a strength and purpose to her movements, like a cat's, that he found appealing.

The back door led into a narrow corridor, mainly used by the waiting staff. A girl in a short skirt was brushing past, with a bottle of champagne in a silver ice bucket. 'Save some for me, babes,' chortled Ollie.

Off the corridor, Maksim opened a pair of double doors, leading into a narrow, long room. It was sparsely decorated, with plain white walls, two strips of neon lighting, and a single desk at one end with a phone on it. It was functional, nothing more, a stark contrast to the opulence and extravagance of the main club. As Steve stepped in, Kolodin was half sitting on the desk. He'd removed his tie, and had opened up a couple of buttons on his crisp white shirt. A pair of his security guards were flanking him, and he was grinding his fists together with an air of impatience.

As the last of the men stepped into the room, Maksim shut the door behind them.

What the hell's going on? wondered Steve. If he wants to give us a bonus for rescuing Aletta, just hand out some sodding brown envelopes and be done with it.

Kolodin glanced around the room. His eyes were cold and determined, with an edge of cruelty, like a snake's. 'There's a job for you men, if you want it,' he said, speaking slowly and deliberately, each word calculated for maximum effect. 'Three days, that is all it will take. And I will pay each man three hundred thousand pounds.'

Five

STEVE COULD SEE THE CALCULATIONS being made in the eyes of each of the men. You didn't need to be a maths genius to do the sums. Even Nick would find them easy enough. Three hundred grand for three days' work. A hundred grand a day. It was an unbelievable sum of money.

A man's big payday, no question about that.

Don't stop and think about it, he told himself sharply. If you start thinking, you'll be tempted. And your mind is already made up.

'We're just here for the football, pal,' said Steve, speaking clearly and decisively.

'And the booze,' said Ian.

'And the birds,' said Dan.

Steve grinned.

He knew the rest of the guys might want to take the job. It was hell of a lot of money. But whatever it was Kolodin had in mind, it was going to be sodding dangerous. Nobody was going to pay that kind of money to get a bunch of blokes to sit around watching Sky Sports for three days. It would definitely mean putting their lives on the line. It might well mean breaking the law as well. He could see that clearly enough. And it was a relief to know the rest of the blokes could see it as well.

In front of them, Kolodin was still grinding his fists together. There was a bull-like strength to the man: powerful, brooding, used to getting his own way. 'Four hundred thousand pounds per man, then,' he said, with the air of someone who didn't have the patience to negotiate. 'Paid upfront.'

Maya stepped forward, standing next to the Russian, her eyes darting from man to man. 'The money can be transferred to your accounts tonight,' she said.

'I'm in,' said Henri curtly.

Steve glanced at the Frenchman. There had been some bad blood between the two of them when they first worked together in Somalia, and he wasn't surprised to see him breaking ranks first. The man was a decent enough soldier, he could respect him for that. But he'd no more trust him than he'd leave Maksie alone with his last bottle of vodka.

'We don't even know what the job is,' snapped Steve.

'It doesn't make any difference to me,' said Henri, with a nonchalant shrug. 'The money will buy me the boat I need for the transatlantic race, and that's all that counts.'

'It doesn't make any difference to me either,' said David. He looked up at Kolodin. 'Count me in as well.'

Steve looked around. None of the other men was saying anything. But their expressions were uncertain. Two of them had already taken the bait. The rest were clearly wavering.

'Why can't you tell us what the job is?' asked Ian suspiciously.

'Five hundred thousand pounds per man, for three days' work,' said Kolodin brusquely. 'And that's my final offer.'

Nick gave a single nod of his head. 'I'll take it.'

A half smile crossed Dan's face. 'I'm in as well.'

Bruce looked across at Ian. 'What about you?' he asked.

'Aye, well, what about you, pal?'

Bruce paused for a second before replying. 'It's the most generous offer any of us will ever get,' he said. He nodded to Kolodin. 'I'm signing up.'

Ian turned his gaze towards Maksim. 'I guess you're already on the payroll.'

'Maksim will get paid the same rate as every other man,' said Kolodin. 'It's his choice whether he takes the assignment or not. There are only volunteers on this job.'

'Half a million,' said Maksim. He laughed to himself. 'You can buy a lot of vodka and whores for that money.'

'It depends on the whores,' said Kolodin, slapping the Spetsnaz man on the back. 'Trust me, I know.'

'That leaves you, Ian,' said Bruce.

'And Steve,' said Ian.

'Well?' asked Bruce.

'The offer's on the table,' interrupted Kolodin. 'But like I said, it's three days' work, starting right now. There's no time to waste on decisions. You're either in or you're out.'

'No one will think any the worse of any man for deciding against,' said Bruce. 'Each man makes his own choices, the same way it's always been.'

Ian looked towards Steve, decided he didn't like what he saw in his eyes, and looked quickly back towards Kolodin. 'I'm in.'

Steve was suddenly aware of everyone looking straight at him. And he, too, had a sense of looking at himself, except from the inside. There was a part of him, somewhere close to his heart, that wanted to go. He missed the camaraderie. He knew he'd wake up in a couple of days wondering where his mates were, how they were getting on, and why he wasn't with them. He knew, as well, that for years to come, there would be get-togethers, where the talk would turn to old times, and the boys would banter about the Russian mission, and he'd regret not having been along for the ride. He could sense all that, and feel the regret already, and knew that it would only get worse over the years. But at the same time, his head was telling him that it was crazy. Every time you took another job, you were gambling, with your own life as the stake.

I've watched three good men die in the last three years. Men who were better soldiers than me, and deserved a bullet with their name on it far less than I did. The payday doesn't matter when you're dead. So whatever my heart might be saying, my head is seeing this right, Steve reminded himself. Have a couple more beers, then get home, and spend a couple of days getting over the hangover.

'Count me out, boys.'

All the men had heard Steve go on about hanging up his AK-47, but they secretly reckoned it was just talk. They didn't believe they'd ever really see it happen. The men in the unit were all equal, of course. They stuck to SAS rules. No ranks, no hierarchies, everyone's voice the same. Even so, it had been Steve who had brought them together, and turned them into a fighting machine. Without him? None of them had contemplated how that would work.

'For Christ's sake, Steve,' protested Ollie. 'Five hundred grand, and you'll be back by Sunday.'

'You'll be on easy street,' said Dan.

'You don't even know where you're bloody going,' growled Steve.

'I'm going to the bank, I know that much,' retorted Ollie. 'And I'm not frightened of taking a few risks along the way.'

'Leave him,' said Ian. 'It's his call.'

'We'll be fine with the men we've got,' said Henri.

Bruce was nodding. 'Like I said, no one will think any the worse of a man for staying at home. Steve's proved himself as courageous as any here. If he wants to sit this one out, then that's his right.'

There was silence

Everything that needed to be said had been said. The decision was made.

Steve turned to leave. He'd get himself another beer, then get a cab back to the apartment Bruce kept for his men in Battersea, and where he usually kipped down for the night when he was in London.

'I'll join you boys for a slap-up meal on Sunday night,' he said with a wry smile. 'I look forward to hearing all about your adventure.'

'Book TGI Friday's,' said Nick. 'With half a million to spend, I reckon the Jack Daniel's ribs are on me.'

'I wouldn't miss that,' said Steve, about to pull open the double doors.

'Wait,' said Maya.

He turned round. She was holding up her iPhone. A small image was playing on its screen.

'Look at this.'

Steve took two steps closer, and took the phone from her hand. The film was simple, home-made, either shot on the phone itself or on a hand-held camera and transferred across. It showed a blonde woman, playing with a small toddler. A boy, judging by his blue Baby-gro. With sandy blond hair that would probably be brown by the time he was grown up. And a goofy, mischievous smile.

Steve recognised the mother at once. His heart thumped inside his chest.

Sam.

The woman who'd walked out on him two years ago. And the boy. Archie. Even though he'd never laid eyes on him before, a man could always recognise his own flesh and blood.

My son.

'Where the fuck is she?' he demanded, glancing angrily between Maya and Kolodin.

The Russian just smiled. 'For you, Mr West, the payment will be half a million plus the address where you can contact this woman and this child. They mean a lot to you, I think.'

Steve was struggling to control his temper. He looked at Maya, his eyes furious. 'You sodding acted like my friend.'

'I just talked to you in the bar for half an hour.'

'That's my child,' snapped Steve.

He took a step closer, his manner aggressive. His shoulders were thrust forwards, and his fists were tightened into balls, like a man ready to start a fight. 'If you've harmed her . . .'

Maya pointed towards the phone. 'Who says she's harmed?' she said angrily. 'We found her for you, didn't we? Which was a damned sight more than you could do for yourself.'

Steve moved forward angrily, but Ollie and Dan grabbed hold of his shoulders and held him back. 'Easy, mate,' growled Ollie.

Maya hadn't flinched. There wasn't a trace of fear evident in her face, noted Bruce; for a slender woman, with a man as strong as Steve moving aggressively towards her, that could only be admired.

'We tracked her down, and we paid for this film to be taken, because we knew that finding Samantha Sharratt and her son – your son – was probably the only thing that would persuade you to take this job,' said Maya. 'We haven't touched her. We haven't even met her.'

'And if you are such a great father, then how come you don't know where this child is?' asked Kolodin. That smile again, noticed Steve. Like a cat's. Sinister and knowing, as if he could look right inside a man, and find his weakness. 'How come you aren't there to protect them? Answer me that.'

Steve remained silent.

Kolodin took a step forward. 'We are giving you a chance to find them. The one missing piece of your life. And we offer to fix it for you in exchange for a lousy three days' work.' He chuckled softly to himself. 'And you get angry with us. You should be grateful, man.'

'So are you in or are you out?' asked Maya. 'There's a car waiting, and we've no time to waste.'

'The address?' asked Steve.

Maya nodded.

'On Sunday?'

'Yes,' replied Maya quickly. 'And the money now.'

Steve took only a second to reply. He knew that whatever choice he had in this had just evaporated. He'd never forgive himself if he said no.

'I'm in.'

Kolodin grinned, but only briefly.

Just one more victory, noted Steve, with a touch of bitterness. One more example of making people do precisely what he wanted them to. One among hundreds, no doubt.

I'm starting to hate the man already.

'Welcome to the Ice Force, gentlemen,' he said, nodding towards the door. 'And welcome to my payroll. There's just one thing I want to say to you before we start. I'm not saying I've met the devil myself. Not in person. But I've drunk his wine, and I've slept with his women, and I believe I'm better acquainted with him than any man on this earth. So be prepared for a hell of a ride.'

Six

THE KNIGHT XV WASN'T LIKE any armoured vehicle Steve had ever been in before. Then again, with a basic price of £325,000, rising to £650,000 once you added in all the extras, you'd expect something special. Even a Bentley didn't cost that much. Based on the chassis of a humble Ford pick-up truck, it had been punched up by the Canadian firm Knight Conquest to be the last word in heavily guarded luxury. Its thick black skin had enough armour on it to withstand heavy arms fire for twenty-four hours. It was designed to survive bomb blasts, and it included oxygen masks and a fire extinguisher as well as a firewall between the engine and the main cabin, to protect the passengers from an explosion. It had night-vision cameras, armoured glass and run-flat tyres so it could keep going even after the wheels had been shot to shreds. Nothing short of a cruise missile was going to do it much damage. But despite all the heavy armour, it was more comfortable than a five-star hotel suite. The Knight came with six leather seats, Wilton carpets, and laptops wired into the four rear seats, each with an internet connection. There was a drinks cabinet, two television sets and curtains that closed across the windows at the flick of a switch. There was even a cigar box, fully stocked.

Three of the machines were waiting outside the club, the engines already humming on the big 6.8 litre V10 engines. A million and a half quid's worth of motor, noted Steve. And that's just to get us down to the airport.

Kolodin took the first vehicle, accompanied by three of his security staff. Maya directed Steve, Nick, Dan and Ollie into the second vehicle. Then she climbed into the third with Bruce, David, Ian and Henri. Just as well she's not here, thought Steve. She's the last person I want to be sitting next to right now.

'When you've got a billion or two in the bank, and a lot of people trying to kill you, then I guess this is the vehicle you'd choose,' said Dan, as they settled back into the deep leather seats.

'I want one,' said Nick. 'I reckon you could seriously pull in one of these in Swansea on a Saturday night.'

'Yeah, but in Swansea you could pull in an Astra, mate,' said Steve.

'Not with Olga, though,' answered Nick. 'I was wondering if I could borrow one of your Jags.'

'Even with an Aston Martin DB5, you've no chance of scoring a date there, pal.'

'I'm seeing her next Tuesday,' said Nick. 'Right after we get back from this job.'

'Blimey,' muttered Steve, with a shake of the head.

'So, like I said, any chance of a loan of a Jag?'

'I've got a blue Mark II you can have,' said Steve. He glanced at Nick, then laughed. 'But any stains on the back seat, lad, and I'll bloody kill you.'

The Knight XV pulled swiftly away from the kerb. It was

driven by a tall, good-looking black guy, in a dark suit and crisp white shirt, who concentrated on the road and didn't say a word to the men in the back. Part of Kolodin's personal team of chauffeurs, reckoned Steve. The cars steered south across Westminster Bridge, then started to drive down towards Croydon.

Biggin Hill, decided Steve, looking at the road ahead. The private airport used by all bankers and politicians and billionaires flying in and out of London. Wherever the hell this Russian is taking us, it's certainly not in Britain. We'll be flown straight into some hellhole, we can be sure of that. And probably with a one-way ticket.

'The Ice Force, that's what he called us,' said Steve, looking across at Ollie. 'What the hell does that mean?'

'Dubai maybe,' said Ollie, laughing.

'Very witty, mate.'

'Siberia, perhaps,' said Dan. 'The bloke's a Russian, isn't he? There's a lot of Russia that's frozen most of the year.'

'Well, I hope you've packed some warm socks,' said Ollie.

Just keep focused on Sam and Archie, Steve reminded himself. Next week, you'll know where they are. And even if she doesn't want me around – and she probably won't – at least I can meet the boy.

The Knight XV pulled up on the perimeter of the airfield. It was two in the morning now, and apart from a skeleton staff, the place was deserted. Night take-offs weren't usually allowed – they would wake up half of South London – but Kolodin had clearly managed to wangle himself an exception. Just about everything was for sale for the right money, thought Steve. And Kolodin was a man who knew all the prices.

The plane was sitting on the tarmac. They'd all brought their passports with them because they needed ID to be admitted to the executive box at Stamford Bridge, and it only took a moment to be cleared through immigration control. The single immigration officer on the desk looked at them slightly suspiciously but let them through. She was used to the small armies of private security guards who escorted billionaires through Biggin Hill.

Maya led them towards the waiting plane. The airport had two landing strips. The longer north–south runway measured 1,802 metres, making it long enough to handle aircraft up to the size of a Boeing 737 or an Airbus A320. Tonight, an A319C was waiting, its engine already running, and ready to fly. The unit walked across the runway, and started to climb up the steps leading to the door. The A319C was a standard Airbus A320 adapted as a corporate jet. But, despite being basically the same plane you found on dozens of commercial flights, the machine had been completely transformed. The corporate version was slighter shorter and lighter than the standard plane, and it had removable extra fuel tanks where all the passenger luggage would usually go, giving it a total range of 6,900 miles, enough to get to most places in the world in a single hop. The plane could carry up to thirty people, but usually carried far fewer. It was split into two cabins. Kolodin was up front in the executive suite, which came complete with a bar, an office, and a full-size bed, but the rest of the plane was just as plushly kitted out. There were sixteen leather seats in total, arranged in eight rows of two; another well-stocked bar; a small office; two big flat-screen televisions, and a carpet so thick that Steve would have been quite happy to curl up on the floor and have a kip right there.

'I want one of these as well as that motor that drove us down here,' said Dan, sitting down in one of the luxuriously upholstered leather seats.

'And a drink to celebrate,' said Ollie.

'Seats for take-off, please, gentlemen,' said the elegantly dressed blonde stewardess, tapping him on the side of the arm.

Ollie finished pouring himself and Bruce a generous measure of single malt Scotch, then sat down in the seat next to Steve, burped, and glanced out of the window. The doors had been shut, the pilot was already pushing the plane back, and the engines were roaring as they prepared for take-off.

'Looks like the fun is about to start, old sausage,' said Ollie. 'And the amount this bloke is paying, we're getting about ten grand just for sitting through the flight.'

'He'll get his money's worth, we can be sure of that,' said Steve.

The plane started to cruise out on to the runway, then took off smoothly into the night sky. It was a clear evening, with only a scattering of cloud, and with a light payload, the A319C climbed quickly to its cruising altitude of 41,000 feet. The corporate plane flew slightly higher than the commercial version, which gave it a slightly longer range. It also allows us to look down on the easyJet and Ryanair planes, if we happen to pass one, reflected Steve. Which was probably the real reason the engineers at Airbus's Toulouse headquarters decided to make this version fly higher.

'Can you see which way we're going?' asked Ian.

Steve was looking through the window. He reckoned he could already see the lights along the south coast disappear beneath them.

'North, I reckon,' he replied crisply.

'It's bloody Siberia,' said Dan. 'We're going to sodding freeze.'

'Not much chance of a barbecue or a beach, that's for sure,' said Henri.

Steve settled back into his seat. It was just about the most comfortable chair he'd ever been in, either on or off a plane: soft, but with enough support in all the right places to allow you to rest. The stewardesses had laid out a selection of sandwiches and dips on the bar, as well as some beers and wine and spirits. Henri and Dan were tucking into the food, while Maksim and Ollie were doing some work on the vodka. At the back of the plane, Nick had switched on the Xbox 360 that was hooked up to one of the TVs, and had loaded up *Call of Duty: Black Ops*.

'Just getting in a bit of practice, mate,' he explained when Ian came over to see what he was up to.

They'd flown for two hours, and Steve had spent one of them dozing, when Kolodin strode through to their cabin. Maya was at his side. It was four in the morning now, London time, but the man looked as fresh as if he'd just woken from a blissful ten-hour sleep. His face was clean-shaven, his skin gleaming, and his shirt crisp, as if it had just been pressed. He poured himself a measure of vodka from the bar, and knocked it back in one swig. Then his sharp, penetrating eyes glanced around the men in front of him, appraising them in the same way a hyena might appraise its prey.

'Here's where we are,' he said suddenly, pointing to the screen behind him.

The pilot had flashed up a screen showing the A319's

progress. They had crossed the North Sea, flown over Germany, then headed across the Baltic Sea and St Petersburg. The plane was flying over Russia, still heading north, straight into the frozen wastelands of Siberia, and then into the Arctic Circle.

Sod it, muttered Steve silently to himself. Not the Arctic.

'Twenty-seven days ago, another plane was flying a very similar route to this one,' he said, taking another hit on the vodka. 'An A319, converted to private use, and owned by a man called Pavel Markov.'

Steve looked at him closely, noticing the hardening of Kolodin's tone as he pronounced the name. He'd heard of Markov, and he already knew what had happened to his plane. He was another fabulously wealthy Russian oil tycoon, one of the small group of oligarchs who'd emerged from the chaos of the post-Communist Soviet Union owning vast chunks of the nation's mineral and energy wealth. He'd dated a couple of film stars, married a supermodel, and was known for his lavish parties, and a massive yacht he cruised around the Mediterranean in for most of the summer, hosting parties for film stars and politicians, which got written up extensively in the gossip magazines. Three weeks ago, his private jet had crashed. It had been a big story for a couple of days. It had come down in the Arctic Circle somewhere. No one knew what had happened to it, and the plane had not been found. It was a mystery. But the man was dead, that much was clear.

So why the hell was Kolodin talking about it now?

'The plane came down,' the Russian continued. 'We don't know precisely where, and we don't know why. Nobody has been able to find the black box.' He paused, his eyes flicking from man to man. 'I want you to go and get it for me.'

A black box? thought Steve. In the sodding Arctic? He must be crazy.

Maya stepped next to the screen, and Kolodin respectfully made way for her.

'Every plane, as you probably know, has two black box recorders,' she started. 'They detail everything that happens on the plane, and the last half-hour of conversation in the cockpit. But this plane came down in a remote region of the Arctic. There was a fearsome storm that night, and it raged for another five days after the crash. The wreckage was buried beneath a ton of frozen snow and ice. There have been investigators from Airbus, and from the Russian government, all out looking for it, but so far without any success. Only by finding the black box is there any way of discovering what happened to the plane.'

On the plasma screen behind her, she flashed up a map. Steve could feel the plane judder, but it was only a spot of turbulence, and it soon stabilised as the pilot dropped the Airbus down a thousand feet.

Maya pointed to the map. 'We've narrowed the area down to fifty square miles. The last contact with ground control was here,' she said, pointing at the screen. 'The plane should have made radio contact ten minutes later, from here.' She pointed again, then looked back at the men. 'It didn't, so we have to assume it came down somewhere between the two points.'

'You said this job would take three days,' interrupted Ian. 'If the experts have been out looking for it for three weeks, how the hell are we expected to find it in three days?'

'Every black box comes equipped with a radio signalling device, designed to make it easier to find if the plane comes down in a remote region, or else in the sea,' answered Kolodin.

'It has a radius of ten miles. There's one problem. The signal only lasts for thirty days.' He paused, looking back towards Maya. 'In three days' time, the battery will die, and the signal will switch off. The winter blizzards will bury the plane in hundreds of feet of snow and ice, and it will never be seen again. If the black box isn't found in the next seventy-two hours, it never will be.'

There was a pause after he finished speaking that was interrupted by the pilot telling the cabin crew to prepare for landing. The safety belt lights were switched on, and Steve could feel the plane making an alarmingly steep descent. It was coming down hard and fast, the kind of flying he'd experienced on military aircraft rather than civilian flights.

'Get back to your seats,' said Maya. 'We'll continue the briefing on the ground.'

'I don't suppose they could turn it around, maybe drop us off at Dan's bar back in Spain,' said Ollie, settling back into his seat and snapping his belt into position. 'Christ, looking for a black box in the Arctic Circle . . . with only seventy-two hours to find it.'

'It was your idea to take the job,' said Steve sourly.

'I know,' said Ollie. 'Remind me never to listen to my own advice again.'

Seven

YEARS IN THE ARMY, THEN a few more fighting as a mercenary, has taken me to some miserable hellholes, reflected Steve as they stepped off the A319C. Iraq, Helmand, Somalia, the war-ravaged armpits of Africa, and the shell-cratered ruins of Bosnia during the civil war. But Dikson makes most of them look like luxury five-star resorts.

The plane had landed bumpily, and it had taken just a few moments for the ground crew to get a staircase up to the aircraft. A blast of cold air, the chilliest Steve had ever felt in his life, hit him in the face as soon as the doors were opened. They stepped down on to the tarmac, struggling to see through the murky light.

'This is worse than sodding Barry Bay in January,' said Nick, pulling the collar of his coat up around his neck.

'Aye, worse even than the feckin' Antrim coast in July,' added Ian, chuckling as he delivered the remark.

'Save the freezing jokes, boys,' said Ollie. 'We've got three more days of this to get through, and I reckon this place will seem like Dubai on a sunny August afternoon by the time we're finished.'

Dikson Airport had been built in the early 1950s as a staging post for Soviet strategic bombers on their way to nuke the Americans, and had hardly been developed since. There was a long runway, capable of handling the big Tupolev Tu-4 bombers of the era, but it was worn with age. There was a single, shed-like customs and reception area that had been built with all the care the Red Army reserved for its men and facilities. And there was a vast refuelling dump, now rusting with age. Nothing had been done since to spruce the place up, noted Steve as they walked across the tarmac. It was about as remote and hostile as an airstrip could possibly be.

'Where the hell is this place?' asked Dan, looking around.

'The northernmost settlement in Russia, and one of the furthest north in the whole world,' answered Maksim. 'It was named after the Swedish Arctic explorer Baron Oscar Dickson, although somehow the spelling got changed along the way. The Russians use it as one of their Arctic staging posts. They built a radio station here in nineteen fifteen, and a port in nineteen thirty-five, even though the sea is frozen much of the time. There are a couple of thousand people here, and one of the worst climates anywhere in the world. For ten months of the year, you hardly get any daylight, and for two months none at all.'

'I was wondering why it wasn't really on the tourist map,' said Steve.

Kolodin and Maya were leading the way into the customs building. There were a few lights surrounding the building, but they were low-powered and didn't make much impact on the darkness of the night. The runway lights had been switched off, and so had the Airbus's. The pilots and crew had already disembarked. It would be a few days until they were needed again, Steve reckoned. Sunday night. To take us home, hopefully.

A pair of police officials were manning the simple customs and immigration post inside, but both men snapped to attention as soon as they saw Kolodin. They didn't ask for his passport or look at the single briefcase he was carrying, nor did they check Maya or any of the guards. Steve took his passport from his pocket, but the immigration official only glanced at the cover, and didn't ask to see inside. Usually you needed a visa to get into Russia. But not here. Kolodin owned all the oil and gas wells up in this part of Siberia, and he was the man exploring the offshore fields that stretched out into the Arctic Ocean. That meant he owned the place. And he could bring in whoever he wanted. A pair of local policemen certainly weren't going to challenge him. It was more than their life would be worth.

'Climb aboard, gentlemen,' Kolodin said, nodding towards a black Mercedes minibus.

He climbed into a waiting Lexus limo, along with Maya and one of his security guards, while the rest of the men stepped into the bus. Steve could feel his skin chilling. He'd worn a snug leather jacket and black jeans for the game, and that was fine for London in late November. He wasn't a man who ever felt the cold particularly; after surviving SAS selection out on the Welsh mountains, he hadn't reckoned there were any temperatures low enough to bother him again. He had no hat, no coat, and no scarf, and neither did any of the men except Dan. But out here you needed them. Steve reckoned it was at least thirty below, and that was with all the heat from the airport and its buildings. He hated to think what it would be like once they got out into the Arctic itself.

'Shut that sodding door,' snapped Bruce as the last man climbed aboard. 'And let's get the bloody heater on.'

The bus was driven by a burly local who concentrated on the road. Maksim swapped a few words with him in Russian but couldn't learn anything except that the journey would take half an hour. Steve sat close to the front, slumped back in his seat, keeping his eyes on the road ahead. It was getting on for five in the morning British time, which made it close on eight local time. But it didn't make any difference this far north, at least not in the winter. There was no sign of any sunrise, and there was no point in expecting one. It would be well after Christmas before it got light again around here.

The minibus pulled to a stop on the quayside. A yacht was moored directly on the harbour front. Steve had seen a few luxury boats in his time, and he once spent a week helping bodyguard an American software tycoon around the Aegean when one of Bruce's close protection regulars had been off sick. But he'd never seen anything like this before. The yacht was 560 feet long, making it one of the biggest in the world, even among the trophy-collecting Russian billionaires. It had a sleek black hull, polished so that it gleamed even through the darkness. A strip of chrome ran around its edge, while the deck and cabins were crystal white. There was a helipad, two pools, one indoor and one on the deck, and enough security to make even the Royal Navy feel safe. The name, *Lizaveta*, was stencilled across the stern in gold lettering. But it was the ice-breaking equipment that caught Steve's eye. On the prow of the vessel was a thick slab of steel, hardened sufficiently to crack open the Arctic ice. Most luxury yachts were designed for cruising around the smarter ports of the Med. This one was designed for crushing its way through the winter of the Arctic Ocean, a bizarre mixture of ruggedness and opulence.

The lights up on the deck were shining brightly, cutting through the darkness, and illuminating the small harbour. A stiff wind was blowing in from the north-east, the air slicing into Steve's skin like a knife, it was so cold. The sea was choppy, the waves crashing into the side of the quay, sending packets of freezing spray up into the air. Chunks of ice were floating past: the sea wasn't completely frozen here, but it soon would be, and it certainly wasn't the kind of water you'd want to be dropped into. Dark, forbidding and rough, it looked as if it would freeze you, then drown you, and all within a matter of moments.

'Welcome to the *Lizaveta*,' said Kolodin, ascending the ramp that led up from the quay to the deck. 'The most expensive ice-breaker ever built. And worth every damned rouble.'

Kolodin disappeared quickly inside, talking into the mobile that seemed to be clasped permanently to his ear.

'Igor Voytov here will show you around,' said Maya briskly, nodding towards the burly sailor who met them by the main entrance. 'Then we'll finish the briefing. There's no time to lose.'

Voytov was dressed in a smart uniform, and had a close cropped brown beard. He weighed at least two hundred and fifty pounds, a great whale of a man but fit and sharp, and with a manner that suggested he'd be able to handle himself in a fight.

The tour would only take a few minutes, he explained, as he led them across the open deck, then down into the main cabin. The *Lizaveta* was one of only a handful of luxury ice-breakers ever built, he explained. To crush its way through the frozen sea, it had the hardened metal prow that was clearly visible from the outside, as well as a toughened hull that would allow it to withstand pressure from the frozen water all around it, and extra power in the engines, which it would need to push its way through the blocks of frozen water. The yacht had suites for twenty guests, and a crew of twelve, nearly all of them plucked from the elite of the Russian Navy. The hull was built of steel, and the superstructure of aluminium. It had eight diesel engines, which between them generated 24,000 horsepower, enough to get it up to a top speed of twenty knots. The interior was fitted out in teak, marble and gold, and no expense had been spared. There was a gym, a cinema, and an aquarium, as well as a library, a disco, and a suite of offices. The yacht was fitted with a military-standard missile detection system, all the windows were bullet-proofed, and there was a safe room, into which Kolodin could retreat if the vessel came under serious attack. There was a submarine that could hold six people for an emergency escape. All of the crew were armed and, if it came to a fight, reinforcements could be radioed in at a moment's notice.

'So he named it after the Pushkin character,' said Ian, as they completed the tour.

'Who?'

'Pushkin. Famous Russian storyteller.'

'I've heard of Pushkin,' answered Voytov irritably.

'Lizaveta Ivanovna is a character in *The Queen of Spades*. It's a story about greed, and gambling, and secrets. I guess those are three subjects that would appeal to a man like Kolodin.'

'Spare us the sodding English lit. lessons, mate,' growled Ollie.

'Russian lit.' said Ian. 'Pushkin was Russian.'

'Whatever,' snapped Ollie.

Steve remained silent. They were still up on the deck, and his teeth were chattering from the freezing cold wind swirling all around them. He just wanted to get back inside the boat, where the heating kept the temperature at a constant twenty-three degrees.

Before our balls drop off from the cold.

Down below, the ropes had been unhooked, and the crew had drawn the gangplank back up into the yacht. 'We're off,' said Voytov. 'Enjoy the voyage.'

Steve watched as the coast slowly receded from view. About five miles away, he could see the lights of the airport and, beyond that, of the small town of Dikson itself. But apart from that, there was no light in any direction. Just a flat, endless expanse of darkness, stretching as far as the eye could see. Beneath him, he could hear the churning of the water as the big diesel engines roared into life, and he could feel the icy, angry water splashing up all around them as the boat pushed out into the sea.

'Ever done any Arctic training, mate?' he asked Henri.

'In Commando Hubert? Yes, of course. We did a course in sailing under the ice. Submarine work, infiltration, exfiltration, all the usual stuff . . .'

'But have you ever fought here?'

Henri shook his head.

Steve looked down at the black water. We're out of our depth, he thought to himself, and that's just up here on deck. We haven't a clue what we've signed up for. Nor what might lie ahead of us.

Except for the cold.

Eight

KOLODIN WAS STANDING AT THE front of the cinema, with Maya alongside him, as the men settled into their seats. Steve was rubbing his hands together, soaking in the warmth of the room. There was space for twenty people, seated in huge leather armchairs, and a screen big enough to grace a local Odeon, never mind a private yacht.

'Maybe we could just sit around here for a few days watching movies,' said Nick cheerfully.

'And trying out the local vodka,' grunted Ollie.

'Or catching seals,' said Dan. 'Apparently they aren't too bad if you hit them hard over the head and then grill the blubber.'

'You're making me hungry already,' said Nick.

From a projector, Kolodin flashed a series of numbers on to the screen.

It showed a set of bank transfers, made from an account in Switzerland to the bank in Dubai where Bruce maintained offshore accounts for each of the men in his private army.

'Half a million pounds for each man was transferred while the plane was in the air,' he announced. 'You are being paid upfront, in full and in cash, and there aren't many businesses where you get offered a deal like that. All I ask for in return is total commitment for the next three days.'

Another image flashed on to the screen. A map. Dikson was clearly visible, and so was the coastline they had just sailed from. There was a narrow strip of water, then the polar ice cap, frozen and forbidding.

'This is where we're heading,' said Maya, pointing at the map. A blue line marked out a section of territory. 'It is an area of forty square miles within which we believe the plane came down. We'll sail up as close as we can to it. The polar ice cap changes shape all the time, so we can't say precisely how near we'll get, but it should be within twenty to twenty-five miles of the target. We'll kit you out with everything you need. Then we'll get going.'

She glanced at the watch on her wrist.

'It is ten o'clock now. Thursday morning. We'll be ready to move out in a couple of hours. The signaller on the black box will switch itself off at noon local time on Saturday. That gives us fifty hours to play with, so I suggest we don't waste any of it.'

'Any questions?' asked Kolodin, looking around the room.

'What's so important about it?' asked Steve. 'The plane came down, everyone died. There's nothing that can be done about it now.'

The expression on Kolodin's face turned serious. 'A well-maintained A319 is one of the safest planes in the world,' he said. 'Weather conditions were terrible that night but according to the Airbus crash experts, and my own pilots as well, there was nothing in the weather to bring an A319 down. My pilots have all flown through much worse conditions dozens of times and not worried about a thing. My guess is that it wasn't an accident. Pavel Markov was murdered. And I want to know who killed him and why . . .'

He paused, as if stumbling on what to say next. His English was good, even if delivered through a thick accent, but it clearly wasn't his first language.

'Because, if I don't, they'll be coming after me next. Get that black box, and we can find out who murdered him, and maybe save my life.'

Bruce was leaning forward, his expression puzzled. 'Why us?'

'I've heard of Death Inc.' answered Kolodin crisply. 'The men who can achieve the impossible.'

'You'd be better off with some Arctic explorers,' said Ian.

Kolodin shook his head. 'Like I said, I reckon Markov was murdered. Whoever brought the plane down won't want us to find either the aircraft or the black box. There will be men out there trying to stop you finding it, we can be sure of that.'

'You didn't say anything about fighting,' said Steve.

Kolodin smiled. 'I'm paying five million pounds for the most lethal squad of mercenaries in the world to do three days' work for me,' he replied. 'What did you imagine it involved? A walk in the snow?'

Maya and Voytov led the unit down a single flight of stairs that led to the storeroom and armoury. They were down in the working quarters of the yacht now, and there wasn't so much teak or gilt in evidence, but it was still kitted out to a higher spec than any Navy boat, or commercial cruiser. The walls were clad in wood and aluminium, and no expense had been spared on the equipment. The mission would be a tough one, reflected

Steve. There could be no doubt about that, and for the money Kolodin was paying, they shouldn't expect anything else. But at least nobody was stinting on the kit; they'd head out into the Arctic with everything they needed to survive. After that, it was up to them.

'It's going to be hard enough just making our way through the ice, without some bastards trying to shoot us,' said David.

'Aye, well, what did you expect?' replied Bruce. 'We're soldiers, aren't we? Like the man says, you don't pay Death Inc. to do a job for you unless you expect there to be some rough work.'

'We'll be all right,' said Henri. 'It's going to be dark out there. There's no light, not at this time of year. Even if there are guys out there looking for us, they won't be able to see us. If anything kills us, it will be the cold . . .'

'Thanks, mate,' muttered Steve. 'I've always hoped to freeze to death rather than get shot.'

The storeroom had everything they would need for the fifty hours ahead of them. The yacht should be hitting the ice cap in three to four hours' time. Two Toyota Hilux vehicles kitted out for crossing the Arctic were being prepared for them and would be ready by the time they landed.

Inside the storeroom, Maksim took charge of equipping the unit for the two days that lay ahead of them. Arctic warfare was part of the Spetsnaz basic training. A huge chunk of the polar region was Russian territory and they were busy claiming the bits that weren't already theirs, so their special forces were drilled to fight in the snow and ice. Maksim had never been posted anywhere further north than St Petersburg, as it turned out, but at least he knew the basics.

Each man was wrapped up in four layers of warm, water-proofed clothing, with no part of their skin exposed to the air apart from their eyes and nose. It was going to be dark most of the time, so they took high-powered torches with plenty of spare batteries, and night-vision goggles as well to help them see.

For resting up, they took two simple tents, each one capable of holding five people. They packed one sleeping bag per man. The body sweats at night, Maksim explained, and in the Arctic the moisture would freeze. You could wake up in the morning inside a block of your own perspiration. So they'd take bags with a vapour-proof lining, or VPL, designed to prevent any moisture getting on to the bag itself.

They'd be doing most of the hard work on foot, so their feet would be the most important part of the body to protect. Maksim chose ten pairs of 'mulaks', a kind of thick felt sock with a wide, flat rubber sole and a waterproof outer layer. They'd make walking in the snow easier, and keep your feet warm, he explained. Much better for fighting in the Arctic than a traditional military boot; that would just slip and slide in the ice, and, if it got wet, leave you with frostbitten toes that would have to be amputated when you got back. The gloves, likewise, were crucial. They had to be thick enough to keep your hands dry and warm, but also flexible enough to allow you to use your kit, and fire your weapons if necessary. They would also be secured to their waterproofs with string: they'd need to take them off sometimes but if they got lost you'd lose your fingers to frostbite in no time.

Steve selected four blowtorches. He knew a bit about driving in extreme cold. The engines would freeze as soon as they were turned off. Even adapted to cope with the Arctic, they might need some extra warmth to get them started again.

Dan collected some flints, and plenty of fuel to add to their backpacks. They'd need to light fires to brew up hot drinks and food, and also to melt snow into drinking water. There wasn't any point in weighing themselves down with liquids, when the bottles were just going to freeze as soon as they got off the boat. Matches weren't going to be any use either. They'd get wet. They would light up a fire the old-fashioned way.

'Here, pack some candles,' said Maya, handing across two packs. 'Get those alight, and you can use them to light up everything else you need. These are the traditional kind, made from tallow rather than the chemicals they use these days. If you get stuck, and run out of food, you can eat them as well.'

'Bloody great,' said Nick. 'I'll have that as a side dish, alongside the grilled seal blubber.'

'A couple of packs of tampons as well,' said Ollie, glancing across at Maya. 'If you can spare some.'

'Time of the month, is it?' said Steve. 'I thought you were acting a bit moody.'

Ollie grinned. 'Tampons are part of the standard RAF survival kit for men flying across the Artic. They make the best kindling ever devised for starting a fire in the extreme cold.'

'Fair enough,' said Steve. 'But they are going in your sodding backpack, mate. I don't want to be dug up dead in a couple of thousand years with a pack of tampons on me.'

'Just do what he says,' interrupted Bruce. 'And we'll take plenty of Bovril as well. We'll need a lot of hot drinks to get us through the next days.'

'What the sod is Bovril?' asked Henri.

'Sort of like frogs' legs to the French,' answered Ian. 'A British speciality. No one else in the world can understand why the hell you'd want it, though.'

They changed into their Arctic clothes, and packed their kitbags. They were distributing the weight between them; it was going to be a hard enough slog across the ice without burdening one or two men with the tents. They packed plenty of high-protein food: peanuts, chocolate bars, and cereals, as well as instant soups and the Bovril and stock cubes that would give them a blast of warmth. They included plenty of starchy carbohydrates as well: pasta and boil-in-the-bag rice that they could cook up quickly. In the freezing cold, the body would burn up a lot of energy just trying to stay warm, and they had to reckon on a daily intake of at least five thousand calories simply to stay alive.

'What about some weapons?' asked Dan. 'It's going to be dangerous out there.'

Voytov unlocked the back door of the storeroom. Behind it was a small but well-stocked armoury. There was a row of rifles stacked against one wall, mostly AK-74s, the more modern Russian successor to the legendary AK-47, and one of the most reliable assault rifles in the world. Below that were rows of grenades, knives, sniper rifles, explosives and handguns, mostly of Russian or Eastern European origin.

'What have you got for the Arctic?' asked Dan.

He looked along the row of rifles until he spotted what he wanted. An Accuracy International Arctic Warfare rifle. It was made by the British company Accuracy International, which had won the contract to make a new precision sniper rifle for the Army in the early 1990s. A few years later the Swedish Army had commissioned their own version of the weapon but wanted it upgraded to cope with the extreme cold of the northern winter. The Arctic Warfare, or AW, was the result. A modified version of the standard weapon, it featured a de-icing system that allowed it to be used in temperatures as low as minus forty degrees centigrade. And the stock, bolt and trigger release were all large enough to allow it to be operated while wearing thick Arctic mittens. Most standard rifles couldn't be fired by men wearing gloves, but in the Artic your fingers would freeze while you were still halfway through a firefight.

'We'll take three of those,' said Dan. 'And ten of the AK-74s. Plus plenty of ammo.'

Voytov nodded. 'You'll need some special lubricating oils,' he said, reaching into the boxes below. 'You're going to struggle to keep your weapons working in the cold, but these will help.'

The men kitted themselves out with the guns. The AW was a sniper rifle for long-range combat, while the AKs could be used for close assault, if necessary. Each of them took a Yarygin PYa handgun, the standard sidearm for the Russian military, which had replaced the legendary Makarov in 2003. They packed fifty rounds each of the Russian-made 7N21 armour-piercing bullets, with a bimetal design that allowed the round to punch its way through steel plating or body armour.

'There are polar bears out there,' said Voytov. 'They get hungry during the winter, and they have a great sense of smell. It's one of the biggest risks Arctic explorers face. The bears smell them, and come and attack them in their tents. Use the armour-piercing ammo on them, and it should be powerful enough to get through the fur and hide and do some damage.'

'You're joking,' snapped Nick. 'I don't fancy getting into a scrap with a sodding bear.'

'Scared of a fluffy animal,' mocked Henri.

'Maybe Sandra took away your favourite teddy,' chortled Ian.

'Bloody leave it out,' answered Nick, red-faced. He was looking closely at Voytov. 'What do you mean, *should* be powerful enough?'

'An animal needs a thick hide to survive at the North Pole. Ordinary bullets bounce off them.'

'And they eat people?'

Voytov chuckled. 'Only when they are really hungry,' he replied. 'If you get into a fight with one, remember this. Polar bears are left-handed, so if you attack them from the right you have a better chance.'

Nick was shaking his head. 'I'll think I'll sodding leg it. I don't fancy a punch-up with a polar bear.'

Ian was inspecting the hand grenades, and chose two dozen of the RGN-86, a lethally effective Russian-made weapon, widely used by the Spetsnaz. With a 3.2 to 4-second fuse, it packed 57 grams of TNT, killing anything in an area within 66 square metres of its detonation. He also took a dozen of the RKG-3: a Soviet era anti-tank grenade, the RKG-3 was a high-powered device which, as its name suggested, was capable of taking out a tank. 'We won't be meeting any armoured vehicles, not out on the ice,' he said, as he distributed the weapons amongst the men's kitbags. 'But this has almost as much punch on it as an RPG and it's going to be a lot easier to carry around if we need to cover some ground on foot.'

'I think that's enough weaponry,' said Maya.

'There's one thing you learn in this business,' said Steve sharply. 'You can never have too much firepower. The only blokes who didn't learn that properly are six foot under the ground.'

'It will just slow you down,' said Voytov sharply.

'We'll be faster if we know we're safe,' said Henri.

Maya remained silent while the unit helped themselves to the weapons and ammo they wanted. Maksim had shown them a Spetsnaz technique for fitting webbing underneath a snow suit, but it was soon clear to all of them that they weren't going to be able to carry nearly as much kit with them as they normally would. Steve managed to get a handgun, a knife, and two spare mags into his webbing, along with a medi-pack, a compass and some food, but that was all he could manage. The rest of it would have to go on the vehicles. The most important task was to stay warm – there wasn't any point in having enough gear on you to fight off a whole platoon if you froze to death in the first few hours.

'This will locate the black box for you,' said Maya. She held two radio receivers, both made from matt black metal, and measuring four inches by two. Each had a small, stubby antenna, like an old-fashioned mobile, and a small, electronic screen that flashed up co-ordinates.

'It should have a range of ten kilometres,' she continued, handing one device to Steve, and the second to Maksim. 'It will pick up the signal emitted by the black box, and give you co-ordinates for locating it. But the aircraft is probably buried in a lot of snow, and that is going to reduce the range. And the closer you get to the North Pole, the stronger the magnetic field gets. Particularly during a polar storm, radio signals go crazy. You probably won't get any signal until you are within five kilometres of the plane, and maybe even less.'

Steve glanced at the device, then passed it across to Henri, who slotted it into his webbing, next to the gun. It was going to be a while yet before they needed that.

'We need a couple of satellite phones,' said Bruce. 'Iridium or Imarsat, depending on what you have.'

'No phones,' said Voytov bluntly.

'It's sodding dangerous out there,' growled Bruce. 'We'll do our bloody best, but if we run into trouble we need to be able to call in some help.'

'They could be tracked,' said Maya. 'It's not worth it.'

'Who the hell can track a satphone?' said Ian.

Maya paused before replying. 'The Russian government,' she said finally. 'They can monitor satphone traffic in their own territory and along their borders the same way the CIA can.'

'Hold on,' said Steve. 'Are you saying we're up against the sodding Russian government here?'

'Markov may well have been killed on the orders of the President of the Russian Republic,' said Maya. 'If so, the FSB – the successor body to the KGB – will be making sure they find the black box first, and not us.'

'Jesus,' snapped Steve. 'Nobody mentioned we were taking on the sodding KGB.'

'The FSB,' corrected Voytov.

'It doesn't matter what the hell you call them these days,' said Steve. 'They're still hardly the boys you want to get into a fight with. Not on their own territory.'

'Leave it, Steve,' warned Ian. 'We're being well paid. We shouldn't have expected a walk in the park.'

'But—'

'No phones,' repeated Maya firmly.

Bruce glanced around the rest of the men, then nodded. 'No phones,' he agreed reluctantly. 'You'll see us in two days. God willing . . .'

Nine

THE MEAL WAS HOT AND filling. A selection of pasta, steaks, salad and rice, washed down with plenty of mineral water. Steve piled his plate high, aware that it would be a long time before they got a decent meal again. Dan, Nick, and Maksim had managed to cram even more grub on to a single plate, and Nick had balanced another couple of steaks on his hand.

'Eat all that, and the polar bears won't come close to you,' said Steve, looking at Nick. 'They'll be sodding terrified.'

'I reckon we should bring back a bear head for Nick,' said Ollie. 'Should impress that Olga babe.'

'Leave it,' growled Nick.

Steve sat down at the long wooden table. They were in the canteen used by the crew, and the chef was still busily cooking up more food. There was a slight swell in the sea, and the yacht was rocking as it plunged closer and closer to the North Pole. Occasionally there was a crunching sound, something like a glass being stamped on, as the ice-breaking equipment smashed through the blocks of ice. Each time, the hull shuddered and groaned before the engine steadied the vessel, and supplied enough power to push the obstacles aside and move the yacht forward. Outside, hardly anything was visible through the porthole. It was midday local time, but there wasn't so much as a glimmer of sunshine. Just a faint glow, as if someone had switched on a single light bulb a long way away.

'Get this grub inside you, lads,' said Bruce cheerfully. 'Then take your tablets.'

Steve started to eat. He didn't have much appetite, but he knew he should get as many calories inside him as possible before they headed out into the ice. Maya had already told them they would be landing on the polar shelf in roughly three hours. The ship's doctor had supplied each of them with a high-impact, short-duration sleeping tablet, the kind used in surgery to prepare patients for a full anaesthetic. It would knock them out for a couple of hours, allowing them to briefly recharge their batteries. Before the journey begins, reflected Steve. Into God knows what.

'I don't like the sound of getting mixed up with the Russian government,' said Ollie.

'No worse than the British,' said Ian. 'In fact, I would rather trust Ivan and his mates than some public school tosser from MI6.'

Ollie glowered but remained silent.

Last time around, they'd been stitched up badly by Six, Steve recalled. Ollie had been hoping to find his way back into the regular Army, and, even though they'd come out of the job with a few quid in their pockets, the betrayal still hurt.

'Think we're going to be OK, Maksie?' asked David. 'This is your territory.'

The Russian chewed on a huge mouthful of pasta, his

expression thoughtful. 'A Russian never trusts his government,' he replied eventually. 'History teaches us not to, and we never forget it. But we should be all right up in the Artic. As soon as we get out on to the ice, we're beyond Russian territory.'

'And we're beyond any kind of law at all,' said Henri. 'We'll make our own rules, and that's the way it should be.'

'Take your medicine, lads,' said Bruce sternly.

The sleeping tablets were small, yellow pills, with no brand name on them. Steve could see the sense in taking them. They were all exhausted, and they were on a tight deadline. There wasn't going to be much time, if any, for sleeping once they got on to the ice, and even if there was, the terrible conditions would make it a challenge to get any rest. But back in the Regiment, it was a rule among the men never to take any of the drugs the doctors offered you. Even during both the Gulf Wars, when the threat of chemical attacks from Saddam had been very real, none of the guys would take the tablets designed to combat poison gases. There was too long a history of soldiers being experimented on. Steve took the tablet, and did precisely what he'd always done in the Regiment: slipped it under his tongue, ready to spit away later.

'Get some shut-eye, boys,' said Bruce, standing up. 'We'll reconvene at three local time.'

Ten of the crew had vacated their cabins. Steve slipped into room seven. It was simply but comfortably furnished: a bed, freshly made up, a small desk with a netbook for web access, a wardrobe and a trouser press. Steve took off his shoes, stripped down into his boxer shorts, and splashed some water across his face. Then he lay back down on the bed and closed his eyes. He knew he wasn't likely to sleep. He was always too keyed up before a mission began. His muscles tensed up, and his heart was racing. Just relax, he told himself.

There was a knock on the door, then the handle turned. Maya stepped inside.

Steve looked up, surprised.

'I knew you wouldn't take the tablets,' she said, stepping inside the small cabin. 'It's the same with the guys the Mossad uses. They won't take anything the government gives them either.'

'What are you doing here?' asked Steve.

Maya blinked a couple of times, and, around her eyes and her mouth, Steve noticed an unexpected tenderness. 'I know you're pissed off with me about what happened back in the club.' She shrugged. 'I just wanted to say I'm sorry. We didn't mean anything bad. We just needed to find a way to get you to take the job, and we thought that would make it worthwhile for you.'

'Are Sam and the kid OK?'

'They're fine.' She looked at Steve. 'What happened there? I mean, you obviously care about her, but she doesn't want to see you.'

'Relationships,' said Steve, with a half-smile. 'If you need a bloke to take out a tank, or drop out of a chopper into heavy gunfire, then I'm your man. Somehow it doesn't seem to translate into getting on with women.'

Maya flicked a lock of her black hair out of her face. It was medium length, stopping just beyond the back of her neck, but she pinned it back when she was working. It was loose now, the same way it had been in the nightclub, and it matched the brown of her eyes and the olive, smoky tone of her skin to perfection. 'I'm sure you do OK,' she said softly.

'I can meet them. But I can't make them stay.'

'You probably don't really want them to.'

Steve laughed. 'Five hundred grand *and* some free relationship counselling. This job really is well paid.'

'You need to rest,' said Maya. But she was still perched on the end of the narrow single bed.

Not going anywhere, noticed Steve. Not in a hurry, anyway.

'There's one way to relax before a battle,' said Steve, reaching out to take her in his arms. 'Works better than any sleeping tablet, I've usually found.'

She hesitated for a fraction of a second, her eyes glancing nervously at the door, then she fell into his arms. Their lips met, her tongue darted forward, and Steve could feel his lust rising. A moment ago he was fighting off sleep, but now he was hungry for her, as hungry as he'd ever been for any women in his life. Her body was warm and supple, but with a strength to it that he had never encountered before; the muscles were crisp and lean, toned to perfection, with not so much as an ounce of wasted flesh. He pushed his hand up into her shirt, pulling it off, and flicked his lips up against nipples that were already as hard as nails. She was pushing into him, her breath heavy, her hands and fingernails digging into his flesh, scratching at him, the way a dog might rip into a piece of meat. 'Fuck me rough,' she hissed. 'I like it.'

Steve turned her over on her back, lying her flat on the narrow bed. He let his tongue run down the length of her body, enjoying the smell and taste of her, teasing her, sensing her excitement growing. 'I said fuck me,' she repeated. 'Don't make me wait.'

Steve pressed into her, opening her legs. Their lovemaking

was urgent, passionate, but not rushed, both of them enjoying each other's body. She gasped and writhed as she came, kissing Steve so hard he suspected she might draw blood, before pulling him out of her, and finishing him in her mouth. There had been some wild women over the years, Steve reflected as the waves of pleasure slowly rippled through every nerve ending in his body. Some drunk ones as well. But he wasn't sure he'd ever been with a women who was so in command of her own pleasure and her man's as Maya had been in the last few minutes.

'What the sod do they put in those tablets?' asked Steve as he lay back, cradling Maya in his arms.

'I didn't take one either.'

'I'm bloody pleased to hear it,' said Steve. 'Otherwise I hate to think what Ian and Maksie might be up to right now.'

Maya laughed. 'Like you said, this is the only way to relax before a battle. And afterwards as well.'

'So how does it work in the Caracal Battalion?' asked Steve. 'Are you guys shagging each other's brains out all day?'

Maya snuggled closer into Steve's chest, the passion turning into tenderness. Her fingers were running softly down the side of his chest, pausing only briefly to examine some of the scars that were a legacy of a decade spent fighting in some of the roughest corners of the world.

'It's strictly off limits,' she answered. 'Once we started, we'd never stop.'

Steve knew precisely what she meant. Combat was a sexual stimulant, every soldier was aware of that. It was why so few armies allowed women anywhere near the front line. They wouldn't be safe, and the generals knew it. And it was why so many armies raped their way through conquered territory. The adrenaline, and the closeness of death, turned men into animals. Perhaps the women as well, he mused, holding Maya close to his chest.

'And then you'd never get around to fighting.'

'Exactly.'

She paused, her fingers twisting into his skin, then relaxing again. 'You miss her? Sam, I mean.'

'I hardly knew her,' answered Steve. 'We were on a job in Africa, and she got mixed up with us. We only spent a few days together.'

'You had a baby.'

'Sometimes it only takes a few minutes.'

'But she meant something to you?'

Steve didn't really want to talk about it. Not with another woman lying in his arms, and with the taste of her sweat still on his lips. It didn't seem right.

'I'd just like to meet the boy, that's all.'

'But the mother will come along as well,' said Maya. 'That's the way it works. You can't have one without the other.'

'I guess I can live with that.'

'I don't think she's right for you.'

'And you're the expert, right?' There was a sardonic note to Steve's tone.

'I've been around men like you all my life,' said Maya. 'My family were all Mossad. My father, my grandfather . . .'

'And you think you know what makes us tick?'

'Better than you do yourself.'

Maya rolled over, resting her chin on her elbow. Her breasts, taut and muscular, and yet with a shape that was luxurious and sexy, were pressing into Steve's chest, and the nipples were growing hard again.

'You're a warrior, Steve,' she said. 'You can only be understood by your own kind.'

'And that's you?'

'Maybe, maybe not,' said Maya. She was brushing her nipples into Steve's skin, letting them run through the hairs on his chest. 'We've got another two hours to find out.'

Steve rolled her on to her back, pressing his weight down into her. 'And I know precisely what we can do with them.'

Ten

BOTH THE TOYOTAS WERE KITTED out to survive the
Arctic weather. The engineers had started with a
Toyota Hilux, a mass-market pick-up truck with
a three-litre diesel engine. But that wasn't much more than a
power unit, a chassis and a skin. The standard wheels had
been replaced with far larger Arctic ones fitted with snow tyres.
The outsized wheels meant the suspension had to be lifted
up, but the extra size, plus the studs on the tyres, gave the
vehicle a lot more grip, as well as making the ride softer.
The tyres had been further modified to run at very low pressure,
which again would make it easier to grip the snow and ice. The
arches had been raised to make room for the wheels, and
the diesel engine had been modified to help it cope with
temperatures of minus fifty or sixty degrees. Heaters had
been fitted inside the engine to keep it warm enough to turn
over, and to warm the fuel as it was delivered to the power
unit, and an extra heavy-duty battery had been added to help
start the beast. A hundred-litre auxiliary fuel tank had been
fitted, and winches were strapped to the back of both vehicles.
If either one got stuck in the snow, and it was more than likely

they would, they could use the other one to try and drag it out.

'I think I saw one of these on *Top Gear*,' said Nick admiringly. 'Sodding great truck.'

Dan was the ablest mechanic among them, and had already made a quick inspection of the vehicle. The Russian engineer was running through how the heating systems worked, and detailing all the tricks they'd need to know to keep the machine running through the extreme cold they were about to encounter.

Steve walked over to the side of the yacht, peering into the darkness. He could see the great expanse of ice stretching out into the distance. The yacht was still moving, but only at the pace of a snail. There was simply too much ice in the way. All around then, glaciers that had broken away were floating through the sea, their tips glinting menacingly as the *Lizaveta*'s big lamps flashed past them. The captain was manoeuvring the yacht closer to the edge of the main polar ice cap. Any moment now, thought Steve, pulling his hat down lower over his face to protect himself against the biting wind, we'll be down on the Arctic shelf itself. And the fun will begin.

He glanced across at Maya. She'd dressed in full cold weather survival kit, and was busily making sure the pair of Toyotas were fully equipped for the hours that lay ahead. The essentials they'd carry on their bodies, but the extra supplies of fuel, ammo and tents would all go on the trucks. My kind of woman? he wondered to himself. A warrior, just like me? Maybe, he reflected.

'The end of the world,' said David, standing next to him.

'It's not that bad.'

David laughed. 'I meant geographically speaking.'

Steve grinned. 'Then let's crack on, mate. We don't want to miss any of the fun.'

The *Lizaveta* had pulled up alongside the main ice block, and two of the crew were laying down a ramp across which the Toyotas could drive straight on to the glacier. The ice cap was just a huge block of frozen water floating on top of the Arctic Ocean. They couldn't expect it to be a straight run to their target zone. There could be walls of ice in the way, and there would be the sea to contend with as well. The ice cap wasn't solid, not any more. There were fissures and cracks all over it. It was worse in the summer when much of the ice melted, but even at this time of year they could expect to come across crevices – known as 'leads' among polar explorers – and they would have to find a way to cross them.

'How's the weather looking?' asked Henri, looking at Voytov.

'Not great,' replied the Russian.

'Jesus,' muttered Ollie. 'It's pretty crap already. You mean it's getting worse?'

Voytov nodded. 'There could be a storm some time over the next twenty-four hours.'

'That's the forecast?' asked Bruce.

'Forecasts aren't much use in the Arctic winter,' answered Voytov. 'The weather is all over the place.'

'Think we should postpone?' asked Ian.

'There's no time,' growled Kolodin.

The billionaire strode across the deck to them. He was wearing a heavy overcoat, and a fur hat, but otherwise was dressed more for the Moscow streets than the North Pole.

'We'll stay right here until sixteen hundred hours on Saturday afternoon,' said Kolodin. 'It is fifteen hundred hours on

Thursday now. The signal on the black box gets switched off at midday on Saturday—'

'But if there's a storm . . .' protested Ian.

'Then you'll fight your way through it,' said Kolodin. 'I've hired soldiers for this job, and I've paid them well, because I expect them to battle against anything. Weather, an assault . . .'

He looked at the men.

'I want that black box,' he repeated, his tone hardening. 'There's a hundred thousand bonus for each man when you come back, on top of what you are already being paid, so long as you deliver what I want.'

'Alive or dead,' said Ian sourly.

'It makes no difference to me,' said Kolodin. 'Your next of kin will receive the money if any of you don't make it back.'

'We'll be back, all of us,' said Bruce. 'You can count on that.'

'Then let's go,' said Steve.

The unit started to climb on board the pair of Toyotas. Dan took the wheel of the first vehicle, and Steve, Nick, Ian, and Maya climbed in alongside him. Henri took the wheel of the second, with Ollie, David, Bruce and Maksim as passengers. The big engine growled as Dan kicked it into life, then started to edge forward. The heating was on, though kept low because of their snow suits, and Steve could feel his skin start to thaw out. He looked forward as the hi-beams were switched on. illuminating the track that led down from the yacht on to the ice. The Toyota gripped the metal ramp, then started to edge out on to the snow. Dan was driving carefully, getting used to the feel of the vehicle, and the terrain, before he tried to pick up any speed.

'Get the lead out of your arse, granddad,' shouted Ollie, leaning out of the Toyota behind, and shouting through the cold, dark air. 'Jesus, man, you're slower than my gran on the A30.'

'Sodding hooligans,' yelled Ian, looking around. 'You can't even get away from them at the North bloody Pole.'

Maya had prepared a route on the map. They would drive north-north-east, taking them straight into the target zone. They wouldn't actually get to the North Pole; the zone they were searching stopped a couple of degrees short of the Pole itself. If they kept moving in a straight line, and could make ten or fifteen miles an hour, which was the most they could hope for across the snow and ice, they should be there soon enough. 'So long as we don't hit any water, or any glaciers we can't cross, that is,' she explained to the rest of the men.

Steve settled back to enjoy the ride. As the mission began, he could feel the adrenaline start to kick in. He was rising to the challenge, the same way he always had. Less then fifty hours, he reminded himself. Then I'll be tucked up back in that bed on the yacht, with Maya at my side, and half a million quid in the bank.

Maybe this job isn't so bad after all.

'Anyone brought any music?' he asked, as the first hour passed without any incident.

The first few minutes of the drive had been interesting enough. The flat, frozen icescape was not an environment Steve had ever encountered before, and it wasn't like anywhere else on earth. The surface was rough, pitted with holes and craters, with occasional walls of frozen water rising up like rocks in the desert. It was probably the closest you could get to a different planet without getting on a spaceship, he reflected. But it quickly became monotonous. The hi-beams pierced the soupy, foggy darkness, but only for twenty yards maximum, and it was impossible to see much on either side of the Toyota's cabin. Ten or fifteen yards of ice couldn't hold your interest for very long. And with such limited visibility, it was reckless to take your speed above fifteen miles an hour. I've had more fun on the M25 on a bank holiday afternoon, thought Steve, as the time started to drag.

'What do you want?' said Nick, fishing out his iPod, and plugging the wire into the Toyota's auxiliary socket. 'The Killers? Arcade Fire? Stereophonics?'

'How about some Bruce?' said Steve.

'Sodding hell,' muttered Nick. 'Not "Born To Run" again.'

'Proper fighting music that is,' said Ian sharply.

'Just play the man,' said Henri.

Steve tapped his fingers on the dashboard to himself as the thundering opening chords of the song filled the cabin of the Toyota. He always remembered what his mate Jeff had said to him on the unit's first job together in Afghanistan. When you're in a battle, only the Boss will do. Well, this one's for you, pal, he said to himself. Wherever the hell you are.

Another hour passed quickly enough. The same landscape, rolling out endlessly all around them. One glacier had loomed up in front of them, and they had stopped for a chat with Henri in the second Toyota to find the best way through it. Dan had tried to drive the Toyota up over the steep ascent, but even with a specially modified gear ratio it was impossible to get enough grip to climb the slope. Maya had charted another route, taking them south-south-east, and after two miles they'd managed to skirt round the wall of ice and were heading steadily north again.

As the Bruce track faded on the iPod, Nick replaced it with the Beach Boys' 'California Girls', humming to himself as the poppy chorus boomed out of the speakers.

'Very droll, pal,' said Ian. 'I didn't realise they ever got around to irony at your comp in Swansea.'

'I-sodding-what?'

'Don't worry about it now, lad,' said Steve. 'We'll explain later.'

He glanced out of the side window. One wheel of the Toyota was snagging on a lump of snow, and Dan was revving the engine furiously, trying to push enough power into the back wheels to propel it forward. The machine was hardly moving, and Ollie was already leaning out of the window behind them, cracking jokes about Sunday-afternoon drivers.

'Doesn't that sod ever realise when a gag is past its sell-by date?' muttered Ian.

Dan was tapping the accelerator, taking the revs higher and higher, but the Toyota still wasn't moving. Suddenly the big tyres found some grip, and the truck sped forward, like a greyhound released from its trap. The wheels caught hold of some thickly-packed snow, and the speed rose in a fraction of a second all the way up to thirty. After two hours at no more than fifteen, it felt to Steve like doing a hundred and ten on an A road, a brutal and dangerous burst of speed.

'Brake, brake,' screamed Maya suddenly.

Steve could hear the fear in her voice.

He looked anxiously forward. Even with the hi-beams on, he couldn't see anything. But maybe her eyes were more accustomed to the conditions. Dan was tapping his foot on the brakes, then releasing the pressure, then tapping the brakes again. He'd done military driving during his time in the SASR, and he knew the drill for preventing your vehicle sliding on ice: steady, short stabs on the brakes to gradually slow the machine down, and turning the wheel in the same direction it was travelling to help regain control. He was doing precisely what the textbooks said you should do. But it wasn't doing any good. The acceleration had been too much and the tyre studs had lost their effectiveness. All around them, Steve could hear a cracking noise. At first he thought it was the engine. Maybe the gears were breaking apart. But then he realised it came from outside. A sharp, splintering noise, like a massive chisel breaking into rocks. Up ahead of him, caught in the Toyota's lights, the ground started to open up. A crack, only a few inches at first, then feet. Water, ugly and black, was foaming up, spilling out on to the ice in an angry torrent.

'Left, left,' shouted Henri.

'I'll sodding lose control,' barked Dan.

'You're going in.'

Steve was hanging on desperately to the side of the Toyota. He could hear another cracking noise, much louder this time, then felt the vehicle rock violently. Then it started to slide. Downwards. It paused as the back winch caught on a block of ice, then that too collapsed. And suddenly the Toyota was plunging straight down into the stormy ocean that lay just beneath the ice that they had been driving across over the last few minutes.

The window glass held the water out for a brief fraction of a second. Then it was spilling all around them. It was unbelievably cold. Only a tiny portion of Steve's skin was exposed around the nose and eyes but the icy water still sliced into it like a finely polished blade. It was darker than any water Steve had ever seen before, like black ink, and with a current that whipped into a man and threatened to take him all the way to hell before he realised what was happening to him.

'Get the fuck out of here,' shouted Henri. 'If the current catches you, you're dead.'

Steve could see precisely what he meant. The water was flowing strongly eastwards. Get carried any distance, and you'd disappear under the ice, and never be able to get back to the surface again. You'd die of cold in a few minutes. He pushed on the door. One of the many modifications made to the Toytota was disabling its central locking. If you went into the water, the last thing you wanted was to get trapped inside. He leant hard into it. The Toyota was falling fast through the water, and there was plenty of pressure up against the door, but with a strong heave it opened, and Steve plunged out into the ocean. Even with his eyes fully open, it was hard to see anything, but as he started to focus, he pushed a hand down to help drag Maya and Nick free of the sinking vehicle. Dan and Ian had already swum out via the driver's door. Kicking back with his legs, Steve started to push himself upwards. The snow suit was keeping him dry enough, but his feet were soaking, and so was his face. The water was black and murky, the current fighting back against him, as if it were a man intent on murder. Steve could feel his lungs start to struggle: it had been a minute, maybe a minute and a half, since the vehicle had plunged into the water. There wasn't enough light to tell where the surface was, but he could tell which way was up, and it could only be a few more yards, he reckoned. One more kick, he told himself grimly. You'll live.

He burst to the surface, looking anxiously around. The lead was forty yards wide, and at least a couple of hundred long: an angry, snarling crack in the ice through which the water was bubbling up to the surface. As he glanced forward he could see Henri and the rest of the unit scouring the surface, looking towards them. Twenty yards or so, he reckoned. He started to swim straight towards them, ignoring the cold. The ice around the edge was rough and jagged, with nothing to grab hold of.

An arm reached down to pull him up, and Steve took it gratefully.

'I'd have said it was a bit chilly for a dip, old sausage,' said Ollie cheerfully, hauling Steve up on to the ice. 'Still, each to his own.'

'Bracing,' said Steve. 'The showers at school were a bit like that.'

As he looked around, he could see Henri and David were helping Maya, Nick, Ian and Dan out of the water.

They took a moment to compose themselves, grateful to still be alive, before the magnitude of the disaster struck home.

The Toyota was gone for good, there was no question about that. And with half their transport at the bottom of the ocean, the target zone was going to be a whole lot harder to reach.

'What the hell do we do now?' said Steve sourly.

'Get you warmed up, my friend,' said Henri. 'Then we crack on.'

Eleven

MAKSIM RETRIEVED A CAMPING STOVE from the back of the remaining Toyota and got it alight using his flints. The pale light of the flame made only a small dent in the darkness all around them but the warmth and the light, weak though it was, helped to restore Steve's spirits. The snow suits had protected their bodies from the water but their faces and feet needed warming fast to prevent frostbite. Steve leant his face into the flame, grateful for the flickers of heat that broke up the freezing air, then sat down to put his feet up by the fire.

'Nice slice of hot buttered toast, that's what you need, pal,' said Ollie.

'Stop it,' moaned Nick. 'You're making me hungry.'

Steve waited five minutes, then ten, allowing plenty of time for his blood to start circulating properly again. All of them had taken off their mulaks, and Maksim was beating them dry against the side of the Toyota. The worst thing they could do was put wet footwear back on: their toes would be frostbitten in only a couple of hours.

While they were drying out, Maksim and Henri were

unpacking a pair of sledges that they had stored on the back of the one remaining Toyota. There wasn't going to be enough room in the single vehicle for all ten of them, so five men would have to go in the back of the pick-up. That meant the kit would have to be piled up on the sledges, and towed along behind them. It would slow them down, but there wasn't anything they could do about that.

It's better than sodding walking, reflected Steve.

Maksim brewed up some teas, mixed in plenty of powdered milk and sugar, and handed them round. Steve sipped gratefully on the hot liquid, then started to pull the dry mulaks over his feet, and strapped his gloves back on over his hands. He let the steam rising from the mug blow over his face, drawing in the warmth. It was amazing how a cup of tea could make you feel better, he realised. Even out here, right at the end of the earth.

'Any vodka in this, mate?' asked Dan.

'I sodding wish,' grunted Maksim.

'I can't believe it,' said Ollie. 'We've been in Russia, what, twelve or fifteen hours, and we haven't had a single drink yet.'

'We're not in Russia,' grunted Maksim. 'This is neutral territory. If we cross the border, we'll drink the country dry.'

Steve chuckled. 'Even you might find that a tall order, Maksie.'

He drained the tin mug, cleaned it out with some snow, and then looked around the rest of the unit. 'Right, let's crack on, lads,' he said decisively. 'I don't know about the rest of you, but the sooner I'm sitting back on a sun lounger by a pool somewhere with a cocktail in my hand and a few gorgeous blondes in bikinis to ogle, the happier I'll be.'

'Who's going in the back?' asked Nick.

'The five of us who lost our vehicle, of course,' said Steve. 'That's only right.' Then he paused. 'Except Maya, of course. One of you sods can make way for her.'

'I can ride in the back as well as anyone,' snapped Maya.

'Don't be stupid,' said Steve. 'It's going to be bloody freezing back there.'

Maya turned her dark piercing eyes on Steve, then broke into a knowing smile. 'I'm as strong as any man here. Probably stronger.'

'I'm sure you are,' said Bruce. 'But this unit isn't putting a lady out in the cold. Standards are standards.'

'But—'

'And that's final,' growled Bruce. 'As for the rest of you blokes, we'll draw lots.'

Ollie grinned. 'We'll throw snowballs,' he said. 'Furthest four get to snuggle up to Maya in the cabin.'

He rolled up a snowball, while Maya walked twenty yards into the darkness. As the one person without a stake in the game, she was the only proper judge. Ollie threw first, but couldn't get any kind of swing with his snow suit cramping his arm, and only managed twenty yards. No one else could see where the snowballs landed until Maya returned.

'Steve, Dan, David and Nick are riding up front,' she said when she returned. 'The rest of you can climb in the back.'

'I'll swap with you, mate,' said Nick to Bruce. 'I don't want you catching hypothermia.'

Steve looked at the two men. Bruce was forty-seven this year, far older than the rest of them, and probably too old to be risking his life on a mission like this. But no one ever mentioned his age. All soldiers grew old eventually. But it wasn't something any of them were ever comfortable with.

'I'll be fine, lad,' Bruce growled. 'At least I won't have to listen to any of that terrible music you play on your iPod.'

Before Nick could say anything, Bruce had climbed up into the back of the pick-up truck, and hunkered down on its floor. Maksim climbed in alongside him, with Henri and Ollie filling up the rest of the space. It was cramped, but at least their bodies would help to keep them warm. Dan secured the sledges to the back of the Toyota, then took the wheel, with the rest of the unit climbing on to the front bench. They'd left the engine running all through the stop – turn it off, and it might take an hour at least to get it started again – so Dan just had to release the brakes and tap on the accelerator to get it moving again.

'Where to?' he said, looking across at Maya.

'North-north-east,' she replied crisply. 'We'll get well clear of this lead before we try going due north again. We don't want to risk losing this vehicle as well.'

'How do we know the ice is thick enough?' asked Nick.

'We don't,' replied Maya. 'Most polar explorers use dogs and sledges because you can never tell whether the ice is going to be able to support the weight of a machine this size. If someone walked ahead, they might be able to test the ground. If you sweep away the snow, you'll see the ice change colour where it thins out.'

'That would take days,' said Steve.

'Right,' said Maya. 'And we don't have that kind of time.'

'We'll take our chances,' said Dan. 'If we go down, we'll just sodding well have to swim for it.'

The Toyota was moving steadily over the snow. With the

sledges to pull as well as the men in the back, Dan had slowed right down to less than ten miles an hour. Anything faster might tip the sledges on their side, and the wind chill from any faster movement would turn the rest of the guys into ice blocks. He drove for two miles north-east, getting no closer to their destination, but putting some safe distance from the crack in the ice, then started to steer north, heading deeper into the Arctic and closer to their target. For the first mile, Steve was listening anxiously to every bark and squeal from the tyres as they ground through the snow, waiting for the first slippery sounds of breaking ice, but after twenty minutes he relaxed. If we go down, we won't know about it until it's too late, he reminded himself. No point in worrying about it until then.

He checked his watch. It was just after seven on Thursday night. Only twenty-four hours since he'd been walking out of Fulham Broadway station on his way to the match. Night, he reflected. But it doesn't make any difference up here. The night never ends.

Dan was heading due north now. Steve glanced out of the window, his eyes darting around anxiously, but there was nothing to see except for the flashes of sparkling light caused by the Toyota's hi-beams catching on the glaciers. 'How much further?' he asked, just as the clock ticked towards eight.

'About ten miles,' said Maya. 'We're making good progress. If we can get into the zone in the next two hours, we can get some rest, and start the search in the morning.'

Steve just nodded. An hour or two didn't sound so bad.

But half an hour later, Dan was forced to stop the Toyota.

Straight ahead of them was a giant mound of snow, blocking their path. It rose at least two hundred feet upwards. A glacier that had been buried, reckoned Maya. Together with Dan, Steve climbed from the vehicle to recce the scene. 'How you doing back there?' he yelled towards Ollie.

'Sodding freezing, pal,' he answered. 'Next winter, I'm flying to the Maldives.'

Steve glanced upwards. The hi-beams illuminated the barrier, but the more you could see, the less hope there seemed to be. 'Any chance of driving over it?' he asked.

Dan shook his head. 'Too steep. We'll just slide on the snow.'

'We can push,' said Ollie, climbing out of the truck.

'We'll just kill ourselves,' said Dan. 'We'll drive round it.'

Steve looked up at the sky. It was even blacker now, with thick cloud blanking out the stars. He could feel the wind whipping around him, and a few snowflakes were hitting his snow suit. It was blowing in from the west, cold and vicious, with a power to it that suggested even worse was on the way.

'The storm,' he said, nodding in the direction of the wind. 'It's coming.'

'Then we crack on fast,' said Ollie. 'The last thing we want is to be caught in a storm in this crap hole.'

They drove for another half-hour. The weather was growing worse all the time, with thick snow now falling all around them. The flakes were blowing into the windscreen, obscuring Dan's vision as the Toyota ploughed slowly forwards. The windscreen was heated but it was still hard to see clearly what was ahead of them. The freshly fallen snow on the ground was treacherous and slippery to drive across, and the stiff wind blew up drifts that were sometimes four or five feet high. The Toyota rocked and swerved as it bumped over them. Twice in less than twenty minutes, Bruce knocked on the windscreen to tell them the sledges had tipped over, and they had to stop while Maksim and Nick righted them and hooked them back on to the truck.

Three miles, noted Maya on her map, as they completed half an hour of driving. And still no break in the wall of ice and snow they were trying to find a way past.

'At this sodding rate, we'll be spending Christmas out here,' said Steve.

'Hey, at least it will be a white one,' said Dan cheerfully. 'We don't get any of those back in Oz.'

Maya was studying her map, but it wasn't telling them anything useful. The Arctic wasn't precisely surveyed and, because it consisted simply of ice blocks, it changed shape all the time. The wall of ice could stretch for two miles or twenty. There was no way of knowing. And with the weather worsening all the time, they couldn't risk going too far in the wrong direction. 'We need to survey it on foot, and find a break somewhere we can drive over,' said Maya.

'I'll go,' said Dan.

'I'll come with you,' said Steve. He nodded towards the boys in the back of the Toyota. 'You lads get yourself warmed up in the cabin.'

'And if we're not back in ten minutes, assume we're dead,' said Dan.

'Does that mean I can have your bar in Majorca?' said David.

'Piss off,' muttered Dan.

Henri was checking his watch, then looked across at David, a grin breaking on to his face. 'I reckon it's ours,' he said. 'You can look after the beer, and I'll handle the waitresses.'

Dan ignored the banter. The big, strong Australian had pulled his hood down low over his face, strapped a torch to his chest, and was already striding out into the darkness. Steve caught up with him. The air was freezing, and the wind howling all around them. Snow was buffeting into the side of the ice wall, then getting caught in air pockets and swirling all around them, like one of those snowflake toys that kids play with. Steve was struggling to walk through it, but Dan was pushing through easily enough. He shone his torch towards the barrier. 'Just look for any kind of dip,' he said. 'All we need is a gradient that the Toyota can get some kind of grip on.'

They covered fifty yards, then a hundred. They were feeling their way along the edge of the wall. At times it stretched up to three hundred feet, but at others it dipped right down. 'Here,' said Dan finally.

Steve looked upwards. Dan was right. It was only a hundred and fifty feet to the top of the wall, and the snow blowing into it had created a natural ramp. It was steep, no question about that. On a normal British road you'd take it in first gear, and still be worried about whether your vehicle could make the climb. And this was solid ice.

'I'll stay here,' said Dan. 'You get the Toyota.'

'You think it can climb that?'

'With an empty load, and nine blokes pushing?' Dan shrugged. 'Sod knows. But it's the best chance we have. If we don't get over this bastard, we'll be driving around the bloody Arctic all weekend.'

He's right, thought Steve. We take a crack at it, or we go home.

He started to trudge back to the rest of the unit. As he emerged from the snowstorm, he could see the huddle of men, and one woman, grouped around the remaining vehicle. And against the massive white backdrop, he was reminded of how small and insignificant they were, and how swiftly they could be lost forever.

'We've found a pass,' he said tersely. 'But it's going to take some shoving.'

Henri took the wheel of the Toyota while Steve trudged along beside him to guide him towards Dan. The freshness of the snow, and the minimal visibility, made it tough going, and Steve was just grateful they had one truck left. There was no way they could march through this. He covered a hundred yards, but still couldn't see any sign of a light from Dan's torch, and for a moment thought he'd lost the man, before he heard a strident call breaking through the screeching of the windstorm. 'Sodding over here, mate,' Dan was yelling. 'I'll be a bloody ice cube by the time you get here.'

In the few minutes Steve had been gone. Dan had used his hands to dig some tracks that the snow tyres on the Toyota could get some grip on. Henri steered the Toyota close, then reversed up so they could get a run at it. Dan told Maya to take the wheel. She was by far the lightest of them, and the least able to shove from the back. 'Keep it in first gear,' he told her. 'Build up some speed so you've got some momentum to take you up, but as soon as you feel it sliding, don't brake, just lower the acceleration and let the blokes behind shove it up the hill.'

'I know how to drive, thank you,' she said sharply.

'Of course you do, babes,' said Dan with a grin. 'Just don't start touching up your lipstick in the mirror.'

'Or texting your girlfriends,' said Ian.

Bruce and David and Ollie were chuckling but Maya clearly

didn't see anything funny about it at all. She climbed into the cabin, and slammed the door shut.

'Keep your toes clear of those wheels, pal,' said Steve, nodding towards Dan. 'Back in the Mossad, they run over a few blokes every morning just for fun.'

The Toyota was in position. The men lined up behind it, two on each side, and five directly behind. A swirling mist of exhaust fumes blasted across their faces as Maya tapped the accelerator, pushing the machine forward. The men walked swiftly behind, keeping alongside as it picked up speed, rising through ten, then fifteen miles an hour. Steve could feel a sweat starting to form on his back, and was already worried about it freezing into his skin. The Toyota started to climb, the studs on the tyres gripping into the tracks Dan had dug. The engine was growling as the momentum carried it forward. Ten feet, and then fifteen. Steve was struggling to keep his mulaks gripped to the snow as he climbed alongside it. His breath was short, the cold air stabbing into his chest. The Toyota was slowing, and one of the front wheels was starting to skid, its studs losing traction on the ice. The gradient was steepening all the time, and although the vehicle was just ten feet from the summit, this was going to be the moment of maximum danger.

'Get your shoulders in, lads,' yelled Dan.

Steve was standing right behind the Toyota, with Dan and Maksim and Ollie alongside. They were the biggest and strongest guys in the unit. Steve leant his shoulders into the back of the truck and heaved. Snow and ice was being kicked up by the back tyres, and it was flying into his face, like shrapnel, but freezing cold rather than red-hot. Steve was aware that it could slice him apart as expertly as any knife attack.

'Push, sodding push,' yelled Dan, his voice raw.

The Toyota lurched a few feet up in a burst of acceleration, and the suddenness of its movement knocked Ollie off balance, sending him crashing face down into the ice. Steve resisted the urge to chuckle: Ollie didn't always have the best sense of humour when it came to falling over. Nick leapt from the side of the truck to take over. The Welsh lad was wiry, but tall, with muscles that were strong as well as supple. Maya tapped the accelerator, sending clouds of exhaust straight over them. Dan was yelling at her to give it more power, but over the din of the engine, roaring up through the revs, and through the wailing of the wind, it was impossible for her to hear anything.

'Sodding women drivers,' he yelled. 'They never listen.'

Henri had grabbed Ollie by the hand, and yanked him to his feet, and the two men joined them at the back of the Toyota, adding their shoulders to the struggle. Five men were now pushing it forward, and with their combined efforts it moved up another few feet.

But then the truck's left wheel caught on an ice block right at the cusp of the barrier, and suddenly jolted upwards. The mud cap on the back wheel caught Steve in the shoulder, sending a thumping pain jolting straight through him. But the snow suit was thick enough to prevent it doing too much damage. It had thrown him back into the snow. As he looked up, he could see that the truck had slipped back two feet, and all four wheels were spinning wildly on the ice. Maksim was grunting, his teeth gritted together, as he appeared to be holding the massive weight of the vehicle all by himself. The rest of the unit had lost their grip as it jolted upwards. Steve jumped to his feet, and lunged into the task, slamming his right shoulder into the back of the pick-up alongside the Russian, and summoning up every last ounce of strength to hold the vehicle in place. 'Hold on, Maksie,' he hissed.

He leant his shoulder into the Toyota, and as Bruce and Dan and Ollie thrust their muscles into the task as well, they got the machine under control. Digging their heels into the ground, they pushed and pushed again, until slowly it began to move upwards. An inch at first, then another inch. 'More power,' yelled Dan at Maya.

A tap on the accelerator, and the tyre studs suddenly gripped some solid ground. The Toyota slid forward, pausing for just a fraction of a second, then climbed the top of the ridge. Steve ran after it, watching as it tipped over the top, then slid like a toboggan down the other side, accelerating up to twenty-five miles an hour. Maya had released the steering; it was useless to attempt to control the machine as it hurtled down the hill. Better to allow it to come to a stop by itself.

Steve peered into the darkness.

Through the heavy snow and thick, murky darkness he could barely see anything. But it looked straight enough.

'A clean run towards the target,' he said.

'Let's sodding hope so,' said Ollie. 'I don't fancy doing that again.'

The Toyota had come to a halt fifty yards away. The rest of the unit jogged down to join it.

'How much further?' Steve asked Maya.

'Five miles,' she replied. 'Due north.'

'It's getting bloody further away,' said Nick. 'How's that possible?'

'The ice we're standing on is drifting all the time. Even

by standing still we're moving at two or three knots either towards or away from our target. There's no way of stopping that.'

'Then move,' said Bruce. 'Before it sodding well disappears completely.'

Bruce was about to climb on to the back of the truck, but Steve grabbed his arm. 'Shift change,' he said.

'I'll be fine.'

'No,' said Steve tersely. 'It's only fair. Maya can stay up front because she's a woman, and Dan's the best driver on the team, but David and Nick and me will do this leg of the trip out in the cold.'

Bruce nodded. 'Then wrap up warm.'

'We can cuddle up to Nick.'

'Sod off, mate,' growled Nick.

Steve clambered up into the back of the Toyota. Ollie had already tugged the sledges over the ice wall, and, together with Henri, repacked them and hooked them up to the vehicle. Steve sat down on the floor, wrapping his arms round himself, and tried to stay warm. David, Nick and Ollie were alongside him, with Dan, Maya, Henri, Maksim, and Bruce riding up front. Dan tapped carefully on the accelerator.

Five miles, thought Steve. Maybe an hour or so. I can handle the wind chill for that long.

But as the Toyota started to move forward, he was no longer so sure.

The first mile was not too bad. Dan was taking it slow, rarely trying to push the Toyota above seven or eight miles an hour. But after a mile, he grew in confidence, and took it up to ten or twelve. The storm was getting worse all the time, and the wind was blowing straight across their path, and although the ground temperature was minus forty, Steve reckoned that once you took the wind and the movement of the Toyota into account, it was more like minus sixty or seventy.

'In other words, more than a little parky,' said Ollie, as Steve explained the calculations to him.

'Just a touch, pal.'

Twice they had to stop when Dan was nervous there might be a lead ahead of them. First Steve got out to recce five hundred yards ahead of them, and the second time it was Ollie's turn. Both men walked alone through the biting wind and the gusts of snow hurtling into their faces, with only their torches to illuminate the path in front of them. Both times the ground was judged solid enough to move forward. It was worth the precautions, Steve reminded himself, as he battled through the terrible weather. Lose this vehicle, and they'd be lucky if they ever got home.

It was just before ten at night local time when they finally arrived.

There was nothing to mark the perimeter of their target area. It was just a line Maya had drawn on a map. 'Here,' she said, instructing Dan to bring the Toyota to a stop.

Steve climbed down from the back of the truck. The storm had grown worse in the last hour. The wind was howling over the desolate landscape, and the snow was drifting into great angry clumps. The landscape was rougher than any they had seen so far. Great walls of ice had been thrown up by the shifting of the ground, some of them a hundred feet high or more, arranged in jagged formations like a watery mountain range. The snow was getting blown into drifts, carving craters and valleys into the ice cap.

We're not going to find anything in this hellhole, thought Steve. Not in conditions like this.

'Somewhere straight out there,' said Maya, climbing out of the Toyota, and pointing straight ahead. 'That's where the plane is.'

Bruce fished the radio equipment from his backpack. The two black boxes on the plane should be broadcasting a steady, continuous beeping noise that could be picked up by a simple receiver. That would give them a precise fix on their location.

But first they had to pick up the signal.

Bruce flicked the switch on the radio.

All the men crowded around. This was the moment they had travelled for. Get close enough to the plane, and it should be easy enough to get a trace on the signal. Dig the black boxes out, then they could get back into the Toyota, and be sitting down to a good fry-up for breakfast tomorrow morning.

'What are you getting?' demanded Steve.

Bruce hesitated. You couldn't see much of his face through his thick balaclava but you could tell he wasn't pleased. It was there in the eyes.

'Sod all,' he growled.

'Let me take a look,' said Henri.

'I already told you, there's no sodding signal.'

But the Frenchman had already taken the radio.

He held it tight in his gloves, staring straight at the dial. He shook it angrily.

Nothing.

'Hitting it doesn't make any difference,' said Steve sourly.

'So where's the signal then?' snapped Henri. He was looking angrily towards Maya. Steve wondered why the Frenchman was so worked up. He hadn't trusted Henri when he'd joined them on the last job in Somalia, and although he'd turned out to be all right in the end, Steve was never certain of his motives. The rest of the men he could read like a road sign flashing on the M1. But Henri was a closed book.

'The plane is almost certainly buried by now,' said Maya. Her voice was even and calm, not taking Henri's bait, and Steve admired her for that. 'We might need to be much closer to find the signal.'

'Then we start now,' snapped Henri.

With the radio still in his hand, he started to climb back into the Toyota.

But, out of the swirling wind and snow, Steve could hear something.

They all could.

A chopper.

Steve looked anxiously into the sky.

He couldn't see it. The clouds were too thick, and the blizzards of heavy snow blowing straight across them had reduced visibility to almost nothing. But he could hear it all right. The wheezing, whining screech of a helicopter cutting through rough weather.

What the sod was that doing here?

In the next instant, the thump of a Gatling gun opened up. The bullets were peppering the snow all around them in short angry bursts. The darkness was suddenly broken by a pair of headlamps, beaming down on the unit. The snow around the chopper had been blown roughly away by the machine's big, powerful blades.

'Bloody run,' shouted Bruce. 'Bloody run for it.'

Steve didn't need the command. When a helicopter gunship was putting high-calibre fire straight into you, you hardly needed to be told to leg it. Instinct kicked in. Fifty yards behind the Toyota there was a curling, twisted wall of ice that Dan had steered carefully around as they approached the target zone. Bruce was already running towards it, and Steve and the rest of the unit were hard on his heels. It was brutal work; the mulaks were designed for walking, not running, and the freshly fallen snow was treacherous, sucking your feet down with each step. But Steve pressed forward, kicking the snow out of the way, and sticking as close as possible to the path Bruce had opened up ahead of them.

Steve hurled himself down behind the glacier. He brushed the snow out of his face, then glanced backwards.

One by one the rest of the unit threw themselves behind the wall of ice.

Except for David. He'd stumbled and fallen, and was struggling to pick himself up off the ground.

Steve darted out to help him.

'I'll be sodding fine,' yelled David, lifting himself up on to his feet. 'Find yourself some cover.'

Directly behind him, Steve could hear the chopper turn. The pilot was struggling to keep the machine under control in the high wind; it was wobbling in the air, about fifty feet from the ground, buffeted by the storm blowing across it. Through the heavy snow it was impossible to see what kind of machine it was, or to make out what flag it was flying under. But the Gatling gun spewing out hot lumps of deadly steel and the twin rockets under its main turret were impossible to mistake. It rose twenty feet into the air, spitting fumes as it did so, then swung right. The pilot had seen David in the snow, and was coming in for the kill. Steve ran forward a few yards, grabbed David's arm and pulled him towards him, but he hadn't been injured in the fall, and was moving fast enough now that he was on his feet again. Steve could see the chopper dropping out of the clouds for another run at them, unleashing a deadly barrage of fire from its cannons.

'Drop,' shouted Steve. 'Fucking drop.'

Both men hurled themselves forward, then skidded across the snow. Maksim and Dan reached out and grabbed them, pulling them behind the glacier, where the rest of the unit were already hiding. The bullets chewed into the massive block of ice that was protecting them. But they were merely scratching its surface. It was at least thirty feet thick; it was going to take a lot more than a Gatling gun to make any kind of impact on that.

'We'll be OK for the moment,' said Bruce, his voice tense. 'Just keep your heads down and stay where you are.'

Suddenly there was a blast, followed by a screeching ball of flame. The pilot had fired one of his rockets into the wall of ice. It shuddered, the shock waves vibrating through the frozen water, and hundreds of splinters of ice flew up into the air, falling again from the sky like a barrage of arrows. But the ice held steady. They could feel the vibration as the red-hot rocket melted down into it, cutting a tunnel that led down into the sea. But the cap was a hundred miles long and fifty miles wide and against its massive strength the rocket had all the force of a paper dart lobbed into the backside of a guerrilla. Within a fraction of a second, the attack had been absorbed, then forgotten.

The chopper rose into the clouds, twisting round, as if in preparation for another attack.

Watching it closely, the unit prepared itself for the next hammer blow to fall.

But a minute passed, and then another. And still there was no sign of the chopper.

'Christ, I haven't seen a welcome like that since the last time Chelsea played an away game against Millwall,' said Steve.

'They're certainly not very friendly,' said Ian.

'Who the fuck were they?' asked Ollie.

'It was a Ka-50,' answered Maksim bluntly. 'A Russian attack helicopter also known as the Black Shark.'

'There weren't any markings,' said Bruce.

Steve had noticed that himself. The chopper was painted battleship grey, but with none of the flags that national air forces used to identify themselves.

'It's Russian all right,' said Maksim. 'It's an all-weather helicopter adapted to fly in the Arctic.'

'But sent here by the Russian Army?' asked Ian.

The question was left hanging in the air.

'I've no idea,' said Maksim finally. 'If it was, why don't they want anyone to know they are here?'

'They sell the Black Shark on the open market,' said Bruce. 'A dozen different air forces operate them. It doesn't even need to be an air force. You can buy them used on the black market for a couple of million each.'

'It still means we're sodding fucked,' said Ollie. 'There's ten of us. We can't take on an enemy equipped with attack choppers.'

'In the Arctic, everyone is equal,' insisted Maya. 'There is no law out here, no government. We've as much right to be here as anyone. And in this darkness, and in these conditions, we can outwit anyone.'

'Not tonight,' interrupted Steve. He was looking up at the sky.

The snow was falling more heavily now. Great swirling gusts were blowing straight across their path, and even in the few minutes they had been hiding behind the glacier, a drift a couple of feet high had built up around them. Fifty yards ahead of them, the Toyota was barely visible, so much snow had blown straight into it. It would take ten minutes just to dig the machine out. Driving it was out of the question.

'The pilot of that chopper pissed off home because he can't fly through this storm,' continued Steve. 'And we can't drive through it either.'

'But . . .' started Maya.

'He's right,' said Ollie. 'We put up our tent and hunker down for the night.'

'And make something hot to eat,' said Nick. 'I don't know if I mentioned this already but I'm sodding starving.'

Twelve

I T WAS LIKE SOME KIND of white hell, thought Steve as he stepped out of the tent. Pristine, clean, and with a certain cold beauty, but at the same time malignant and brooding, with a malevolent cruelty to it. Over the course of a rough night, at least ten feet of snow had fallen, and huge drifts had twisted the landscape into a new shape. With the arrival of morning, the clouds had drifted on, the winds had dropped, and the light had improved. But their tent was half buried beneath the snow, and only the roof of the Toyota was visible from the drift that had collected around it.

He unzipped the flies on his suit, and took a piss in the snow. The cold was excruciating, the worst he'd ever felt. It chilled straight through the exposed skin, stabbing at the veins, and sending shivers of pain right through to his spine.

'Be quick, mate,' said Ollie, grinning. 'It'll drop off. And then what will the slappers around your way do for entertainment on a Friday night?'

'At least someone will miss it,' said Steve. 'That's more than you can say.'

'Only Nick's lovely mum.'

'She's already had enough to last her a lifetime, I reckon,' laughed Steve.

'Bloody shut it,' snapped Nick.

Steve zipped himself up, jogging on the spot to try and get the blood circulating through his veins. There had been some uncomfortable nights during his career in the Army, and then working for Death Inc. On his selection for the SAS, he'd spent several days tabbing across the Brecon Beacons in the winter: the Welsh rain had lashed into him every night with a ferocity he didn't think could ever be matched. He'd kipped down in the Iraqi desert during the Gulf War, caught some sleep in the lethal mountain ranges between Afghanistan and Pakistan, and fought his way through the African jungle. But he'd never experienced anything quite as uncomfortable as the night they'd just endured in the Arctic.

After the chopper had disappeared, Dan and Maksim had retrieved the one remaining tent from the Toyota. Just getting it up had taken all their strength in winds that quickly rose to forty miles an hour. Twice it had nearly blown away, and only a desperate lunge from Nick had retrieved it. Once it was securely pegged in place, the entire unit had crawled inside. The tent was designed for a maximum of eight people but the second one had gone down with the Toyota and this was all they had. It was a tight squeeze to get everyone inside. They laid out the ground-sheet, then opened up their waterproofed sleeping bags, but there weren't enough to go round, and four of them had to keep watch while the rest tried to get some kip. Maksim had lit the stove to try and get some warmth, but the winds blowing across the tent made it too dangerous to keep alight. The flames either blew out, or they fanned up and could easily have set them all on fire. Maksim pointed out that burning in your tent was the biggest danger any Arctic military force faced, and they soon realised it wasn't worth the effort, and hunkered down to sleep as well as they could through the cold.

Even when he finally did get his head down, Steve found it was impossible to get any proper rest. He just closed his eyes, and tried to relax as much as he could. His teeth were chattering, and so were those of everyone around him, creating a rackety, infuriating noise, something like trying to sleep next to a busy railway track. Ice quickly formed on his skin where he was sweating, and he could feel a thin film of frozen water inside his snow suit. The tent was flapping in the wind, constantly threatening to tip over, and from his sleeping bag Steve could see the snow piling up outside, so that by morning there was a five-foot-high drift blocking the exit from the tent, and it took Ollie, Dan and Nick ten minutes with their gloved fists just to dig their way out.

Never again, thought Steve as he finally got out of the tent. Not for all the money in the world.

'Time to crack on, chaps,' said Bruce, joining them outside the tent. 'The weather is clear enough to start looking for that black box.'

It was just after ten, Friday morning local time. Twenty-six hours until the signaller on the black box expired. Thirty hours until the rendezvous with Kolodin back on the yacht.

Not much time, thought Steve. Not much time at all.

David and Nick managed to get the stove alight, and slowly melted some snow, then mixed in some stock cubes to make a hot drink. Ian and Maksim were busy taking the tent down, while Dan began the long task of digging the Toyota out of the snow and getting the machine started again.

Bruce and Henri fished the radio from their kitbags. The two men had stopped snarling at one another, and had started working together. The radio was switched on. But there was still no signal.

'It must be buried pretty sodding deep,' growled Bruce, as he checked the radio for the third time.

Maya handed around the tin cups of hot chicken stock, along with some slabs of chocolate. 'It's not exactly the healthiest breakfast we're ever going to eat, but it will keep us going for the next few hours.'

Steve sipped on the steaming liquid. He took it delicately at first. His mouth and lips were so frozen, he didn't want to risk breaking apart his skin with a sudden change of temperature. But once the stock dropped down into his gut, he could feel his body slowly starting to warm up, from the inside at least. He took a bite on the chocolate, chewing it slowly, warming the frozen food up in the back of his throat before he tried to swallow it. But he was surprised at how it tasted of nothing: the extreme cold of the Arctic killed off the taste of everything.

'Don't suppose there's any chance of rustling up a full English on that stove over there, Maksie,' said Steve, glancing across at the Russian.

'One sausage or two, mate?' shouted Nick.

'Three, at least,' said Steve, chuckling. 'With some bacon, eggs, beans and a fried slice.'

'Sorry, sausages are off today,' said Nick.

'Come to think it, the egg, beans and the slice are off as well,' said David.

'Sodding Arctic,' said Steve. 'They need to work on their grub.'

He finished the rest of the chicken stock, and slowly digested the chocolate. The food wasn't great, but it was at least putting some energy back into his body, and that was going to be badly needed in the day ahead of them.

'We'll get ready and then we'll move out,' said Bruce. 'We've no signal yet, so all we can do is start driving around the target zone until we pick something up.'

'And we'll see if we can find Nick here a polar bear to play with,' said Ollie, grinning, and slapped the Welsh boy on the back.

Dan had made a start on digging out the Toyota, but with breakfast finished, the rest of the unit came across to help. It was tough work. The snow was packed tight into the side of the machine, and had frozen over the course of the night, and as he started hacking away, it seemed to Steve that an axe might be more useful than a shovel. It took ten minutes with all of them working together to get it free of the snowdrift. 'All we have to do now is start her,' said Steve.

'Easier said than done, mate,' said Dan.

The Toyota might have been modified, but once the engine was cold, it was a struggle to get it going again. The batteries were still functioning, and the internal heaters fitted to the machine started to melt some of the ice that was hanging from the engine. But Dan still needed to get out the blowtorch they'd brought with them. One by one, he unlocked the main bolts, and defrosted them using the torch before getting Steve to screw them all back into position. When the engine finally kicked into life, it spluttered and stalled a couple of times, before the the fuel tank had warmed up enough for it to run smoothly. The unit clambered on board as Dan took the wheel. The sledges were tied to the back, and they started to edge slowly north again.

It was almost midday by the time they finally started making progress. Exactly twenty-fours hours left that would determine whether this mission was a success or a failure, reflected Steve. He was sitting in the back cabin again, with his snow suit wrapped around his face, trying desperately to keep as warm as possible. Bruce was up front with one radio, and Henri was in the back with another, and both men were constantly scanning the territory for any kind of fix on the black box. But as they covered one mile, then another, driving straight into the heart of the target zone, there was still no signal from it.

At one o'clock, Dan brought the Toyota to a halt. They were lost in semi-darkness, and a massive glacier had diverted them a mile to the east. They were still inside the target zone, but moving closer to its perimeter. The landscape was harsher than anything Steve had yet seen during the long hours they had already spent in the Arctic. A pair of huge glaciers rose two hundred feet into the air, their surface pitted with spikes and turrets, like a castle of ice. Next to them was a snow ridge that stretched for at least half a mile, and small ice boulders were scattered everywhere, like the rocks you might find strewn across a desert. Behind them was a crater that dug deep into the ice cap, and next to that a three-hundred-foot lead through which black, freezing water was swirling angrily upwards.

'Stopping for a tea break, are we?' said Steve, climbing down from the back of the stationary Toyota.

Steve shivered as Dan and Maya and Bruce climbed out of

the cabin. The storm had dropped when they emerged from the tent, but now it was starting to whip up again. The wind was whistling through the two giant glaciers, funnelled into a powerful, icy blast that was blowing straight into them.

'We're still getting sod all sign of a signal,' said Bruce, clutching the receiver in his gloved hands. 'We might need to get out and walk around. If the plane is buried in all this bloody snow, then there might only be a faint signal, and we won't pick it up inside the vehicle.'

'Walk? In this?' As Steve spoke, he was nodding up at the clouds. Snow was starting to fall again, the flakes getting picked up on the wind, and swirling angrily through the glaciers.

'Scared of a bit of snow, are you, pal?' said Henri. 'I thought the SAS were meant to be tough.'

'I'll be fine, Frenchie,' growled Steve.

Somewhere Steve could hear a groaning sound that came up through the surface of the ice, as if the ground itself was in pain. 'What the sod is that?' he asked.

The ground was shaking, as if an explosion had been detonated deep underground, and he had to put his hand up against the Toyota to steady himself.

'It's just the ice caps moving around,' said Maksim. 'It happens all the time up here in the Arctic.'

Steve shook his head. 'Maybe it does,' he said, his voice rising in intensity. 'But that doesn't.' He pointed north.

The Mi-28N attack helicopter had just dropped out of the sky, and was spewing out bullets from its two main cannons. The ammunition was chewing up the ground all around them, and a dozen rounds sliced into the side of the Toyota.

'Cover,' yelled Bruce. 'Take sodding cover.'

Steve started to run first, with Ollie alongside him. A group of circular glaciers, each one at least eight feet high, lay directly behind them. As they moved, they could hear the chopper swooping lower and lower, its cannons in full roar. Steve dived to the ground, throwing his body up to the solid ice of the glacier. He looked around to see Dan jumping into the driver's seat of the Toyota. 'What's that mad Aussie doing?' he growled.

'Rescuing our transport,' snapped Ollie. 'If we leave it there, the chopper is going to chew it to sodding pieces.'

The rest of the unit had already dived for cover, all nine of them huddled behind the ice. But Dan was alone and exposed. Steve doubted the Australian's sanity but he couldn't question his bravery. Dan kicked the vehicle up into second gear, and slammed his foot on the accelerator. Up above him, the chopper was rising into the sky, twisting, and preparing for another run. From the angle and approach of its flight, the pilot clearly had the Toyota straight in his sights. Dan was moving faster all the time, getting up to twenty-five, a near suicidal speed in these conditions and on this surface, but better than getting shot to hell by the attack chopper. The machine swerved between two of the larger glaciers, before Dan used the steering wheel and handbrake to try and bring it back under control. The chopper was swooping now, the bullets spitting from its cannons cascading into the back bumper of the Toyota, sending sparks of molten metal fizzing into the frozen snow. 'Shift some sodding glaciers into place,' shouted Dan, bailing out of the Toyota, and tumbling on to the ground. 'We have to cover this truck.'

Steve, Ollie, Maksim and Henri leapt to their feet.

'Cover us,' snapped Steve.

Bruce, Nick, David, Maya and Ian had already pulled out their rifles. The chopper was rising back into the sky again, and even through the darkness and the snowstorm, it must have been clear to the pilot that his target was still in one piece. A volley of fire blasted into its tail rotor. At this range, and against a machine of this power, rifle fire was never likely to be very effective. Only a shot in a million was going to bring the Mi-28N down. But it would be enough to make the pilot pause for thought. A bullet straight into the gearbox on the rotor blade or straight through the narrow front window could still do a lot of damage. Maybe even destroy it.

The chopper shuddered in the high winds, steadied, and then the cannons continued their murderous barrage.

Steve and Ollie had grabbed one slab of glacier, while Henri and Maksim took another. All four men were leaning hard into the ice, straining their muscles to push it forward.

'Protect the engine,' yelled Dan.

With a sudden movement, the ice moved, rolling like enormous snowballs into the side of the Toyota. The cannon fire was sweeping through them, and all four men dived instinctively to the ground, making themselves as small a target as possible. There was no mistaking the pilot's intention. He was attempting to blow out the engine on the Toyota. Destroy that and they were as good as dead. He could leave them here to die of cold.

The bullets pinged straight into the slabs of ice. Dan was hiding directly behind them, curled in a ball down beside the big raised wheels and the outsized hubcaps on the Toyota. The munitions slammed into the ice, but frozen water is surprisingly resilient. Chips of ice flew everywhere. But the barrier held.

Behind them, Nick had stood up. He was in no danger now. The cannons on the Mi-28N were pointing in the opposite direction. He took aim with his Arctic Warfare sniper rifle, trying to put a bullet straight into the gearbox.

But the shots ricocheted harmlessly away from the rotor blades.

The chopper rose up into the sky, swaying in the high winds.

For a few moments, its lights were visible, but then it disappeared.

'What the sod are they playing at?' growled Steve. 'First they attack us, then they piss off.'

He was scanning the dark sky, looking for the chopper's next angle of attack. But all he could see was the heavy, cold flakes of snow falling straight into his face.

Then, five hundred yards to the east, Steve could see a flash of tracer fire, an arc of brilliant yellow light, which allowed a marksman working at night to get some idea where his bullets were landing.

The first round opened up, followed by a barrage of sustained fire.

'Take cover, boys,' said Steve grimly. 'The chopper was just softening us up.'

Thirteen

'GET DOWN, GET DOWN,' YELLED Bruce.

It was the same tone of voice that had made him such an effective sergeant in the SAS, noted Steve. Bruce had led Scud-busting missions behind the line during the first Iraq War, and a man who could survive that could survive just about anything. He was decisive, commanding and clear, and never afraid to put himself directly in harm's way, exactly as a good sergeant should.

Steve kept his head below the glacier. They were coming under sustained fire and had been ever since the chopper first swooped on them five minutes ago. Round after round of carefully placed munitions were firing straight into them, the bullets chipping away at the ice that was sheltering them.

Steve, Bruce, and Ollie were behind one block, Henri, David and Maya behind another, and Maksim, Nick, Ian and Dan behind a third. In the darkness and through the snowstorm it was impossible to see how many men were attacking them, or what kind of kit they had. Long-range sniper rifles, Steve reckoned, given the accuracy of the rounds they were laying down from between five hundred and seven hundred yards away. There were at least a dozen men, firing from two different locations, and using night-vision goggles to get a fix on their enemy's location.

'You boys all right?' shouted Steve, glancing across at the rest of the unit.

'Living the dream, mate,' shouted Nick, chuckling at his own humour.

'No one hit?' demanded Bruce.

'Not yet,' snapped Ian. 'But it's only a matter of sodding time.'

Steve flinched. A slither of ice had broken away from the main block as a bullet smashed into it, narrowly missing his face, and thumping into the side of his shoulder. If it wasn't for the thickness of his snow suit, it would have done him some serious damage.

Christ, he muttered under his breath. We can't hold out much longer.

He looked across at Bruce. 'What the fuck are they playing at?'

'They're testing our positions,' answered Bruce. 'It's a probing attack. They want to find out how many of us there are, and what kind of kit we have.'

'Sod all,' said Ollie.

Steve had unpacked his AK-74 and bombed the mag into place. He'd tried lining up a couple of shots, but in these conditions, and without a sniper rifle, it was pointless. You were just shooting into the snow.

'I mean, we've got fuck all to fight back with,' continued Ollie. 'An AK each, some handguns, and a few bloody grenades. We haven't got any hard hats, or body armour, or RPG . . .'

'Well, don't let them know that,' said Bruce. 'Make them think we've got more kit than we have.'

Steve looked across to the next glacier.

There was only one man on the team who could make a big and ugly bang out of very little. 'Hey, bomber, we need some fireworks,' he hissed.

But before Ian could reply, another volley of fire and a burst of tracer lit up the dark, snowy sky. This time it was coming from the north-north-east, about three hundred yards from the last round. Another attack unit? wondered Steve. Or maybe they are moving around, probing us from different positions, and trying to get an idea of our vulnerabilities.

He levelled himself with the glacier.

One bullet had crashed into the ice, about two feet above his head. Another pair of rounds had spat into the snow about five yards in front of him.

They are getting closer, he told himself grimly. Too sodding close.

'Move around,' yelled Ollie.

All three men shifted a few feet around the glacier, so that they now had more protection from the gunfire. But they had no way of knowing where the next assault would come from. The marksmen were using tracer fire on about one round in five. With a small pyrotechnic charge attached to the bullet, the tracer arced through the night sky, and allowed a shooter to judge where his rounds were going when visibility was poor. But it also allowed the enemy to know where you were firing from, and any skilled soldier would use it sparingly: a few rounds, to assess the target, then a barrage of fire that would appear out of the darkness without warning. For the moment, they had some idea where the assault was coming from, but it could change at any second. And right now, they were easy, defenceless targets.

'I said, can you rustle up some fireworks, bomber?' yelled Steve.

'What's the feckin' point?' shouted Ian.

It was a strain to be heard above the snowstorm and the rattle of gunfire, but the anger in Ian's voice was evident enough. None of them had been expecting to come under this kind of sustained assault. If they'd known the level of attack they'd be facing, they would have demanded more weaponry. None of them minded getting into a scrap if they had to. It was part of the job. But not with nothing to fight back with. That was never part of the deal.

'We need to make them think we're a formidable force,' shouted Bruce. 'Otherwise, they are just going to close in for the kill.'

Ian paused for a second. 'We use the RKG-3,' he said finally. 'It's got a sod of a big bang on it, and it should make them pause.'

'Then bloody go,' said Steve.

Ian had a dozen of the Soviet anti-tank grenades. With a thick handle and conical, charged nose, the RKG weighed just over a kilogram, and packed enough punch to disable a tank if it was delivered at the right angle. But it had a maximum range of thirty yards at most, and their attackers were at least five or six hundred yards away. The RKG had a small parachute attached which opened after the pin was pulled; it stabilised it in the air, allowing it to hit its target at the ninety-degree angle that would maximise the damage it could cause. But with no idea where the target was, that wasn't likely to be much use to them.

'I'll make a rocket from them,' growled Ian. 'Make the bastards think we've got some RPGs down here, and they might back off.'

'OK,' said Bruce. 'We'll put some fire down until then.'

Each man loosed off five rounds from their AK-74s. There was no way they were going to hit anything from here. The AK wasn't a precision rifle, and anyway, through the snowstorm they couldn't even see their enemy, let alone aim at it. Each man had packed two hundred AK rounds in his pack, and they had another three hundred rounds for the Artic Warfare rifles. But after that, they were out of munitions.

'Aim north-north-east,' said Ollie, putting down a couple of rounds from his own AK-74. 'That's where the last round of tracers came from.'

Shot followed shot, as twenty rounds in total were fired through the darkness. They had no tracer rounds on them, so at least they weren't revealing their position directly. But the noise of the gunfire would allow their attackers to figure out where they were soon enough. 'Move fifty yards to the right,' shouted Bruce. 'They know where we are now.'

Each man in the unit picked himself up from the ground and started to hurtle through the darkness. The plateau of ice on which they were standing was flat enough on this side of the ridge, and they were still some way short of the lead, so the ground was easy enough to cover. There was another big, jagged glacier ahead of them, this one twenty feet high and fifteen feet wide, and as Steve stumbled straight up to it, the rest of the unit swiftly followed.

By the time they reassembled, all of them were gasping for breath. Running through the snow in the extreme cold took a toll on even the fittest lungs, and none of them could sprint the way they could on normal terrain.

'They've stopped,' said David, peering round the side of the glacier, and looking in the direction the last volley of gunfire had come from.

'They're just trying to figure where we are,' said Steve.

'I wish they'd sodding well come down and take us on,' said Dan. 'Make it a fair fight.'

'Why should they?' answered Henri. 'They can just keep plugging away at us until they wear us down and without taking any risks themselves.'

'That's why we need to level things up,' said Ian.

The Irishman had assembled three of the RKGs inside a spare mulak, and linked the chargers, so that the grenades should detonate simultaneously. He repeated the operation three more times, so that the dozen grenades were turned into four highly potent missiles.

'I need a volunteer,' said Ian. 'We need two blokes to get within a hundred yards of their position.'

There was a silence among the men.

'Don't all sodding jump at the chance,' said Ian sourly.

'I'll go,' said Maya.

'No you bloody won't,' said Ollie quickly.

'Very gallant,' said Maya. 'But this is no time to play the gentleman. It's my fault we haven't got the right kit with us. If there's a risk to be run, it should be me putting my life on the line.'

She was right, thought Steve. They'd have taken more kit from the armoury if Maya hadn't stopped them.

But then, maybe she hadn't known they'd be facing anything rougher than a few polar bears out here.

Why should she?

'I'll go,' said Steve.

'No.'

'He said he'd go,' snapped Bruce. 'And I'll go with him.' He looked around at the rest of the men. 'Cover us,' he said flatly. 'And if you don't hear a big bang in the next five minutes, assume we're dead.'

Steve grabbed two of the mulaks that Ian had shaped into missiles, and started to walk out into the snow before anyone could say another word. Bruce was walking at his side, with two more missiles gripped in his gloves.

Another volley of fire descended on their position, the rounds fizzing through the cold snow as they stepped forward, but it was met with a round of covering fire from their own unit. Steve ignored the bullets. He'd learned to stay calm under fire many years ago, and it wasn't a talent that ever left you. The wind was blowing the snow sideways into him and reducing visibility to a few yards. The tracer fire had given them a fix on the enemy: five hundreds to the north-north-east, up close to the massive ridge of ice, on a plateau that appeared to be a hundred feet up. Steve trudged steadily forward. It was hard going through the snow, and there was no point in trying to hurry. Even with the mulaks, his feet were sinking at least a foot into the snow with every step. Bruce was keeping tight beside him, and there was exchange of fire flying over their heads, but the two men pressed on relentlessly.

Two hundred yards melted away, then three.

They were getting closer all the time.

'Another hundred yards or so,' hissed Bruce.

He was keeping his voice low. Noise travelled in the frozen

air, and even though the storm and the sporadic exchange of gunfire were creating plenty of noise, they had to assume they were close enough for any sudden burst of conversation to be overheard.

'Right,' whispered Steve. 'Just keep going.'

A flash of fire revealed just how close they were to the enemy. A hundred and fifty yards, no more. Practically under the bastards' noses, realised Steve with a momentary flash of anxiety. If they were seen now, a short burst of concentrated fire would probably finish them off. He walked more carefully. Their pale, off-white snow suits allowed them to blend into the storm as easily as a leopard blends into the jungle, but he'd strapped his AK-74 to his back for easy access in case they got caught in a sudden firefight, and the glint of its steel barrel might easily give them away if there was a sudden burst of light from a tracer round. He put his head down, ignored the danger, and ploughed forward.

A hundred and twenty-five yards.

Then a hundred.

'Here,' whispered Bruce, his voice no louder than the wind blowing through them.

There were two units right ahead of them, reckoned Steve. Up on the plateau, about fifty yards apart. He heard a voice, but as soon as he caught it, it was carried away by the howling wind, and it was impossible to catch what was being said or even what language was being spoken.

'One each,' whispered Bruce.

Steve nodded.

One mulak was steady in each hand. The improvised device had a weight of three kilos, and the chargers had been linked together so that they could be detonated with a single pin. Steve took a second to assess the target. He was straining his eyes, but through the snow he still couldn't see the enemy closely. He was aiming simply for where the last round of tracer fire had come from. He assessed the weight of his missile, the force it would need to travel, then glanced towards Bruce. 'Ready?'

Bruce nodded tersely.

Taking off his right glove, Steve winced as the cold air assaulted his fingers. He prised the pin, and started to pull. It was freezing to the touch, and he knew he couldn't hold it for more than a couple of seconds without risking permanent damage to his hand. Ian had rolled them around in his hands before reassembling the chargers to warm the metal but it had frozen again in the few minutes they had been walking. Steve yanked at it hard, and as the pin came out, he tossed it to the ground.

He started to swing both arms. He needed to build up some momentum if the projectile was going to cover the required distance. Once, twice, then three times. The mulak swung through the air, then, released from his grip, started to arc through the sky.

One mulak, followed swiftly by the second.

The two missiles disappeared into the storm. Ian had adapted the detonators, so that the fuse now had a lead time of six seconds. The grenades had been wedged together so they would impact with the force of an RPG and, with any luck, convince the opposition they were facing a well-armed force.

Steve glanced at Bruce.

His two missiles had already been dispatched.

'Fall back,' he hissed.

Steve turned round and started to move. He was ticking down the seconds in his head, counting them aloud as he pushed back through the snow towards the rest of the unit.

'Three, two, one . . .' he muttered, the words no more than a whisper.

It was the pristine emptiness of the environment that made the blast so formidable. The four missiles detonated one after another, in a rolling cascade of explosions that cracked through the air. There was a blast of yellow light, like an egg yolk suddenly spilling open, which burst through the sombre, permanent darkness of the Arctic winter. No flash of lightning could ever match its intensity. For a brief moment, even the storm was stilled by the ferocity of the explosion: the wind stopped blowing, and the snow was frozen somewhere in the clouds, evaporated by the ugly blast of fire and smoke that rolled up from the ridge of ice where the missiles had exploded.

Steve looked up. In the flash of light, he could see the rest of the unit, emerging from behind the glacier like pale white ghosts. Their AKs were slammed to automatic, and there was a blast of gunfire, an attack designed to wipe out their unseen enemy while they were both visible and vulnerable. Then a bullet crashed in to the snow a yard to Steve's left, followed by another one a foot to his right. He'd been spotted, he realised immediately. The light from the explosion had illuminated the plateau, and made him a simple enough target. He started to run, pushing forward, but it was impossible to get up any speed through the freshly fallen snow. The bullets were getting closer all the time, and Steve sensed it was only a fraction of a second before one hit home. Make yourself as hard a target as possible, he told himself. Survive the next few seconds. He dropped to the ground, rolling as deeply into the snow as possible. It was soft, and easily worked, and he buried himself in it, face down, so that his back would blend into the ground. His face was freezing, and it was hard to breathe but he disciplined himself to remain in place. Only amateurs run when the bullets are slamming into them, he reminded himself; the professional soldier knows that sometimes it is better to stay put, the same as you would when attacked by a wild dog.

One second passed, then another. Steve could hear bullets flying in the air above him but had no idea whether they were fired by his side or the enemy, nor whether any of them had hit home.

On five, he started to lever himself up from the ground, He shook the snow from his face and, still squatting, looked around. The afterburn of the four missiles had faded completely, and the Arctic winter had reasserted its dark authority. He could see nothing in any direction, and the gunfire had stopped.

'Bruce,' Steve hissed. 'Where the sod are you, mate?'

Silence.

Silence and darkness, like death.

Steve got to his feet.

He walked a few paces forward, but he was disorientated, with no real idea where he was going. He had a torch on him, but didn't want to switch it on: the enemy would be looking for a light, and it would be greeted by a barrage of fire.

'Bruce, mate, where the sod are you?'

Nothing.

Maybe he was already back with the rest of the unit. Maybe he'd been shot in the assault.

Steve kept walking. Five yards, then another five yards. He

was trying to follow the same path they'd taken, a path he felt certain would lead him back to the unit, but he couldn't be sure. He'd lost his orientation, and in the blackness it was impossible to get a clear fix on which direction he should be walking.

A figure.

A black shape was moving a dozen yards away, no more than a silhouette in the darkness. The snow was falling heavily again, and the figure was moving in and out of view.

'Bruce . . .'

A shot.

It fizzed through the air, narrowly missing Steve.

He ducked, an instinctive movement, then reached for the AK-74 strapped to the back of his snow suit. For a brief moment, he cursed the fact they didn't have the more familiar AK-47. He had taken that rifle into combat a hundred times, and knew its whims and quirks the same way a man celebrating his golden wedding anniversary would know his wife's foibles. He'd never fought with the 74 and although in many ways it was a superior rifle, it wasn't so instinctively familiar. It slipped into his hands, but the trigger wasn't adapted for the Arctic, and he had to rip the glove off his right hand before he could fire it. Precious time was slipping away as he fumbled with the manoeuvre, fractions of a second that might mean the difference between life and death. Never go into battle without taking a weapon you are familiar with, he reminded himself. It's the kind of mistake that costs men their lives. He flicked the gun into automatic, slamming his finger into the trigger, and unleashing a brutal volley of fire into the man he'd seen moments earlier.

The rounds emptied into the darkness.

Another shot.

Fired slightly to his left, but closer this time.

The shadow was moving, running. The man was wearing a dark snow suit, and blended into the night, making it impossible to catch more than a fleeting glimpse of him. He was firing at the direction of Steve's weapon, shooting at the same time.

'Christ,' muttered Steve angrily.

The AK-74 had thirty rounds in its clip, and those had all been spent in his first angry burst of fire. Steve stabbed a hand inside his webbing, reaching for the spare mag. But it was frozen solid. He yanked once, twice, but there was no moving the thing; he'd have to strip off and defrost it, but there was no way he could do that in the middle of a firefight in a snowstorm. He slipped the Yarygin from his webbing, and slotted the handgun into his right hand, pulling the slide back, and looking for something to aim at.

But the shadow had vanished.

Steve held himself still, reluctant to even breathe.

The snow was blowing into his face, and visibility was down to a few yards at most. A movement. To his left, he felt certain of it. He twisted, levelled the Yarygin, and fired. One shot, then two, but he'd lost track of the shadow, and no longer had any idea what he was shooting at. A noise. Somewhere to his right. A man or the screeching of the wind? He couldn't be sure. He spun, his ankles stuck in the snow, but his body twisting round. Another shot, then another. He could hear something falling. Snow? Or the shadow? He fired again, then again, then again, determined to finish the enemy. The rapid rounds blasted through the empty air, the racket of the recoil rising above the howl of the wind. But on the third shot, there was only the dull, metallic click of an empty mag. The bullets were gone.

'Christ,' Steve muttered out loud.

He reached into his webbing, but the spare mag for the Yarygin was frozen as well.

He was alone. In the darkness. With no weapons left. And a silent, unseen enemy stalking him.

He looked around. The snow was whistling through the plateau, the cold cutting into skin. He was trying to judge his direction, but the last encounter had only disorientated him even further. The glove was still off his right hand, and the bare skin was freezing, but he fished back inside his webbing and took out a compass before hurriedly slipping the glove back on.

The compass gave him a rough idea of north, and the unit should be south-south-west if he was to retrace his steps. But he was well aware that compasses didn't always work accurately this close to the Pole. The magnetic fields played havoc with them. They might well be as lost as I am, he reflected bitterly. Sodding Arctic. It's fucked us both.

He started to walk.

It was slow, painful progress, pushing straight into the wind.

The unit should only be five hundred yards away, a matter of a thousand steps or so, he told himself. He started to count. Don't go too far in the wrong direction, he warned himself. Get lost in this place, and in this darkness, and you're a dead man. They'll never find you, and you'll have frozen within hours.

Five hundred steps, then a thousand.

Steve paused.

He looked straight ahead, then right and left.

The shooting had stopped, and he hadn't seen any lights anywhere, nor heard any sound apart from the wind, for the last five minutes. He could only see five or six yards in any direction. Nothing. No sign of the unit.

'Br . . .'

Steve was about to call out.

Then he stopped himself, suddenly nervous.

What if they were still out there, the shadows? Stalking him, waiting for the moment to kill.

'Christ,' he muttered silently.

He couldn't see, and he couldn't call.

He took another two hundred steps, then decided it was useless. He must be going in the wrong direction. He'd have seen or heard the unit by now. I have to turn round, he told himself. But which way? He consulted the compass again, but the direction of its needle had changed, and it was clear it wasn't working. Cursing, he turned round, and started to retrace his steps. Twelve hundred paces back, he told himself, then veer off to the right. Just keep searching for them, and you'll be all right.

The walk was slow and painful. Five hundred steps, then another five hundred, each one counted out. Steve paused, listening. Nothing, apart from the wind. Another two hundred steps, then he turned right. He tried to keep as straight a path as possible, retracing his tracks precisely, but the snow was heavy, and even in the few minutes he'd been walking, his footprints had already been covered up. He had no way of knowing whether he was back where he started, nor in which direction to turn next.

He trudged forward, whistling softly to keep his spirits up. It was twenty minutes now since he'd lost sight of Bruce. They'll be there, waiting, he told himself. Ian and that French bastard are probably arguing that they should leave me to die in the snow but Ollie and Dan and David will be telling them they can't leave without me. At least I sodding hope so.

A gust of wind whipped through him, stronger than anything he'd felt so far. Steve whistled louder, slipping into the refrain from *The Great Escape* that he was familiar with from watching England games, then put his head down, and walked faster. A thousand steps melted away, then twelve hundred. 'Sodding fuck it,' he muttered under his breath.

Nothing.

He'd taken the wrong direction. Again.

Maybe left, he thought to himself. Or maybe I started from the wrong place.

He began to retrace his steps, wading back through the thick snow. Jesus, he thought, this mission is bollocks. We haven't got the kit to fight whoever is attacking us. We haven't got RPGs, or machine guns, or proper armoured vehicles or radios that work or satellite phones to contact each other if we got lost.

He could feel an anger beating somewhere close to his chest.

Anger and despair.

He checked his watch. Two thirty local time. Forty minutes had passed since he'd lost sight of Bruce.

And still nothing.

He was freezing and losing strength and there was a sweat forming on his body from all the walking, a sweat that he knew would soon turn to ice. A terrible thirst was scratching at his throat. He reached for his water bottle but it was frozen solid, and he didn't have a stove to thaw it out.

He turned left, and walked three hundred steps. Nothing. No

lights, no sound. Another three hundred steps. Fear was starting to fill him, a thick, dark cloud of anxiety and confusion that drifted across his mind, blanking everything else out.

'Bruce,' he shouted, breaking his silence.

There was no point in worrying about the enemy hearing him any more.

'Ollie . . .' he yelled.

Nothing.

Just the snow and the wind.

Christ, thought Steve. I'm going to die out here.

'Bruce. Ollie. Where are you, you sods?'

The yell was louder this time, a bark that broke through the snowstorm and was carried across the ice plateau.

But still there was no reply.

Steve ploughed forward. The sweat was getting worse, and so was the thirst. He knelt down, and grabbed a handful of snow, rolling it between his gloves, trying to thaw it out, then slipped some into his mouth. But it felt dry, like paper, and did nothing for his thirst.

He was shivering, and shaking, still kneeling in the snow. Get up, he commanded himself. Keep going.

But where?

He was lost, in the most hostile environment on earth. And hope was fast evaporating.

Steve had thought about dying plenty of times. You couldn't be a professional soldier without coming to terms with death, making your reckoning with it, and finding a way of letting it accompany you on every mission. It was always there alongside you, lurking in the shadows, sometimes a friend and sometimes an enemy. But he'd always counted on dying in the heat and fire of combat, with his mates around him. Not freezing to death. Alone. In the unending darkness.

A light. Fifteen, twenty yards away.

'Steve . . . Steve . . .'

He recognised Nick's voice instantly. A flashlight was advancing out of the snowstorm.

'Nick,' yelled Steve. His voice was ragged.

Nick started to push forward, fighting through the snow. He grabbed Steve by the arm, and pulled him upwards. Steve was shaking with cold, his bones chilled, his eyes wet, and Nick held him tight, clutching him to his chest. It wasn't just the cold making him tremble, Steve knew, and he sensed in the way that Nick was holding him that the Welshman realised it as well. It was the fear, the fear of dying out here alone.

'You all right, mate?' said Nick, letting go of him eventually.

Steve pulled away sharply, suddenly embarrassed by the state Nick had found him in. 'Living the dream, pal, as you might put it,' he said with a rueful shake of the head. 'Living the sodding dream . . .'

'This way,' said Nick, nodding to the frozen wasteland behind them.

The flashlight broke through the snowstorm and the two men had only walked fifty paces before Steve could see the rest of the unit another hundred paces in front of them. He'd been close to them all along, he noted, but his voice hadn't broken through the storm, and he realised as he looked around how lucky he'd been. Get separated from your mates in this kind of weather in this environment, and even if it was only a few hundred yards that separated you, you'd never find them again.

Steve's pace quickened as he covered the last fifty steps, and his face broke into a smile as he closed in on the rest of the group. The men were grouped around the Toyota, and the stove was lit, with Bruce and Dan brewing up cups of Bovril. He could see the flash of a grin on Ollie's face as he stepped out to greet him.

'Steve bloody West,' said Ollie. 'We were wondering where the sod had got to. Thought you might have done a Captain Oates on us.'

'I was hoping you'd stepped out for a few tins of lager,' said Dan.

'Or a bottle of vodka,' said Maksim, chuckling.

'Sorry, boys,' said Steve. 'I've got some snow if you want.'

'I think we'll sodding pass,' said Ian.

Steve took the cup of Bovril, and drank it thankfully. He didn't much care for the stuff usually, and he'd never make it at home, but right now it was about the best drink he'd ever had.

'So what the hell happened?' he asked, looking up at Bruce.

'Some fucker was out stalking us,' said Bruce, 'trying to nab us in the snow. I was lucky, I headed off in the right direction, but you must have got lost.'

'I'd have left you,' said Henri. 'We've wasted a whole hour.'

'I know you would have, Frenchie,' said Steve warily. 'And I'll do the same for you one day, you can count on that.'

'Leave Steve?' said David. 'We couldn't do that. What would we do for laughs?'

'Maya's out looking for you,' interrupted Nick, nodding to the north. 'I'll go get her.'

'Is she going to be OK?' Steve tried to hide the note of anxiety in his voice but he could hear it there anyway.

'We agreed not to go more than a hundred paces in any direction,' said Nick.

Steve watched until he disappeared from view, then told himself to calm down. They'll be back in a few moments. He took another swig of the Bovril, then refilled his cup from the small pan Maksim had brewing on the stove. 'And what happened to the attack?' he asked.

'The plan worked,' said Bruce. 'The explosions were big enough to convince them they were facing a major, well-equipped force. Not just a few blokes with some frozen rifles. They'll think twice before they take us on again.'

'Or maybe they don't want to finish us off,' said Ian, joining the conversation. 'Not yet anyway.'

'Meaning?' said Bruce.

'They've got choppers, and they've got RPGs,' said Ian. 'I reckon if they wanted to they could come in for the kill. It's a warning. They want us out of here.'

'Why?' asked Steve.

'We're out here looking for the wreck of the plane,' answered Ian with a shrug. 'Maybe they're looking for the same thing. Who knows? We don't even have any real idea who they feckin' are. But there's something I don't like about this place, and it's not just the sodding snow.'

Steve drained his drink, and looked back out into the storm. There was some truth to what the Irishman was saying. Ian was a cynical, untrusting man. Life had dealt him a rough hand, and he had learned to treat the world with the same suspicion it treated him. But there was something strange about the attack.

Something not quite right. If I'd been leading it, I'd have finished us off as well, he thought to himself. We were at their mercy. So why didn't they?

'We'll see,' he said finally. 'Whoever the hell they are, and whatever the hell they want, we need to crack on, and get out of this crap hole.'

A flashlight was breaking through the darkness and the storm. As Maya walked with Nick out of the snow, she had a beauty to her that Steve found striking, Her skin was frozen a pale white, like an ice statue, and her protective suit made her look more like a bloated Michelin man than the attractive women he knew lurked somewhere underneath all that thermal clothing, but the brightness of her eyes had a warmth that could light up even this place.

'You OK?' she said to him.

'Fine,' he said tersely. 'But we mustn't split up. Once you get lost out there by yourself, you'll be a dead man in no time.'

'But splitting up is precisely what we need to do,' said Maya.

'What the hell do you mean?' asked Ollie.

'It is three o'clock local time,' answered Maya after a quick glance at her watch. 'We have precisely twenty-one hours left to find that black box, and twenty-five hours to get back to the yacht. If we split up into three units, we can cover three times as much ground. The sooner we find it, the sooner we can get out of here.'

'And the sooner we can all get lost and die,' snapped Ollie.

'We can find each other,' said Maya. Her tone was firm but calm. 'None of us will be alone, and we'll have the right kit with us.'

There was a silence among the men.

'She's right,' said Steve eventually.

He was reluctant, and from the looks on their faces he could tell the rest of the blokes were as well. In conditions like this, everyone wanted to stick together. But her logic couldn't be denied. There was a lot of ground to cover, and the snowstorm would stop them moving very fast. Their radios might not pick up the signal from the black box unless they were walking right across it. The more units they had scouring the ground, the less time it would take.

'Then let's sort out the teams,' said Bruce. 'The sooner we get started, the sooner we get home.'

Fourteen

OLLIE WAS LEADING THE WAY through the storm.

His head was bowed, and his shoulders were leaning into the wind, ploughing his way through the snow like a battering ram. There was a strength to the man Steve had learned to respect on the three missions they'd fought through together already. A steeliness that existed somewhere inside him, and which allowed him to meet impossible odds with a calm, even deluded, assuredness. He wasn't the quickest soldier Steve had ever met, and not always the smartest either. But he was the most rugged, and the most enduring, and that always made him the man you most wanted on your team.

One step followed another as they moved relentlessly forward.

Steve and Maya were following a few yards behind, using the track that Ollie had opened up for them. It had taken them half an hour to prepare, and they'd been walking for an hour now. David, Nick, Henri and Maksim had taken the Toyota, planning on driving to the other end of the target zone, and starting a more detailed search from there. Bruce, Ian and Dan made up the other unit. Most of the heavy supplies, and the tent, had been taken on the Toyota, but both of the foot units had bought along a single sledge. They packed in spare clothes, some food, their rifles and the remaining ammo, a camping stove to melt some snow so they could drink, and, most importantly of all, a pack of flares. If they needed each other, or if they found the plane, a flare would go up, and that was the signal for the other two units to come to their assistance. Their invisible enemy might see it, or they might not; that was just a risk they were going to have to take. At noon tomorrow, if they still hadn't found the plane, David would put up a flare from the Toyota, and the two foot units would converge on that, and they'd all ride back to the yacht together.

If we don't find the plane, it doesn't matter that much to any of us, reflected Steve as he trudged relentlessly forward. We just want to get home.

It was just after four thirty when Steve checked his watch. They'd been walking in a north-north-west direction, creating a triangle with the second foot unit that would allow them to search as much ground as possible. Less than twenty hours to go, and half of that was night time, not that it made much difference out here in the permanent winter darkness. Less than a day before Kolodin sailed his yacht back to civilisation and left them all to die out here.

Behind him, Maya paused to check the radio. Every twenty yards one of them stopped to check for a signal. Only by constantly monitoring the ground beneath them could they hope to find the plane. The snowstorm had ebbed now, and although the clouds were still thick in the sky, the going was getting a little easier, and visibility had improved. As he looked back at her, Steve thought for a second he detected a smile of triumph on Maya's face, as if she'd picked up a reading, but it was soon replaced by a frown that creased up her lips, and he could tell the reading from the radio was as blank as it had been ever since they'd arrived in the target zone.

'Nothing?' he said, as she hurried to catch up with him.

She shook her head tersely.

'You think it's really here somewhere?'

Maya attempted a smile. 'It's not as if someone is going to come along and clear away a whole Airbus, is it?' she said. 'Not in these conditions.'

'No, I suppose not.'

She looked around, exasperated. 'I just don't understand why we can't find it.'

They walked steadily forward, putting their heads down into the freezing wind. At five in the afternoon, Steve took over the sledge from Ollie. Ollie still led the way; he seemed to prefer to be up front, forging a path the other two could follow, and Steve wasn't about to stop him. It was easier to pull the sledge through the path Ollie had carved and that suited him just fine. Another twenty minutes slipped by, and then another. Steve felt hungry and thirsty and tired, but he could live with that. They had travelled at least a mile since they set off, he reckoned, and it was only another four until they reached the end of their zone. After that, they would have done what they could, and if they didn't find the plane, it wasn't really his problem.

'Fucking, fucking, bloody fuck,' yelled Ollie.

It was a howling cry of pain that punctured the air.

Steve looked up. Ollie had fallen to the ground.

Maya rushed up to help him, but Steve was held back by the sledge and it took a couple of minutes to close the twenty yards that separated them; there was no way you could rush through the snow with the sledge weighing you down. By the time he got there, Maya was already helping Ollie to his feet. He was a big man, more than six foot, and weighed at least two hundred and twenty pounds, and probably a lot more once his snow suit and kit were added into the calculation. Maya was struggling to handle his bulk. 'Here,' said Steve, pushing out an arm and then a shoulder for Ollie to grab hold of. 'Take this.'

Ollie gripped Steve's arm, and levered himself up out of the snow. It had been a bad fall, Steve could tell that immediately from the way Ollie was wincing. He'd caught his leg in a crack in the ice, and tumbled to the ground, crashing down on his foot with his full body weight. It was the kind of fall you might see on a football pitch any Saturday afternoon. At best, it meant the stretcher was coming out and the subs were going to start warming up; at worst, it meant the manager was going to be looking for a new player.

'You all right?' said Steve.

'I'm fine,' said Ollie gruffly.

But from the expression on his face, Steve could tell that wasn't true.

'No you're not,' said Maya sharply.

Ollie was resting on Steve's shoulder. There was sweat on his brow, and an expression of fierce determination set into his lips. He was fighting back the pain, as if he could defeat it through sheer doggedness and determination.

But broken bones don't respect willpower, reflected Steve. You can't deal with them through defiance alone.

'Let's get your socks off and take a look,' said Steve.

'I'll bloody freeze,' said Ollie.

'Just do it,' said Maya. 'It might only be twisted.'

Steve sat Ollie down on the side of the sledge and yanked off his mulak, and then peeled away the thick, thermal sock that was covering the right foot. Steve had never broken an ankle himself, but he'd done first aid training back in the Regiment, and he knew how to tell the difference between a snapped bone and a bad strain that would fix itself with a couple of hours' rest. He held the foot in his hand, and started to run his finger along the edge. Usually the smell would be pretty bad after all this walking, but the extreme cold meant every kind of odour was killed off. Even Ollie's feet. The joint around the ankle was crooked and lumpy, twisted out of shape, a sure sign that it had fractured. It was swollen, and the skin and flesh around the foot was already numb. Steve tapped the side of the ankle, close to where it was twisted, with his knuckles, but he didn't need to ask Ollie whether it hurt. He could see it on his face.

'It's broken, mate,' said Steve flatly.

'Bugger, bugger, bugger . . .'

Steve knew precisely what he meant. Broken ankles were the one thing that really scared polar explorers. The icy surface of the Arctic was easy to slip on, and there was nowhere easier in the world to break a bone. It meant you couldn't walk. And out here, particularly in winter, that could easily mean you were dead. It was the most common cause of fatalities in the Arctic.

Steve started to pull the sock back on, careful not to move the ankle any more than he had to, then slipped the mulak back over that. Ollie was a strong man, with a heart of solid oak, but there was a limit to how much pain he could take.

'I'll call Henri and the blokes with the Toyota,' said Steve.

He was already reaching into his webbing to pull out a flare. 'We need to get you out of here.'

'I'll be all right,' said Ollie, starting to stand up. 'It's only another day. The doctor on Kolodin's yacht will patch me up. I'll be all right till then.'

'You'll sodding cripple yourself,' said Steve.

'I said I'd be all right.'

Steve let go of his shoulder, thrusting Ollie away.

'Let's see you sodding well walk then.'

Ollie tried to put his foot down, but the pain was too great. His strong face crumpled in pain and he was wobbling. He put out a hand to steady himself on Steve's shoulders. 'We can't abort the mission,' he said.

'If we have to, we have to.'

'I'll be OK right here,' said Ollie. 'Just give me some food, and let me have a stove, and I'll get some kip. You can pick me up when you've found the plane.'

That dogged determination again, noted Steve. The man never knew when he was beaten. Most of the time it was a strength. In combat, a certainty of victory was the most valuable weapon you could have. But it could be a form of madness as well. Sometimes you *were* beaten, and all you could do was accept that fact.

'You'll freeze to death,' growled Steve. 'And anyway, we might never find you.'

Ollie looked worried.

'We can find him some shelter,' said Maya.

'Some shelter?' asked Steve. He was scanning the frozen darkness. 'If I happen to see a Travelodge I'll check him in, but I can't seem to see one.'

'There's a network of Arctic base camps,' said Maya. 'Polar explorers and adventurers use them if they run into trouble on a trip. They keep them supplied with food and heating and medicines.'

'And how are we meant to find one?'

'I brought a map from the yacht.'

Not for the first time, Steve found himself admiring her foresight and intelligence. The Israeli Army hadn't managed to fend off the armies of countries ten or fifteen times its size for a couple of generations by accident. No other military force in the world paid so much attention to detail, nor did any other combine ferocity and intelligence in such lethal quantities.

'That'll be just the job then,' said Ollie. He was sounding more cheerful already. 'I'll get my feet up, get a good night's shut-eye, then you chaps can collect me on the way home, and let me have my cut of the money.' He chuckled to himself. 'It'll be the easiest half million I ever made.'

'Where's the nearest base?' asked Steve.

Maya had drawn the map from her webbing. It gave the precise co-ordinates of every base station, along with detailed instructions on how to find it, and what equipment was stashed there. 'About half a mile to the west,' she said.

'Then let's crack on.'

Ignoring Ollie's protests, Steve strapped him on to the sledge. If Ollie tried to walk on the broken ankle, he risked doing it permanent damage. In this kind of weather, he might even lose the foot. 'I'm already used to you being an emotional cripple, mate,' Steve said, brushing aside the objections. 'I don't think I could handle a physical cripple as well.'

It was hard going. Steve strapped the sledge back into the

harness and fitted it over his snow suit. At first he could scarcely move at all. The weight of Ollie plus all the kit was too much for him. The harness was tugging into his shoulders, and each step was a battle against the elements. As he got into his stride, it got slightly easier. The momentum of the sledge over the freshly fallen snow started to pick up, and after twenty minutes he was making a decent pace. They were crossing a flat plateau of snow and ice, with Maya marking out the path for them to follow, cutting a trail through the snow that Steve could glide through.

'If you were a motor, you'd be a second-hand Rover, pal,' chuckled Ollie from the sledge. 'I've been on faster tricycle rides.'

'Next time, I'm leaving you to die, mate,' growled Steve.

There were some ridges of high ice up ahead, but Maya scouted the ground, and managed to find a way around them. It added a quarter of a mile to the journey, but it was easier than trying to haul Ollie up and over a small mountain. Steve just followed Maya relentlessly forward, ignoring the fatigue and thirst and hunger that were eating away at him.

'Here,' said Maya finally.

'Where exactly?' said Steve. 'It just looks like more sodding snow to me.'

Visibility was ten yards in each direction, and Steve couldn't see anything apart from a dense mass of white snow, and the ridge of ice they had just left behind. But when Maya flashed a torch to the north, he could make out the top of a flagpole, painted blue, sticking about a yard above the ground. In summer when the snow was melting, the base station would be visible to the naked eye, but during the long Arctic winter, with its endless snowstorms, poles were needed to mark out depots that would otherwise be completely buried. Maya walked across to it, using the collapsible shovel from her kitbag to start digging out the entrance. The steps leading down were buried under five feet of snow, and after a couple of feet some of it had frozen into ice and had to be hacked out by using the shovel as an axe. But after ten minutes, they had cleared enough of the snow for Ollie to lever himself down into the tin shack.

Steve shone a torch down.

'You OK, mate?' he shouted.

'Never better, mate,' yelled Ollie up through the ice.

'We'll be back to get you in twenty hours at the most.'

'I'll get a nice cup of tea brewed, and maybe some Pot Noodles. And I'll try and get the footie scores for you. See if those Chelsea boys are still losing every week.'

Steve grinned.

Ollie would be OK.

He looked across at Maya. 'Let's go and find this sodding plane. Before anything else goes wrong.'

Fifteen

DAN WAS BRUSHING OFF THE snow as if it were no more than raindrops. With his face to the wind, his shoulders were powering him forward, and his thick sturdy legs were tramping rapidly across the ice.

But Bruce and Ian were finding it harder to keep up.

Neither man was as fit as the Australian. Ian had smoked while he was in jail, and his lungs had never fully recovered, while Bruce was approaching fifty, an age at which even the toughest of men can start to feel the clock catching up with them.

'Do you think we should ask him to slow down?' asked Bruce.

'Or maybe give us a lift on the sledge,' said Ian.

The trio had covered two miles in the two hours since the unit had split into three. There had been very little easy, flat ground to cross. For the first half-hour, they had been climbing a steep incline that in places turned into a treacherous mountain. They'd taken a five-hundred-yard detour to try and slip round it, but quickly concluded it was impassable, and decided to climb over the barrier instead. But with their backpacks to carry as well as their own weight, their progress was slow and agonising. Even Dan had stopped for breath a couple of times, before cheerily waving them forward. In their second hour, they'd encountered a small lead. Dan had only just managed to avoid falling into it, and the hazards strewn in their path tested even his reserves of humour and resilience. Avoiding the black, foaming water spilling up through the crack in the ice took them another seven hundred yards out of their way, and meant climbing another hill.

With the time approaching five in the afternoon, they had reached a relatively flat plateau of ice and snow. But the wind and the snow had picked up force, swirling straight into them, freezing their bones and skin, and reducing visibility to just a few yards. There were moments when Dan vanished into the darkness completely, and Ian had to shout after him to wait for them to catch up. Lose him now, and they might never see him again. 'Take your time to enjoy the scenery, boys,' he joked as they struggled to cover the ground he'd put between them. 'None of us are in any hurry here.'

'Do you think the plane is in the ocean?' asked Ian, as they paused to rest their aching limbs, rub some warmth back into their faces, and check for a signal on the radio.

'What do you mean?' asked Bruce.

'We're getting fuck all of a signal,' said Ian. 'There are leads all over this feckin' sea. If the plane came down in one of those, then it's just going to sink right to the bottom of the sodding ocean.'

'It's possible,' said Bruce.

'Then we're wasting our time,' said Dan angrily.

'We're getting paid to look for the plane,' said Ian. 'If there's nothing there then it isn't our problem.'

Bruce could tell everyone was on edge, but figured it was the cold and the hunger and the exhaustion that was getting to them. A long march through difficult terrain was always one of the toughest military manoeuvres. It was hard to keep the spirits of the men up. They were trained to fight, and when they weren't fighting they were trained to relax, and prep themselves up for the their next round of combat. But this was neither fighting nor relaxing. It was just an endless slog through the darkness in pursuit of a target that didn't even appear to exist.

'Only a couple more miles, lads,' he said, forcing a note of cheeriness into his voice. 'If it's not there, it's not there, and there is sod all we can do about that. Just think about all the money we'll collect when the job is done.'

After a break of a few minutes, and after Dan had checked the radio a couple more times, they set off again. They were heading in a straight line but had to veer east to avoid a huge glacier that loomed in front of them. The plates of ice groaned as they moved against each other, and a couple of times Bruce was certain he could feel the ground move beneath his feet, but he ignored it, and pushed himself endlessly forward. He kept Dan close to him this time, the three men walking in a line, with no one in the lead. The Australian was not a man who could be left alone, Bruce reminded himself. He was a man of action, not a thinker, and if you left him with his thoughts for too long, he grew uncomfortable. Dan had done a year in a military jail after being held responsible for the deaths of a pair of kids in Afghanistan while fighting with the Australian SASR, and the experience had left him scarred in a way that Bruce suspected he didn't begin to realise. Keep him alongside, and keep him talking, he decided. That's the only way he'll be OK.

'Just think of the work you'll get done on the bar with all the money you'll make,' said Bruce, glancing towards Dan as they trudged relentlessly forward.

'I'll pay off my tax bill, that's for starters,' said Dan. 'Get some new beers in. Maybe some Japanese ones. We're getting a few of the Nips on the island these days, and I reckon they'd like a taste of home. Say what you like about the bastards, they know how to drink. Ten bottles of beer with ten single malt chasers, and that's just to get started. Even Maksie would have trouble keeping up with them.'

'What kind of beer?' asked Ian.

'Taisetsu Ji Bīru. It won the Japanese Beer Grand Prix two years in a row. They make it in a microbrewery in Asahikawa, up in Hokkaido. And once those Japs start making something, they don't stop working on it until they are making the best in the world.'

From the tone of his voice, Bruce could tell he was cheering up, finding the fighting spirit that made him such a formidable soldier. All he needed was some talk from his mates. Simple really.

They walked for another twenty minutes, alternately discussing Dan's beer bar in Majorca and Ian's website for helping out former IRA men. There were dozens of former Provos who'd been released under the Good Friday Agreement. Most of them were men who, like Ian, had expected to die in jail and had gradually accustomed themselves to their fate. When they were released, they had no idea what to do with themselves or how to live the lives that had suddenly been handed back to them. Nor did the world have much of a place for them. As Ian liked to put it, a decade in the IRA and a

Matt Lynn

decade in the Maze didn't add up to the kind of CV that the desk monkeys in HR wanted to waste any time on. Many of them took to crime, supplying the muscle for the most desperate gangs in the world. There wasn't any kind of cruelty a former Provo couldn't inflict, and those were the only skills they had that the world had any respect for. Ian designed the website as a way of putting them all in touch with one another, recreating some of the camaraderie they'd learned about in the prison yards in Belfast. But it was more than that. There were links to charities, to counsellors, and to employment agencies, any one of which might point them towards a better life. Bruce didn't have much time for terrorists. He'd fought the IRA when the Regiment was patrolling the savage border country between the Republic and Ulster, and he'd known too many good men die to have any sympathy for their assassins. But every man deserved a second chance in life. Sometimes three or four, if that was what it took to get them straightened out. That was the principle on which Dudley Emergency Forces based its recruitment. And he'd never seen any reason for changing it just because a man happened to be a terrorist rather than an official soldier.

Ian and Dan had both done time in jail, rightly in Ian's case, and wrongly in Dan's. But the rights and wrongs of it didn't make much difference after a while. What counted was that they found some way of redeeming their lives, reflected Bruce. Even if it did mean trekking through the sodding Arctic in the middle of winter.

'Ready for another climb, boys?' said Dan.

Another high ridge was straight in front of them. Bruce had just checked the radio again, but there was still no signal. He paused for a moment to recover his breath, and to look at the time. It was five in the afternoon. Nineteen hours remained before the signal switched itself off. It's only forty sodding square miles, Bruce reminded himself sharply. We must be able to find it.

He started to climb. Dan was leading the way. They used their torches to scan the area, but the ridge stretched for as far as they could see and there was no point in burning up precious hours and energy when they could climb over it instead. The incline was easy enough to start with, but steepened significantly ten feet up, until there was a five-foot wall of ice running along its top that they would need to vault across. Dan was using his shovel to chip some hand and foot grips into the ice, hacking away at it with a brutal strength. The snowstorm had eased slightly; the flakes were still falling, but with nothing like the same ferocity as they had earlier. Bruce hauled himself to the top of the ridge, then looked out into the ice that lay below them. At this height, visibility improved slightly, and he could see the shifting contours of a glacier stretching a couple of hundred yards into the distance. He was studying the shape of the ground, looking to see if he could make out a hump or a hill where a plane might be buried.

But instead something was moving, About a hundred yards away. Where the folds in the ridge of ice and snow started to fade away into a fresh plateau of flat ground.

Bruce focused hard. It was a light. A torch perhaps, otherwise he would never have been able to see it in the darkness. A gust of wind blew a drift of snowflakes right across his face, obscuring his view. He waited for them to pass, then looked again, squinting. 'There's something there,' he hissed.

Ian and Dan looked at him sharply, then dropped behind the five-foot ice wall. All three men sheltered behind it, their faces strained and anxious.

'What?' hissed Ian.

'A bloke,' said Bruce. 'About a hundred yards away. I'm sure of it.'

'In this darkness?'

'I saw someone, I tell you.'

Ian fished his night-vision goggles from his kitbag, along with his Yarygin handgun. He checked the mag on the pistol, then pulled back the slide to make sure there was a bullet in the chamber, before slotting the goggles over the balaclava that was masking most of his face. He peered carefully up over the ice, looked for only a fraction of a second, then ducked down again.

'One bloke, but more like two hundred yards away,' he said.

Bruce nodded grimly.

'Armed?' asked Dan.

'A rifle,' said Ian. 'Ready to fire, by the looks of it.'

'What kind?'

'Christ, how the hell should I know?' hissed Ian irritably. 'Go and sodding ask him if you want to know.'

Bruce slotted his own goggles into place, and so did Dan. Both men permitted themselves a brief glance over the ice to establish the position of the man, and whether he had any company. But he was alone. A single figure, sheltering behind a stubby, four-foot-high glacier.

'What do you think he's doing?' asked Dan.

'Waiting for a bus,' snapped Ian.

'Steady, boys,' growled Bruce. 'It's a fair question.' He looked at Dan. 'I reckon he's a watchman. He's not going anywhere. He's just sitting there keeping an eye on things.'

'The same people who attacked us earlier?'

Bruce shrugged. 'Probably. This whole place is crawling with more heavily armed nutters than Basra in two thousand and five. What they hell they're all doing here I have no idea.'

'Looking for the plane?' said Dan.

'Or trying to stop anyone else from finding it,' said Ian.

'Could be either,' said Bruce. 'I reckon we should find out.'

'Meaning?' asked Ian.

'There's three of us, and only one of him,' said Bruce. 'I reckon that means the odds are on our side. So I think we should pop down and have a friendly chat with our pal down there. See who the hell he is, and what the sod is going on around here.'

Ian glanced up over the ice wall, using the hazy greenish light of the night-vision goggles to get a fix on the man. He was jigging up and down, with his gun over his back, jogging on the spot to keep himself warm. There are some godforsaken spots in the world where a soldier might be posted as a watchman, he thought. He'd done plenty of wet and wintry nights keeping an eye on arms dumps during his days in the Provos. But there couldn't be anywhere in the world God had abandoned quite so completely as this place.

'Here's what we do,' he said to Dan and Bruce. 'I go fifty yards right, and you two boys go fifty yards left. We slide down the side of the ice ridge on our backsides so that we don't create any kind of body profile that he can see in this darkness. We lie completely still, but get the Yarygins cocked and ready to fire. Every fifteen minutes or so, that bugger gets up for a bit of a jig around. He has to, I reckon. Sit still in these conditions, and you'll just freeze into a block of ice. He has to put his rifle down. When he does, the three of us rise up out of the snow and walk straight towards him, pointing the Yarygins straight into his face. Tell him to drop his weapon, and start talking. Or else choose which ice block he'd like to be buried in.'

'You sound like you've done this before,' said Dan.

'We took out a few British sentries that way back in the good old days.' He chuckled to himself. 'You should have seen the looks on their faces when three boyos walked towards them with guns cocked.'

'Some of them were my mates,' said Bruce sharply. Then his face softened. 'But it's a good enough plan. Let's crack on.'

Bruce and Dan started to move to the left. They were crouching down low behind the wall of ice, making sure they remained invisible from the plateau below. Dan checked once that the soldier wasn't looking up before hoisting himself up and over the barrier. He lay flat on his side, then started to slither straight down the side of the mound, going head first, like a human sledge. The way the wind had been blowing meant there was plenty of fresh snow, and he slipped down easily enough. Bruce followed in the path he had cut, then veered further to the left, so that when the moment came to attack, the three men would surround the soldier, squeezing him in a triangle from which there was no escape.

Bruce used his elbows to bring himself to a halt. He was still flat on the ground. There had been some noise as they came down, but the wind rustling and moaning through the desolate landscape and the creaking of the ice beneath them combined to create an environment that was noisy enough for small sounds to remain undetected. He looked up towards the soldier. The man was fifty yards away. He was stockily built, his frame bulked out even more by his cold-weather suit. He was wearing short, stubby skis, the kind used mainly for snow walking, and he was carrying a compact sub-machine gun. At this distance, Bruce guessed it was an 9A-91, a Russian-made assault weapon used widely by both police forces and armies throughout both Russia and Eastern Europe. But it was impossible to be sure. The man was standing still, the wind battering into him as he surveyed the ground around him.

Wait for him to try to warm up, Bruce told himself. That will be our moment.

A minute passed, and then another. Bruce could feel the cold starting to eat into him. He was lying face down in the snow, his body right in the ice. The flakes were starting to fall more heavily again from the sky, and had covered his back already with a fresh layer of snow. True, it's making me harder to spot, he reflected grimly. But it's also freezing my bollocks off.

Another minute. Then another.

Christ, thought Bruce. I can't lie here like this for much sodding longer.

The soldier turned. He took a couple of paces forward, moving skilfully on his skis. Bruce held his breath. If the man was moving out on a patrol, he might easily spot them. It might be three against one, but the sub-machine gun could empty its twenty-round mag in a fraction of a second. Their handguns couldn't begin to match its rate of fire. He stopped, and Bruce breathed out again. The man was now moving a couple of paces to the right, closer to where Ian was lying in wait.

He scratched himself.

Put the gun away, you bastard, thought Bruce.

The man was standing still again, leaning against the side of the glacier.

Another two minutes ticked by. Bruce could feel the cold slowly destroying him. His face was starting to numb up, as if he was under anaesthetic, and his lips were starting to crack. The freezing air was settling into his lungs, shortening his breath, and slowing his pulse.

You could die like this, he reflected grimly. In just a few hours.

Then the soldier put down his rifle. He'd unzipped his cold weather suit and started to take a piss into the snow. Bruce knew exactly how he felt. The freezing temperatures were playing havoc with his bladder as well; it was only the fear of exposing his tackle to the cold that was stopping him going more often. He glanced across to where Dan was lying. A count of five, from when the soldier put his gun down. That was what they'd agreed.

Three, four . . .

Bruce stood up in a single swift movement. At the same time, he whipped his glove from his right hand and thrust the Yarygin straight out in front of him. Twenty yards away in either direction, both Dan and Ian had jumped to their feet, like vengeful white ghosts rising up from the graveyard. All three men started walking simultaneously, their guns stretched out in front of them, closing the soldier in a human vice.

'Stand fucking still or we'll shoot,' shouted Bruce across the fifty yards that separated them. Whether the man understood English or not they had no way of knowing. But every soldier understood the barrel of a gun; that was one language that was universal.

He let go of his cock, but piss was still dribbling down his leg, melting a small patch of snow around him. There was a look of panic in the soldier's eyes, but it was swiftly replaced by one of steely determination. The gun was right by his leg and his hand started to reach down, going for the weapon.

'We'll sodding shoot,' yelled Ian, from one side.

'So stand fucking still and throw the gun away,' yelled Dan.

But the soldier ignored them.

His right hand grabbed for the 9A-91, flipping it upwards and into his hands.

Suicide, thought Bruce. It's three against one. But if the sod wants to die, it's his choice.

'I said drop your sodding weapon or we'll kill you, right here, and right now,' he shouted.

Bruce slammed his finger into the trigger of the Yarygin, releasing a single bullet from its seventeen-round, double-column magazine. He was aiming to wound not kill, looking to place the bullet into the man's shoulder. He still wanted to talk to him if he could; unless they knew who was out here looking for them, and what their capabilities were, he didn't rate their chances of surviving very highly. But the Yarygin only had an effective range of fifty metres, and he was right at the edge of that, so he knew that he wouldn't have much control over where the bullet landed. As he fired, he could hear the retort of Ian and Dan's guns firing, then a ghostly echo as the blast of gunfire bounced back off the ice ridge behind them, and reverberated across the plateau they were standing on.

The bullets flew through the air. But Bruce couldn't tell whether any of them struck their target. Snow suits were so thick, it was perfectly possible for a bullet to pass right through it and chew up the man underneath, and it would be minutes before any blood managed to seep through the thick layer of protective clothing. He might well be wearing body armour underneath. As far as he could tell, the man hadn't been injured so far.

Bruce fired twice more. This time to kill.

The solider had gripped the 9A-91 in his hands, flipped it to automatic, and sprayed a steady stream of bullets straight into his attackers. Fire and smoke was spitting from its barrel. He was turning on his hips, moving the sub-machine gun through the air, so that its rapid fire could mow all three of them down in a fraction of a second. Bruce fired again, but his focus was gone, and he knew he'd missed even before the bullet had left the chamber of the Yarygin. As he felt a bullet whiz pass him, and heard it ricochet off the ice wall behind him, he threw himself to the ground, wincing as his face collided with the snow.

The burst of fire from the 9A-91 was terrifying but brief. It chattered as the bullets flew out of its barrel, the soldier spinning. But the mag was emptied in an instant. Even before it had finished firing, however, the soldier had spun round, kicking back with his right leg, creating enough momentum for his skis to start carrying him away. Directly to the south, the plateau dipped down. The soldier was heading straight for the gradient, using the slope to build up speed.

Even without poles, he was soon moving away from them at thirty miles an hour.

As Bruce glanced up, he could see that Ian had dropped to the ground, precisely the same way he had. But Dan had remained upright, ignoring the danger. He'd run after the soldier as best he could, emptying the mag on his handgun. But the man was too fast for him. He'd already vanished into the darkness and the falling snow. Dan turned around, trudging back to the other two men.

Bruce levered himself up off the ground. He slotted the Yarygin back into his webbing, then rubbed his right hand as hard as he could, trying to get the blood circulating properly again before slipping his glove back on.

'Christ, who the sod are they?' he said, looking up at Ian and Dan as the three men regrouped.

'They're good, whoever they feckin' are,' said Ian.

Bruce nodded, his expression sombre.

'It took guts to fight back like that,' he said finally. 'It was three against one, from different angles. Even Maksim might have surrendered.'

'They know this territory like the back of their hands as well,' said Dan. 'Did you see the way he skied out of here? He knew precisely where he was going.'

'Maybe we should piss off,' said Ian. 'Whoever they are, this is their territory, and they don't seem very friendly to outsiders.'

'Turning chicken, are you, bomber?' sneered Dan. 'I always reckoned you Provos would clear off if you ever found yourself in a fair fight.'

'Ian's got a point,' interrupted Bruce, his tone hardening. 'There's no sense in getting into a scrap you can't win. That's just brawling in a pub, not soldiering.'

'If we haven't got the kit or the training to take these boys on then there's no point in being here,' said Ian, looking sharply at Dan.

'You want to piss off?' said Dan. His tone was angry. 'Well, you go if you want to, mate. I've never backed out of a fight in my life.'

Ian looked at Bruce. 'What do you reckon?' he asked.

The snow was falling steadily, and the sky had darkened, reducing visibility down to just a few feet. All three men were exhausted. Their sledge was back up the ridge and would have to be retrieved before they could make any more progress.

'I don't like it, not one bit,' said Bruce finally. 'We're up against a skilled and well-trained enemy we don't know anything about on territory we don't understand.'

'Then like I said, we piss off,' said Ian. 'There's no point in throwing our lives away.'

Bruce shook his head. 'The only way home is walking back to Kolodin's yacht. It's too far, in this weather, without a vehicle, and I don't reckon he'll be too pleased too see us come home early without his sodding black box.' He looked at each man in turn. 'I don't like the hand we've been dealt but we've no choice now but to play it.'

'Then let's sodding well move on,' said Dan. 'I reckon that bastard will have hooked up with his mates. And when he has, they'll be back to finish us off.'

Sixteen

THE TOYOTA WAS MAKING PAINFULLY slow progress. Henri was at the wheel, steering the machine as best he could through the brutal terrain, while Nick, David and Maksim sat alongside him, keeping their eyes peeled on the ground in front of them. Nick was flicking through the tracks on his iPod, playing Coldplay, until Henri snapped at him to put some Springsteen on, and they settled on listening to the whole of *The Rising*. The booming chords of the music managed to briefly calm the anxiety that was eating away at each of them, and Maksim singing along to the chorus of 'Waiting For A Sunny Day' cracked everyone up. But as they peered out into the darkness, and felt the crunching of the ice underneath the tracks of their vehicle, and wondered where the next attack was going to come from, it was impossible for any of them to settle.

A fear is coming over us, thought David. A fear of the darkness, and a fear of the unknown. And a soldier can have no greater enemy.

The first hour passed easily enough. The plan was to drive straight across the target zone in a single run, then, once they got to the other side, start working their way back, stopping every five hundred yards to get out and check the radio for any sign of a signal from the black box. They'd meet up with the other two units somewhere in the middle, or else at the plane, if any of them managed to get a trace on it. They covered the first three miles easily enough. The ice was rough in places, there were glaciers they had to detour around, and one lead that they only narrowly managed to avoid, but it was nothing that held them up. The second hour was tougher. They hit a patch of fierce snow, falling so thickly from the clouds that it took their visibility down to less than a yard even with the big head-lamps on. Henri could literally not see where he was driving. Twice they drove straight into big blocks of ice, and even though they were only doing five miles an hour, it still sent a judder right through the machine. The second collision took out a chunk of the hubcap, but they decided they could live without that, and tossed it in the back of the pick-up truck to be fixed later.

They ignored those setbacks, and just pressed on. At five thirty, they hit a glacier that was so high there was no way they could drive over it, or push the Toyota up its steep slope. They drove round it, taking a detour that took them a mile in the wrong direction, until they finally found a break in the barrier through which they could drive. When they got to the other side, they were suddenly plunging down a deep ravine. Momentarily, Henri lost control of the steering completely as the vehicle skidded across shiny, snow-free ice. The Toyota picked up speed, climbing up through twenty and then twenty-five miles an hour, a suicidal acceleration in these conditions, but with the wheels losing all grip on the surface there was no point in trying to brake. In the darkness, they had no idea where they were going. Henri was fretting that they might hit a wall of ice or sink into a lead, and suggested bailing out, but Maksim refused, insisting that they would be all right. After three seconds, the incline turned upwards, and the Toyota rapidly slowed, until eventually the tyres re-established their grip, and Henri could bring the vehicle under control again, but it had been yet another close run with death, and none of the men was sure they could carry on driving blind for much longer.

'Jesus, I'd rather be back in sodding Somalia,' said Nick, as they finally got back to driving across a flat plateau. 'And I never thought anything would make me say that.'

It was six by the time they reached the other side of the target zone. Henri stopped the Toyota, but left the engine running as he stepped out. They had a radio, and although they'd kept it switched on during the drive, they hadn't expected to pick up a signal from inside a moving vehicle. They had all agreed by now that the plane must be buried under deep snow, and that was what was making it so hard to find. The hi-beams on the Toyota were providing some light, but the snow had picked up force again, and the wind was blowing it straight on to them, making it hard to see for a more than a few yards in any direction. David and Henri huddled over the radio, trying to find some trace of a signal, while Nick and Maxim lit a camp stove and started to melt some ice so they could all have a drink. When it was melted, Nick opened up a big bar of chocolate, and for a few minutes the men just huddled round the stove, drawing whatever warmth they could from its pale blue flame, and drank the cold water and chewed on the rock-hard chocolate, taking some strength from the sugar and liquid.

'I could murder a Pot Noodle,' said Nick finally, his tone wistful.

'A King Pot,' said David ruefully. 'Now that would go down a treat right now.'

'Or the new Doner Kebab Pot,' said Nick. 'I think that's taken over from the Bombay Bad Boy as my favourite.'

'If only they could launch a Vodka Pot,' chuckled Maksim. 'I mean, I usually add a shot to a chicken King Pot, but it would be good if they saved you the trouble.'

'What are these Pot Noodles?' asked Henri.

'Don't they sell them in France, then?' asked Nick.

'I don't think I've ever seen them. What are they?'

'Proper Welsh grub, that's what it is,' said Nick.

'I think you'll find the noodle originated in China, not Wales,' said David.

'Leave it out, mate,' said Nick. 'They make them up near Newport. My mate Darren went out with this bird once who worked in the factory. A hundred and fifty million pots a year they make. Sodding amazing.'

'Classy, was she, Nick?' said David.

'Right classy,' said Nick. 'A real looker, and she got all these free Pots. We were dead jealous, we were.'

'I can understand why,' said David. 'What more could a man possibly hope for in a woman?'

By the time the chocolate and water was finished, it was already half past six. They checked the radio once again, and carried it three hundred yards in every direction without picking up any trace of a signal. The four men packed themselves into the Toyota and drove five hundred yards back towards the centre of the zone, then Nick got out and walked in a long circle a hundred yards from the vehicle, checking the radio every few paces. Another five hundred yards, and then David got out and walked, followed by Maksim and Henri. There was no other option but to do this the slow way, driving for short distances, then getting out to search. It was cold and slow work, and they would struggle to keep their spirits up if it went on for many more hours. But for now they couldn't think of any other way of making sure they covered the ground they needed to.

By seven, they had covered a mile. Another couple of miles, and they'd be right back in the centre of the zone. 'Maybe we'll bump into Steve and Ollie,' said Nick, climbing out of the Toyota to search the area where they had just pulled up. 'Or Ian and Bruce.'

'They're probably putting their feet up somewhere,' said David. 'Making a nice cup of tea, and leaving us to do all the hard work.'

'It wouldn't be the first time,' replied Nick, with a shake of the head.

He walked out into the snowstorm. Henri had pulled the Toyota up close to the edge of an ice crater. There was a dip in the surface, and as they drove down into it, Henri had briefly lost control of the machine. The ground was squeezed together into an increasingly narrow valley, while on either side, thirty yards from the track they were driving through, there were big glaciers rising twenty feet or more upwards. All around them the ground was littered with twisted, jagged lumps of ice, through which Henri had to steer the Toyota as if it were a slalom course.

The hi-beams from the vehicle illuminated a few yards in

front of him, but after that Nick had to switch his torch on. He walked straight into the icy darkness, shivering as he did so. After twenty yards, he couldn't even see the Toyota any more. He was keeping a straight line, aware of how Steve had got lost in the snow even when he was just a few hundred yards away from the rest of the unit. Just keep an eye on how to get home, he reminded himself, as a gust of freezing wind whipped across his face and cut into his exposed lips and nostrils. That way you'll be OK.

A hundred yards, noted Nick, with a sense of relief. Close enough anyway. He checked the radio. Nothing. 'Sod it,' he muttered under his breath.

He turned to his left, readying himself to complete a full circle round the Toyota. Ten paces, then twenty.

And then he froze in his tracks.

A shot.

At first Nick thought it was just the echo of a chunk of ice being blown off a glacier. He still hadn't got used to how noisy the Arctic was, and he wasn't sure he ever would. The place was constantly creaking and snapping as if the surface of the ground itself was in pain. But that wasn't ice breaking down, or an avalanche, or a plate moving.

That was gunfire. Nick was sure of it.

Somewhere behind him, he decided. But amid the swirling snow and wind, it was impossible to get much sense of location. Another shot. Sniper fire, he guessed. Not an automatic weapon, but single bullets fired from a great distance.

He looked around once more, and then he started to run.

A hundred yards away, the bullet struck the Toyota just below the engine casing. It splintered the thick layer of steel wrapped across the bonnet, sending a plume of smoke upwards as it chewed its way into the engine.

'What the sod was that?' snapped David, glancing over at Henri and Maksim. David was sitting up front, with Henri next to him at the wheel. 'Have you hit another glacier? Christ, from now on, we're getting Dan to do the driving.'

'We haven't bloody hit anything,' growled Henri. 'We're not even moving, in case you hadn't noticed.'

Another bullet.

This time it smashed its way through the driver's side windscreen, narrowly missing Henri and lodging itself in the gearbox. Splinters of glass had sprayed across all three men like confetti as the window was shattered, and a freezing blast of wind was whipping straight through the passenger cabin as the cold air collided with the hot.

Bugger it, bullets, thought David. We're under attack.

Then he noticed that the gearbox had started to burn.

Incendiaries, he realised. Ordinary bullets, but with a tiny charge drilled into them that ignited on striking their target. Perfect for setting a vehicle on fire. Along with everyone inside it.

'Out, get sodding out,' he yelled, his lungs roaring out the words.

But Henri had already slammed his foot on the accelerator. The Toyota leapt forward, its big wheels kicking back suddenly against the drifts of snow that had built up all around it during the few minutes they had been stationary. It skidded, and Henri was cursing in French as he thought he'd lost control of the steering again, but then the wheels found some traction, and the vehicle started to power forward.

'I said sodding well get out,' yelled David. 'Can't you see they're bloody shooting at us.'

Maksim started to move. But Henri turned to face him, his expression calm.

'And you want us to stay here, like sitting ducks, do you?' he growled. 'We're driving the hell out of here while we still can.'

David was about to shout back. But then he stopped himself, strangling the words on his throat. The French bastard is right, he told himself. We've got more chance of getting out of here alive inside the Toyota than outside.

The smoke rising from the engine was getting worse. At first David had assumed it was just the snow getting inside the bonnet, and turning into steam. But this was thick black smoke, mixed with diesel fumes. The Toyota swerved suddenly. A bullet had struck one of the tyres, bursting into flames inside, and ripping the rubber to shreds. Henri was gripping the wheel, sweat pouring down his face. He tried to shift gear, hoping to get more control of the machine, but the gearstick was far too hot to touch, and looked to be broken beyond repair. He started to softly touch the brake, but it didn't make any difference. The Toyota was picking up speed. Another bullet struck the engine, and then another blew open the back window, and there were flames both inside and outside the cabin. Suddenly, the Toyota swerved uncontrollably into a deep snowdrift, ploughing into its centre before coming to an abrupt stop.

Henri turned towards David, a rough grin creasing up his face.

'All right, you win,' he said. 'We're getting out.'

'About sodding time,' snapped David.

The door was already open, and all three men rolled out of

the passenger side, hurling themselves into the snow. David went first, followed by Maksim, then by Henri. Behind them, the plumes of black smoke were rising thickly from the engine, and some flames were starting to spit out of the vehicle, their yellow light illuminating the ground around them.

David was kicking back with his feet, putting as much distance between himself and the vehicle as possible, while staying as close to the ground as he could. The sniper was clearly an expert; give him any kind of target to aim at, and he'd blow your head off.

But behind him, Maksim had jumped to his feet.

'Get down, you sodding fool,' shouted Henri.

The Frenchman reached out a hand to grab hold of the Russian but Maksim was too strong for him. 'Our kit is all in there,' he growled.

'You'll sodding die,' yelled David. 'It's about to blow.'

Maksim ignored the warning. With his head down, like a bull, he charged towards the Toyota. David and Henri watched, aware there was nothing they could do without sacrificing their own lives. The flames starting to leap out of the engine were casting a pale light across the surrounding snow but Maksim was already disappearing into the darkness. David heard the crack of gunfire, and glanced upwards. It was coming from straight ahead of them, somewhere in the glacier that ran down the side of the crater, but a skilled sniper could be making these shots from five hundred yards, and an expert from a thousand. He pulled the Yarygin from his webbing, and fired a pair of rounds up towards the sniper's position. But he couldn't see his target, and even if he could, at this range a handgun wasn't going to hit anything.

It just felt better to be firing back, he reflected grimly. Like you weren't about to die without a struggle.

Suddenly, a terrifying explosion ripped through the air. The flames had reached the Toyota's fuel tank. A jet of flame shot straight into the air, rising twenty feet upwards, like a yellowy-blue water fountain. Then the tank blew apart, the flames turning into a giant ball of sparks and smoke that swelled up like a balloon, obliterating everything in their path. There was a cracking sound as the engine exploded, and then the remaining tyres burst. Next, the jerry cans stored in the back of the pick-up truck ignited, sending fresh jets of burning fuel straight up into the sky. A thousand fragments of steel and glass and rubber flew in every direction, each one a molten dagger that could slice into a man and kill him in a fraction of a second. A wind started to howl, as the fire consumed the oxygen all around the burning vehicle, sucking the snow falling from the clouds into the fire, creating a stormy haze of white and yellow. As he watched with grim fascination, David wasn't sure he'd ever seen an explosion that was quite so hellish. Nor one that was quite so devastating even to the men who survived it.

The flames subsided as quickly as they had erupted, engulfed and then dampened by the snow, but thick clouds of smoke were still billowing out from the wreckage of the burnt-out machine.

'Maksie,' shouted David. He knelt on the ground, confident that the sniper couldn't see him through the smoke. 'Maksie? Where the hell are you?'

Maksim stepped through the black smoke, his face and snow suit black with soot. Like some kind of devil arisen from the ice. He was holding a single kitbag in his hand. There were some cuts to his skin, and a streak of blood across his forehead where a slither of flying steel had caught him a glancing blow, cutting through the balaclava and down into the skin below. But his eyes were clear, and there was a hint of a grin on his face.

Madman, thought David. But at least the sod is on our side.

'Did you rescue us a bottle of vodka, Maksie?' called out David.

'You wish.' He walked up to David and Henri, and put the kitbag down.

How the man had survived the blast, David had no idea. He must have been right in the centre of the explosion. Maybe he really was made of Kevlar after all.

'All I got was this,' he said, his tone hardening. 'One kitbag. A bit of food, a camping stove, and a few spare rounds. Sod all.'

'We'll be all right,' said David tersely.

'I wouldn't count on it,' said Henri.

David was about to get some disinfectant out of the medi-pack he was carrying in his webbing, but the Russian brushed him aside. He rubbed some fresh snow into the cut on his face, reassuring David that the freezing temperatures would be more than enough to kill off any bacteria. The smoke was clearing from the blast, the black soot caught up in the wind and the snow turning the ground a smudged grey colour. As it cleared, David could see the charred remains of the Toyota sinking fast. The red-hot metal chassis was cutting a hole straight through the ice, twisting as it did so, until it had cut all the way through to the ocean underneath, and sank straight towards the bottom.

'Bugger,' muttered David, his lips tightening as he watched the machine disappear. He rubbed his hands together, trying to keep warm, but also trying to keep up spirits that were rapidly fading. 'Without transport, we're fucked,' he said, his voice resigned.

Henri was scanning the horizon. There was still some burning rubber scattered around them from the explosion, and that was providing a brief, flickering light that broke up the darkness. Through it, the ridge where sniper fire had come from was faintly visible but, although he was looking for a glint from a steel rifle barrel that might reveal an enemy he could take his revenge on, there was no sign of any form of life.

'Think they're still out there?' he asked.

David shrugged. 'If they are, I don't think we're going to find them,' he answered. 'I don't think we're going to find anything in this hellhole.'

A hundred yards to the west, Nick had watched the explosion with a sense of horror. He didn't need to be close up to know precisely what had just happened. The flames would have been visible hundreds of yards away, even through the snow. He'd dropped down to his knees, putting his kitbag over his head to avoid getting hit by any falling debris or shards of metal. But with one eye he watched the fireball burst into the sky, roll into the clouds, then collapse in on itself. And as he lay still on the ice, he knew that their chances of getting home had probably gone up in smoke along with the Toyota.

He waited a couple of minutes before getting up again.

He could see the black fumes still swirling into the air. Nick put his head down, and started walking straight towards it. He ignored the wind and snow blowing into him, and didn't bother to check the radio for signals. As he walked, his feet getting sucked down at times by the snow, he could feel a fear beating inside his chest. What the hell had just happened to them? he wondered. The Toyota had blown up, that was for sodding sure. But were David and Henri and Maksim inside it at the time? If they'd been hit by a missile, or by chopper fire, it was quite possible.

'Shit,' he muttered out loud.

Stuck out here alone. Miles from the yacht. Miles from the rest of the unit. Nick's right hand fumbled inside his webbing. He searched around desperately for a few seconds before he found it. A flare. Thank Christ for that, he thought. At least I can signal to the others if I am alone out here.

He pressed on. Step after step. It was almost impossible to run in these conditions. The thick snow kept holding you back. But he was trying as hard as he could.

Just close down that hundred yards as fast as possible, he told himself.

'Nick, Nick,' cried a voice.

He recognized it at once. Maksie.

Nick didn't reckon he'd ever been quite so pleased to hear the Russian's voice. This was the fourth mission he'd been on with this unit. Afghanistan, Africa, Somalia and now the sodding Arctic, he reflected to himself. But this was the first time it had ever occurred to him that he might die.

Today he could sense it. Death was hovering next to his shoulder, like a shadow that he couldn't escape.

'Where's the others?' he asked, as Maksim grabbed hold of him in a tight bear hug.

'Looking for you, you sod,' growled the Russian.

Thank Christ, thought Nick. We're not alone out here.

Maksim yelled. The three men had split up to look for Nick but had agreed not to go more than twenty paces in any direction. The flames from the Toyota's debris were being quickly extinguished by the snow, and their meagre light was fading, plunging the plateau back into the eerie darkness they were now all so depressingly familiar with.

'The Toyota's gone,' explained David quickly, when the four men were reunited.

'Sod it, how are we getting home?' demanded Nick.

'We're walking, I reckon,' answered Henri.

'It's bloody miles.'

The Frenchman nodded. His expression was tight, and from the look on his face, Nick guessed that he was painfully aware it was going to be close to impossible to get back to the yacht in one piece without any transport.

'We'll do it,' said David.

He was trying to put some confidence into his voice. But it wasn't convincing. You could hear the nervousness in each word, the same nervousness all of them felt at the scale of the challenge ahead.

'First we find the rest of our unit,' said Henri.

'And what about the plane?' asked Nick.

'I reckon if we stumble across the plane, then all well and good,' said Henri. 'But from here on, getting our unit back together and getting out of this hellhole alive has to be our first priority.'

'But . . .' started Maksim.

'Nothing else counts, Maksie,' said David sharply. 'I'm not dying here, that's for bloody sure.'

'Then let's move,' growled Henri.

Maksim stomped into the snow. The wind was blowing in harder, and the flames were all out now. Somewhere out on the ridge, the sniper might well still be tracking them. With the right kind of rifle and night-vision sights he could pick them off one by one if he wanted to. There was nothing they could do about that now, however; the first they'd probably know about it was when a bullet lodged itself in one of their backs.

Maybe he won't even bother wasting his sodding ammo, thought David grimly. Without transport, maybe he knows that we're corpses already. He can let the Arctic kill us, and save himself the trouble.

The four men walked in single file, the Russian up front, then Henri and Nick, with David bringing up the rear. They were moving purposefully enough, but their shoulders were starting to sag, and there was none of the good-humoured banter that might otherwise have kept their spirits up in the tight corner they were now in.

'Christ,' David muttered to himself, then stifled the words under his breath. We've really dropped ourselves in it this time.

Seventeen

OLLIE CLOSED HIS EYES FOR the twentieth time, but still he couldn't sleep.

He was lying back on a simple wooden bed frame. The shack was buried several feet below the snow and ice, but it had walls that had been decently constructed out of planking, and a sheet of corrugated iron that was used as a floor, and it was a lot warmer than above ground.

It had been built by one of the polar exploration companies that ran trips up to the North Pole for anyone who didn't mind paying a few thousand for an adventure they wouldn't experience anywhere else on earth. There was a whole network of them throughout the Arctic, maintained by an informal group of explorers who made sure the shelters were resupplied at least once a year with the basics of food and medicine, so that they could be used by anyone who got into trouble. But they were mainly used in the summer months, when the weather, although freezing, was far better; only a few madmen determined to get themselves in the *Guinness Book of Records* ventured into the Arctic in the middle of winter.

After he had dropped down the shaft that led into the shack,

Ollie had spent ten minutes with a spade hacking away at the ice that had frozen across its surface before he got in. During the summer, the top layer of ice melted, making the shelters easier to access, but at this time of year, they were about as easy to get into as a Swiss bank vault.

Once inside, though, Ollie was grateful for the shelter. The shack measured ten feet by five. There was a cot in one corner: no mattress, no sheets, and certainly not a pillow, but a man could put his head down inside his snow suit and be reasonably comfortable. There were three metal chests in the corner. None of them was locked, but the lids on all three were frozen solid. Ollie propped his torch up in one corner and, squatting so that he didn't put any pressure on his broken ankle, used his knife to start prising them open. It took ten minutes of hacking away at the frozen metal to get the first lid up, and just as long for the other two. The first contained a set of basic medicines: antibiotics, painkillers, bandages and disinfectants. The second had food: tinned fruit and meat and dried pasta and rice that would last for years in these frozen conditions. The third contained a small stove, some candles, matches, and a basic tool kit for fixing broken skis and sledges.

'We'll be all right with this lot,' grunted Ollie to himself, as he opened each box in turn. 'A man could survive on this grub until next spring.'

He lit a candle and switched off his torch. There was no point in wasting the batteries when he had no idea how long he might be down here. It cast a pale light through the small shack, and his shadow flicked monstrously behind him. At least there's no mirror, he thought to himself as he rubbed the stubble on his face. I must look like crap. After lighting the candle, he got the stove going and boiled up some pasta, tipping a tin of tuna on top of it, and ate the food slowly with a tin spoon from his kitbag. Next he opened up some peaches and ate them straight from the tin. The food started to make him feel better, the way it always did. The first rule of soldiering, he reckoned, was always to get some grub inside you whenever you could. Finally, he rummaged through the medicines. He didn't fancy taking his mulaks or socks off, it was way too cold for that. Instead, he just swallowed a couple of Vicodin, a high-strength American-made painkiller he found in the medicine chest, and hoped that would make his ankle hurt a little less.

By the time all that was done, it was past seven o'clock in the evening, and Ollie reckoned there wasn't much else to do other than get his head down and try and get some kip. He switched off the stove but left the candle on, and lay down on the wooden cot. He shut his eyes, but it wasn't much use. As soon as he tried to get off to sleep, the throbbing from his ankle only seemed to get worse. Ollie was usually a good sleeper. He'd learned at boarding school to get some kip just about anywhere, and he still reckoned it was the most valuable lesson he'd learned in the place. But today was different. Maybe it was the pain. Maybe it was the howling of the wind from the storm that was still raging outside. Maybe it was knowing his mates were out there, facing danger without him. Whatever it was, it was keeping him awake, and there didn't seem to be anything he could do about it.

He reckoned at least two hours had passed before he decided it was useless. He dragged himself out of bed, and re-lit the stove. He stepped outside for a moment, careful to use his foot as little as possible, and grabbed a few handfuls of snow to melt on the pot on the stove. It took several minutes before he had enough water to fill a couple of centimetres at the bottom of his tin mug, but he drank it anyway, and took a couple of bites of a chocolate bar, chewing on it in a slow, thoughtful way. He'd lost a tooth on the Somalia mission and had a fair few fillings in the rest of his mouth, and was aware that any kind of dental work had a tendency to fall apart under the extreme Arctic cold. Be careful, he reminded himself, sucking rather than chewing on the chocolate so that it slowly melted in his mouth. You're already in bad enough shape without a sodding tooth falling out.

He warmed his hands on the small stove and began to feel a bit better. The painkillers had started to kick in and his foot wasn't hurting as much as it had been. There was a thick swelling around the ankle, but that too was helping to dull the pain. His teeth were still chattering, but he was getting used to that now. He reckoned it would take a couple of months in Dubai in midsummer before he started to feel warm again.

He checked his watch. It was getting close to ten, Friday night. Another fourteen hours until the signaller switched itself off. Eighteen hours until the yacht departed. The boys would be out there, doing their best to find the plane, Ollie felt sure of that. Death Inc. had never failed in a mission yet, and they weren't planning to start now. Not if Bruce had anything to do with it. The reputation of the firm rested on its ability to achieve the impossible and, if that was ever tarnished, they were just a bunch of ugly old soldiers with not much to recommend them. But even if they couldn't find it, there was just tonight and the next morning to get through. And then the lads will pick me up in the Toyota and we can get the hell out of here.

I'll be fine, Ollie reassured himself. I just have to sit tight and keep myself out of trouble.

He'd already searched through the cabin once, but he still hadn't checked the log book. He dragged himself towards the small shelf next to the entry shaft, and looked down at the small notepad. There was a pencil next to it, attached to the wall with a piece of string. Anyone visiting the shack was meant to write down their name, give brief details of how long they'd stayed, where they were heading, a description of the weather, and details of any supplies they'd used. Next to the log was a tin can, where you were supposed to put some money to pay for what you used. American or Canadian dollars were preferred, it added. Ollie hadn't brought any money with him, but he made a mental note of the email address of the Canadian exploration company that resupplied the shack every summer, and reminded himself to wire them a hundred quid when he got home. Most expensive plate of pasta and tuna I've probably ever had, he thought to himself with a rough grin. But worth every sodding penny.

He started to leaf through the pages, immersing himself in some of the stories of the men who'd used the shelter over the years. It stretched back to 1995. At most, the shack had been used three times a year. Last summer it had been visited by a group of five Korean women trying to become the first female team from their country to reach the North Pole on foot. Crazy girls, thought Ollie as he read the entry. Why the hell were you trying to do that? The year before, some German students had spent a couple of nights here when one of them had got frostbite, and the same summer an American team had sheltered here while walking home from the Pole. They'd lost all their food and fuel in a lead, and had decided to stay in the shelter while they waited for the helicopter they'd radioed for to come and collect them.

Most of the stories were roughly the same. Adventurers and explorers, who ventured out into the greatest wilderness left on the planet but found themselves defeated by the rugged icescape and retreated in here for some respite from the brutal conditions. There was a hint of regret in each of the entries, but also of pride. After all, anyone who'd made it this far was doing OK, reflected Ollie as he read back through the notes they'd left behind. There was no shame in getting beaten by the Arctic. Many men had buckled before far lesser enemies.

One entry caught Ollie's eye. It was from a pair of Norwegian students, on a trek to the North Pole in the spring of 2003. Henning Carew and Torstein Knudsen. Big strapping lads, reckoned Ollie, just from reading their names and looking at their strong, purposeful handwriting. Vikings. They'd taken refuge here after breaking their skis: there was enough kit here to make them good. It had been a warm summer, by Arctic standards, and the shack was visible from the surface. 'A hundred yards north-north-east, we found a fascinating historical site,' Torstein had noted in impeccable English. 'When we get home, we should notify the history department at the University of Oslo. The guys who work on World War Two. It would merit further investigation.'

The entry ended right there.

Ollie closed the log book, and placed it back on the shelf. He'd make his own entry, but he'd leave that until tomorrow, when the rest of the boys picked him up. On the stove, the snow had melted, and he had enough water now for a full cup. He drank the tepid water, surprised at how thirsty he was, then staggered back to the door to collect another few handfuls of snow to melt.

Ten thirty, he noted, checking his watch.

He put the snow on to melt, then lay back on the cot, and closed his eyes.

For a few seconds he could feel himself drifting off. Every muscle in his body ached, his head was throbbing with pain, and his ankle was swollen and numb. Sleep was so close, he felt he could reach out and grab it. But then it vanished again. Like trying to catch a shadow, as soon as you reached out for it, it flitted away into the darkness.

Ollie rolled on to his side, but that only disturbed the muscles in his foot. Bolts of terrible pain started to roll though his whole body, waking him up again. He climbed out of the cot, and started looking for some more painkillers.

Christ, just thirteen more hours, he told himself, checking his watch for the hundredth time.

Just hold on that long.

Eighteen

STEVE STOPPED TO CHECK THE radio.

He was holding the slim, black device tight between his gloves. The snow was swirling all around them, the wind was blowing in hard from the east, and he had to use his hand to wipe the small screen clear before he could see it clearly.

But it didn't make any difference how many times you looked. There was still nothing there.

'What are you getting?' asked Maya.

'Sod all,' said Steve.

He glanced around. There was one big glacier directly to the left of them and, straight ahead, a dip in the ground, where the ice plateau faded away into a long thin crater. It had taken them three hours to cover a mile since they'd dropped Ollie off at the shelter, and it had been a slow, hard slog. Almost every yard had been a struggle. Maya had struck out ahead, while Steve harnessed the sledge to his back and followed the trail she was carving through the snow. They immediately encountered one large ridge which, in the darkness, seemed simple enough to climb at first but turned into a solid wall of ice once they got further up. They had to come back down again, then trek east for half a mile before they found a spot where they could push through. They were stopping every hundred yards to check the radio, but so far they had come up with nothing, and each time they tried, they lost a little more hope. After they made their way through the ridge, they were a long way off course. Maya had mapped out the target zone into three distinct sectors for the units to search; unless they covered the territory methodically, she kept insisting, they were never going to find the plane. They tabbed their way slowly back to the path they were meant to be following, but the way was constantly blocked by great sheets of ice that rose suddenly out of the ground like freak waves at sea. As they trekked forward, they were getting hungrier and thirstier all the time. Their bodies were dehydrating despite the intense cold and the calories were burning up inside them as their bodies struggled to make progress across the rough terrain and to keep themselves warm at the same time.

'We press on,' said Maya.

There was a note of determination in her voice that Steve couldn't help but admire. She reminded him of Ollie. Except smarter, of course, and a lot better looking, he noted to himself with a rough smile. She had the same bull-like determination. The same stamina and fortitude. The same refusal to admit defeat. Maya was a formidable force. Of that there was no question. And Steve wasn't sure he'd ever met anyone quite like her before.

'We need some food and water,' said Steve.

'It will just waste time.'

Steve shook his head. He was already unpacking the stove from the sledge. 'If we don't get some calories and some liquid inside us, we're going to collapse out here,' he said firmly. 'And then we're no use to anyone.'

'We've only fourteen hours . . .'

'We'll drop if we don't rest.'

Reluctantly, she sat down on the side of the sledge. The wind was blowing hard across the ice, and as soon as you stopped moving, the cold started to get to you. She was shivering, and her teeth were chattering. Steve placed the stove behind her, using both their bodies as a shield from the wind, then attempted to light it with a flint. It took a couple of goes, but finally the small blue flame came to life. He put some snow into a pot, keeping his back to the wind to shelter the stove from the storm. It took several minutes before the snow started to thaw out, but finally he had enough liquid to fill two tin cups. He waited a few more minutes until it was bubbling, then stirred in a Bovril cube, and handed one across to Maya.

She took a sip of the liquid, then pulled a face.

'In England, people really drink this stuff?' she asked. 'For pleasure, I mean.'

'We're raised on it.'

Steve put his lips to the cup and drank carefully. He was so cold he didn't want to suddenly gulp down the hot liquid, it would be too much of a shock to the system. He took a small sip, and swilled it around his throat for a few seconds, before letting it sink down to his stomach. Much like Maya, he didn't much care for the stuff. His mum had never served it to them back in Bromley, and if you didn't grow up on Bovril, it was unlikely you were going to develop a taste for it later in life. But there was a strength to its beefy flavouring that hit the spot at just this moment. And as he drank, he could feel some warmth returning to his stomach, and some colour to his frozen cheeks.

'Some date you are, Steve West,' she said. 'Sitting in the frozen snow with a cup of Bovril.' She was attempting to smile, but her lips were frozen, and the skin around them was starting to crack, and it was impossible for her to crease up her mouth.

'Classy, eh,' said Steve, grinning. 'I know how to treat a lady.'

'Where's next? A jungle, maybe? Or a desert?'

'I was thinking more like a five-star hotel. Maybe in Greece or Turkey. Somewhere hot, anyway. With a few pools, and a spa, and a beach, and a balcony overlooking the sea, and all the food you can eat, and a bucket of chilled champagne in the corner of the room.'

'A spa,' said Maya, wrapping her arms round herself, rubbing to try to keep warm. 'That would be nice.'

'If I could get a signal on my mobile I'd reserve it right now.'

'You can book it when we get back to the yacht. If we make it . . .'

Steve paused for a second before replying.

'Don't say that,' he said finally. 'We'll be fine.'

'We're stuck in the middle of nowhere, Steve,' she said. 'It's forty below, possibly more. There's a snowstorm, we've lost one of our vehicles, and there are guys everywhere who know this territory a lot better than we do trying to shoot us. I'd say there was a possibility we're not going to make it.'

She cradled the tin cup in her hands, drawing a few remaining flickers of warmth from the liquid, then drained the cup. But the Bovril was already stone cold; in these temperatures, it only took a minute for a drink to lose all its heat, and two minutes for it to turn back into ice.

'Funny,' she continued. 'I always thought I'd die in Israel. And be buried beneath the shade of an olive tree.'

'You're being defeatist,' said Steve. He didn't like the way she was talking. There was one rule he'd learned in the Regiment. You never contemplated the possibility of defeat. It was bad for the soul. There were no finer fighting forces in the world than Israel's front-line troops. But he was surprised they hadn't learned the same lesson.

'Keep our chins up, and we'll be fine.'

'I'm just being realistic.'

'They've got Maksie in the Toyota. The bloke's a nutter. He won't let anything happen to it.'

'Let's hope so.'

Steve drained the rest of his cold Bovril. The wind had blown the flame out on the stove. He switched it off, and started to pack it away with the rest of the kit on the sledge, then hooked it on to his back.

'Anyway, it was your idea not to bring a satphone,' he said.

Steve started to walk out into the ice. The snow and the wind were blowing into his face, but they had hit a flat stretch of ground, and it wasn't too hard to walk across, even with the extra weight to pull.

'It could be used to track us,' said Maya.

'It could also be used to get us the hell out of here,' growled Steve. 'If we got stuck, we could call in and ask for help.'

'I know,' said Maya.

'So why the hell didn't we?'

'Kolodin didn't want us to,' said Maya. 'He kept insisting that it wasn't safe.'

'How much do you know about the guy?' asked Steve.

Maya was walking steadily behind him, two yards distant, but as he asked the question she quickened her pace so that they were walking alongside one another, battling straight into the oncoming snow.

'He's rich and tough and manipulative, but I suppose that doesn't make him any different from any other billionaire,' she replied. 'Certainly the Russian ones.'

'Is he on the level?'

'We don't know. He's invested a lot of money in Israel, like a lot of the Russian oligarchs. Most of them are Jewish, and there is such a tradition of anti-Semitism in Russia, they like to keep a foothold in Israel. An insurance policy against the return of the bad old days. The Mossad looks after them. They feed them information that's useful for business deals, provide protection and security, and in exchange they expect the investment to keep flowing. Kolodin is part of that network, but I haven't been able to find out much more about him.'

Steve used his glove to wipe some snow out of his face. There was two days of stubble on his cheeks, and the snow was starting to freeze on the short spiky hairs, creating a mess of little ice cubes that clung to his skin. 'Are you working for the Mossad?'

'It's the same as the Regiment, I guess,' answered Maya. 'Once you're in, they can always call on you for favours, contacts. There's a whole network of people the Bureau can call on. The Sayanim, that's what they call it. There are thousands of them around the world. The Bureau taps their expertise when it is needed.'

'But do you know why Kolodin wants to find this plane so much?'

Maya was shaking her head. 'Only what's he's told us. He

believes that someone murdered Markov, and whoever they are, they might be coming for him next.'

'And the Mossad believes that?'

She hesitated, and she missed a couple of steps, so that she was walking a pace behind Steve again.

But she didn't answer the question.

'Are you reporting back to the Bureau?' Steve turned to face her, his expression angry.

'Of course I report back,' she snapped suddenly. 'I'm ex-Caracal. The Bureau placed me on the man's security team. I tell them what's happening.'

'Shit,' barked Steve. 'Who the hell are we working for out here? The Russians? The Israelis?'

He took a couple of swift paces forward. If it wasn't so sodding cold, my face would be burning red with anger, he thought.

'We're just looking for the plane, Steve,' insisted Maya. 'The Bureau don't believe it was a crash either. They think something happened to it. So when I told them a unit was being put together to carry out a last-minute search, they said to go right ahead. They're interested in the results, that's all.'

'As far as you know.'

Maya nodded. 'As far as I know,' she said quietly.

'I don't like it,' said Steve.

'Neither do I,' said Maya. 'But let's just concentrate on finding the plane. And then see if we can get out of here alive.'

Steve put his head down, and battled forward through the snow. They reached a steep hill, and he paused to check the radio, but there was still no signal. He looked at his watch. It was just after eleven. Another hour, and they'd be into the final day of the job. He took a moment to catch his breath, and relax his aching muscles, then steeled himself for the climb. The first few yards weren't too bad, but then the ridge steepened. His breath was short, and there was a stabbing pain close to his lungs, where the freezing cold oxygen was rattling through him. He cursed to himself, then took another couple of steps forward. He plunged a foot down into the snow, then hauled the other up behind it, but lost his balance. The sledge was slipping on the steep slope, its weight dragging him backwards, and suddenly he could feel himself tumbling down, unable to stop himself. Christ, he thought. Don't let me break a sodding bone like Ollie. Maya caught him in her arms. 'I'm on your side, Steve,' she said gently. 'Don't worry about it.'

'We're all on the same side in the grave,' answered Steve. 'And that's where we'll be quite soon the way this sodding job is going.'

She helped him back on to his feet. 'I'll take the sledge for a bit.'

'I'll be fine,' said Steve gruffly.

He steadied himself, adjusted the harness that was keeping the sledge attached to his back, and took a couple of steps up the hill. It was a hard climb, but his balance was back, and he was soon on the other side. He looked down. There was a narrow plateau of level ground, flanked on either side by huge ridges of ice that rose forty or fifty feet into the air in solid, impassable walls. For a brief second he thought he saw a glint of steel on the left-hand side, and was about to warn Maya to dive for cover, but as he looked closer he could see it was only the reflection from his torch beam catching on a jagged ice crystal. Steady yourself, mate, he told himself. You're getting jumpy.

He put his head down, and started to descend the slope into

the plateau. The sledge slid easily across the snow and, going downhill, hardly weighed anything. Steve ploughed forward, glad to have less of a weight to lug, but as he hit the flat ice, it was harder going again. The snow was still falling relentlessly, and the clock was ticking towards midnight.

And still we're no closer to finding the sodding plane, thought Steve.

They walked alongside each other for the few hundred yards of the ice plateau. As he pressed forward, Steve felt bad for doubting Maya earlier. She was just an ex-soldier, the same as he was. Something weird had happened out here, and they'd been plunged into a fight that none of them understood, but she wasn't involved, he felt certain of that. She was an extraordinary, formidable women, sexy yet tough, brutal when she needed to be, yet tender as well when it was necessary. He was a bit scared of her, he didn't mind admitting that to himself, although he wouldn't own up about that to anyone else. But he also felt reassured to have her at his side. There weren't many blokes he could say that of, and certainly no women. Not until he'd met her, anyway.

'What will you do when you see Archie?' asked Maya.

It was past midnight, and they managed another quarter of a mile through terrible conditions. They stopped five times to check the radio, but still there was nothing. The valley they had walked through had protected them from the worst of the storm, but as they got through to the other side, there was another high ridge to climb across, followed by a crater littered with thick, chunky blocks of ice they had to weave their way around, a kind of frozen maze which stopped them making any decent progress.

Matt Lynn

'Make him a nice cup of hot chocolate,' said Steve. 'With marshmallows in it. And some hot buttered toast on the side.'

'Stop it,' said Maya. 'You're making me hungry.'

'I don't know. I don't think one-year-olds drink hot chocolate, do they?'

'I haven't met many.'

'I have a couple of nieces and a nephew. I don't see as much of them as I should. My brother is a banker. The golden boy. My family never approved of my joining the Army. Still don't.'

'Not even when you got into the Regiment? That's bloody difficult.'

'It's all military to them. They don't like any of it.' He paused to free up the sledge which had got stuck between two blocks of ice. 'How about you? I can't imagine your old man was too happy when you said you were joining the Army permanently.'

'I come from a Bureau family,' said Maya. 'My grandfather came from the Ukraine. Most of his family went to the concentration camps, and my grandmother died at Auschwitz. But he made his way south and crossed the Mediterranean, and joined Menachem Begin's Irgun group fighting for an independent state of Israel. Afterwards, he was Army, then Bureau.'

'Christ, I'm sorry . . .'

'No need,' said Maya. 'It's ancient history. My father was Army, then Bureau as well. A Kidon. One of the Bureau's licensed assassins. And I'm his only child. I'm sure he'd much rather have had a son, but he didn't so it was up to me to carry on the fight.'

'And did he mind you leaving?'

'He died four years ago,' said Maya. 'Cancer. They smoke like crazy at the Bureau. And the Kidon as well. All that hanging around, waiting to assassinate people, I suppose.' She attempted a smile, but the joke had fallen flat. 'If he was still alive, I don't think I could have left the service. He'd have been too disappointed.'

Steve paused to decide on which direction they should take. There was a massive wall of ice straight in front of them but with two valleys to the left and right that they could walk through. Both looked as if they would take them in the right direction, but there was no way of knowing what further obstacles might obstruct their path. He flashed his torch, but the beam of light only illuminated the way ahead for twenty yards, and although it looked clear on both sides, he'd learned enough about the treacherous geography of the Arctic in the last twenty-four hours not to trust a single yard of the place. 'Right or left?' he asked Maya.

'Left,' she said, her tone firm and decisive.

Steve nodded, and turned left, pushing himself forward. It didn't make any difference to him. The valleys were cut through the ice, each about fifty yards wide, with steep banks of snow on either side. The wind caught in the channel, the air accelerating, so that it was blowing hard into his face. Steve leant into the wind, letting it blow right around him, and pulled forward. The sledge was straining on his back; the mound of kit piled on to it was creating some wind resistance, slowing him down even further. Maya was following right behind him, but when the weather was as severe as this, it was impossible to talk any more. The snow would gust straight into your lungs. For a moment, Steve just shut his eyes, no longer even looking where he was going. And, if he was being honest with himself, not caring very much any more either.

It was getting close to one in the morning by the time they broke through the valley and out into the ice plateau on the other side. The wind had dropped now that it no longer had the ice blocks to swirl through, and there was less fresh snow falling from the skies. Steve shone his torch forwards. With better weather, the beam illuminated twenty-five yards of ground. The snow was rolling outwards in small mounds and drifts, but the ice beneath it was flat, and the terrain was passable. He flashed the torch left and right, then arced it round again, trying to decide which path to take across the plateau.

'Straight on,' said Maya, standing beside him.

Steve flashed the torch again. To his right.

He'd seen something. He felt certain of it.

'There,' he said.

From her webbing, Maya drew her gun.

'No,' said Steve. He reached out with his hand to touch her arm, and she put the gun away. 'Not a soldier. An object.'

He started to walk, his pace quickening.

It was a mound of snow, like thousands they had seen since they started this hunt. But it had a tall, triangular shape. Something like the tail wing of an aircraft.

Don't get too excited, mate, he warned himself, as he strode towards it. It's probably just a strangely shaped lump of snow. The wind can twist it into any kind of shape it wants.

But maybe . . .

It was twenty yards away, right at the limit of his torch's arc of illumination, but Steve closed that space in less than a minute. He flashed the light over the mound. Snow, snow, and more sodding snow. And then a chunk of what look like metal. Steve put the torch down and reached out to grab it with both hands.

It was lodged deep in the drift, and ice had frozen it into place, but with a hard yank it came free. Steel, painted white, but covered with black soot marks. It measured six feet in length, by two across. Steve had spent plenty of time at airports over the years, and he'd been up in a lot of military jets. He didn't need to be an aeronautical engineer to know what he was holding in his hands.

A chunk of a tail wing. From an Airbus A319.

'Christ, we've found it,' said Steve, looking back towards Maya.

Steve laid the charred metal down on the snow. Maya knelt down and ran her glove along the side of the object, shining her torch on to it. The metal was twisted in several places, and there were signs of melting where the flames that engulfed it must have been hot enough to turn even its hardened steel into liquid. But there was no question about what it was.

'Where's the rest of the plane?' she asked quickly, looking around as she posed the question.

She stood up, and got the radio out. Steve leant across her, looking down at the small screen. But there was still no sign of a signal from the black box.

'I don't understand,' said Steve. 'If that's the sodding fuselage, why aren't we getting a signal?'

Maya looked anxious. She turned the radio on and off again, double-checking that it was working properly. But still there was nothing.

'We've found a bit of the plane,' she said finally. 'But it might have broken up in mid-air. The main fuselage could have travelled another half-mile or more.'

'Christ,' said Steve angrily. 'I thought we were close.'

'We are,' said Maya. 'It can't be that far away.'

They started to walk across the plateau. Steve was striding out across the snow and ice with renewed vigour in his step. A plane might break up in mid-air, it was possible. But only if there was a cataclysmic explosion. If it crash-landed, and that was more likely, chunks of the plane would spin off in every direction when it impacted with the ground. But the main fuselage wouldn't travel more than a few hundred feet.

The bastard has to be here somewhere, he told himself.

Another mound. Steve flashed the torch on to it, and started to dig. A wing section, perhaps. He could see it in the shape of the snow. He plunged his hands deep into the freezing drift, angrily using his fist to shovel it away. One foot and then another. Nothing. He took the spade out of the sledge and started to dig even more furiously, until he pushed aside five feet of snow. There was a sweat on his brow from the exertion, and the icicles that had formed on his stubble were starting to melt away.

'There's nothing there, Steve,' said Maya finally.

'Then where the sod is it?' demanded Steve angrily.

They kept walking forward. Fifty yards, then a hundred. The snow had lessened and it was getting easier to see: their torches sometimes lit up a path thirty or forty yards ahead. There was no debris they could spot on the open ground, but Steve wasn't expecting that any more. It was a month since the plane had come down, and the snow would have buried everything. They tried two more mounds, Steve digging into them with his shovel, but found nothing.

'Jesus,' he muttered to himself angrily.

'Maybe we should split up,' said Maya.

'In this sodding darkness?' growled Steve. 'No way. We'll never find each other again.'

As he spoke, he was flashing the torch east. There was a shape in the snow, about forty yards away, with what looked like a black spear sticking out of it. He walked swiftly across to it, his pulse quickening. As he got closer, he was no longer in any doubt. It was part of a wheel. An axle maybe. Or one of the hydraulic levers that operated the undercarriage on take-off and landing. He gripped the metal and started to tug, but there was no give in it. Using his gloves, he started to push away the snow all around it. Until the wheel was exposed.

It wasn't in one piece any more. The tyre had been shredded, and the axles had broken apart, but it was clearly identifiable as an aircraft wheel.

'We must be close,' said Maya.

'But where's the sodding plane?' growled Steve.

He was flashing his torch from east to west, casting long beams of light. He scoured the landscape for any kind of mound or hill. The length of an A319 fuselage measured 111 feet. It wasn't exactly easily hidden, thought Steve to himself. Right now, however, it seemed to have melted into nothingness. The ground rolled away in the distance, like white meadowland, but there was nothing that looked like a buried plane.

'We need to follow its trajectory,' said Maya. 'The tail wing came off two hundred yards south-east of here. The wheels dropped off right here.' She was tracing her hand through the sky, trying to figure out the descent of the stricken plane. 'The pilot might have been trying to crash-land.' She looked thoughtful, working out the angles. 'In which case, it should have come down two to three hundred yards north-north-west of here.'

Steve started to walk. He shone his torch forward, looking for any kind of hill. Nothing.

'Christ,' he muttered. 'Where is it?'

He was standing right where Maya reckoned the A319 should have come down. But there wasn't any kind of mound. Instead, the ground fell away into a kind of snow ditch. The way it might if a huge plane had cut a hole into the ice, Steve realised suddenly.

We're not looking for a hill. We're looking for a trench.

He plunged the shovel into the ground, and started to dig, working slowly and methodically, convinced that he was right. The freshly fallen snow was easy enough to work through, but as he got past a foot he was cutting into stuff that had packed tight, frozen into a hard icy substance that had the strength of rock.

Maya was standing over him, shining her torch down into the hole he was digging. He was down three feet, leaning hard into the spade with his back as he smashed the packed snow apart. Then there was a different kind of sound. Metal on metal. Steve smashed harder with the spade, breaking apart a huge lump of snow, then knelt down, using his hands to scramble away the mess of ice fragments at the bottom of his pit.

He was touching steel. White, with a streak of black soot along its surface, and frozen to the touch even through his thick gloves.

Steve looked up at Maya.

'Here's your man's plane,' he said simply.

Nineteen

MAKSIM WAS LEADING THE WAY, with Nick and David following in his path, and Henri bringing up the rear. It was three hours now since they'd lost the Toyota, thought David. And the mood hadn't lightened at all. A sombre weariness had descended on all four of them when the vehicle went down, as if it had taken their lives into the ocean with it, and now they were walking through this ghostly, desolate landscape with all the spirit and determination of dead men. They were silent, trudging forward, stopping every two hundred yards to check the radio for a signal, but without much conviction that they'd find one, or that they would ever get the black box back to the yacht even if they did.

At midnight, they stopped for a rest, and some food and water. Nick got the stove going, while Nick and David collected some fistfuls of snow to put in the pot. They'd distributed the supplies Maksim had managed to rescue from the Toyota into their four backpacks. They had some food, and a tin of paraffin. Henri fished out a pair of stock cubes to mix into the warm water, and David got out some shortbread biscuits and a slab of chocolate. Once the water was melted, and hot enough to dissolve the stock, the four men sat around the small blue flame, drinking and eating but not saying anything.

'How much paraffin have we got left?' asked David finally, looking across at Henri.

'A litre.'

'Christ, it's not much.'

'I reckon it will be enough to get us home.'

'How'd you work that out?' asked Nick.

'A litre should be enough for ten fires to burn long enough to melt enough snow for a litre of water. Ten litres is a litre for each of us. We've got some pasta and rice, enough for at least one decent meal. It should be enough to get us back.'

'We've got some candles as well,' said David. 'We can eat those if it gets really bad.'

'It could be ten miles back to the yacht,' said Nick. 'I'm not sure I'm going to make it all the way back on a sodding candle.'

'And we might get another bad snowstorm,' said Maksim. 'If we have to lay up for a time then we aren't going to make it back to the yacht.'

'Then we're done for anyway,' said Henri. 'If we don't make it back to the yacht in time, and with both Toyotas down, and no satellite phones, I don't give us much chance of surviving. We're not going to make it through the winter, are we? And no one is going to come and rescue us. Apart from Kolodin, no one knows we're here, and I don't reckon *he* cares enough to bother.'

'There's always seal meat,' said Maksim cheerfully. 'Club a few of those bastards on the head, and we'll be all right. You can eat the meat, use the oil for heating, and the skins to build a tent.'

'I'm almost looking forward to it, Maksie,' said David.

'At least you won't have to go home to the twins,' said Maksim.

'Or the alimony,' said Nick.

David chuckled. He was pleased to get some banter back among the boys. So long as they could keep their spirits up, they had a chance, even if only a slim one. That was one of the first rules of military life.

They finished the stock cubes, ate the chocolate and biscuits, then switched off the stove. Its flame didn't generate much heat, and certainly not enough to make any dent in the storm, but if you leant right in close, there was some warmth to be drawn from it. They couldn't keep it on for too long, however; as Henri said, a litre of paraffin wasn't going to last long, and they had no way of knowing any more how they might get home. Reluctantly, they put it out, then repacked their kit, and started to march forward at just after midnight.

'The start of a new day,' said Henri, urging the men forward. 'The last of the mission.'

'That's something to be sodding grateful for.'

'I don't know, I'm starting to like it out here,' said Nick cheerfully. 'It's sort of peaceful.'

Henri led the way this time, with Nick and David in the middle, and Maksim bringing up the rear. They had only managed a mile over the last two hours, and they were still another mile from the centre of the target zone. The terrain had been rough, huge glaciers and valleys to manoeuvre around, treacherous leads, and craters that appeared out of nowhere, and at times seemed to sink right into the ocean itself. It had been hard enough going in the Toyota, but it was far harder on foot, and none of them was looking forward to the prospect of trying to make it all the way back to the yacht. They'd planned to meet up with the rest of the unit close to the centre of the target zone. Flares would alert them to where each unit was, and would tell them if the plane had been found by any of the three search parties. But so far, there was no sign of their mates trying to get in touch with them. And, given that the hunting party had tracked them down and taken out the Toyota, they could no longer guarantee they were still alive.

'Stop,' shouted Henri.

It was just after one in the morning. The Frenchman was twenty yards ahead of them, using his torch to try and navigate his way through a glacier that at one point rose fifty feet into the air in a twisted yet at times magnificent mess of frozen water.

'I see something,' he hissed.

David, Nick and Maksim all drew their handguns. They advanced steadily towards the glacier. David was flashing his torch forward, while Henri stalked along the ridge.

'What was it?' hissed Nick.

But the Frenchman was twenty yards in front of him. The storm was blowing snow straight across them, and his words got lost on the wind.

Ahead, Henri walked silently forward. He'd switched off his torch, and if he could tell the boys behind him to do the same he would, but he was aware that saying anything out loud would make him a target. Something had been moving in the shadows, he felt certain of it. A soldier, perhaps? One of the men who had been attacking them since they landed in this godforsaken place? If he could capture one of them, then at least he might find out who they were. They might even have a vehicle they could nick to take them home. He looked left and right, but saw nothing. Pausing for a moment, he fished his night-vision goggles from his kitbag and slotted them over his face. He scanned the ground ahead carefully. The ice had a strange luminescent quality when looked at through the goggles, as if he had suddenly been transported to a strange, glowing planet. But ice wasn't what he was looking for. Any kind of body would show up in red, its heat marked out by the night-vision kit.

He took another five paces forward, moving along the edge of the glacier, until he approached a point where it tumbled down into a mass of small blocks, like the debris from a landslide. It was rough, jagged terrain, precisely the kind of place a soldier might decide to lose himself while he stalked his prey, decided Henri.

He gripped the Yarygin in his right hand as he walked forward, making sure it was ready to fire.

A shape.

A small trace of red, like a cloud drifting across the sky. It was to the left of him, behind a small glacier.

'*Merde*,' muttered Henri out loud.

It wasn't a soldier. It wasn't even human. No man could have that shape.

It was an animal of some sort.

Henri froze in his tracks. The shape was moving. So far it was just a trace on the screen of his night-vision goggles. It was behind an ice block, but clearly visible. A polar bear, he realised grimly. Polar bears have such a thick layer of blubber and fur to protect them from the harshness of their environment that they lose practically no body heat, and don't show up on infra-red cameras or on the heat-seeking sensors of night-vision goggles. Apart from their breath, which is just warm enough to be captured, they are quite literally invisible.

But that doesn't make them any less deadly, thought Henri.

The animal was moving away from him right now, but whether it was retreating or simply feeling its way around the terrain, Henri had no way of knowing.

'You all right, mate?' shouted Nick.

Shut the sod up, thought Henri to himself.

Nick was at least twenty yards behind him, reckoned Henri, judging by the sound of his voice. Stay quiet, he thought grimly. Don't frighten the big bastard.

'I said, where the hell are you?' shouted Nick, a tone of anxiety in his voice.

The animal moved suddenly. Startled, reckoned Henri. It won't have heard any human voices out here. It started to move, picking up speed alarmingly quickly. Henri stayed rock steady. Remain completely still, he told himself. It works for wild dogs, and it works for wolves. Whether it worked for polar bears, he had no idea, but it was worth a try. The shape was moving faster, a streak of red across his night-vision goggles, but thin, and spread out, as the goggles were only capturing its breath. Moving straight towards him. He could feel his heart thumping in his chest, and sweat pouring off his back. The beast was twenty yards away but fast closing the space between them. Whether it could see him or smell him, Henri had no idea, and didn't reckon it made any difference. The bear had marked him as an enemy, or supper, and was focused only on its target.

Henri felt a moment of indecision. He knew that nothing

was ever as fatal for a soldier as being unable to make up his mind; it was usually better to make the wrong response quickly than the right one several minutes too late. But he could not reach any settled conclusion. Stand still, and the bear might walk right past him, the way a dog would. Or it might just tear him to shreds. Flee, and that might make him even more of a target. Or it might just save his life.

Henri wrestled with the options, cursing the fact he'd only had basic Arctic survival training. And the couple of seconds that separated him from a mauling were fast evaporating.

'Christ, man, it's a sodding bear . . .' yelled Nick from somewhere behind him.

The noise startled the animal. It was hissing and snorting, its way of preparing for an attack. It was just ten yards in front of Henri now, suddenly breaking out of the darkness. Its head was lowered as it charged straight towards its prey. Henri could feel a flicker of panic close to his heart. Something he'd never felt before. He'd faced danger plenty of times, and met it calmly enough, but he had never taken on an opponent as strange or as fearsome as this. Ten yards closed to five. The beast was standing up now. It was massive, ten feet tall when it was up on its hind legs, and weighed four hundred pounds. It was almost twice Henri's height, and double his weight. Each paw was a foot wide, with claws that glistened even in the darkness, and which it managed to keep immaculately free of ice. Three yards. The beast was about to pounce. Henri didn't need to imagine what kind of damage a single blow from one of those paws would do to a man: it would rip him up as certainly as any sword. He held the Yarygin steady in his hand, and started to pump the bullets from its chamber. There was no distance to the target, and despite his mounting fear, Henri managed to hold the gun steady enough to hit the target. The first two bullets struck the bear's massive chest, and the second two flew into its neck, but none of them had the stopping power to bring the animal down. It fell forward, hissing as it did so, and Henri ducked out of the way, throwing himself to the ground, but as he did so, the bear caught him with a glancing blow across the side of his chest. The sharp claws ripped through the protective clothing on his right arm, then slipped easily into the skin below. Henri roared out in pain, and the startled bear fell away, taking a chunk of flesh with it.

Henri turned on the ground, and rolled away into the snow. By kicking back with his legs, and using the slope of the ground, and the slipperiness of the ice, he managed to cover twelve yards before he came to a halt. As he looked back, the bear appeared disorientated, confused by the speed and agility of its prey, but it quickly swung round. At least two of the bullets had penetrated its chest, and from the look on its face, the animal was angry, and in terrible pain. It hissed, snorted, then swivelled on its thick, stout hind legs, and started a fresh charge. Henri pumped two more bullets straight into its chest. The dual-stack mag on the Yarygin held seventeen rounds, so he had plenty of ammo left, but he couldn't fire it any quicker than the gun would allow, and his right arm had blood pouring from the wound where the bear had ripped into his skin. The pain was intense, like having hot coals pressed into your raw flesh, and there were tears of agony streaming down his face as he kept his finger on the trigger, pumping round after round into his predator. But the bear was massively strong, its tough frame absorbing bullet after bullet, growling in pain, but moving slowly forward, so that it was now just five yards from where his prey was lying helpless on the ground.

The Yarygin had jammed.

Twelve rounds fired. And the mag had frozen solid.

Henri glanced behind him.

Nick, David and Maksim were crouched down in a neat wall, their guns drawn.

'Get your bloody head down, mate,' snapped David.

'Go for the heart,' said Maksim. 'The skulls on these fuckers are so thick the bullets bounce off them like tanks.'

'Sounds like you, Maksie,' said Nick.

'Just fucking fire, will you?' yelled Henri, his voice raw and ragged.

The three men opened up with a lethal barrage of gunfire. For bringing down a polar bear, you really needed a high-calibre hunting rifle, or else a double-action shotgun, but sometimes sheer firepower was enough to get the job done even when you didn't have the right kit. A volley of bullets flew into the bear's heart, tearing it from a dozen different directions, until finally its strength gave out. The animal hissed, and lunged forward once more in a last desperate attempt to kill Henri, but fell a yard short of its target. It lay face down in the snow, grunting as the last embers of life flickered out, then closed its eyes.

Henri watched in silent fascination, too frightened to move even as the guns behind him fell silent.

Maksim rushed up to the bear, and slotted a couple of rounds into the left ear, where the bone of the skull would be soft enough to allow the bullets to do their grisly work. 'I'm not taking any chance with this bastard,' he grunted. 'I want him dead.'

Nick and David had already run across to Henri. They rolled

him over in the snow so that he was lying flat on his back. His snow suit was ripped into shreds along his right arm, and there was a deep gash in the skin between the elbow and the shoulder: three neat grooves from the claws, as if he had been sliced by a trio of knives simultaneously.

'You OK, pal?' asked David.

'I've been better,' grunted Henri.

'We need to get that cleaned up,' said David.

Nick pulled the shreds of snow suit out of the way, while David pulled out the medi-kit he'd stashed into his webbing. He had a small bottle of disinfectant, and some bandages and tape. 'Hold him down,' he said to Nick. Then he looked at Henri. 'I'm afraid this is going to hurt,' he said.

'I bloody know that,' snapped Henri. 'Get on with it.'

'That man needs some vodka,' said Maksim.

'Right, well, if we had some we'd sodding well give it to him,' snapped David. 'As it is, we'll just have to manage.'

Maksim reached inside his webbing and pulled out a small drinking flask. He handed it across to David. 'Strictly for medicinal purposes.'

Henri glanced upwards. 'Your secret stash, Maksie,' he said. 'I'm touched.'

'So you sodding should be,' answered the Russian crisply. 'I was keeping that in case *I* got into an emergency.'

David took the flask, and held it to Henri's lips. 'Here, take a sip, mate.'

Depending on the alcohol content, vodka freezes at minus twenty to forty degrees centigrade, and Maksim's packed plenty of punch, so although there were flecks of ice in it, it was running smoothly from the flask.

Henri took a swig, then handed it back to David with a half smile. He nodded just once to indicate he was ready.

'Maksie, Nick, hold his shoulders and legs,' said David. 'I need the bugger still.'

Maksim grabbed hold of the Frenchman's shoulders, using both fists to hold them down. Nick put his weight down on the legs. David pushed away the snow suit, then tipped the disinfectant straight into the open flesh wound. Henri grunted and bucked upwards viciously as the pain shot through him, but Nick and Maksim were strong enough to hold him in position. David took off his gloves, rubbed some disinfectant in his own hands, then picked up clumps of snow, rubbing it into the wound to clean away any dirt. Henri roared again. The disinfectant was colliding with the cold to create a pain with an intensity to it he had never felt before. 'Fucking, fucking shit,' he cried out.

'Steady, pal,' said David.

Henri pushed his back down into the snow, trying to control the agony. David rubbed two more handfuls of snow into the wound, then started to wrap the bandage round it, tying it tightly into position.

'Job done, mate,' he said finally. 'You'll be all right. I reckon even the bacteria can't live in this crap hole, so it shouldn't get infected.'

Henri grimaced, and sat up. He reached out for the vodka flask, took a second swig, then handed it across to David and Nick. Both men took a small sip, before passing it back to Maksim.

'Don't sodding drink all of it,' growled the Russian. 'If I'm going to freeze to death out here in the next couple of days I'm going to need a flask of vodka in my hand.'

223

'There's another bottle in your webbing somewhere, pal,' said David.

'There sodding isn't,' snapped Maksim. 'And the one thing I've always promised myself is that I'm not going to die sober.'

Nick retrieved some tape from his own medi-kit. He had a spare thermal vest in his backpack, and he tore that in half so that he could wrap it round Henri's arm where the snow suit had been ripped. He taped it into position. It wasn't perfect, and it wasn't going to protect him from the cold nearly as well as the suit, but it was the best they could do.

'You going to be warm enough?' he asked.

Henri shook his head. 'What do you sodding think?' he growled.

David checked his Yarygin handgun, then slotted it back into his webbing. 'I used up a whole mag, and I've got one fully loaded spare,' he said. 'How about you boys?'

'I used up a mag in the last contact,' said Nick. 'I've only got three rounds left.'

'Last mag, eight rounds,' said Maksim.

'Five rounds,' said Henri. 'When a ton of polar bear is charging you, you don't exactly stop to think about saving ammo.'

David stood up, looking out into the horizon, even though his torch was only illuminating the way ahead for twenty yards. The wind was blowing harder across the plateau, and whistling through the ice ridge to one side of them. He pulled his gloves on, and rubbed his frozen hands together to try and get the blood moving again. It was just after one in the morning, but time seemed to have lost any meaning, its usual discipline extinguished by the constant darkness.

'We've no transport, not much food or fuel, and we're dangerously low on ammo,' he said. 'We better hope nothing else goes wrong, because I don't think we're in any shape to deal with any more crap being thrown at us.'

Twenty

BRUCE KNEW ABOUT SOLDIERS LOSING their spirit. He'd seen it before, both in the Regiment itself and in the private military corporations. Shoulders would sag, the pace of a march would slow to a crawl, and the banter amongst the men would start to dry up. The better trained a military force was, the better looked after, and the better led, the less chance there was of its spirit breaking, but even in the SAS it happened sometimes. Morale was hard to sustain in the face of impossible odds, stupid decisions and terrible suffering. And right now, thought Bruce, we are dealing with all three.

It was just after one in the morning, and they had been trudging through the dispiriting darkness for hours now. They couldn't see anything that was more than a few yards away, the cold was brutal, and the storm rough. They were swapping the sledge around from man to man every hour, but it was still a lot of extra weight to carry, and both Ian and Bruce had already realised they weren't in good enough physical shape to venture out into the Arctic in the middle of winter. The search for the plane was proving far harder than any of them had realised, they hadn't brought the right kit with them, and the terrain was far harsher than any of them had allowed for. It was a bad plan, poorly executed, and Bruce was already feeling pissed off with himself for allowing the unit to be thrown into such a brutal mission.

I should have said no in the nightclub, he reflected bitterly as he climbed wearily up the side of yet another steep ridge of ice. Some jobs just aren't worth it. And this is turning into one of them.

'I expected to go to hell one day,' said Ian. 'I've made my peace with the idea. A man can't have done the kind of things I've done and expect any other outcome. But I was expecting to at least have the pleasure of sodding well dying before I got there.'

'Are you a believer then?' asked Dan.

Ian glanced up at the sky. The snow was falling steadily from the thick, low clouds, and getting blown straight across the plateau at them like a swarm of angry insects.

'It's hard to believe in a god out here,' he said. 'But I grew up in Belfast. A good Catholic family.'

'I thought you came from a long line of Provos,' said Bruce.

'My father and my grandfather, and I'm feckin' proud of it as well,' said Ian. 'There's nothing in the Bible that says you can't blow up English fuckers.'

'He's right there,' said Dan. 'I reckon the good Lord takes a very relaxed view of taking down the Poms.'

Both men chuckled to themselves, and marched steadily forward. They weren't making much speed. The ground was too tough for that. But they were managing to cover half a mile an hour, which in these conditions Bruce reckoned wasn't too bad.

'Another square mile, lads, that's all,' said Bruce. 'A few more hours and we'll have done it. And if there's no sign of the plane after that, then we'll call it a day, round up the rest of the boys, and start making our way home.'

'How about we stop for something to eat?' said Dan. 'I'm bloody starving.'

'We're all starving, mate,' said Bruce. 'It's only an hour since our last break. We agreed, we'd only eat every two hours. It we don't stick to that schedule, our food will run out in no time.'

'I don't think I've ever been this sodding hungry,' said Dan grumpily. 'Not even in Afghanistan.'

'Not even in that military jail?'

'Maybe,' said Dan. 'I was bloody hungry in there, I don't mind admitting that. But nothing like this.'

'You'll live, mate.'

'I wouldn't count on it,' said Dan. 'I'm already starting to wonder how I can club a seal.'

'A nice roasted seal cub wouldn't be too bad, I reckon,' said Bruce. 'Put it on a spit, and eat it in great chunks with some bread on the side to mop up the oil.'

'Stop it, mate, you're making my stomach hurt.'

'It's a very dark, oily meat apparently. Sort of like eating a giant anchovy.'

'I'd have two of them right now. I don't care.'

Bruce chuckled to himself. He'd read somewhere that seal meat tasted like anchovy, but although he'd eaten most living creatures during a long military career, he'd never tried seal, so he had no way of knowing. It was good to get the man talking, though. In good humour, Dan could accomplish just about anything.

'Shut the fuck up, will you,' snapped Ian angrily.

'I'll bloody talk if I want to,' said Dan. 'Like I said, I'm hungry.'

'I'm getting a signal.'

Ian was standing fifteen yards away from the other two men. He'd climbed a ridge of ice, and was standing on top of it, partly shrouded in darkness, and only just visible amidst the snow swirling all around his short, stocky frame. Bruce was walking towards him, but quickly broke into the nearest he could manage to a run on the thick snow. Dan was close behind. Ian was standing with his shoulders hunched, his back to them, staring down into the tiny screen.

'You've got something?' said Bruce. He was gasping for breath, standing next to Ian, looking down at the radio.

'See,' said Ian.

But Bruce couldn't see anything.

'It's feckin' gone,' snapped Ian. 'Jesus, it was there, I'm telling you.'

Bruce looked straight ahead. There was a long ice plateau, with two deep valleys cut into it. The wind was swirling through it, blowing up swirls of cold snow. 'Anything could get lost in that,' he said grimly. 'A man, a polar bear, even a radio signal.'

'Which way was it?' asked Dan.

'Due north,' said Ian.

'Towards the Pole?' asked Dan.

Ian nodded.

'How far?'

'I don't feckin' know, do I?' he snapped.

Dan started to walk down the side of the ridge, down on to

the plateau that lay below. 'Then we find it,' he said. 'We'll pick up the signal again soon enough.'

The three men started to stride out, heading straight into the storm. The wind was blowing hard into their faces, making progress painfully slow. At moments the gusts of snow battering into them took visibility down to less than two yards. But they had renewed vigour in their step, noted Bruce. Ian had seen the signal, there couldn't be any question about that. The Irishman was sly and cynical, but for a man to survive as an IRA bomb-maker took superb technical skill and steady nerves, and if he said he'd seen it, then it was true. They were close, he felt certain of it. The black box was found.

'Got it,' said Ian. There was a note of triumph in his voice.

They'd been walking north for twenty minutes, covering five hundred yards.

Bruce and Dan crowded around. There was no doubt about it this time. The signal was clearly visible on the tiny screen.

'Where's it coming from?' asked Bruce.

'Still due north,' said Ian. 'A mile from here. Maybe slightly less.'

The three men started to walk even faster. The reading from the radio was getting clearer all the time. They no longer had any doubt they were on the right track; another hour, or two at most, and they would have the plane.

'Have you noticed something odd?' asked Ian, as they marched relentlessly forward.

'It's bloody cold,' said Dan with a grin.

'And it's dark all the time,' added Bruce.

'Aye, that's true enough, but there's something else as well.'

He looked round at both men. 'If the signal we're getting from the black box is right, it's outside the target zone.'

Bruce stopped. He took out the map Maya had supplied each unit with, and pointed his torch down on to it. The paper was laminated to keep it dry and protect it from the falling snow, and the target area was marked out clearly enough.

'You're right,' said Bruce, after locating first their position and then the position the signal appeared to be coming from. 'It's at least half a mile outside the zone.'

'It's not surprising we can't find the plane then,' said Ian. 'We've been looking in the wrong sodding place.'

'Maybe she made a mistake,' said Dan.

'Does Maya look like the kind of women who makes mistakes?'

'It can't be that easy to determine where a plane comes down.'

'Ian's right,' said Bruce. 'Kolodin has all the money in the world to spend on any expert he wants. There was one signal from the plane that was picked up by air traffic control, then it failed to make the next one. There shouldn't be any mistake about where it came down.'

'So why would they send us to the wrong place?' demanded Dan.

'A Russian billionaire and some bitch from the Mossad,' snorted Ian. 'Who knows what the hell they are up to? Maybe they just want to kill us for the sheer fun of it.'

'If they don't want us to find the plane, they wouldn't be spending millions getting us to come out here and look for it,' said Dan.

Bruce shook his head. 'It doesn't make any kind of sense,' he said. 'Nothing has, ever since we set foot in this sodding place.'

'Maybe when we find the plane we'll find out what the hell is going on out here,' said Ian, striding into the snow blizzard that lay in front of them. 'And what precisely it is we've been dropped into.'

Twenty-One

STEVE WAS PUTTING ALL THE muscle he could manage into the shovel. He was leaning into the blade, stabbing it down into the snow and ice. He'd been working for twenty minutes now, and there was sweat all over his body. His shoulders were aching from the work, and his gloves were starting to stick to his hands. But that's not the worst of it, he thought to himself. The worst of it is, I'm not getting anywhere.

He'd dug down five feet into the snow. At the bottom of the short trench, the fuselage of the A319 was clearly visible. The white metal was scratched in places, and charred with the remnants of a fire, but was clearly recognisable as the main body of a plane. It must have crashed right here, and in the nearly four weeks since then the snow had gradually buried it until it was completely obscured from view. But all he'd uncovered so far was the top of the fuselage; digging down to one of the doors was going to take a lot more work.

'That'll make a nice grave for someone,' he said bitterly, nodding down at the trench. 'But it's sod all use for getting into the plane.'

Maya climbed down into the ditch. She knelt and brushed

away the snow and ice with her gloves, looking closely at the metal underneath.

'It's a plane, Sherlock,' said Steve sourly. 'I think we've established that beyond any reasonable doubt.'

Maya turned back to look at him, and smiled. 'I know that,' she replied. 'I'm trying to figure what section of the plane this is.'

'What difference does it make?'

'The A319 has doors at the front and rear of the plane,' she said. 'Plus it has an emergency over-wing exit. If we can figure out where we are on the plane, then we don't need to dig out the whole thing.'

Steve nodded. 'The over-wing exit would be best,' he said. 'It's going to be higher up, so we don't need to dig so far to get to it.'

'Right,' said Maya.

She climbed out of the pit, back on to the fresh snow. The storm was still blowing across the plateau, and fresh flakes were drifting on to them all the time, burying the plane even further. 'I reckon we're about two-thirds along the plane,' she said, starting to pace forwards. 'If you take the total length of the A319, that means the wing should be about thirty feet away.'

She walked the distance, and dug her snow shovel in the ground. 'Or right about here.'

Steve caught up with her, his own shovel slung under his arm. The radio was in his hand, and he was examining its screen.

'So why aren't we getting a signal?' he asked. 'We should be right on top of the sodding black box. It's two in the morning, so it shouldn't be switching itself off for another ten hours.'

He was looking at her suspiciously. Maya dug her shovel into the ground, sliced up a scoop of snow, and tossed it to one side.

'I don't know,' she said. 'Maybe the batteries gave out earlier than expected.'

'Is that possible?'

'I don't know. I'm hardly an expert on black boxes, am I?'

She'd taken another shovel of snow, and was about to toss it aside, but Steve grabbed hold of her arm. 'Is there something you're not telling me?'

'Of course not,' she said angrily.

'Because whoever it is who builds these things, I reckon they put a sodding decent battery in it,' he said. 'Not some cheap bit of rubbish. Something that lasts the full twenty-eight days.'

Maya put her spade down. 'So what's your theory, Einstein?' she said, looking straight at him. 'We've found the plane all right. And a bloody miracle it is as well, since there isn't a black box signal to guide us towards it. Why do you think we're not picking up anything on the radio?'

Steve thought for a moment.

Ian might have a theory, he reckoned. Perhaps even Bruce. But he was stumped.

'I don't know,' he answered finally.

'Then I suggest we start digging until we find out.'

Steve stabbed his shovel into the snow, and tossed the snow aside.

Then he paused.

'I'm calling the others,' he said. 'I'll put up a flare so that they know we've found the plane.'

Maya looked at him anxiously. 'There are soldiers out here looking for us. They'll see the flare as well.'

'We need some help digging the plane out,' snapped Steve.

'It's not worth the risk.'

Steve eyed her suspiciously. He'd trusted her absolutely so far, but over the last few minutes nothing she'd been saying made much sense. 'There's one lesson you need to learn about Death Inc.,' he said firmly. 'When we say we'll do something for our mates then we do it. Those are the only rules we know, and I'm not breaking them now.'

'But Steve . . .' She reached out to touch his hand.

'We said we'd send up a flare if we found the plane,' he growled. 'So the flare's going up. And that's final.'

Twenty-Two

OLLIE WOKE UP WITH A start.

He'd left an oil lamp burning in the corner of the shack, but it had extinguished itself. His foot was throbbing with pain, and so was his head. The painkillers had worn off and everything was hurting again. Outside, he could hear the wind howling across the open Arctic, as the storm that seemed to blow endlessly through its long, dark winter gathered force. For a second, he could hardly even remember where he was, but then it all came back to him, and he permitted himself a brief, weary smile.

You're stuck in hell with a broken ankle, and no idea where your mates have got to, old sausage, he reminded himself. You'd have been better off not remembering.

He closed his eyes again, trying to get back to sleep. He'd been dreaming about something, he was sure of it. A rugby game back at school. He was playing inside centre, the position he always had in the team. A good, dependable all-rounder's position, perfect for a boy who could run a bit when he needed to and who could also bring down any of the blokes on the other side, no matter how big they were. In the dream, they'd been twenty up, with a minute to go, but still lost. What the hell does that mean? he reflected to himself.

He tried to get back to sleep but it was useless. It had grown colder in the last couple of hours, he felt certain of it, even though it was hard to imagine how anywhere could be colder than this place already was. His teeth were chattering uncontrollably, and there seemed to be something frozen next to his skin. Inside his snow suit he reckoned his sweat had turned to ice. He was wondering if he should strip off and try and give himself a wash. It would probably do him some good, but he didn't reckon he had the strength.

I'd rather get my kit off at my gran's old people's home than this place, he thought with a wry smile. Chuckling to himself, he wished Steve or David were around to listen to the joke. This wasn't the kind of place a man wanted to be by himself. You needed some banter around you to keep your spirits up.

Ollie checked his watch. It was just after two in the morning. He didn't know precisely what time he'd finally dropped off to sleep. Maybe around eleven. That meant he'd had three hours' kip. Not bad for this hellhole. He wasn't likely to get any more.

He levered himself up out of the small cot, and flicked on the torch. The light instantly started to make him feel better. He didn't much care for the darkness. He checked the pot of snow he'd left by the candle, hoping its warmth might melt it down into water, but it was still nothing but dry flakes. His throat was scratchy, and he coughed violently a couple of times to try and clear it, but only some water would help. With a limited amount of fuel left, however, he didn't want to use it frivolously. He'd eaten and drunk a few hours ago. He'd be all right for now.

Ollie hobbled to the door of the shack. He pushed it open. A gust of wind blew a drift of snow right into his face, and he stepped backwards, briefly frightened by the violence of the storm outside. He grabbed hold of his shovel, and started to step outside. In these conditions, the entrance to the shelter could easily get completely buried, he realised. If the rest of the blokes can't find me, I could be stuck here until spring.

He hacked away at the snow, clearing away a path that led up to the surface. Briefly, the work cheered him up. It was always better to be busy. As he finished, he flashed his torch out on to the horizon, half hoping that he'd see the rest of the boys walking towards him, perhaps even with the sodding black box tucked under their arm. But he couldn't see anything apart from the snow blowing relentlessly into his face.

It could be hours yet, he reckoned. They could have been a long way from finding the plane, and even when they did locate it, they still had to get inside to retrieve the black box.

He glanced to his right. The notebook he'd been studying said the Second World War relic was just a hundred yards north-north-east of here. After a moment's reflection, Ollie steadied himself, using the snow shovel as a makeshift crutch, and started to climb up out of the shelter.

I'll take a look, he thought to himself. I need something to keep myself busy. Otherwise I'm just going to die of cold and boredom down here. And anyway, maybe there's some kind of snow tractor there. If there was, and if we could get it started, it might be useful for getting home again.

He checked his compass, working out the direction. Gripping his torch with his right hand, and still using the shovel as a crutch, he started to walk. The pain in his ankle was bad, even though he was making sure he put as little pressure on that leg as possible. But he ignored it. Some pain wasn't so bad, he reflected, so long as you were expecting it, and you had a purpose.

He counted out the distance. With his broken ankle, he couldn't make any strides more than a foot, so he needed three hundred steps to cover the distance. The ground was flat enough, a few hillocks where the snow had drifted up into piles three or four feet high but nothing insurmountable. The wind had picked up force over the course of the night and was blowing with a ferocity that Ollie hadn't yet encountered since they landed on the Arctic. It was gusting almost straight into him, making it hard to walk, and a couple of times he was almost thrown to the ground by a harsh blast of air. But he put his head down, and ploughed forward, ignoring the weather, and concentrating on closing the distance between his shelter and his target.

As he walked, he wondered what it might be. History had been one of the few subjects that really interested Ollie at school. He'd always been more of a sports boy than a scholar. But the battles and wars of the history books had captured his imagination. He'd done projects on longbows used by the British archers at Agincourt, and the muskets used by the British at the Battle of Waterloo, and could still draw a precise diagram of the airframe of a Spitfire from the fantastically detailed research he'd done in the upper third. But the history of the Arctic had just about passed him by. Maybe I was asleep during that lesson, he thought with a wry smile. Or maybe we just never got around to it.

He paused. Ten more steps to his target. Given the difficulty of measuring precise yardage while walking through fierce snow, it could be anywhere around here. He swept his torch round in a long, raking circle but couldn't see anything except pristine white snow, interrupted by the occasional jagged glacier. Ollie walked forward another five steps, then ten. Right here, he told himself. This is where it should be.

But still he couldn't see anything.

It's winter, he reminded himself. The Norwegian lads were here in summer, the only time of year when any sane person would venture into this hellhole, and the site might well be buried under a layer snow at this time of the year. He leant on his shovel, examining the ground for unusual dents or hills that might indicate some sort of structure, but he couldn't see anything apart from rolling snowdrifts. Ollie stabbed his shovel into the ground, and started to dig. He tossed the snow aside, then pushed down again, shovelling aside the freshly fallen snow, until he reached the harder, packed ice below it. It was hard work, and he didn't want to use either of his feet to push on the spade: his ankle wasn't in any state for that kind of work. I'll give this ten minutes, he thought to himself. And if I haven't seen any sign of it by then, I'll go back to the shelter and try and get some kip and wait for the rest of the boys to find me.

Ten minutes ticked by, then twelve. Ollie was digging a long, shallow trench that cleared away the surface snow to see if there was anything underneath. He'd covered about ten yards, still heading north-north-east. Time to quit, old sausage, he told himself. Unless . . .

He looked straight down. There was a wooden beam, clearly visible under the snow he'd just cleared away. He gripped his torch in his right hand, and knelt down to take a closer look. A beam all right, he decided with a sense of satisfaction. Made of pine, by the looks of it, but treated with something very tough that would allow it to survive the Arctic winter. He pushed aside some more snow with his gloves, then took a closer look. A roof. Some kind of shelter, he felt certain of it, but probably much older than the one he'd been staying in. He cleared some more snow away with his shovel, until more of the roof was revealed. It seemed to measure at least twenty feet by ten, and there was a trapdoor a few feet in from its left corner where, Ollie guessed, you could drop down into the shelter.

He crawled across to the door, and took a closer look. There was a metal hook sunk into the wood at one end. Ollie pulled, but the trapdoor was frozen solid, and there was no give in it at all. He pulled again, harder this time, but the door wasn't budging. 'Sod it,' muttered Ollie out loud. 'Nothing works out in this bloody wilderness.'

He pulled his knife from his webbing, and stabbed it into the ice that had frozen up around the entrance. It had been built with a gap around its edges to allow space for the ice, and broke away easily enough as Ollie smashed into it. Within a couple of minutes, he had hacked it all away. He pressed his fingers into the hook, and pulled again. This time it started to move, slowly at first, but as he tugged harder, it came up in his hand.

Ollie flashed his torch down into the shelter.

There was a smell of dust and rotting wood. From the trapdoor, it was a drop of just six feet down into the shelter, and there was a knotted rope hanging next to it to help you down. Ollie shone the torch through the interior. He was worried that if he dropped down, he might never get up again, but there was an ancient desk and a chair in one corner, and if he needed to he could climb on top of that. Carefully, he lowered himself into position. He tucked his torch into his webbing, and pressed his left hand on to the side of the trapdoor, while his right reached out for the rope. Carefully he gripped it in his glove, tugged it a couple of times to make sure it could hold his weight, then swung on to the rope, lowering himself gently down on to his left leg. Only when he hit the ground and had steadied himself without putting any pressure on his broken right foot, did he let go of the rope.

He retrieved the torch from his webbing, and flashed it on.

The interior of the shelter was small, cramped, but far from derelict. It was made of wood, solidly enough constructed to keep out the worst of the weather. There was a sprinkling of dust on the floor, but given how many years it might have been since anyone apart from the Norwegian lads set foot in here, the place was remarkably clean. That's the Arctic for you, noted Ollie. Too sodding cold even for the dirt.

The ground was covered with floorboards. There were a pair of bunk beds in one corner, just wooden frames, with no springs, or bedding, but four blokes could kip down there if they wanted to. Close to that was a cast-iron black stove, and a small pile of coal next to it, and a chimney that would let the smoke out into the air above. Across the shelter was the desk. And there were four slits built into the wooden structure, one on each wall, but up high, five feet off the ground.

Ollie glanced at each one in turn, puzzled momentarily, before he realised what they were.

This wasn't a shelter. It was a bunker. Only a military force would build slits like that. They are for shooting out of, while protecting yourself from incoming fire.

He started to hobble across the floor, towards the desk.

Maybe there was a drawer with some papers inside that would tell him more about who built this place and why. It was only seven feet, but he was going carefully: the pain had flared up again in his ankle, and he was wincing with every step.

Suddenly, a board cracked. There was a splintering noise, and Ollie could feel his left foot dropping into thin air. He tripped and crashed heavily to the ground, his left foot still trapped in the broken floorboard. 'Bugger, bugger, bugger,' he shouted, spitting as he did so.

The pain in his broken ankle was excruciating. And now his left foot was trapped as well.

Ollie lay still for a moment, trying to compose himself. Christ knows what I'll do if the other foot is crocked, he thought grimly. Lie here and slowly freeze to death. He twitched the toes in his left foot. They seemed to be working OK. Bruised maybe, but it didn't feel like they were broken. He slowly used his forearms to lever himself up, then pulled his foot free of the trap into which it had fallen. For a moment, he sat still on the floor, wiping the sweat from his brow, and thanking God he hadn't smashed any more bones.

Then he turned to look at the hole.

He flashed his torch downwards. He'd assumed the bunker had been built straight into the ice pack with nothing underneath but snow. But there was something down there.

A secret chamber.

It made a kind of twisted logic, he decided. If this was a military bunker, you'd want a position to fight from, but also somewhere you could hide if the going got too rough, or the odds looked overwhelming. If I was building it, I'd put another bunker lower down. A trench, where you'd be protected from artillery fire. And the same logic had been applied by whoever had constructed this place.

Ollie shone the torch down again, but it was too murky. He couldn't see anything.

His foot had smashed open a gap in the floorboard about a foot long. Using his fist, he levered up the rest of the board. The wood was well-preserved, but the nails that held it in place had rusted over the years, and a six-foot section of board came away easily enough in his hand. He pulled up the next board, then the next one, until he had created a space big enough to drop down into.

He swung his feet into position first, then using his arms for support lowered himself gradually into the lower bunker. It was only five feet high, and Ollie was over six foot, so he could drop down easily enough, and land just on his left foot. Whoever built this place clearly didn't have the comfort of the blokes who'd be using it uppermost in his mind. Any normal-sized man coming down here would have to stoop.

Ollie steadied himself, then switched the torch back on.

The bunker was ten yards long, by five wide, almost the same size as the room above it. The floor was made from straw and some rough planking, and the walls were made of wood, but far less well finished than the upstairs room.

As he looked ahead, Ollie froze in his tracks. A shiver of fear ran down his spine.

Straight ahead of him were five dead bodies, sitting on a bench.

Ollie took a step forward. He shone the torch into their lifeless faces.

They were young blokes, he could tell that right away.

Nineteen or twenty years old. They were frozen solid, like statues, their corpses encased in a block of solid ice. They looked as fresh as if they'd come down here this morning, although their faces were twisted into expressions of agony.

And they were wearing uniforms. Nazi uniforms.

Ollie shone the torch on to their tunics to make sure. But there was no mistaking the field grey of their uniforms, nor the shape of the helmets secured to the sides of their jackets. They were instantly recognisable from a hundred war movies. Nor was there any mistaking the insignia on their shoulders. The double lightning bolts of the Waffen SS.

'Shit,' muttered Ollie, speaking out loud.

His words echoed in the tiny space. And, as he listened to the echo, he felt alone and afraid.

Twenty-Three

NICK SAW THE SIGNAL FIRST.

'Look,' he shouted, pointing up at the dark, cloudy sky.

David, Henri and Maksim all stopped walking, and turned their gaze upwards.

The four men had been marching steadily through the snow for another hour, growing ever more weary with each step. There were constant obstacles in their path, and the storm whipping across the barren, empty land made the journey a battle against the weather as well as the terrain. The temperature was dropping because of the wind, and even their snow suits seemed a flimsy protection against the biting cold.

'Up there,' said Nick.

The swirling snowstorm made it difficult to see anything. All four men were grouped in a tight circle, scanning the sky. Nick was pointing with his finger. The flare was clearly visible now: a bright yellow arc of light that burst violently through the clouds and the snow. It was the signal they had agreed on. One of the teams had found the plane.

'Due east, I reckon,' said Henri. 'About a mile.'

'Then let's crack on,' said David. 'They might need help.'

They started to march in close formation. The flare burnt for a few minutes, then fizzled away, its light quickly snuffed out. Maksim led the way, followed by Nick and David, with Henri bringing up the rear. They were marching as fast as they could through the treacherous conditions; once they got close, actually finding the men they were looking for might well be tricky, so any time they could make up closing the distance between them would help.

The first half-hour was easy enough. It was just after three in the morning, and the ground was flat. The wind was bad, blowing straight into them, but with their spirits lifted by the discovery of the plane, they were strong enough to fight their way through. They covered three-quarters of a mile in the next half-hour, virtually a sprint by the standards of Arctic travel. All the time, they were scanning the sky for another flare, but after the first one there was no further signal. At three forty-five they hit a huge glacier, and had to detour five hundred yards over rough ground to get round it. 'We're close, lads, we're close,' said David, trying to keep everyone's spirits up. 'One more leg, and we'll have found that damned plane, and we'll be on our way home to a nice hot bath on that luxury yacht.'

'Stop,' said Maksim, flashing his torch forward.

He'd seen something.

They'd just rounded the glacier, and were heading out on to an ice plateau that should take them straight to the position the flare had come from. Another quarter of a mile, they reckoned. A third at most.

Maksim switched his torch off, hissing at the others to do the same. He put on his night-vision goggles and peered cautiously round the glacier. On the plateau ahead of them he could see a smudge of red across the green screen. The body heat of a force of men.

'There's five of then,' he hissed. 'At least.'

'Going where?' asked Henri.

'Straight towards our target,' answered Maksim. 'I reckon they must have seen the flare as well.'

'It might be Bruce's unit,' said Nick. 'Or Steve's. We don't even know who put the flare up.'

'There's five men,' said Henri. 'Bruce's unit has three blokes in it, and so does Steve's.'

'Definitely five, Maksie?' asked David.

The Russian nodded.

The other three, all now wearing their night-vision goggles, peered round the glacier in turn, taking a look for themselves. The men were moving in a single file, patrol formation, about four hundred yards away. At this distance, they could make out how many of them there were but not what weapons they were carrying.

One by one, each man took his Yarygin out of his webbing, and chambered the handgun so that it was ready to fire.

'Reckon we can move out?' asked Nick.

'If we can see them, they can see us,' cautioned Henri. 'And we haven't got enough ammo left to risk getting into a firefight.'

'We can't just leave our mates,' said David. 'If they're closing in on Steve or Bruce's unit, then they are going to need some help.'

'Give it two minutes,' said Henri. 'Let them get a safe distance in front of us, then we move out.'

David looked round the glacier. The unit of men was still

moving away from them. It was four hundred and fifty yards or so ahead, and closing in on the position where the flare had come from.

He tightened the Yarygin in his hand. They might not have much ammo left but if a scrap kicked off they weren't going to be able to stay out of it.

Ian was studying the radio signal. It was fading in and out, but he reckoned that was due to interference from the magnetic fields around the North Pole. As they got closer and closer to the Pole, radio signals and compass readings were going to get steadily worse, until eventually they wouldn't have any idea where they were at all.

But for now he reckoned they were about three-quarters of a mile away from where the black box signal was coming from.

'How much longer do you think it will take us to get there?' asked Dan.

They'd made little progress in the last hour. When they'd picked up the signal on the radio, the ground had been clear enough but they'd soon run into a series of crevasses that plunged straight down into the ice and were impassable without ropes, or ladders that could be slung across them like bridges. They'd had to walk around each one, but in the darkness, and with the snow blowing straight into them, it had been a hard slog, and a couple of times they nearly lost a man in one of these deep cracks, and that made them cautious. At times, they were inching forward, using their torches to check each yard of ground before they attempted to traverse it, and roping themselves together so that they could catch one another if they fell.

'It could be an hour, it could be three,' replied Ian, glancing between Dan and Bruce. 'The ground is so rough, it's impossible to say how long it will take us to cover that distance.'

Bruce checked his watch. It was just after three in the morning. 'We've got another nine hours until the black box is switched off,' he said. 'We should have plenty of time.'

He was looking forward, preparing himself for the next leg of the journey, so he didn't notice the flare at first. But Ian was standing in front of him, looking back at the ground they had just covered, and saw its brilliant yellow light breaking through the fierce storm and briefly illuminating the desolate landscape.

'A signal,' he snapped, pointing upwards.

Both Bruce and Dan looked round, their necks craning upwards.

'I wonder who it is,' said Dan.

'They've found the plane,' said Bruce, 'whoever it is.'

He took his compass out and got a reading on where the flare was coming from, and its estimated distance from their current location.

'About two miles,' he said, when he'd finished the calculations. 'South-south-west of here.'

'That means going back through those sodding crevasses,' said Dan.

'It means something else as well,' said Ian. He was pointing back to where the flare had come from. 'If they've found the plane over in that direction, then how come we're getting the signal from the black box off to the north.'

Bruce was looking south, then north, then south again. 'It doesn't make any sense.'

'Maybe the lads are in trouble,' said Dan. 'The flare doesn't have to mean they've found the plane. It might mean they're in a scrap and they need some back-up.'

'Then we better get our arses moving and go and help them,' said Bruce. There was a note of steely determination in his voice.

'If we lose the signal we might never find the plane,' Ian pointed out.

'Jesus, are you seriously suggesting we don't go and help our mates?' said Dan angrily.

'I'm suggesting that we came here to find the feckin' black box and we're close to it, and if we lose it now, we may never pick up the sodding signal again.'

'And our pals are in trouble.'

'We don't even know who put up that flare,' snapped Ian. His face was reddening with anger, but so was Dan's. The Australian took a step towards him, his burly form even more menacing than usual when it was bulked up by his snow suit.

'Easy, boys,' growled Bruce. 'Nobody needs to lose their rag.' He looked at Ian. 'Dan and I are going to go see who's in trouble and whether we can help them. Whether you're coming with us is up to you.'

Twenty-Four

I F STEVE HAD EVER HAD to work harder, he wasn't sure he could remember when. There had been gruelling training sessions first in the Paras and then in the Regiment: digging trenches in the pouring rain, climbing mountains with a backpack full of bricks, and white-water rafting down rapids that could tear a man in two. But nothing came close to the punishment a man took when trying to dig through the Arctic ice in the middle of a winter storm.

He hacked his shovel into the packed snow, then swore as the blade bounced off the hard ice, leaving barely a dent in it. They had been digging for almost an hour now, and the sweat was building up inside his snow suit, making his skin scratchy and uncomfortable. The perspiration was starting to collect on his body and already icicles were forming around his legs and feet. If he was to avoid frostbite, he'd need to get his kit off and get rid of them, but in this cold it wasn't a prospect he was looking forward to.

They had hacked their way about six feet down into the packed snow, striking the wing of the downed plane, and were smashing into the ice that had frozen up around the emergency exit. It was half an hour now since they had put up the flare, and there was still no sign of the other two units. Steve wasn't too worried about that, not yet anyway. They could well be a mile or more away, and across ground this rough it might take two or three hours for them to get here. One more hour and he'd put up another of the three flares he had in his kitbag, but until then he'd just keep on digging. They could use some help. Dan or Maksim's muscle was precisely what they needed to smash their way through the remaining ice. But until they arrived, they'd just have to carry on by themselves.

'We're getting near the door,' said Steve.

Maya put down her shovel, taking a brief rest.

They could see the door clearly now. The A319 had just a single over-wing emergency exit, unlike the A320 which had two: aircraft safety rules demanded that any plane must be able to be fully evacuated in ninety seconds, and for a small plane like the A319 a single escape hatch was enough. It was slightly larger than a window and, unlike a door, came away in a single piece, allowing the passengers to climb out on to the wing after an emergency landing, and complete their escape from there. But there was no handle on it. From the inside, there was a lever that opened it up, but there was no mechanism for opening it from the outside. It was designed to get people out in a hurry, not to get them in.

'We'll need to blow it open,' said Maya, nodding towards the door.

Steve was examining it closely.

Christ, he thought to himself. She's right. There's no other way into the plane.

'Ian would know how to do it,' he said. 'The guy was a

bomb-maker for the IRA. He can blow up anything.'

'We can't wait,' said Maya. 'We'll use a grenade.'

'Christ, are you serious?'

Maya was already digging into her kitbag. She pulled out the single RGN-86, the Russian-made hand grenade she'd stashed in there when they were packing their weapons. 'I've only got one of these,' she said. 'And no explosives. So we better make sure it works.'

'And what are you going to do exactly?' said Steve. 'Just lob a sodding grenade into the door?'

Maya shrugged. 'That's roughly the plan, yes.'

'I thought the Mossad were famous for their subtle tactics. Christ, we might as well have asked Dan or Maksie.'

'What's your problem?'

Steve pointed down at the wing. There was still a foot or so of ice and snow covering it, but the white metal was clearly visible underneath.

'Unless I've missed something, the A319 has a fuel tank in both wings,' he said, his voice rising. 'A grenade could blow the whole thing. If the whole plane goes bang, its going to take us with it.'

'This plane crash-landed,' said Maya. 'There's no mechanism for dumping fuel on an A319 but the pilot would have burnt off as much as he could before bringing it down. It's standard procedure.'

'You reckon the wing tanks are empty?'

'They might be.'

'But you can't be sure.'

'Have you got any better ideas?' she said. 'We need to get into that plane.'

Steve looked at the frozen door. He was thinking, trying to figure out the angles. They were taking a terrible risk using the grenade, no question about that. If the plane exploded, it would create a massive fireball. They'd lose the black box, that was for certain. They might well get killed themselves. The RGN-86 had a fuse that lasted for three to four seconds, which wouldn't give them enough time to get far enough away to survive an explosion of that size. Not through the snow. If Ian was here, he could remove the TNT from the grenade and shape a charge that would take out the door without damaging the wing. But Steve didn't have the expertise to do that. If the rest of the blokes were here, they could dig down to the front or rear passenger doors: they had handles that allowed them to be opened from the outside, and would be a lot easier to access. But between the two of them, it might take hours more work to clear that much snow.

'So have you got any better ideas?'

There was a mocking tone to the way Maya repeated the question that Steve wasn't sure he liked.

'All right,' he said gruffly. 'Let's sodding do it.'

Maya took a step towards the door. The grenade was in her hand, held tight in her right fist. Steve reached out and touched her fist. 'You stand well back,' he said. 'I'll do this.'

'It's my idea,' she replied sharply. 'I'll take the risk.'

'I said I'll sodding do it.'

'I'm a soldier, the same as the rest of you.' said Maya. 'In the Caracal Battalion we don't expect the men to be constantly opening doors for us, you know. We're trained to fight exactly the same way they do, and we learn not to expect any special treatment.' She was staring straight at him, a look of defiance on her face.

Steve was about to snap back, but then he stopped himself.

Maybe she's right, he thought. Maybe I'm not treating her with the respect she deserves. After all, she's probably a better soldier than any of us. All the same. I'm not sodding well scarpering while a bird lobs in a grenade for me.

'I'm just saying I'm the bloke who's getting paid to find this black box, so it's my job to put the grenade in,' which wasn't strictly true, but he was trying to sound as persuasive as he could. 'Please . . .'

Maya nodded curtly. 'OK, if that's the way you want it.'

Her tone was still pissed off. She placed the RGN-86 in his hand. 'You know where the pin is, I presume.'

'Duhhhhh,' said Steve with a rough grin. 'Of course I know where the sodding pin is.' He took the grenade, and glanced back at her. 'Now clear off to a safe distance,' he said. 'And if I go up in the fireball, no carnations at the funeral please. Lilies.'

'White or pink?'

'White, of course. Do I look like I want pink flowers? We'll save those for Ollie.'

'Any poppies?'

'Piss off,' said Steve, grinning. 'Let me get on with this.'

Maya had already started climbing out of the ditch they'd dug. As she scrambled back on to the ground, Steve took a deep breath, glanced down at the grenade, then across to the emergency exit on the plane. There was still a sheet of ice across it but there was no point in hacking that away now. The blast would rip straight through it. He'd done plenty of ballistics training in the Regiment, and knew all the basics of breaking down doors. Usually, you'd use an RPG at a safe distance. On their last job they'd used one of the new Israeli-designed GREM munitions, a flat grenade fired from a rifle that diffused energy around a sealed door and literally knocked it right off its hinges. We could use some of that kit here, he thought bitterly. In fact, we could use any kit at all. All we've got are handguns, a few AKs, and one explosive.

He packed up some snow and ice to make a cradle for the grenade. He needed to shape the blast, so that it blew inwards and upwards, with enough force to knock out the door, and not down into the wing. The work was cold, but only took a moment. When it was done, Steve placed the device carefully in the cradle he'd made for it, on its side, with the pin clearly visible.

'Let's hope there's four seconds in you, you little sod,' he whispered to the few pounds of inert metal.

Steve leant into the pin, and pulled it free. In the same swift movement, he turned on his heels, and threw his hands up to the top of the ditch. Kicking back with his legs, he hurled himself upwards, but stumbled as he did so, so that he was lying face down in the snow.

'Christ,' he muttered to himself. That's at least two of my seconds gone.

He pushed back with his legs, starting to run as if he were in a sprint, but in a snow suit, and with mulaks on his feet, it was impossible to get any kind of speed. Another second flashed by, and Steve had covered maybe three yards. He could see Maya thirty or forty yards away, nestled behind a crater, flashing her torch at him. Steve's lungs were bursting as he scrambled to put some more distance between himself and the plane. He heard a crack, then a flash of noise echoing up and around the still landscape. He flung himself to the ground. The grenade had blasted, and if it was going to ignite the fuel in the wing tanks, it would blow any second. He was lying face down in the snow, panting for breath. I'm less than ten yards from the plane, he thought grimly. If it goes up, I'm a dead man.

One, two, he counted.

His face was freezing from the cold. And the sweat inside his snow suit had turned into torturous strips of ice.

Three, four . . .

At least it will be quick, he thought.

Five, six . . .

On seven, Steve glanced nervously backwards. Smoke was rising from the ditch they had dug, and there was a yellow glow. Flames. 'Shit,' he muttered. He started to lever himself up from the ground, using his elbows for support, and was about to start running towards Maya. But she was already running towards him. Shouting.

And behind her, there was a rattle of gunfire.

'Jesus, it's really not our sodding day,' muttered Steve angrily.

'Move it, move it,' Maya was shouting. She was ten yards in front of him now. 'Get into the fucking plane.'

Steve couldn't see the enemy, but he could hear them all right. The murderous chatter of automatic weapons was filling the air, and it was only the darkness, and the intensity of the snowstorm, that was keeping them alive. If their enemy could see them, they'd already be dead.

Maya was right. The plane was the only place they could hide. If the door had been blown off. And as long as it wasn't about to explode.

Steve turned, bounced over the few yards that separated him from the ditch, and threw himself down on to the wing. As he landed, he could see tiny gobbets of fire spread out across the wing. Fragments of the grenade must have split open, and ignited. There was smoke everywhere, thick and black, with a taste of charred metal to it. Steve choked on the fumes as he stripped off the jacket of his snow suit and used it to beat out the flames. One fire was put out, then another. Maya jumped down, landing behind him, and looked around anxiously, taking in the extent of the damage the grenade had caused. 'There's at least three units of men up there, with snow tractors,' she said hurriedly. 'We have to get into the plane. It's our only chance.'

Steve doused two more small fires, and reckoned he'd dealt with the worst of it. There were some lumps of red-hot metal across the wing, with smoke rising off them, but you had to reckon the A319 was built to take plenty of punishment: electrical storms, engine explosions, that kind of thing. It should be able to handle a bit of heat.

He advanced towards the emergency exit. It had been blown off its hinges but looked to have snagged on its frame. Steve grabbed hold of it, but immediately released it from his grip. The metal burnt right through the fabric of his gloves. 'Sodding hell,' he shouted, jumping back.

The sound of gunfire was getting close.

'Use your jacket,' snapped Maya.

Steve wrapped his hands in the snow suit, and plunged them back on to the exit. It felt hot, but through the thick fabric it was bearable. He gripped tight, then pulled hard.

The exit came away in his hands.

'Get into the plane,' hissed Maya.

Twenty-Five

T HE SOLDIERS WERE PERFECTLY PRESERVED. Ollie shone his torch from man to man, the light slicing through the block of ice that encased them. Their faces were afraid, and hurt, as if something very bad had happened to them just before they died, but there was no blood on their uniforms, nor were there any signs of bullet wounds anywhere. The ice had frozen them very soon after they died, reckoned Ollie. Or maybe while they were still alive. And it had preserved them as perfectly as if they'd been put in a deep freeze.

Ollie took a step closer, so that he was just a few inches from the ice block. Something about the corpses unnerved him, he didn't mind admitting that. He'd seen plenty of dead bodies. And he'd been responsible for putting a fair few men in that condition over the years. But he'd never seen a corpse that was more than sixty years old. And he'd never seen a Nazi before. Not one you could reach out and touch.

He shone the torch into their faces. Three of them were blond, one dark, and one had dusty brown hair. They all looked toughly built. Perfect Aryans, thought Ollie. You could see why they passed selection for the SS.

He looked more closely at the insignia on their jackets. The double lightning bolts worn by all SS troops were clearly visible. Next to them was a badge Ollie was less familiar with. It looked like an asterisk in black with white edging, encased within a shield. Ollie was thinking back through all the books he had studied for his school projects on the Second World War. The Hagelrune, he realised eventually. Every SS division wore the lightning bolts, but also the insignia of their own unit.

And the Hagelrune was the . . .

Ollie racked his brains. It was there somewhere.

The 6th SS Mountain Division Nord. That's what these sods had belonged to. Hitler's crack mountain and Arctic troops. Men who had fought in Operation Barbarossa, the invasion of the Soviet Union. And who been in the thick of the vicious fighting that stretched all the way up into the North Pole itself.

'Christ, boys,' said Ollie out loud. 'You're a long way from home.'

He flashed his torch to the left.

There was another block of ice, and inside it a set of metal crates. Ollie had a fair idea what they were. It didn't make any difference whether it was the Wehrmacht, the SS or indeed the Household Cavalry. Any military operation was roughly the same. You didn't head into a scrap without bringing plenty of kit with you.

Those were weapons boxes.

'I don't know what you boys were doing here,' said Ollie, a wry grin creasing up his face. 'But I don't reckon you were on your holidays.'

He approached the first box. A thick layer of ice had formed around it. He hacked his snow shovel into the side of the box and it came away easily enough. A couple more blows and the ice broke apart. A padlock had been slotted into the crate's lock, but no one had secured it. Whatever had happened down here, there had been no time to pack everything away neatly. Ollie tried to lift the crate open with his hands, but the metal had frozen together. 'Bugger,' he muttered under his breath. He levered his shovel into a tiny crevice that had opened up between the lock and the crate, leaning down hard into it. Suddenly it snapped open.

Ollie steadied himself. His broken ankle was hurting, and he knew he had to watch carefully how much weight he put on it.

He put his shovel to one side, and picked up the torch.

Guns.

Ollie leant down, and picked up one of the rifles. He'd only ever seen one in a museum, but it was unmistakable. The StG 44. One of the main SS weapons, and the first of the modern assault rifles. Ollie held it in his hands, and found it impossible not to admire the sleek black metal of its barrel and the chunky wooden stock, all of it perfectly preserved. The StG was a shortening of the German word Sturmgewehr, meaning 'storm rifle', and that was precisely what it was. The weapon had first been introduced in 1942. At the start of the war, the German infantry carried the standard weapons of the day: a mixture of conventional bolt-action rifles and machine guns. But the high command soon worked out that most of the fighting was being done by men less than three hundred metres apart and they came up with the StG as a new kind of battlefield rifle. It combined the very rapid rate of automatic fire of the machine gun with the flexibility of a standard rifle. It was brutally effective on the Eastern Front in particular. And although there were plenty of improvements still to be made, the StG was the template for the AK-47 later developed for the Soviet Union and the FN-FL assault rifle that was to become standard issue for the NATO troops who opposed them.

Ollie counted the weapons. There were ten rifles in this box, and next to them a dozen spare magazines, and an additional thousand rounds of the StG's 7.92mm 'Kurz', or short, rounds.

Picking up his shovel, Ollie started to hack open the next crate, and then the next one.

Within ten minutes, he'd unpacked a tremendous range of weaponry.

He had a crate of the Model 24 Stielhandgranate, the standard-issue hand grenade for the German Army during the Second World War. Unlike the Allies, the Germans put the explosive charge on the end of a wooden stick, which, although it looked clumsy, acted as a lever, and significantly improved the throwing distance of the device. The grenade could be thrown thirty or forty yards, compared with fifteen yards that the British grenades could be thrown.

He had three MG 42s, the key German machine gun of the Second World War. With an awesome 1,200 rounds a minute firepower, the MG 42 could spew out ammunition at twice the rate of the British Vickers machine gun or the American Browning. He had a dozen Walther PPs, the standard-issue handgun for SS troops and high-ranking Nazi officials, which later, in its PPK variant, became more famous as James Bond's preferred pistol, and a dozen sticks of TNT. And he had a Flammenwerfer 35, the deadly German flame-thrower that spat out fire and was used for clearing trenches and buildings that might still have surviving enemy soldiers within them.

And as far as Ollie could tell, it was all in perfect working order.

'I'll say this for you boys,' he said, glancing across at the five corpses, sitting frozen and silent inside their icy tomb, 'whoever the hell it was you were planning to get into a scrap with, you weren't going to be short of gear. The quartermaster must have loved you.'

Twenty-Six

DAVID PUT A HAND ON Maksim's shoulder.

'Steady, mate,' he said, his voice tense.

'They're in trouble,' growled Maksim. 'And we're just sodding sitting here.'

David glanced up ahead. Five hundred yards ahead of him, through his night-vision goggles, he could see three snow tractors, each with at least three armed men on board. Behind those, he could see another two units of five men each. That made a total of nineteen men, all of them well-equipped, and armed to the teeth. The five men they had seen earlier had just been an advance guard. This was the main force. And damned formidable it looks as well, thought David to himself. Whoever the hell it was must have spotted the flare and now had the guys up ahead trapped.

'He's right,' said Nick, glancing between David and Maksim. 'Our mates are in trouble and we're just sitting on our sodding arses.'

David took a moment to assess the situation. They were hiding behind a thick, stubby glacier. As far as he could tell, they were out of sight. But if the enemy had any kind of decent heat-seeking equipment, they'd find them easily enough. They could watch and wait here. But if the guys up ahead were in serious trouble, and it looked as if they were, that was sod all use to anyone.

He looked at Henri. 'What do you reckon?'

'There's four of us and all we've got are these handguns,' replied the Frenchman. 'We haven't even got enough ammo left in them to make a fair fight of it.'

David nodded. Henri was right.

'We'll wait for the other unit,' he said. 'A few minutes won't make any difference.'

'And I said they're in trouble,' growled Maksim.

'We heard you, mate,' snapped David. He looked at Nick. Death Inc. had always modelled itself on Regiment rules. They made decisions jointly. Everyone's voice was equal. 'What about you, mate?'

Nick was holding the Yarygin in his hand. He was toying with the weapon thoughtfully. He lined up the sites, as if he was about to take a shot at the men on the horizon. But with a mere handgun, across hundreds of yards, in the darkness, and through a fierce snowstorm, not even a marksman of Nick's ability stood a chance of making the shot.

'We'll give it ten minutes,' he said. 'If we haven't seen the rest of the blokes by them, we'll have to do something on our own.'

David nodded. 'Looks like that's the consensus, lads,' he said.

The four men dug in behind the glacier. The storm was blowing right across the plateau ahead of them, and at times they couldn't see anything of the attackers, not even through the goggles. A couple of times they heard the rattle of gunfire, and Maksim had to be physically restrained from bursting into an immediate assault. The minutes ticked by and all of them knew they'd have to do something soon. They couldn't just leave the others to die there.

'Look, behind us,' said Nick suddenly. He turned and pointed.

Three shapes were clearly visible across the screens of their goggles.

Men.

'Who the hell are they?' hissed Henri.

They were about two hundred yards behind them, walking purposefully, in a straight line, with their middle man towing a sledge.

'The lads?' asked David.

'Can't tell from here,' answered Nick. 'It could be our boys. It could be the enemy.'

'Get your guns ready,' said Henri.

The men were closer now. A hundred and fifty yards, no more. Whether they could see them yet, there was no way of knowing. Probably not, reckoned David. If they could see us, they'd take more precautions. He chambered his Yarygin. They might not have much ammo left, but if there was a scrap, they'd have to use what they had, and they could worry about how to fight their way home later. The men were veering left, heading for where they must have calculated the flare had come from, but on the trajectory they'd set themselves, they were going to miss it by a couple of hundred yards.

'I reckon its Bruce's lads,' said Henri. 'The enemy is going to have radios to communicate with, I reckon. These boys are off course, which means it's probably our lot.'

Less than a hundred yards separated them now.

Maksim stepped out from behind the glacier.

'Jesus, Maksie,' started David, putting a hand on his shoulder.

Maksim pushed the hand away. 'Let me step up to them. Be ready with some covering fire if there is any trouble.'

The Russian walked out on to the plateau. The three men were climbing up towards a higher ridge of ground, taking them away from the plane. A gust of wind whisked up a blizzard of snow that left Maksim completely invisible.

'If he's not back in three minutes, we're going after him,' said Nick.

Both David and Henri nodded. Their guns were chambered and ready to fire.

A minute passed. Then another.

Nick was looking edgy, switching his gun from hand to hand.

Then a figure emerged out of the blizzard. Maksim. Followed by three more men. Bruce, Dan, and Ian.

'Fancy running into you lads here,' said Bruce with a grin. He reached out and shook Nick, David and Henri by the hand.

'I don't suppose you boys have whipped up any grub, have you?' said Ian with a crooked smile. 'I was hoping you might have some tea and crumpets ready for us.'

'Or steak and eggs,' said Dan.

'Leave it out,' growled Nick. 'My stomach's hurting.'

Bruce looked round the glacier where they were sheltering.

'Where's the Toyota?' he asked briskly.

'Gone,' answered David.

'Christ, what happened?'

'An attack with incendiary bullets,' said Henri. 'We managed to escape with our lives, which was sodding lucky, but they took out the vehicle.'

'It's official then,' said Ian morosely. 'We're completely fucked.'

'We're still alive, and that means we're still in the game,' said Bruce sharply.

'And how the feck are we getting home, then?'

'Like the man says, we'll worry about that later,' snapped David.

'What's the situation?' Bruce asked.

'Looks like Steve and his unit have found the plane, but they're under attack from whoever the hell is out here looking for it as well.'

'How many blokes?' asked Dan.

'We counted almost twenty,' said Nick. 'But it could easily be more. You can't see a sodding thing through this snow.'

Up ahead, there was a sudden burst of automatic fire, followed by some shouting, but through the storm it was impossible even to make out what language was being spoken, never mind figure out what was being said.

Maksim was looking straight ahead, his gun at the ready.

'We have to do something,' said Nick. The tension was evident in his voice.

'How much kit did we lose with the Toyota?' asked Bruce.

'Just about all of it,' said David. 'It was on fire, and about to blow. Maksie got our handguns, and some fuel, but that was it.'

'Like I said, we're officially feckin' fucked,' muttered Ian.

'What have you boys got?' asked Henri.

'We've got our Yarygins and one AK-74 each,' said Dan.

'And about thirty rounds for the handguns, and two mags for the rifles.'

'We've just got the Yarygins,' said Nick. 'And only a few rounds left each.'

'You lost the Arctic Warfare sniper rifles?' asked Dan.

'Afraid so. They went down with the Toyota.'

'Jesus.'

All seven men looked at the plateau ahead of them.

Through their night-vision goggles, they could make out the shapes of the men, as well as a formidable array of weaponry. Assault rifles, machine guns, RPGs. And probably plenty more tucked away, reflected David sourly.

Another round of gunfire burst across the snowy plateau.

'We're going in,' said Maksim.

'Jesus, man, how many times do I have to hold you back?' growled David. 'If you want to throw your life away, go ahead.'

'We can't just leave them,' said Nick. 'They need help and they need it now.'

Bruce was looking forward. 'He's right,' he said flatly.

Twenty-Seven

I T WAS PITCH BLACK INSIDE the plane.

Steve dropped down through the emergency exit, and clambered over the seat next to the wing. He reached out a hand and helped Maya through the small exit, then jammed the door back into place.

He switched on his torch, and glanced around.

The A319 was a private jet, similar to Kolodin's plane that had flown them to Russia. There was a main cabin for the bulk of the passengers but the central portion of the plane had been turned into a private cabin, presumably for Pavel Markov's personal use. There was a thick, well-upholstered leather seat next to each wing, a small office with a computer and a desk, a bar and eating area, a shower, and a flat bed that still had a sheet on it. There was one door leading to the cockpit, and another leading back into the main body of the aircraft.

Steve looked out on to the wing.

There was a flash of gunfire on the ground above and he could see the shadows of men moving around.

He drew his handgun, and fired a couple of shots upwards. Steve knew he wasn't going to hit anything. But he wanted to let them know he was inside the plane, and in no mood to be taken alive. If they wanted a scrap, he was going to give them one, no matter how overwhelming the odds against them might be.

'Stop,' shouted Maya.

'We need to sodding well let them know we're ready to fight,' said Steve.

'Those soldiers aren't interested in us,' she said briskly. 'If they were, we'd be dead by now.'

'Then what?'

'There's something on this plane they want.'

Steve paused. She's right, he reckoned. If they wanted to take us out, they could have done it. They aren't interested in whether we're alive or dead.

'The black box?'

'Maybe, maybe not,' said Maya. 'Who knows what was on this aircraft.'

She glanced out across the wing.

She could see the foot of a soldier about to climb down into the trench they'd dug. She pulled her Yarygin from her webbing, and fired a single shot straight towards him. It missed, but it was enough to make the man withdraw.

Climbing into a defended ditch was committing suicide, reflected Steve. Maksim might try it. But no sane soldier would risk his life in that way. They could hold this plane if they wanted to.

Steve removed the emergency exit door again, and climbed out on to the wing. He flashed his torch upwards, but he couldn't see anyone.

'We've got a grenade rigged to these fuel tanks,' he shouted. 'You bastards try and storm the plane, and we'll blow it to hell.'

He slipped back down into the fuselage, glancing across at Maya.

'That should hold them,' he said. 'If you're right, and it's something on the plane they want, then they can't risk storming it.'

Maya nodded. 'But they'll find a way of digging down into the plane by another route,' she said. 'We might have bought ourselves some time, but that's all.'

'Time is what we need,' said Steve. 'We put up a flare. The rest of the boys will be here soon to help us out.'

'You have a lot of faith in those guys,' said Maya.

'So would you if you'd fought alongside them before.'

Maya peered into the murky, freezing interior of the plane. Even after it had crash-landed, the cabin had clearly remained completely sealed and, because it had been buried in snow, it had stayed slightly warmer than the ground above. It was about twenty degrees below freezing, she reckoned, but dry, and that meant the snow and ice outside hadn't managed to do any damage to its interior.

'So what do we do now?' she asked, her tone turning nervous.

'We hunker down and wait for the sodding cavalry to show up,' answered Steve. 'And in the meantime, we might as well try and find out what the hell happened on this plane, and where that black box is.'

Twenty-Eight

G ETTING OUT OF THE LOWER bunker was a lot harder than getting in.

Ollie levered himself upwards. He was standing on a couple of the ammunition crates and using his forearms to pull himself up through the hole in the floorboard he'd made earlier; but without being able to put any pressure on his right foot, it was a struggle to get enough lift. He grunted, spat, and heaved upwards again. Briefly, he slipped back, but on the third go, he got enough traction on the floorboards, and once he had his chest on the floor, it was a simple enough matter to haul his legs up as well.

Ollie checked the main part of the shelter one more time, flashing his torch around the small room to check there was nothing there that might be of use for the journey home. He'd strapped one StG to his chest. He wasn't sure if he'd be able to come back here and he wanted a gun as a souvenir. It was already past four in the morning, which meant there were less than eight hours until the black box stopped transmitting, and twelve until they had to be back at the yacht. He didn't have a place of his own, but if he ever got around to buying that house in Dorset he'd always thought about, then an StG to hang on one of the walls would be quite something. And there would be a hell of a story to go with it, he reflected.

Picking up his snow shovel to use as a crutch, he hobbled towards the exit. The moment the wind hit his face, he regretted it. Down in the bunker it had been relatively dry and warm, but out here the weather laid into you with the ferocity of a tanked-up drunk. Ollie bowed his head, gritted his teeth, and hobbled a few yards out into the storm to get himself on to level ground, and started to prepare himself mentally for the short walk back to the shelter where the rest of the lads would come and pick him up when the job was finished.

At least I filled in some of the waiting time, he thought to himself. And I found something sodding interesting as well. The Norwegian lads were right. Some proper historians should come and dig that bunker out one day.

Then he heard something. Ollie turned his head sharply to the north. Maybe it was just the storm cracking some ice apart. He listened, loosening the hood of his snow jacket a fraction so that he could hear better, even if it meant his ears started to freeze from the cold.

I know what that is, he thought grimly. Gunfire.

It was impossible to gauge how far away it was. When the wind was blowing flat across the ground, and in the right direction, it could carry a sound a mile or more. But, if he was forced to guess, Ollie reckoned it was about half a mile.

There's a scrap on. Involving our boys.

Ollie looked back towards the shelter, then north again.

They're going to need help. And there's no point in me sitting around on my arse. If they don't prevail in this fight, I'm a dead man anyway. I'm never going to be able to get home by myself. Not in this state, through this weather. If I'm going to die, I'd rather go down with my mates, fighting to the last breath.

Ollie dug his shovel into the ground and, using that as a crutch, started to hobble towards the sound of gunfire.

Nick had volunteered to scout out the position for them, but now that he was up here he was starting to regret it. He was lying flat in the snow, two hundred yards from the enemy position, in a dip in the ground where he hoped he was invisible even to their night-vision goggles. He'd been watching them for five minutes now, and the cold was starting to get to him. The ice crept up from the ground, seeping into his skin and bones, until it felt as if it he were freezing from the inside. Nick had never minded the cold much. He'd go out on the lash in Swansea in the middle of January dressed in just a T-shirt, the same way most of his mates would. But this was something different. A cold that rotted a man, until he lost the will to fight back.

Nick looked forward, making a mental note of what precisely they were up against. There were nineteen men in total, as they had calculated earlier, with three big snow tractors between them. They were equipped with assault rifles, precision sniper rifles, handguns, RPGs and grenades. There were machine guns strapped to the front of the snow tractors, turning them into a kind of wintry tank. And they had all the shovels, picks, and ropes they needed.

'Shit,' muttered Nick, not for the first time. And all we've got are these sodding handguns.

The contours of the plane were clearly visible and, Nick reckoned, Steve's unit must be inside it. The enemy had surrounded the site, placing two men at each of its four corners, creating a cordon that was well-defended and was going to be very tough to break through. Another ten men were digging at one end of the site, working methodically with picks and shovels. One bloke was in charge. Same as any unit, thought Nick. One Rupert who sits on his arse not doing anything.

Nick checked again to make sure he'd got it all straight, then wriggled round. He didn't want to risk standing up. The men on guard duty at the four corners of the site looked well trained and alert, and it would be simple enough for them to spot a standing figure on their night-vision equipment. A sniper rifle could easily bring him down at two hundred yards. His only hope of getting back to the boys with blood still running through his veins was to stay as flat as possible.

It was slow, cold work. He was using his hands and his elbows to lever himself forward, but it was impossible to keep himself dry as he pushed his way through the snow, and he could feel his teeth chattering and his hands shaking as he inched his way forward. It took a full ten minutes before he reached the glacier where the rest of the lads were holed up, and by the time he got there, he was exhausted.

'How's it looking?' asked Bruce.

Once he was behind the glacier, Nick stood up, and started to jog on the spot, in an effort to get the blood moving around his veins again.

'Tough,' he said simply.

He started to explain, detailing how many men they were up against and what kit they had with them. As he spoke, he could see the faces of the men falling. They'd known it was bad. Just not that bad.

'Like I said, we're feckin' fucked,' sighed Ian.

'Will you sodding leave it out,' snapped David. 'You're getting me down.'

'Aye, well, is there another way you'd like to describe it?' said Ian.

'Easy, boys,' said Bruce. He looked at Nick. 'What would you say are their vulnerabilities?'

Nick shrugged. 'The men digging, I guess. You can't hold a shovel and a gun at the same time.'

'The Provos can,' said David, with a sour glance towards Ian. 'It's in their blood.'

'Watch it,' growled Ian. He curled his fists into a ball and took a step towards David.

'Bruce already told you boys to sodding leave it,' snapped Dan, standing between them. 'Jesus, we've got enough problems without fighting between ourselves.'

Both men backed away, their expressions surly.

'Maybe the lad is on to something,' Dan said. 'The blokes doing the digging are out of action. It's going to take them thirty seconds minimum to drop their shovels. That gives us a chance to slot the bastards.'

'That still leaves eight guards, each one armed,' said Henri. 'And how precisely are we going to creep up on the guys with the spades without anyone noticing?'

Dan fell silent.

'All right, all right, we're just kicking around ideas,' said Bruce. He looked at Nick. 'They're digging down towards the plane, so how long do you reckon we've got?'

'It'll be easy enough for Steve to hold one entrance,' chipped in Henri. 'One man with a gun, or even just a length of steel ripped from inside the plane, can do that easily enough. But if they can come in from two or three places at once, then they've got him.'

'An hour maybe,' said Nick. 'And that's tops.'

Bruce nodded. 'We need to come up with a plan.'

'Or else we just storm them with all guns blazing, and hope for the best,' said Maksim with a rough grin.

'Right, that's Plan B then,' said David. 'When all else fails, throw Maksie at the bastards. And start saying our prayers.'

Twenty-Nine

STEVE TRIED TO OPEN THE door separating the private cabin from the rest of the plane. It was frozen solid. In the sub-zero temperatures, the metal around the handle mechanism had locked up tight, and there was no give in the thing. He put his torch down to one side, then threw his shoulder against the door. He thumped into it hard, and bounced straight off. 'Shit,' he muttered.

'Like me to try?' said Maya.

Steve ignored the question.

He took three steps back and turned sideways so that his right shoulder was directly facing the door. He breathed once, then charged, putting as much force into the attack as he could muster.

'Shit,' he muttered again as he bounced back off it.

He kicked at it with his right foot, but the mulaks on his feet were designed for gliding across soft snow, not for kicking down metal doors.

Maya edged him aside.

She tore a strip of metal from the casing that held the computer on the desk, and fashioned it into a simple lever. She worked it into the slight space between the lock and the door's outer casing until it was wedged a centimetre in, then started to lean into it. The door creaked, and she pushed harder, her brow furrowing in concentration, until the door burst open with a sudden movement. The lever dropped to the floor with a clang.

Maya gestured to Steve to walk through.

'My Caracal instructor used to say that if you combine brains with brawn there is nothing you can't achieve,' she said.

'I'll try and keep that in mind,' answered Steve.

He flashed his torch forward, and turned right, towards the main cabin.

His torch was lighting up the path in front of him. Two bodies were lying across the entrance to the cabin, and one of them had wedged the door open slightly. Steve looked down at them. Both women, they were dressed in dark blue stewardess uniforms. They were both blonde, and very, very pretty; the ordinary airlines might have ditched the whole 'trolley dolly' concept when it came to hiring the cabin crew, but on the private jets model-style looks were clearly the first thing you had to have on your CV. The freezing cold weather meant the bodies hadn't started to decompose at all. But they had taken a battering; there was bruising and dried blood across their faces.

Steve flinched. He'd seen plenty of dead bodies in his time. Probably more than he wanted to. But they'd all been big ugly brutes, with guns in their hands and knives in their boots. These girls didn't look like they deserved to die.

He stepped over the two dead bodies, and on into the main cabin. It had room for more people than Kolodin's jet. On either side of the main aisle were twenty comfortable leather seats, arranged in ten rows. There was a bar at the back, and a television screen for each passenger.

Twelve of the seats were occupied, nine of them by men, and three by women.

They were all smartly dressed, the men in dark suits, with ties, although a couple of them were loosened around the collar. The women were wearing skirts and blouses; two looked in their early forties, the third was a girl in her twenties, not much older than the two stewardesses.

Steve flashed his torch from face to face.

They looked calm and peaceful. Each person was strapped into their seats, and looked as if they were simply resting. Their expressions were frozen solid, and their faces had turned almost as white as the snow outside, but it didn't look as though any of them had tried to move before they died.

Steve reached into his webbing, and pulled out the Yarygin. He checked that it was chambered, and pulled the slide.

Then he turned round and pointed it straight at Maya.

'I suggest you tell me what the fuck is going on here,' he said coldly.

'Steve, what—'

'I might not be the sharpest thorn on the tree, but I'm not completely sodding thick,' he said. He took another step forward, so that the Yarygin was pointing straight into her face. 'Now tell me what's going on, or you can end up like this lot.'

Thirty

OLLIE STAGGERED FORWARDS, DRIVEN BY a fierce determination. The storm was blowing hard across the plateau, and the snow was hitting him directly in the face, but he ignored it, and kept his head bowed into the wind, ploughing relentlessly forward.

He paused, and checked his watch.

Four thirty in the morning.

Time was slipping away from them.

He'd been walking for twenty minutes, and he reckoned he was making steady progress. The going had been tough, but the ground was flat, and that made it far easier to walk across. The pain in his ankle was growing all the time but he brushed aside any worries about the long-term damage he might be doing to his foot. There were only a few hours of this job left, and either he'd be dead, in which case he hardly needed to worry about his ankle, or else he'd be on a luxury yacht with all the medical care he needed to get it sorted.

For now, he just had to press on and help his mates. That was all that counted.

'Stop right there,' snapped a voice.

It was delivered in a loud and clear voice, from ten yards away.

'Or else I'll shoot.'

'Jesus, I didn't imagine the Abominable Snowman was a sodding Aussie,' said Ollie.

'Christ, Ollie, what the hell are you doing here?' asked Dan.

Ollie hobbled forward, until he was standing next to the Australian.

'Looking for you boys,' he said. 'And seeing if you need some help with the scrap.'

Dan let Ollie put his arm across his shoulder for support, and together the two men walked carefully back towards the glacier where the rest of the men were sheltering. Dan had been out on a short patrol, checking for any enemy forces that might be out searching the area. It was pure luck that he happened to run into Ollie looking for them, he reflected. Otherwise the guy could have stumbled straight into the plane and been shot on the spot.

'What happened to you, mate?' asked Ian as they joined the others.

Ollie briefly explained how he'd broken his ankle.

'So it must be just Steve and Maya trapped in that plane up there,' said Bruce.

'The plane?' asked Ollie.

Bruce briefly explained that they reckoned Steve had found the plane but was trapped inside it. Almost twenty enemy soldiers had surrounded the site and were digging down towards the fuselage.

'Then what are we waiting for?' said Ollie. 'There's eight of us, for Christ's sake, against nineteen of them. We've faced far worse odds than that in the past. Is this unit losing its bottle?'

'No one's worried about a scrap,' growled Ian.

'The Toyota's gone,' said David. 'And most of the weapons with it. All we've got are our handguns and a couple of AK-74s.'

Ollie grinned. 'Looks like I showed up at just the right time, then.'

'What do you mean?' asked David.

'I found a stash of Nazi weapons in an old Second World War shelter,' said Ollie. 'Rifles, grenades, machine guns . . . the works.'

The rest of the men looked at each other before Bruce finally spoke.

'Then what the hell are we waiting for?' he said. 'Let's go get them right now, and start taking the fight back to these sods.'

Four men formed a group to go and collect the kit.

Ollie led the way. His foot wasn't necessarily up to the journey, but they needed him to show them the way. Dan and Henri let him rest on their shoulders, while Nick scouted the way ahead, making sure they didn't stumble across any of the enemy forces. A blizzard of snow battered into them as they moved forward but there was a renewed vigour in the step of each man. Finding a hidden stash of Nazi weapons was the first bit of good luck they'd had since they'd landed in this godforsaken place, reflected Ollie, as the big shoulders of his two pals dragged him forward. Maybe, just maybe, it was a sign that their fortunes were starting to change.

'Straight down here,' said Ollie, when they finally arrived at the entrance to the bunker.

A dusting of snow had fallen across the entrance, but the place was clear enough and they quickly dropped down into the first bunker. Ollie pointed to the secret chamber underneath. 'That's where you'll find Fritz and his pals,' he said. 'Grab the crates, and we'll get out of here.'

Ollie didn't want to risk damaging his foot any further by dropping down another level, so he stayed upstairs while Dan, Henri and Nick went down below.

Dan turned his torch on to the five frozen SS men.

'Jesus, Nazis,' he muttered.

Henri took a step towards them, shining his torch into their faces. 'My grandfather was killed by bastards like these,' he said. 'Oradour-sur-Glane, nineteen forty-four. The SS rounded up all the men in the village, in reprisal for an attack on the local garrison. They forced them into a barn and shot them all in the legs so they couldn't move. Then they doused the barn in petrol, and set fire to it. They burnt the poor bastards alive, and made the women and children listen to the screams of their husbands and fathers. Most of them were just farmers. Not Resistance at all.' He glanced at Nick and Dan. 'Think they're dead in there?' he asked. 'I mean, they're not going to defrost and come back to life or anything, are they? Because if they are, I'm going to put a few bullets through them just to make sure.'

'They're dead all right,' said Dan. 'Let bygones be bygones.'

'That's easy for you to say. Your country wasn't occupied by these filth.'

'Let's get the kit and go,' said Nick. 'Steve needs us.'

Dan made a brief inspection of the weaponry. He'd liked to have spent more time getting to know it, but Nick was right. Every minute they wasted was another minute the enemy had to dig down to Steve's position. They took a dozen of the StG assault rifles, and two thousand rounds of ammo; the Walther pistols; two machine guns and ammo belts to feed them; two boxes of grenades; the TNT and the flame-thrower.

'This lot should give those boys something to think about,' said Dan, lifting the final crate up to the floor above.

'Do you reckon there's any Nazi grub down here?' asked Nick. 'I'm sodding starving.'

'What did the SS get in their rations anyway?' asked Henri.

'I've no idea,' said Dan. 'But I reckon old Adolf wouldn't have sent these lads this far north without a few special treats. A nice bit of bratwurst, that's for sure.'

Nick opened up another crate.

'Here,' he announced triumphantly. 'Grub.'

'Just grab a few tins, we can look at them later,' said Henri. 'We haven't got time to sit down for a meal now.'

'But I'm—'

'We know, Nick,' growled Ollie from the floor above. 'You're sodding starving. But there's a scrap on, and we need to get moving.'

Thirty-One

'WHAT THE HELL ARE YOU talking about, Steve?'

Maya was looking straight at him. There was a fierce anger in her eyes. A hardness and a ferocity he hadn't see before. That's what I should expect, he reminded himself sharply. She was a soldier with one of the finest armies ever seen. She may well be an agent for the most lethal intelligence agency in the world. If you put her into a corner, you have to expect her to fight back like a tiger.

'Reach into your webbing, and give me your weapon,' said Steve.

'Fuck off.'

Steve held the Yarygin steady in his hand, so that the tip of its barrel was pointing straight at her forehead. It wasn't the most powerful handgun in the world, nor the most accurate, but there were only five yards separating them, and at this distance, and in his hands, it was going to blow her brains clean out with a single shot.

'I said, retrieve your gun and give it to me.'

'You're not going to use that thing.'

Steve weighed the Yarygin in his hand. It was perfectly

balanced and he'd used it enough times to know that its aim was true. He'd already thought about whether he'd shoot her or not, weighing that decision in his mind with the same precision that he weighed the handgun. And although he'd rather not, the answer was still as clear as the crystals of snow falling outside. He'd shoot her if he had to. Without hesitation.

'Are you willing to risk finding out?'

'Listen, Steve . . .' she started.

Some doubt was starting to creep into her voice.

But not enough.

He pulled the trigger.

The sound of the bullet echoed around the cramped space, bouncing down the cabin of the A319. Steve had aimed slightly to her left, and the bullet struck the partition wall, breaking through it, and lodging itself in the private cabin on the other side.

'That's the warning shot,' he said. 'You get just one of them. The next bullet is the one that kills you.'

'Just tell me why you're doing this.'

Steve shook his head. 'First I want your weapon.'

'Why the hell . . .'

Steve gestured with his head to the corpses sitting neatly in their seats.

'There's plenty of bodies on this plane already,' he growled. 'One more isn't going to make any difference.'

Maya looked at him closely. She could see something in his eyes. A coldness. The certainty of a man who was about to perform an execution without a moment of regret.

She reached inside her snow suit, and into the webbing. She pulled the Yarygin free, unclipped its magazine, and handed it across to Steve. Then she placed the harmless handgun down on the seat next to her.

'OK, I'm defenceless,' she said, looking sharply at Steve.

He pointed to the corpse closest to them. It was one seat behind where Steve was standing. A man in his thirties, handsome, with dark hair, and wearing a charcoal-grey suit. There was an iPod on his lap. His face was white and peaceful but with the eerie calm that Steve had seen on the faces of dead men before.

'Now, I suggest you tell me what the fuck happened on this plane. Because I'm getting fed up with people lying to me.'

Thirty-Two

NICK LED THE WAY THROUGH the snow.

The storm was swirling drifts of snow up into ridges that were three or sometimes four foot high, turning ground that had been flat on the way out into a rippling assault course that threatened to sap what little remained of their strength.

He paused, and glanced backwards. For a brief moment, he'd lost sight of the rest of the unit, then he spotted Henri and Ollie, with Dan bringing up the rear, and he grinned, shouted out a few words of encouragement, and turned his face back into the storm.

A few more hundred yards, he reminded himself. Then we'll be back with the rest of the lads. And we can start cracking into whoever the hell is attacking Steve.

Inside the bunker, they had ripped up some of the floorboards and fashioned them into two roughly made sledges. They placed two crates on each, one containing the assault rifles, the pistols and their ammo, the other, the machine guns, flamethrower, the TNT and the grenades, plus a selection of tinned food that Nick had managed to pack in alongside them. Nick was hauling one sledge, and Dan the other. Henri was helping Ollie hobble across the snow.

'We were just starting to wonder where you boys had got to,' said Bruce, stepping out from behind the glacier as he spotted them on the horizon. 'We thought you might have scarpered.'

'And miss out on the scrap?' said Nick. 'Not on your life.'

Bruce grinned, and helped the Welsh boy haul his sledge into the small base camp they'd constructed behind the glacier.

'Let's have a look at what we've got,' said Ian.

Ollie knelt down, then ran though the kit piece by piece.

As he did so, each man was examining the weapons, judging its capabilities, and calculating how it might be used in an assault.

'Look at these beauties,' said Ian, cradling one of the grenades in his hands. 'Perfectly weighted, and with an elegant polish to the wood on the handle. Quality, that's what that is. They don't make explosives like this any more.'

'I reckon we should test it,' said David. 'We've got no idea if it still works.'

Bruce nodded in the direction of the plane. The enemy was only five hundred yards away, and through the storm and the howling of the wind, they could hear the sound of digging, the engines of the snow tractors, and the occasional burst of gunfire.

'We're too close,' he said. 'Let any of this kit off, and its going to make a hell of a bang. They'll be on to us in seconds.'

'Don't worry, it'll work,' said Dan. 'Vorsprung durch Technik, remember. Those boys knew what they were doing.'

Ian grinned. 'He's right,' he said. 'If the SS didn't make kit to last, then no one did.'

'All right,' said David reluctantly. 'So what's the plan?'

They all looked out towards the plane.

It was impossible to tell at this distance how far the digging had progressed. It was just after five in the morning, and they'd been excavating the plane for an hour now. They must be close to getting down to the cockpit window, reckoned Bruce. The guards were still on patrol, pacing in tight circles around the perimeter of the plane, their guns ready to fire. Every few minutes, they'd put a few rounds of fire into the ditch. Bruce reckoned that was just a warning to Steve, to keep him on his toes, and make sure he was occupied guarding the entrance he'd already dug into. When they were ready, they'd find another way into the plane. And that moment couldn't be far away.

'We could use some high ground,' said Dan, cradling the machine gun in his hand. 'That way, if we turn this beast on them we can do some serious damage.'

He was peering out on to the plateau where the plane was lying. It was in a dip in the ground, and off to the right, two hundred yards away, there was a ridge of ice. 'Two guns up there could do a lot of damage,' he said.

'Right,' said Bruce crisply. 'I think you've just volunteered. Who do you want with you?'

Dan glanced around the men.

'I'll go,' said Henri, stepping forward.

'Make sure you know how to work those things, and how to feed the belts then,' said Bruce. He looked at Ian. 'Those snow tractors are a big problem. Reckon you can take them out?'

Ian was still cradling a grenade in his hand. 'The Stielhandgranate has a range of up to fifty yards. That's what the handle is for. But I reckon that's when thrown by an SS lad who has been using them for years. I don't think we should count on more than thirty.'

'I said, can you take them out?'

Ian assessed the position of the tractors, and the lay of the land. Five hundred yards separated the tractors from the glacier where they were hiding. They would have to crawl across most of it, then put the grenades in when they were close enough to make sure they made an impact.

'With a bit of luck, yes.'

'We're all going to need that,' said Bruce.

He looked at Maksim, then at the flame-thrower.

'I heard you used one of these in Afghanistan, Maksie,' he said.

Maksim nodded. 'An American one, yes. But the Nazis invented the flame-thrower. They used them on our boys all the time in the Great Patriotic War. I reckon I should be able to handle it.'

'Then you take that,' said Bruce crisply. 'Spend a few minutes familiarising yourself with the thing. And try not to set fire to any of us.'

Maksim chuckled to himself, and started to unpack the Flammenwerfer 35 from the crate. The machine burned Flammöl 19, a mixture of petrol and tar. The tar made the flames heavier, and gave it a better range, allowing the flame-thrower to shoot a burning jet up to twenty-five yards. It had a three-gallon can of petrol, plus a metal canister of tar to mix into it. Whether the fuels would still work after all these years they had no way of knowing. Steve reckoned they would. Modern petrol had all kinds of chemical additives that deteriorated over time, but the old stuff, the kind the cars in his garage ran on, was just distilled crude. It was simpler, so there was nothing to degrade. Maksim started mixing the two liquids together, and pouring them into the fuel container on the Flammenwerfer. He'd find out whether it worked when they switched it on.

Bruce glanced around at the rest of the men. 'Dan and Henri will take the high ground with the machine guns, Ian will attack the snow tractors with the hand grenades, and Maksie will take charge of the flame-thrower. That leaves me and David and Nick to attack the bastards with the assault rifles.'

'What about me?' said Ollie.

'You're injured, so you're staying right here.'

Ollie started to struggle to his feet. 'Sodding hell—'

David reached across and pushed him back down.

'For Christ's sake man, sit this one out,' he said. 'You're in no fit state for a scrap.'

'I'll be all right,' growled Ollie.

'No you won't,' snapped Bruce. 'Grab yourself a rifle. If we're in real trouble, come and rescue us.'

Bruce picked up three StGs and handed one across to Nick, another to David and kept one for himself.

'Anyone ever fired one of these?' he asked.

'They've got them in *Call of Duty*,' said Nick.

There was a silence.

'In a video game, Nick?' said Henri finally. 'You've fired one in a video game?'

'Not just any video game,' answered Nick. 'It's sodding *Call of Duty* we're talking about here. On Xbox Live as well. I was champion for the whole of the Swansea region.'

David patted Nick on the back, grinning. 'I don't think we've got anything to worry about then.'

'Bloody good weapon,' said Nick, examining the StG and checking that the mag was full.

Bruce looked from man to man. 'I reckon we've got half an hour max, lads,' he said. 'Get your weapons ready, make sure they're oiled and you've got enough ammo. I want everyone ready to kick off this scrap in thirty minutes.'

Thirty-Three

STEVE COULD HEAR THE SOUND of digging. Axes were smashing against ice. And men were grunting and swearing at each other in a language that he couldn't understand.

A few more minutes and they'll be all over this plane, he thought to himself.

Maya's eyes were burning with anger. Steve reached down and took her Yarygin, slotting it inside his own webbing. He didn't want her pointing a weapon at him, even with the magazine removed. Not while he said what he was about to say.

He pointed towards the closest corpse. The man in a suit. Looking perfectly peaceful.

'Does he look like he died in a plane crash to you?'

Maya leant forward. She examined the corpse, peering into the lifeless yet pallid face. Slowly she shook her head. 'No,' she replied.

'Sodding right,' said Steve angrily. 'When a plane crash-lands, people panic. They brace themselves for the impact. They run around and try and get out. It's chaos. They don't sit back in their chairs looking like they're enjoying the in-flight movie.'

Steve took a couple of paces forward, pointing at the next corpse. An older man, about fifty, with greying hair, and a blue suit. 'Look at this geezer,' he said. 'He looks like he's had a couple of stiff drinks and has just dropped off for a quiet snooze.'

He took two more paces along the central aisle of the A319, pointing at corpse after corpse. They were all the same. Men and women strapped into their seats, calm, relaxed, with iPods and laptops and books and magazines on their laps. 'None of them look as if they died in a plane crash, do they? And they don't look like anyone told them the pilot was about to attempt an emergency landing in the middle of the bloody Arctic either.'

Maya shook her head but remained silent.

'Maybe the pilot didn't tell them,' she said finally.

'Not sodding likely, is it?' said Steve. 'If I was on a plane and it started its descent when we were nowhere near an airport, I think I'd notice whether the pilot told me or not. And when I looked out of the window and saw that we were about to land, and there wasn't anything that looked like a runway outside, or an airport, I think I'd brace myself for a bit of a bumpy ride, don't you?'

Maya fell silent again, just looking into the frozen faces of the corpses all around them.

Steve kept on walking.

He stepped over the bodies of the two young stewardesses, past the private cabin, and up towards the cockpit. The door was shut but not locked and although the handle was frozen solid it gave way with a shove. Steve stepped inside. It was a standard cockpit, the same as you'd see on any Airbus. A wide window across the front, now buried in snow. Dials and switches everywhere. Two big seats where the pilot and the co-pilot sat. Steve flashed his torch forward. Both pilots were still in their chairs, wearing crisp blue uniforms. Steve stepped to one side, shining the torch into their faces. Dead.

'Here, take this,' said Steve, handing Maya the torch.

He pulled off his gloves, leant forward and grabbed the head of the captain. The hair was cold to the touch and matted to the man's head. Steve used his fingers to brush aside the man's black hair. 'Look,' he said roughly.

Maya leant forward.

Steve was pointing to a small neat hole in the back of the man's head. It was half a centimetre in diameter, drilled straight into the bone. There were some signs of further damage to the skull around the wound, but otherwise the hole was a neat one.

'A nine-millimetre bullet,' said Maya. Her voice was quiet.

Steve took a step across the cockpit. The co-pilot was slightly younger than the captain. A man of about thirty, thin, with a wiry strength to him, and hair that reached the collar of his perfectly ironed white shirt. Steve used his fingers to part the hair. The same neat hole, an inch up from the back of the collar. The same burn marks where the bullet had penetrated the skull.

'Another one,' said Steve roughly.

He let the man's hair fall back into place, covering the bullet hole.

'I wouldn't say these two boys died in plane crash either, would you?'

Maya shook her head.

'In fact, I'd say some bastard shot them in the back of the head.'

Maya just nodded.

'Which is a sodding strange thing to do,' continued Steve, pressing on with his train of thought. 'The plane is in trouble in a storm. You walk into the cockpit, and you shoot both the pilots . . .'

He was looking straight at Maya as if he was expecting some form of explanation.

'So why don't you start telling me what this sodding job is all about,' he snarled. 'Because it certainly isn't about investigating a plane crash.'

'I don't know any more than you do.'

Steve held the handgun up so that it was pointing straight at her.

'I'm telling you, Steve, I don't know anything.'

Steve took a step towards her, the barrel of the gun still pointing directly at her face.

But suddenly there was a huge explosion.

The cockpit, even though it was encased in ice, shook from side to side. Steve lost his balance, and fell heavily to the floor. He hung on to his Yarygin, steadying the weapon in his hand, and pointing it straight towards Maya. Instinctively, he was expecting her to use the chaos of the moment to rip the gun from his hand. But she'd fallen to the floor as well, and even though she steadied herself before he did, she didn't make any attempt to disarm him. Instead, she grabbed hold of his shoulders and helped him to his feet.

Steve looked around anxiously.

Much of the ice around the window of the cockpit had been cleared by the explosion. There was now a clear path from the ground down into the cabin.

'They've blown their way through,' said Steve through gritted teeth. 'They'll be inside the plane in a moment.'

'Then we better find a way of holding them off,' said Maya.

Thirty-Four

'I T'S SODDING WELL STARTED,' said Nick.

He'd taken up a forward position right at the front of the glacier, keeping a watch on the enemy force five hundred yards in front of them. The rest of the blokes might have been taking the piss, he reflected ruefully, but as it turned out he was more familiar with the workings of the StG than the rest of them. He'd stripped and cleaned his weapon in no time, oiled it, and slotted the mag into position, and although there was no time to either test or zero it, he was confident that it would work perfectly. While the rest of the guys prepared their weapons, he'd kept a close eye on the plane, counting down the minutes until the attack would kick off. He'd seen a flurry of activity where the men were digging, and he'd seen the snow tractors move into closer positions, then he'd seen the fire and smoke of an explosion as a well-targeted stick of dynamite was used to break through the remaining ice, and clear away an access route to the buried plane.

'What's the flap, mate?' hissed David, joining him.

Nick pointed straight ahead.

'An explosion,' he replied. 'The bastards are blowing their way in.'

'Christ,' muttered David. 'We're not ready.'

'Well, we sodding well have to be ready, don't we?' said Nick. 'If we leave it any longer, Steve will be dead.'

David nodded. He turned round to get the others.

'We're going in, lads,' he said. 'They're about to break into the plane.'

No one spoke.

'They outnumber us two to one, and I reckon their kit might be a bit more up-to-date,' said Bruce. He spoke in a tone of steely determination. 'But I don't reckon they've got the same kind of fighting spirit we do and that makes it a more than even match. So let's crack on, and good luck to each man.'

'Everyone know the drill?' said David.

Each man nodded in turn.

'Then take up your positions. Dan and Henri get as far up that ridge as you can, then unleash as much fire as possible. Ian, you get some grenades into the tractors. Maksie, you get into position with that flame-thrower. Each man is going to have fuel on him to survive in this weather, and the vehicles will have spare cans of diesel on them, so get any kind of flame on to the buggers and they are going to go up like a firework. The rest of us will lay up with these assault rifles and finish off any of the sods that don't get what's coming to them in the first assault. The more firepower we put into them in the first few seconds, the more chance we've got, so start counting, and no matter where you are, kick off in a minute and a half.' He glanced around the unit. 'Any questions?'

The men remained silent.

'Right then,' he said crisply. 'Let's give them the good news.'

Nick dropped to the ground, with Bruce and David alongside him. Each man had prepped his StG, with one thirty-round mag in the chamber, and two more spares in his webbing. The guns were switched to automatic. They started to wriggle across the snow, using their elbows to pull themselves forward. It was slow, brutal work, with the cold biting into their skin, but they had to stay as flat to the ground as possible to avoid being seen. The StG had an effective range of two hundred yards; it had been designed for the close-quarters combat that characterised the Second World War. The closer they could get to the enemy in the next ninety seconds, the greater the chance that at least some of their bullets would find their target.

To their right, Dan and Henri crouched down, and started to move swiftly towards the ridge of high ground that overlooked the plateau where the plane was buried. They followed the arc of the ice, moving silently along its natural contours, hoping that would shield them from detection. Both men were carrying one machine gun each, plus two ammo belts. The MG 42 was not a heavy weapon. It weighed just twenty-five pounds, and had been designed to be carried in the field by one man unaided. During the war, it was nicknamed Hitler's buzz saw by the Allied troops because its 1,200-rounds a minute rate of fire was so rapid that it was impossible for the human ear to distinguish the sound of individual bullets being fired. It didn't chatter like standard machine guns, just made a noisy buzzing sound. Dan kept the gun at his side, and counted out the seconds. 'Here,' he whispered on the count of forty.

They were only a dozen feet up into the ridge, and three hundred yards away from the enemy, but there was a dip in the ice that made a natural foxhole, and Dan reckoned they had to allow at least thirty or forty seconds to get the guns set up and aimed.

Henri nodded, saying nothing.

Both men dropped down into the foxhole. The MG 42 had a simple steel tripod. Dan spiked his into the ground, and slotted the gun on top of it. It had a range of a thousand yards, plenty for the distance they needed to cover. But belts held 250 rounds. Using both of them, Dan reckoned they'd both have enough ammo for twenty-five seconds of sustained fire. The MG 42 had been designed on the principle that in combat there were only very brief moments when a solider could put any rounds into the enemy, and it was more important to create short but lethal bursts of fire than sustain longer attacks. It worked for the Nazis and it will work fine for us as well, decided Dan as he slotted the first belt into place. If we haven't dealt with these sods in the first twenty-five seconds, we probably never will.

'You ready?' hissed Dan, looking across at Henri.

The Frenchman nodded. 'Ready,' he replied.

'Ten more seconds,' said Dan. 'Then we can let them have it.'

Down below, Ian was advancing steadily towards the three snow tractors. He was kneeling on the ground, crawling through the snow like a dog. He'd prepped six of the Stielhandgranates, two for each vehicle. Whether they were going to work, he had no idea. But they looked in good enough nick. If they don't explode, he reflected grimly, we'll just have to think of something else.

Maksim was following right behind him. He'd attached the Flammenwerfer 35 to his back, and prepared the petrol-tar mix. The whole piece of kit weighed almost eighty pounds, but

Maksim was strong enough to carry that kind of load on his back even while crouching to avoid detection. The petrol-tar mix was pushed through a long tube, then lit by a hydrogen-fuelled igniter as it left the nozzle. Like any flame-thrower, it was a volatile piece of kit, and often burned its operator to death. But within range, it was lethal, delivering an immediate and painful death on the enemy. The plan was for Ian to move in first with the grenades, and for Maksim to follow swiftly in his wake with the Flammenwerfer. If the explosive didn't destroy the tractors, with any luck the fire would finish the job.

'Ten seconds, Maksie,' muttered Ian. 'And may God be with us.'

Twenty yards to his left, Bruce put a hand up to indicate to Nick and David to stop. There were ten seconds to go. They'd advanced to within two hundred yards of the enemy, and that was close enough. 'Ten seconds, lads,' he hissed.

The enemy was clearly visible from here. Eight guards were patrolling the perimeter in pairs. Each man looked alert, well prepared, and fighting fit. They were carrying assault rifles, and, Bruce reckoned, they'd have handguns and grenades in their webbing as well. To the right, close to where Dan and Henri would be leading the assault, were the three snow tractors. They were big, heavy machines, with massive tyres designed for crossing the Arctic, and with sledges behind them for carrying supplies. Each one had been fitted with a machine gun on its front. From this distance, Bruce couldn't tell what make the guns were, but he reckoned they'd be up to date, and capable of spewing out an awesome quantity of munitions on anyone unlucky enough to find themselves caught in their line of fire. As far as Bruce could see, there was one driver on each vehicle, who would no doubt double up as a machine-gunner once the fun kicked off. Another eight men were in charge of the digging. They had just used an explosive charge to blow their way through the last few feet of ice blocking the way into the plane, and now it looked as if they were clearing away the debris left by the dynamite. None of the diggers had any weapons in their hands but they would have plenty of weaponry tucked into their webbing.

'If Ian and Maksie can deal with the tractors, and Dan and Henri can take out the guards with the machine guns, then we can deal with the diggers before they have a chance to get their weapons out,' hissed Bruce, glancing towards Nick and David.

Both men simply nodded their agreement.

'We'll be fine so long as it goes according to plan,' said Nick.

'Since when has that ever happened?' said David.

'There's a first for everything,' said Bruce. 'Let's just hope this is it.'

He looked forward. 'Eighty,' he muttered aloud, then mouthed the next couple of numbers silently. He was counting down the last few seconds until the attack began. Up ahead, the guards were still on patrol, calmly going about their business. They clearly had no idea of the brutal firepower that was about to be unleashed upon them. That at least is on our side, reflected Bruce. There's no more lethal weapon in any arsenal than surprise.

Twenty yards away, Ian counted down towards eighty-seven. He was reckoning on a three-second delay on the fuses of the grenades. That meant he had to launch his weapon a fraction before the rest of the assault opened up. He looked back towards Maksim, grinned roughly, then stood up. It made him visible, and the moment he leapt to his feet Ian was acutely aware of how vulnerable a target he'd just become, but there was no other choice. He couldn't get the distance on the grenades unless he could swing his arms, and he couldn't do that crouching down. He took a second to get a fix on the location of the first tractor. With its engine running, it burned as a bright splodge of red on the screen of his night-vision goggles. Then he pulled the pin and hurled the grenade straight into the air, followed swiftly by a second one. Moving slightly on his heels, he located the second tractor, then the third, and in a fraction of a second launched the next two pairs of grenades. The storm was still blowing snow fiercely across the plateau, and within moments of the Stielhandgranates leaving his hand he'd lost track of them in the dark sky.

He looked back at Maksim. 'Pray, man, feckin' pray,' he muttered.

Up on the ridge, Dan glanced towards Henri. 'Ready?' he hissed.

The Frenchmen nodded, his expression sombre.

Dan swivelled the MG 42 into position. It was resting on its tripod, and pointing directly into a pair of the guards.

'Go,' he snapped, slamming his finger into the weapon's automatic trigger.

For a brief second, nothing happened. Dan could feel a beat of panic close to his heart. We're fucked, he muttered to himself. But at his side, he could hear a screeching buzzing noise as Henri's gun leapt into life and in the next instant his own weapon opened up. The strength of the kickback took him by surprise. The gun practically jumped out of his hands. He slammed his left fist down on the centre of the gun barrel, while holding his finger on the trigger to keep the bullets spitting out. The first couple of seconds of fire had been wasted. As he lost control of the gun, the barrel had pointed too far into the distance, and the munitions had sprayed harmlessly into the glacier a hundred yards beyond their target. As he regained control of the gun, he could see that Henri had already shredded the pair of guards he'd had in his initial sights, leaving both men dead on the ground, and had turned his fire on to the secondary target. The bullets were raining down on them, but they'd seen their comrades fall to the ground and already taken evasive action. Dan cursed the way he's squandered the first few valuable seconds of the assault. He trained his gun on the two men he'd planned to target first. They'd already thrown themselves into the snow, making themselves as hard to hit as possible. He aimed the MG 42 at them, releasing an awesome rate of fire straight into their position. As the ammo belt expired, he fed the second belt into the machine gun, and directed his fire towards the second pair of guards. But whether he was inflicting any damage, it was impossible to tell at this range.

'I told you the sodding Aussies couldn't count,' grunted David from his position down below. 'There's no way that's ninety seconds.'

In unison, Bruce, David and Nick stood up, and started to march into the heart of the battle. Their StGs were held in front of them, but they hadn't started firing yet. Until they had a closer view of the scrap, there was no point in burning through their mags. They walked steadily forward. 'Hold the line, lads,' grunted Bruce. 'We're the poor bloody infantry of this scrap, and it's our job to hold our fire until we see the whites of the sods' eyes.'

The wind was blowing up flurries of snow that whistled straight across the plateau. Visibility was sometimes as little as a few yards, making the battle hard to follow, and even harder to fight. As they marched forward, Bruce heard a sudden explosion cracking through the storm. A blast of brilliant light shot upwards, followed by a deafening explosion as one of the three snow tractors ignited. As first its fuel tank and then the spare supplies fixed to its sledge caught fire, a ball of flame rolled into the air, briefly illuminating the entire plateau in a glowing yellow light. It was followed by a thunderous snapping noise, as all the munitions on board exploded piece after piece. Smoke billowed out of the stricken tractor, and somewhere in the centre of the chaos the ghostly scream of a man being incinerated could be heard.

'One down,' said Ian.

He looked forward. Through the snow and wind he could see and then hear a rolling set of explosions. One, two, three, then four, as one grenade after another detonated. Flashes of white, intense light broke through the darkness, one after another, creating a strobe effect, like some kind of mutant, hellish disco. Ian was straining to tell how much damage they had done. But through the smoke rising out of the first tractor and the snow blowing hard across the battlefield, it was hard to make out anything at all.

'Get ready with that flame-thrower, Maksie,' he said. 'There will be stragglers to deal with.'

He ripped his StG from his back and slotted a mag into place.

At his side, Maksim was cursing. 'It's not working,' he hissed.

He was pulling on the ignition lever, but although a jet of

fuel and tar was spouting from the nozzle, nothing was setting it alight.

'I think the lighter's fucked,' snapped Maksim.

'Then get it working,' growled Ian. 'Or else we're all done for.'

Up on the ridge, Dan ran through the second belt of ammo. The massive rate of fire on the MG 42 meant even two belts lasted for less than a minute of sustained fire. At his side, Henri's gun had fallen silent as well. 'How many?' asked the Frenchman, glancing across at Dan.

'One, I reckon,' said Dan. 'You?'

'Three,' said Henri.

'Well done, mate.'

'It's not a competition,' said Henri with a shrug. 'There's a fair bit of fighting left to be done yet.'

Both men were looking down at the battlefield. They'd seen three of the eight guards fall, and one tractor explode in the initial assault. They could hear the shouts of men, and the rattle of gunfire, but it was impossible to see who was alive and who was dead. One thing was clear, though. They hadn't knocked them out in the initial assault the way they'd hoped to. There was plenty of fight left in the opposition yet.

'Let's move, then,' said Dan.

Both men snapped their StGs into position, and started to run down the side of the ridge.

Below, Bruce, Nick and David were moving steadily forward.

They advanced in a neat line, each man one foot apart, their guns stretched out in front of them. A hundred and fifty yards, then a hundred. They were so close, they could smell the debris from where the grenades had exploded, but through the thick snow they still couldn't see how much damage had been done, or what kind of numbers still opposed them.

Two men appeared from the left. Nick saw them first. He snapped a command and turned his StG towards them, unleashing a volley of bullets straight into their chests. David and Bruce turned in the same instant. The men had started to fire but they were too slow. The storm of munitions ripped into them with a ferocity that knocked the life from them before they had a chance to respond. The StG was a smooth, efficient gun, as lethal today as it had had been on the Eastern Front. By the time half their thirty-round mags were emptied, Nick had signalled to stop firing. Both men were already dead.

'We can stop and see who they are later,' said Bruce, his tone harsh. 'There's a battle to be won first.'

They kept marching steadily on.

They were looking left and right, searching for their opponents, but although they could hear shouts and bursts of gunfire, they couldn't see anyone. The smoke from the burning tractor was still too thick; it was rising into the air, then getting pushed back down again by the wind. Two men appeared out of the snowstorm to their left. David snapped round and was about to loosen off the remaining rounds from his assault rifle when one of them cried out.

'It's us, mate.'

David's finger rested on the trigger.

Dan. With Henri following closely behind him.

'How many did you get?' growled Bruce.

'Three, for sure,' said Henri, as the two men ran up. 'Maybe more. It's hard to see through all this crap.'

'We've got two here, and at least one tractor is gone,' said Nick.

'There's plenty left then,' said Dan. His expression was grim. He unhooked his StG from his back, and slotted the mag into place.

The three-man line had become five.

A gust of wind ripped across the plateau, stronger than anything they had experienced for several minutes, and although it brought blizzards of snow sweeping across them, it also cleared the smoke. As the visibility improved, they could all see what was confronting them.

They froze in their tracks.

One snow tractor had been destroyed, and a second had been damaged, but the third was intact.

The driver of the undamaged tractor was turning the machine straight on to them. Fixed to its front they could see clearly now what kind of machine gun it was carrying. The Kord 12.7, a heavy-calibre Russian machine gun designed during the 1990s. Light, simple to operate, with a brutal killing capacity. Behind it was a line of six guards, all carrying AK-74 assault rifles. Behind that was the damaged tractor; it couldn't move but its guns would still work.

The line was advancing straight on to them.

The intact tractor would punch through first, like a snow tank, while the men behind it would mop up any survivors. If there were any.

Classic close-quarters armoured warfare, thought Bruce grimly. And they were less than two hundred yards away.

'Return fire, return fire,' yelled Bruce, his voice raw and angry.

All five men opened up with a burst of fire from the StGs.

The volley of fire ripped across the plateau. They could see the line of men move to take cover behind the snow tractor. But their bullets were making no impact on the machine, even if they were hitting it. And the big beast was moving relentlessly forward.

David glanced to his right.

Ian and Maksim were less than a hundred yards away. The Russian was struggling with his flame-thrower, while the Irishman was prepping another pair of grenades.

'Put some grenades into them,' yelled David.

Ian glanced across.

The smoke had only just cleared enough for him to see what was confronting them. Ian started to take a run, pulling the pin from a grenade, waiting a second and a half, then lobbing the device high into the air. It arced forward, caught on the fierce wind, lost its course, and landed several feet short of the tractor.

The Kord machine gun opened up with a sudden burst of fire.

'Drop, drop,' yelled Bruce.

All five men hurled themselves to the ground. They were still firing spasmodically, but they weren't even holding the enemy back.

The grenade detonated. A flash of flame shot upwards, followed by a flurry of snow and ice that kicked up into the air, then a swirling mass of black smoke. But still the Kord kept firing. Its huge 12.7mm rounds, each bullet 4.3 inches long, were peppering the ground around them, splintering open chunks of ice as they hit the ground.

'Retreat, lads,' growled Bruce. 'We're going to get murdered out here.'

'We're not sodding well going back,' snapped Dan.

'Of course we bloody are,' snarled David. 'We have to regroup.'

'If we back off now we're done for,' said Nick. 'We'll never get back into the fight.' His voice was tense, raw with emotion.

'We're dead men if we stay,' shouted Henri. 'Do what he sodding says.'

The men looked at one another. Then they rose as a single unit.

'I'll put down some covering fire,' growled Bruce. 'You blokes leg it.'

Bruce knelt down, his StG held tight into his chest. He unleashed a volley of fire into the advancing tractor and the men crouching behind it.

Behind him, Nick, David, Henri and Dan started to run back towards the glacier they had been hiding behind.

To the right, Ian watched them run.

'We're retreating, Maksie,' he shouted, looking around.

But the Russian was still grappling with the ignition on his flame-thrower.

'I've never retreated in my life,' he growled. 'And I'm not planning on starting now.'

Ian ran to him and tugged him on his shoulder. But Maksim pushed him away.

'You're a bloody madman,' Ian yelled into his face.

Maksim just smiled roughly. 'Either stay here and help me fix this sodding machine, or piss off.'

Ian shook his head in disgust. Then he started to run back through the thick snow towards the glacier.

Thirty-Five

STEVE GLANCED UP THROUGH THE tunnel of ice that led from the cockpit to the surface. 'Looks like the cavalry finally showed up,' he said, as the racket of machine-gun fire filtered down into the interior of the plane. 'And about sodding time as well.'

'Who's up there?' asked Maya.

Steve shook his head. 'How the hell should I know?' he said simply.

He drew his gun. Maya was already looking at him nervously as the weapon flashed into his right hand. But the Yarygin wasn't aimed at her this time. He pointed it straight at the glass of the cockpit. He fired. Steve was expecting the bullet to smash through the glass and shatter it. But instead it simply bounced off the surface of the window and ricocheted dangerously around the small cabin, until finally it lodged itself in one of the control panels.

'Shit,' muttered Steve, wiping the sweat off his brow.

'This is an aeroplane,' said Maya, raising her right eyebrow. 'You think they don't make the glass in the cockpit strong enough to withstand a single nine-millimetre bullet?'

'All right,' growled Steve. 'If you're so sodding smart, how do we get out of here exactly?'

'Why would we want to get out?' demanded Maya.

'We need to help the lads,' answered Steve. 'Slide our way up that tunnel and we can slot a few of these bastards in the back.'

Maya nodded just once.

She rummaged around on the floor of the cockpit. 'Help me,' she said. 'There should be an emergency tool kit down here somewhere.'

Steve pointed the torch downwards. The floor was covered in grey carpet tiles. He started trying to peel one back, but they were frozen solid to the metal of the aircraft's deck. He took a knife from his webbing, and started to lever away at the edges of the tile until finally he managed to prise one up.

There was nothing underneath apart from cold steel.

'Back here,' hissed Maya. 'It should be directly behind the pilot's seat.'

Steve levered up another tile, then another. Nothing. Then on the third tile, there was a bolt. He pulled it, but it was frozen solid. 'Christ,' he muttered, the frustration evident in his voice. 'Nothing works in this sodding place.'

'Stay calm,' said Maya harshly.

She pulled one of the candles from her webbing and lit its wick. It added a pale yellow light to the cockpit. Leaning forward, she held the flame as close as she could to the bolt, cupping her hands to it so it didn't blow out.

'We just need to defrost it,' she said.

Steve stood up. He was standing right next to the cockpit window, leaning into the cold glass. He could see a flash of light, followed by another, and then, as he stretched his neck, he reckoned he could see clouds of dark smoke. There was the chatter of gunfire. Machine guns, he noted. What type he couldn't tell. Not from here. But high-calibre, he could tell that much. And that meant lethal.

It's a hell of scrap, he thought to himself grimly. And our boys haven't got the right kit for that kind of fight. Not even close.

'Got it,' said Maya, a note of triumph in her voice.

By the time Steve turned round, she'd already pulled out an emergency toolbox. Amid the screwdriver, fuses, and spanners, there was a glass-breaking hammer. With a massive red plastic grip, it had a series of zinc-plated heads designed for crashing through the toughest barriers.

'Give me that,' said Steve.

He took the hammer from her hand, and with a single blow that released all his pent-up anger, smashed it straight into the glass. It vibrated for a split second, then began to crack. Steve swung again. The glass splintered, falling into the cabin in a dozen places.

A draught of freezing air swept across Steve's face.

He used the hammer to clear away the remaining glass. The sound of gunfire was far louder now, echoing down the tunnel, and straight into the cockpit.

Steve gripped the Yargin tight in his right hand.

Using his left hand, he started to lever himself out of the small window. It was easily wide enough for a man to climb through, but the sharp edges of the remains of the glass meant he had to be careful.

Maya was following close behind.

'I need my gun,' she hissed.

Steve turned round to look at her.

'You're joking, right?' he said sharply.

'There's a battle on up there. We need all the hands we can get.'

'I don't trust anything about this job,' snapped Steve. 'If I give you a gun, you'll put a bullet straight in my back.'

'Jesus, Steve, I've had enough chances to kill you,' she shouted. 'I'd have done it by now if I wanted to.'

'You're working for Kolodin. He knows a lot more about this job than he told us, and for now that means I'm not trusting you.'

Maya reached out to touch him, but Steve just brushed her hand away.

'Just wait here,' he said.

Thirty-Six

MAKSIM WAS LYING FACE DOWN on the ground.

The bullets from the Kord machine gun were slicing open the ground all around him. Chunks of frozen water were spitting up into the air, mixing with the snow and wind to create a hailstorm of metal and ice. His back was already starting to ache from the debris pounding into him, and it was only by staying flat in a dip in the land that he was managing to stay alive.

But the tractor was advancing relentlessly forward.

'Work, you bastard, work,' he hissed.

He was fiddling furiously with the ignition on the Flammenwerfer 35. It used a flint to create the spark that would ignite the fuel as it left the nozzle. But it had degraded over the years, and it didn't matter how many times he tried, he couldn't bring it back to life.

'Sod it,' grunted Maksim.

He reached inside his webbing, and pulled out a standard cigarette lighter.

I'll just set fire to it as it leaves the tube. And if it blows me up? I'll take my chances. I'm a dead man anyway if I stay here.

A hundred yards back, Bruce glanced round the side of the glacier, then looked back at the rest of the men. They were exhausted, out of breath, and dirty. Their clothes were a mess, and there was sweat dripping down their faces, and none of them understood their sixty-year-old kit properly. Ollie was sitting slumped on an empty weapons crate, holding his rifle in his hand, with his head bowed. Bruce didn't reckon he'd ever seen a more ragged-looking fighting force, nor one less able to take the battle back to the enemy. But he knew he couldn't allow any of those thoughts to show on his face or in the tone of his voice. He'd learned that as a sergeant in the Regiment. The first rule of command was confidence. Let that slip for a second, and you were as good as dead.

'Maksim's a gonner, lads,' he said grittily. 'No one can survive that kind of assault.'

'So what's the plan?' growled Dan.

'Get back in there,' snapped Nick. He was toying with his rifle anxiously. Two of his mates, Steve and Maksim, were in mortal danger. Quite possibly already dead. He was coiled up, ready to launch the counter-strike.

'No suicide jobs, lads,' growled Bruce. 'That won't do anyone any good.'

'Sitting around on our arses and getting shot at while our mates get blown to pieces isn't doing anyone any sodding good either,' snapped Nick angrily.

He moved swiftly, emerging from behind the glacier and releasing a volley of fire from his StG in the direction of the snow tractor. The bullets spat from the barrel of the gun, then disappeared into the darkness. Suddenly a burst of sniper fire chipped away at the glacier just inches from Nick's face. Ollie lunged forward, grabbing Nick by the shoulders and pulling him back to safety. 'For Christ's sake, cool it, man.'

Nick resisted momentarily, then allowed Ollie to drag him back behind the glacier. He chucked the empty magazine to the ground angrily, then slotted a fresh one into the rifle.

Bruce turned round. 'Dan and Henri, you get those machine guns fed with fresh ammo. Put down some covering fire straight into the tractor. David and I will veer off to the left. Nick and Ian, you head right. We'll try and distract them with the machine-gun fire and then squeeze them in a pincer movement.'

It was a desperate plan, with not much chance of success. They'd probably be spotted as soon as they tried to move out, and mowed down by machine-gun fire. But it was better than doing nothing.

'What about me?' said Ollie.

'Christ, we already told you, you're in no fit state to fight,' said Bruce.

'And I'm not staying here to freeze to death after the rest of you get shot.'

Ian handed him a crate of grenades. 'Lob these into the sods as soon as we open up with the machine guns,' he said. 'It might hold them up for a bit.'

'Right, boys,' said Bruce. 'Let's get to work. Thirty seconds . . .'

The men moved silently into action. They had a plan and a sense of purpose again, and that alone had started to restore their spirits even though the dice were stacked against them. Dan and Henri grabbed new belt feeds, and slotted the MG 42s on to their tripods, while Ollie prepped half a dozen grenades, and the rest of the men bombed fresh mags into their StGs.

Matt Lynn

Up ahead, Maksim muttered a silent prayer. He could feel the snow and ice on his back, and the cold seeping into his skin. The bullets were getting closer all the time, turning the ground into a splintered mess. I'd have preferred somewhere better to die, he thought grimly. A whorehouse in Moscow, preferably. Or at least a bar.

But if it's here it's here.

So be it.

He took a healthy swig from the bottle of vodka hidden in his webbing, and as the alcohol sluiced around the back of his throat, he permitted himself a brief, tense smile. At least I'm keeping one promise to myself, he reflected. I won't die sober.

Then he torched up the lighter, shielding its flame from the wind and snow blowing across him. In the next instant, he released the fuel from the canister strapped to his back, and scrambled to his knees. He held the nozzle with his right hand. For a brief second he waited until a jet of fuel escaped, then he slammed the lighter into it. It ignited in a terrible ball of fire, blowing up like a balloon, and Maksim could feel the skin on his face singeing as the sudden blast of heat swept into him. But he held himself steady on the ground, kept hold of the nozzle, and started to march straight forward.

The Flammenwerfer had a range of twenty-five metres, and could fire in ten-second bursts. The jet of flame arced out of the nozzle, like the water from a garden hose, dropping down into the snow, melting it instantly on contact. Maksim could see the tractor thirty-five to forty yards ahead of him. The bullets were spiting straight towards him from its machine gun, but he ignored them, moving relentlessly forward.

Close, he thought grimly. Too close for the bastards to turn round.

'The nutter is going in,' yelled David from the side of the glacier.

Everyone could see the great yellow balloon of flame marching across the snow.

'Move, lads . . .'

The unit fanned out seamlessly. Dan and Henri slotted the machine guns into place, Ollie started to move forward, hobbling on his broken foot, while Bruce and David ran to one side of the battlefield, and Nick and Ian to the other.

'Hold your fire,' shouted Bruce as he started to move across the thick snow. 'We don't want to kill the Russian.'

Up ahead, Maksim was quickening his pace. The Flammenwerfer had been burning for three seconds now. Seven left. The tractor had stopped. The driver was turning the machine gun straight towards him. All the man has to do is fire straight into the centre of the fireball, realised Maksim. He can't miss.

He lunged forward desperately, turning up the fuel supply beyond maximum, trying to eke a few more metres of range from the machine. If it blows up on me, it doesn't make any difference now, he told himself grimly. I can only die once.

The flame started to lick up to the edge of the tractor. The Kord was firing furiously, but Maksim managed another foot forward. A scream ripped through the air. Followed by a sudden shaking of the ground.

A plume of smoke swirled upwards as the spare fuel tanks on the tractor caught fire first. Then the machine itself detonated. The ice shook as the force of the explosion rattled through the plates. The tractor blew apart as tank after tank of diesel was set alight, then exploded, sending jets of flame and volleys of molten shrapnel spinning in every direction. The flames licked out to one soldier standing behind the tractor, igniting the spare fuel canister in his backpack and exploding on contact. The man literally blew apart, his chest bursting open, and one severed arm flew furiously out into the cold air.

Something hit Maksim on the side of his snow suit. He spun round, dropping the nozzle of the flame-thrower, then crashed hard into the ice. He head was spinning, and he could taste blood in his mouth. Fire was still spitting from the flame-thrower, but he could no longer see well enough to switch it off, nor find the strength to push it away from him.

A brothel or a bar, that's where I wanted to die, he thought to himself again as he felt consciousness slipping away from him. Not the sodding Arctic.

Out of the smoke, three soldiers emerged, running towards the glacier, their AK-74s on automatic, unleashing volleys of fire into the men sheltering there. But they were running straight into Dan and Henri's guns. The MG 42s buzzed as they mowed the soldiers down, bullet after bullet slicing into their veins, cutting them to ribbons and sending them tumbling to the ground.

Behind them, Ollie had started to hobble forward, lobbing the first of his grenades into the air, aiming so that it would land in the mass of black smoke still swirling up from the tractor. Somewhere inside, he could hear men screaming, and the more punishment they could put into the enemy while they were wounded and disorientated, the quicker their victory would be.

Bruce signalled to David to keep running. It was hard going

across the thick snow, but the force of the explosion had temporarily cleared away the storm and when they looked away from the smoke the visibility improved. The tractor had taken out most of the rest of the men immediately surrounding it when it exploded but up around the plane there were at least five more guards and one more tractor which, while it had been immobilised in the earlier attack, was still manned, and capable of turning its machine-gun fire on anyone that came close to it.

'Pincer, pincer,' hissed Bruce.

David knew precisely what he meant.

They had to take them from the flanks, and hope that Ian and Nick would be in position to do the same. 'Twenty yards, then fire,' said Bruce.

They two men ploughed steadily forward. They could see their targets clearly now. Men who were disorientated, and alarmed, but still had plenty of fight left in them. Suddenly one of them spotted Bruce and David. A shout was followed by a blast of gunfire. Both men dropped to their knees, steadied themselves, then released a barrage of fire from the StGs.

Thirty yards to the east, Nick and Ian snapped to attention at the sound of gunfire.

'It's feckin' started,' said Ian.

Nick had already lined up a shot. He had a clear view of the man in his sights, and even though the StG was not a high-precision weapon, even by the standards of the 1940s, he was confident he could make the shot. 'Kill,' he muttered softly, squeezing the trigger.

The man fell face forward in the snow, the back of his skull fractured by the bullet.

At Nick's side, Ian was squatting in the snow, his StG on automatic, putting a barrage of fire into the opposition.

The group of soldiers was caught in a blizzard of crossfire. The bullets were slamming into their position from left and right, shredding them to pieces. The landscape offered no possibility of cover, and not much of escape. Two of them started to run, dashing back towards the safety of the third tractor. But they were cut down before they could cover more than a few yards, their legs shot from beneath them, and as they fell to the ground their heads and chests were ripped open in a brutal hailstorm of munitions.

Up by the plane, Steve was crawling up from the cockpit, through the tunnel, and back up towards the ground. It was six feet up, and he needed to use both his hands, so he tucked the Yarygin into his mouth for ease of access. The frozen metal hurt his teeth, and he was sure he could feel a filling coming loose, but he ignored the pain, using his shoulder muscles to lever himself upwards. All around him he could hear gunfire and explosions echoing across the plateau, but he had no idea who was winning, only that the fight was a vicious one. As he looked up, he suddenly saw a man's face peering down. It was dark and ugly, a balaclava covering most of the skin, and with the hood of his snow suit tied tight over his forehead. In one swift movement, Steve swung his legs up, so that he wedged himself into the tunnel with his feet and his shoulders. With his right hand now free, he whipped the handgun from his mouth, and in the same moment fired once, then twice. One round struck the soldier in the left eye, while the second rocketed through his mouth and chewed into his brain. The man slumped forward, blood pouring from his open mouth into the tunnel, dripping over Steve. He ignored it, slotted the Yarygin back into his mouth, and levered himself up the three remaining feet to the surface. He shunted the body aside, and crawled carefully on to the ground, taking the gun back into his hand as he did so.

He glanced anxiously around.

Debris from the two shattered tractors was scattered across a landscape that was stained with crimson. There were bodies lying where they had fallen and, a hundred yards ahead of him, he could see an exchange of gunfire still in progress. Right in front of him, there was the third tractor. One wheel had been blown away by a grenade, but the main body of the machine was still intact, although leaning badly to its left side where the wheel had fallen away. Three soldiers were sheltering behind it, facing forward and oblivious to what had happened to the man who'd been trying to retreat down the tunnel. A third had climbed up to the heavy Kord machine gun on its front, and had opened up a murderous barrage of fire on the attackers a hundred yards away.

Those must be our boys he's shooting at, realised Steve.

A hundred yards away, Ian and Nick were running across the open ground. Their StGs were still on automatic, putting round after round into the men lying on the ground, making sure they were dead. Bruce and David closed in from the opposite direction, only releasing their fingers from the triggers when they were certain the enemy was completely disposed off.

'Job done,' said Bruce tersely. 'Good work, lads.'

The men rested their guns, each of them blowing on their fingers, trying to restore some warmth to them.

Then a burst of gunfire opened up from the Kord.

The bullets were breaking up the ground all around them.

'Christ,' muttered David, as he dived to the ground.

All four dropped down, lying flat amongst the corpses of the men they had just killed. The ice all around them had been broken up by the gunfire, and the snow was stained crimson from the victims' blood.

'Get back behind that glacier,' shouted Bruce.

'If we start running we'll be sodding slaughtered,' snapped Nick.

'The bodies,' growled Ian. 'Shunt them together to form a barrier.'

There was a momentary silence as the gunfire stopped. As they looked ahead, they could see that the man up on the tractor was re-sighting his weapon, trying to get a more accurate fix on his enemy. Nick grabbed one of the bodies, while David got another and Bruce a third. They piled the men one on top of the other. Each was badly shot up, suffering multiple bullet wounds before they died, but their thick snow suits had held their shattered bodies together and staunched the worst of the bleeding. The corpses formed a makeshift barricade that would at least hold off the worst of the fire.

Nick slotted his StG over the bodies, resting it in the small of a dead man's back. He glanced towards the tractor, lined up a shot into the steering cabin, then took a deep breath. 'Kill,' he muttered, and squeezed the trigger.

'You feckin' missed, sharpshooter,' said Ian sourly.

'You try then,' snapped Nick.

Another hundred yards back, Dan and Henri were striding across the snow. They could see the Kord had opened up again, but reckoned that in this weather, with little light, they were too hard a target to hit.

'There,' said Dan, pointing towards where Maksim was lying on the ground.

'There's no time,' said Henri. 'We'll help the others first.'

Dan just nodded. Every instinct was telling him to go and help the Russian, but his battlefield training reminded him that he had to deal with the enemy first, and the wounded second. You couldn't help your mates if you were getting shot at. And if they were already dead, there was no point in throwing your life away.

Both Henri and Dan dived behind the barrier where the rest of the unit were sheltering. As they did so, the gunner was alerted by the movement of their bodies, and opened up with an intense volley of fire. A barrage of bullets slammed into the man on top of the pile, knocking him over so that he fell on to Nick.

'Pull the bodies on top of you,' snapped Bruce.

Each man lay flat on the ground, pulling one of the corpses on top of them to try and provide some shelter from the munitions flying into their position.

'We're getting murdered,' said Ian, his tone grim. 'Someone needs to get in there and put some return fire into the bastards.'

They glanced at one another.

'Any volunteers?' asked Bruce eventually.

Nobody said anything. It was a death sentence, and each of them knew it.

'Aye, well, I'm the oldest man here, so I guess I've got fewer years left on the clock to lose than anyone,' said Bruce finally. 'Ian, you get me a grenade prepped, and the rest of you sods ready some covering fire, and I'll charge the fucker.'

The gunfire stopped. The gunner was feeding a new ammo

belt into the Kord, Bruce reckoned, and adjusting his sights, ready to open up with a fresh barrage of bullets.

And in the brief moment of silence, Ian got a grenade ready, and the rest of the men slotted fresh mags into their StGs.

Up ahead, Steve crouched down in the snow.

The gunner had stopped firing, his belt spent. But that was only a brief respite. Three remaining soldiers were hiding behind the tractor, but in the lull in the attack two of them knelt down, and started to crawl through the snow, one heading left, the other right. Steve could tell at once what they were planning. The gunner would pin the unit down with a fresh round of fire. His two mates would sneak round the sides and launch their own attack.

They'd make mincemeat of their opponents.

Steve took two more paces forward. The gunner was clearly visible now. A man of medium height, wearing a thermal snow hat pulled down tight over his head. No helmet. It was too cold for that. Under his snow suit, Steve reckoned he'd have some kind of Kevlar plating. A bullet to the back, although the easiest target to aim for, would just bounce off him. The head, thought Steve. That was the only target worth aiming for.

He raised the Yarygin, lined up the shot in its metal sights, and muttered a short, silent prayer. Then squeezed the trigger.

The man slumped forward.

His body twitched once, then remained still.

By the side of the tractor, the one remaining soldier turned round. He fired once into the darkness. But he hadn't had time to locate his enemy, let alone take an accurate aim at him. Steve started to run forward, pumping out round after round from his

Yarygin straight into him. The first two bullets perforated his snow suit but were deflected by the Kevlar underneath. But a third caught him on the side of the neck, ripping out a huge chunk of flesh. Blood started to gush from the open wound. The man fell to his knees, his AK-74 firing wildly. Steve swerved. Like a wounded tiger, the man was at his most dangerous now. Desperate, vengeful, suffering terrible pain, and frightened of his own imminent death, he would lash out with terrifying force. Coming at him from the right, Steve took aim at his head, pumping round after round into his exposed skull. The man spun, roaring with pain, then fell forward. His finger was still locked on to the AK-74, bullets spewing from its barrel, but its mag was soon spent, and the weapon fell silent.

Steve looked out into the open plateau. Only two men left. Then they are defeated.

He could see someone running. The unit was launching an assault, he realised.

Bruce was racing across the open plateau. Behind him a volley of covering fire opened up.

'Gunner down, gunner down,' yelled Steve from behind the tractor.

But his voice died on the wind raging across the plateau.

As he looked up, Steve could see some kind of missile arcing through the air. It bounced no more than a foot from him, right at the base of the tractor. Steve knew he had only a split second to make a decision. Run for it, before the device exploded, or try and chuck it away. On that choice, to be made in an instant, he knew his life would depend.

He glanced around. There was no cover, and the missile would ignite the fuel tanks on the tractor when it exploded, creating a hellish inferno of ice and fire that would burn up anyone within twenty or thirty yards. He couldn't make that kind of distance in the time available. He lunged forward, his mind made up. The missile was some kind of grenade, he could tell that much, but not one he'd ever seen before, even if there was something about it that seemed strangely familiar. Where the hell Bruce had got hold of it, he had no idea. He gripped the wooden handle, and lobbed it to the left of the tractor. The grenade spun into the air, exploding less than a second after it left his hand. A thunderbolt opened up in the sky, and the fierce light of the explosion briefly illuminated the plateau in a magical yellow light. A shower of sparks hissed down, and Steve could feel the shock wave roll through him with the force of a punch. But it quickly died away, its power spent.

A burst of gunfire opened up from Bruce's rifle. Steve hid behind the tractor, waiting. Bruce was running straight towards him, his weapon on automatic, but the bullets were merely hitting the tractor and bouncing harmlessly into the snow. 'It's me,' shouted Steve. 'The gunner is sodding down, you mad bastard.'

Bruce was just feet away now. His took his finger from the trigger of his gun, slowed down, and then walked up towards the tractor. Steve edged carefully out from behind the machine. There were still two enemy soldiers out there, he reminded himself. But as he looked out over the landscape, he could see two men disappearing to the eastern side of the plateau, losing themselves in the glaciers that lay beyond it. They knew they were outgunned, reflected Steve. Their unit had been wiped out, and they'd decided to flee rather than join their mates in an icy grave.

Bruce was striding towards him, a broad grin on his face. He stopped a few inches short of him, and put down his StG.

Steve glanced down at the odd-looking rifle. For a moment he was puzzled but then he remembered where he'd seen it before, and the grenade as well. In the Commando comics he used to read as a kid.

He picked it up, running his hands along the smooth wood of its stock. 'Bloody hell,' he said with a smile. 'I was hoping to get rescued. But I wasn't expecting the sodding SS.'

Thirty-Seven

OLLIE STAGGERED OUT ACROSS THE snow.

He'd been following the battle as closely as he could, but even using his night-vision goggles he could only hear it, not see it. And that didn't tell you anything except that the contest was a fierce one. One in which there would be heavy casualties on one side or the other. But there was no way of knowing which.

It was ten minutes now since the fun kicked off. So either our lads have already won, or I might as well go and make a last stand, he told himself grimly. He picked up a spare StG and started hobbling forward. I'd rather go down in a hail of bullets than die of cold anyway, he decided.

Maksim's body was lying in his path.

Ollie knelt down, and brushed the snow out of the Russian's face. 'Christ, Maksie,' he muttered.

The man was as cold as the ice that surrounded him, and there was no sign of any breath on his lips. There was some blood around the side of his face where a piece of shrapnel had opened a cut in his forehead, but the cold had staunched the wound before he'd lost much blood. Ollie started to reach around for a pulse, but had to push his fingers up into the sleeve of his snow suit to find his wrist.

'What the fuck?' muttered Maksim, coming round with a start. He looked up, confused. 'Where the hell am I?'

'In a whorehouse, mate,' said Ollie. 'I've just asked a couple of blonde sisters to get a room ready for you. Apparently they are quite a double act.'

'Did you order some vodka as well?'

'Of course, pal.'

'And champagne for the ladies?'

'The best in the house.'

Maksim grinned. 'I knew it,' he growled. 'I must have died and gone to heaven.'

'Sorry to disappoint you, old sausage,' said Ollie, starting to lift Maksim to his feet. 'I'm afraid you're stuck in the sodding Arctic, with a gash in your head, miles from anywhere, with only a bloke with a crocked foot to help you home.'

Maksim shook his head sadly. 'I knew it was too good to be true.'

The two men propped each other up and, with their arms over each other's shoulders, started to stagger towards where the main battle had been fought. The guns were silent now. By the time they got there, everyone had gathered around the remaining tractor.

Steve and Henri stepped out to help Ollie and Maksim.

'Good to see you, mein Kommandant,' said Steve, gripping Ollie's shoulder, while Henri took Maksim.

'Heil Hitler,' replied Ollie, raising his right arm in a Nazi salute.

Steve grinned. He reckoned they could keep this joke going

for the rest of the day, but there were more important things to worry about. He steered Ollie towards the rest of the unit.

'You all right?' said Bruce, checking him over.

Ollie nodded. 'Never better. All I need is a nice cup of tea, and everything will be perfect.' He looked around. There were six bodies scattered around the few yards that separated the damaged snow tractor from the plane wreck, all of them lying where they had fallen. 'These sods all dead?' he asked.

'We're still checking,' answered Steve.

'This one's alive,' shouted Nick from a few yards away. 'Get Maksim. He speaks Russian.'

Maksim walked swiftly across the ground. He leant down into the man's face and put his hand to his mouth. There was just a trace of breath escaping from his lungs but it was weak. Maksim slapped him hard across the face twice. The man still had enough life left in him to wince from the pain. He coughed, hacking up a ball of phlegm and blood.

'Who the fuck are you?' growled Maksim.

The man grunted, then spat.

Maksim repeated the question, louder this time.

But still there was no reply.

Maksim looked up at Nick and Dan and grinned. 'Strip him,' he said. 'In this temperature, that should get him talking. It's the most brutal torture any of us could inflict.'

Nick nodded curtly and, together with Dan, started to remove the man's trousers. He struggled momentarily, but there wasn't the strength left in him to put up any serious resistance. They took off the snow jacket, Dan pinning down his arms, while Nick started to unhook the Kevlar jacket that protected his chest. Next, he started to cut away the layers of thermal vests with a knife. The man had taken three bullet wounds to the arms and neck, and as the cloth came away, the blood started to pour out of him. Maksim slapped him around the face again, repeating his question, this time in Russian.

The man suddenly started talking, the words flooding out of him as quickly as the blood from his wounds.

Maksim nodded, listening intently.

Then he pulled the Yarygin from his webbing, slotted one of his few remaining bullets into the mag, chambered it, and placed the barrel of the gun into the man's mouth. He mouthed a few words in Russian. 'Good luck in the next life,' he said, this time in English. And then he squeezed the trigger, blowing the man's brains clean out of the back of his skull.

'Christ, mate,' said Dan. 'That was a bit rough, even by Russian standards.'

'It was his last wish,' said Maksim standing up. 'A quick and honourable death.' There was a sombre note to his voice.

'Who the hell were they?' asked Dan.

'Spetsnaz,' answered Maksim. 'An Arctic unit.'

'They haven't got any insignia,' said Bruce.

'I know,' answered Maksim, with a curt nod of the head. 'Usually, the Spetsnaz have a panther symbol on their uniforms. Like the dagger that the SAS wears. Not these guys, though. They'd removed all identifying symbols before coming up here.'

He was looking around at the corpses, noticed Steve. He glanced at Bruce. Both men nodded silently to one another. They were thinking the same thing. Maksim had been Spetsnaz himself, and there were loyalties there that time couldn't unwind. Neither of them would feel comfortable killing Regiment men, no matter how many years had passed or what kind of battle they might be engaged on. It was the same for Maksie, reflected Steve. They would have to watch out for him over the next few hours. This was going to be tough for the guy.

'We're not in Russia, are we?' said Ian.

'The Arctic is officially meant to be neutral territory,' said Maksim. 'But the Russian government is trying to claim it because it has the last great untapped oil reserves in the world. For any Russian troops to be discovered up here would cause a major diplomatic incident. They were sent up here to find the plane – and to make sure no one else found it. That's why they were attacking us.'

'What's so feckin' important about this plane?' said Ian.

'Wait until you see what's inside it,' said Steve.

'What do you mean?' asked David.

'Follow me, and I'll show you,' said Steve crisply. 'If you think a bunch of Spetsnaz boys trying to kill you is weird, wait until you see this.'

He started to lead the way back to the narrow tunnel. He pushed aside the corpse of the man who had fallen near the exit, then started to climb down the few feet that led to the broken window of the cockpit. As he stepped inside, he nodded curtly to Maya. If she was relieved they'd won the battle, and not the Spetsnaz unit, then there was no sign of it on her face, he noted. He helped the rest of the men down into the plane until the cockpit was full, and Dan and Henri and Nick had to move out through the door to make space for everyone.

Steve showed them the neat, expertly drilled bullet holes in the back of both the pilots' heads.

And then he led the men back into the main cabin of the

plane, showing them the bloodied bodies of the two steward-esses, and the strangely peaceful corpses of the passengers in the main cabin of the A319.

'So you see,' he said, turning round from the back of the cabin and looking the rest of the men in the eyes. 'Something seriously fucked up happened on this plane. And we need to work out what the hell it was.'

Maya pushed herself forward, looking at Steve.

'I think I can tell you,' she said quietly.

Thirty-Eight

ACH MAN TURNED TO LOOK at Maya. Even the corpses strapped into their seats appeared to be turning their glassy dead eyes on to her, as if seeking an explanation of their own demise.

'Don't listen to her,' said Steve angrily. 'She's a plant from Kolodin.'

'Let her speak,' said Bruce. 'We don't have to believe what she says but we might as well hear her out.'

'Why do you think she's a plant?' asked Ian.

'Can't you sodding see it? This plane didn't crash, that much is obvious. The pilots were shot. Kolodin's playing at something, and she's working for him.'

'Maybe he's playing with her as well,' said Nick.

'We're on his payroll too,' said David. 'No different from her.'

Steve remained silent. Those were possibilities that had occurred to him. But he still didn't see why they should trust her.

Maya glanced from man to man. 'So shall I tell you what happened here?'

'We'll listen,' said Bruce firmly. 'And then we'll judge.'

'I've had ten minutes alone down here while you were dealing with the soldiers up on the ground, and that's given me a chance to have a good look around,' she said, speaking with a composed, natural authority. 'Look at these corpses,' she continued, pointing to the man in the well-tailored business suit sitting next to her. 'As Steve pointed out earlier, they clearly had no idea what was happening to them. Any normal person braces themselves for a crash landing. They panic. Not this lot.'

She paused again, glancing from face to face. She had their attention. They were hanging on her every word. 'The only logical conclusion is that they were either already dead or unconsciousness before this plane came down.'

'Already dead?' said David. 'How could you kill all these people?'

'It's a plane,' said Maya. 'There's no natural air supply. It's all recycled, and that process is controlled by the pilot. I think the pilot switched off the normal oxygen supply coming into the cabin, and replaced it with a powerful sleeping gas.'

She rested her hand on the head of the suited corpse next to her. 'If you did a post-mortem on this guy, I think you'd find he was knocked out by some kind of anaesthetic before the plane came down. He actually died many hours later of hypothermia, and so did the rest of them.'

Steve looked at the corpse at his side. A woman with the earplugs on her iPod still hooked into her ears. Reluctantly, he had to admit Maya's explanation made sense. How else could they end up like this?

'The pilot deliberately killed each and every one of them,' Maya continued, her tone flat.

Her eyes flicked up towards Steve. There were nine of them standing along the main aisle of the plane, but it's just me she's speaking to, he realised.

'Then he crashed-landed the plane.' She waved a hand. 'Take a look at this aircraft. The tail wing came off a hundred yards back. But it didn't break up in the sky, and there is no sign the engines failed. It was brought down deliberately.'

'That's a hell of a big claim,' interrupted Ian.

'Perhaps,' answered Maya with a shrug. 'But think about it. Pilots fly across the Arctic all the time. It is one of the main routes between Europe and Japan or Korea. There are diversion airports if they run into trouble. But pilots are also taught how to crash-land on the ice. They drop down low, circle, look for a few hundred yards of thick, straight ice, then bring the plane down. With a bit of luck, it isn't going to be much harder than landing at Heathrow.'

Steve listened carefully. It was hard to disagree. They'd seen the engines, and there was no sign of the power units burning up. There was no evidence of internal or external damage. Nothing that would make it crash.

'What about the weather?' he asked. 'We know there was a heavy storm that night. Maybe that bought the plane down.'

'Do we know there was a storm?' answered Maya. 'For sure? Kolodin told us, but I think we already know he hasn't been levelling with us from the start. We can check the weather records when we get back. But even if there was a storm, this is a modern, well-maintained aircraft. They are built to withstand the worst weather imaginable. Planes crash when there is a combination of bad weather and mechanical failure. It's hardly ever the weather alone that brings them down.'

'But why the hell would the pilot kill all the passengers?' asked Ian. 'And how did the two pilots end up dead themselves? I can hear what you're saying but it still doesn't make any sense to me.'

Maya walked the length of the main fuselage, then pointed to the private cabin, and on to the cockpit. 'You missed something else which is very odd,' she said. She was looking directly at Steve again.

But he remained silent. He was racking his brains. What else did we miss?

'Where's Markov?' she said.

Steve looked from body to body. She was right. They'd seen pictures of the Russian billionaire who was meant to have died on this plane, and there was no sign of his corpse.

She was several steps ahead of them in this game, he realised. All they could do was listen.

'This is what I reckon happened,' Maya continued. 'The pilot was paid by someone to assassinate Markov. He fed sleeping gas into the air system to knock everyone out, and put on an oxygen mask himself. Then he planned to crash-land the plane. The whole thing was going to be made to look like an accident. The two pilots would have walked away from the whole incident without any blame, and Markov would have been murdered. Just about the perfect crime, when you come to think of it.'

Her brow furrowed up, as if she was thinking the whole plot through as she explained it to the men in front of her.

'But Markov realised what was happening. I reckon he was expecting an attempt on his life, possibly on this flight, and when the sleeping gas started pumping through the system, he jumped into action. Together with his bodyguard, he smashed his way into the front of the plane.'

She walked a few paces forward, to where the bodies of the two young women lay on the floor. 'Take a look at these hostesses. They've clearly been bludgeoned to death. They are the only corpses on this plane, apart from the pilots of course, who show any sign of injuries. I reckon they were in on the plot, and Markov and his bodyguard had to fight their way past them. Once they got into the cockpit, I think they turned their guns on them, grabbed oxygen masks for themselves, and forced them to bring the plane down. After they'd done so, probably when the plane was skidding along the ice, they shot both pilots in the back of the head.' She looked around at the men. 'There are just two questions we need to answer. Who was the pilot working for? And where's Markov?'

Ian took a step forward. 'I don't know about the first question,' he said. 'But I think I can answer the second one.'

Thirty-Nine

IAN WAS STANDING HALFWAY ALONG the plane's central aisle. Next to him was the corpse of a woman in her thirties, a brunette, smartly dressed, with a Russian novel open on her lap. Her eyes were closed, but her head was tilted back, so it looked as if she was looking straight up at him.

'He's about a mile north-north-east of here,' he said.

'What?' said Maya.

Steve glanced from Ian to Maya and back again. She was right about what happened to the plane, he felt certain of that. It was a bizarre series of events, no question about that, but the evidence was all there right in front of their eyes, and there was no other way of making sense of it. This wasn't a search for a black box they were involved in. It was a murder investigation.

I was wrong to question her, he thought to himself. She never knew more about this job than the rest of us.

'Just before we saw the flare Steve put up we located the signal from the black box,' Ian said. 'It was just outside the zone we were searching, about a mile away. I reckon Markov took it with him when he made his escape from this plane.'

'You're saying the black box isn't here?' asked Henri.

347

'That's precisely what I'm saying. We haven't picked up a signal from it, even though we are right inside the plane. That means someone took it.'

'Maybe it's broken' said Nick.

'They're indestructible,' growled Ian. 'That's the whole point of a feckin' black box. If the plane blows up, the black box still survives. And this plane isn't even badly damaged.'

'But why the hell would he take the black box?' asked David.

'Why don't we go ask him?' replied Ian. 'I reckon he's still with it.'

'Still with it?' questioned Maya.

Ian was a step ahead of her now, noticed Steve. And it didn't look as if she liked that much.

'Why not?' answered Ian with a shrug. 'The man was meant to have died in this plane crash. If he'd suddenly turned up in the four weeks since then I think we'd have seen something about it on the news.'

'OK,' said Maya tentatively. 'You might be right. Then let's go and find him.'

'We'll check whether the black box is on the plane first,' said Bruce firmly. 'That's what we were paid to do and we'll finish the job. If it's not here, we'll head out to where we got the signal, and see if we can finally find the sodding box, and the man as well if he's with it.'

Bruce and David organised the unit into search parties. Steve, Ian and Nick took the back of the plane, Bruce, David and Henri took the middle section, while Maya and Dan took the front. Ollie was resting his foot up in the cockpit with Maksim. While the rest of the men searched, Ollie used the emergency medical kit stashed in the pilot's compartment to clean and bandage the wound on Maksim's head, and to finally remove the sock from his broken ankle, clean the sore, bruised flesh underneath, and carefully put his mulak back on. 'Afraid there's no duty-free on this flight, old boy,' said Ollie as he finished. 'I reckon we could both have used a drop of the hard stuff.'

The search only took a matter of minutes. The A319 was not a big plane. Each unit checked the passenger areas, dropped down into the luggage hold, and used their torches to search through the engines, inside the wings, and up into the broken tail section. But they all sensed even before they began that they weren't going to find anything, and it was no great surprise to anyone when they all reconvened in the central aisle of the plane without anyone having found the black box.

'It's not here,' said Bruce when he'd checked the results of the search with each unit. 'I think that means Ian's right. The black box is out where we picked up the signal earlier.'

'Something else is missing as well,' said Henri. 'Every plane flying over the Arctic is legally required to carry a basic survival kit in the hold. At least two cold-weather suits, food, and a medical kit. The idea is to give any surviving passengers after a crash a decent chance of staying alive until a rescue party can reach them.'

'And it's not there?' said Maya.

Henri shook his head. 'It should be in the luggage hold, where it's easily accessible. But it's gone.'

'So has the inflatable dinghy,' said Steve. 'Every plane has to carry one of those in case it comes down at sea. But that's gone too.'

'You don't need a dinghy out here,' said Nick.

Matt Lynn

'No,' said Steve, with a shake of his head. 'But I reckon it might make a pretty good shelter if you were planning to cross the Arctic by foot.'

'Markov must be out there somewhere,' said Bruce. 'And it's our job to go and find him.'

Steve checked his watch. It was almost ten in the morning local time. They had two hours until the black box was switched off forever.

'Let's crack on, boys,' he said firmly. 'The sooner we can find our man, the sooner we can get out of here and get our feet up by the fire with a nice round of hot toast and big glass of brandy.'

Forty

THE STORM WAS BLOWING IN hard from the east now. The wind was whipping across the icy plateau with the force of an artillery battery, hurtling across them in vicious eddies and gusts that could knock a man sideways. The unit was marching in two columns of five men. Henri and Dan were leading the way, using their torches to cut a path through the valleys and ridges that littered their path. Steve and Bruce followed a few steps behind them, both men equipped with StGs chambered and ready to fire. They were aware that at least one man had escaped from the battle for the plane and might well have managed to call for reinforcements. Maksim and Nick were pulling a sledge into which they'd strapped Ollie, along with the rest of the spare guns and ammo they'd stolen from the SS bunker. And Ian, David and Maya bought up the rear, watching the ground behind them, staying alert for any sign of an attack.

They covered the first half-mile easily enough, but as the march stretched on, they were growing wearier and wearier. They were all exhausted. It was close on two days now since they had slept properly, and although they were all strong, and they kept themselves in good shape, their bodies were being pushed beyond the limits of even the fittest of men. Henri had lost part of his snow suit in the tussle with the polar bear, and even with the patched-up cloth covering his arm, the intense cold was starting to get to him, chilling his blood and his bones, and gradually sapping his spirit. But they pushed on regardless, digging deep into reserves of fortitude and endurance to keep going.

The second half-mile was harder going. The ice suddenly dipped into a deep valley. Henri and Dan were nervous a lead might be ahead of them, and Dan sent the Frenchman ahead with his torch to find a path through. The storm was blowing up so fiercely, visibility was down to just a couple of feet, even with his torch switched to full power. The wind had taken the temperatures down to fifty or sixty below zero, and even though their bodies had become hardened to the terrifying cold of the Arctic, there was a bitterness to the air now that none of the men would have imagined possible. Henri established that there was no break in the ice, and summoned the rest of the unit down the path he had cut through the snow, but they were immediately confronted by a high ridge of ice that rose thirty or forty feet into the air. An attempt to scout their way round it proved futile, and with the clock ticking against them, they quickly concluded there was no choice but to try and get over it. It was a brutal climb upwards, with the wind against them, and there was no way even three or four men could pull Ollie up on a sledge, so instead they lifted him up. Steve and Dan took him on their shoulders, ignoring Ollie's constant protests that he'd be fine so long as they let him walk for himself.

'Just keep going, lads,' said Bruce. 'There's a week in the Caribbean on Death Inc. for anyone who makes it out of this sodding mission alive.'

'Not hot enough, mate,' said David. 'I want to go to Dubai in August. Now that's really scorching.'

'The Gobi desert,' said Henri. 'Dubai never gets above forty-five degrees. You can hardly even get a suntan.'

'Or Death Valley,' said Steve. 'I've heard it can get so hot there the tyres on your car start to melt.'

'Blackpool in September will suit me fine,' said Ian. 'I'll never complain about a wet and windy bank holiday again.'

'We'll book you in for a week in a guest house,' said Steve.

'Paradise,' answered Ian, chuckling, 'after this place.'

The ridge climbed, they kept marching. The downward slope was far easier, and it led them through a narrow channel sided by two high ice mountains, so high that their peaks were obscured by the storm. There was some respite from the wind, as the ridges shielded them from the worst of its fury, and they managed to pick up some speed, covering the next few hundred yards at something approaching a normal walking pace. They'd crossed the zone they'd originally been searching and were now moving into the territory where Ian reckoned Markov was hiding. They should find him at any moment. If he's still there, thought Steve as he battled his way through the snow still falling steadily from the sky.

'Anything?' said Bruce, looking towards Ian.

Ian was checking his radio. But there was no sign of a signal.

'Nothing,' he replied tersely.

'Christ, we must be close,' complained Steve.

'Aye, and we're close to the feckin' North Pole as well,' said

353

Ian. 'We might not pick anything up until we're practically tripping over the bastard.'

'Keep going, lads,' said Bruce. 'But use your torches and your eyes as well. We may have to search our man out the old-fashioned way.'

They moved steadily forward. It was eleven fifteen local time. The black box would switch itself off before the hour was out. And with that gone, the last chance of finding both the device and the man who'd taken it from the plane might well have slipped away from them.

The ridges on either side suddenly turned in on themselves, steering the unit through a narrow channel, no more than thirty feet wide, with great blocks of ice on either side. A gust of wind suddenly whipped through it, increasing in force as the ridges created a tunnel, pushing the air speed close to forty miles an hour. Nick was knocked over, and had to be helped back on to his feet. As soon as they'd steadied themselves, the unit put their heads down and forced their way forward. There was a turning in the ice up ahead, noticed Steve. Get past that, and it should provide some shelter.

'I'm getting something,' shouted Ian.

Bruce and Steve stopped to look at the radio. It was picking up a signal only two hundred yards away.

'Right around that corner,' said Steve, pointing. 'Where there's some shelter from the wind.'

'We're almost there, boys,' said Bruce.

Dan and Henri led the way. Their torches were switched on, but the light was struggling to cut through the falling snow. They were advancing steadily, with Steve and Bruce following close behind them, their guns ready to fire. None of them had any idea what kind of reception they might get, and they'd seen enough of the Arctic to expect the worst. Dan rounded the corner first, flashing his torch into a small plateau enclosed by ridges of ice on each side. It made a natural enclave, sheltered from the worst of the storms that raged across the ice caps, yet also hidden away from anyone who might be searching for you.

'There's something there,' shouted Dan to the men behind him.

Suddenly a burst of gunfire rang out.

The bullets spat through the air, narrowly missing the two men at whom they were fired, before smashing harmlessly into the glacier behind them.

'Fire, fire,' yelled Henri.

Dan and Henri had dropped instantly to the ground. Both men had started to draw their weapons, but it was to Bruce and Steve they were looking for instant retaliation. Both men ripped off their gloves and slammed their fingers into the triggers of the StGs. Whoever was up there needed to know they were in a scrap, and not one they were necessarily going to live through.

'A grenade, Ian,' shouted Steve. 'Put a sodding grenade into them.'

Up ahead, a gun was still firing at them, but Dan and Henri had managed to wriggle backwards, retreating behind the curve in the ice. Both men had drawn their handguns and were pumping bullets into the enclave. Ian ran up behind them, a grenade in his hand, already prepped and ready to be launched.

'No,' snapped Bruce, grabbing him by the arm.

'We need to sodding well deal with them,' shouted Steve.

'There's only one bloke firing at us,' yelled Brice. 'Listen.'

Steve and Ian both paused.

The gunner fired a few more rounds from what sounded like a semi-automatic assault rifle, then fell silent. He's right, thought Steve. There's just one bloke up there.

'We don't want to kill Markov,' said Bruce. He looked at Ian. 'Lob that grenade to the side. Make sure you don't kill anyone. Just let him know he's heavily outnumbered and outgunned.'

Ian nodded curtly, and pulled the pin. The Stielhandgranate curved up into the air, travelling at a right angle to the enclave ahead of them, and bounced once on top of one of the surrounding glaciers before detonating. A jet of yellowy-black flame shot upwards, kicking up a cloud of splintered ice, and a plume of dirty smoke rose into the air before the snowstorm extinguished the flames and smothered the explosion.

'Put down your weapon, man,' yelled Bruce round the corner. 'There's a lot more where that came from.'

To emphasise the point, David organised Nick, Dan, Henri, Maya and Maksim into a column, and instructed them to unleash a brutal volley of fire from their StGs. The bullets smashed through the ice in a three-second burst of co-ordinated fire designed to impress rather than kill.

'I said lay down your weapon,' yelled Bruce as the guns fell silent. 'This is your last chance.'

Steve listened closely. But all he could hear was the wind whistling through the ice.

'I said lay down your weapon,' shouted Bruce.

'It's done,' cried a voice.

The man spoke in clear English but with a heavy Russian accent.

Henri and Dan stood up and started to advance round the

corner. Their weapons were ready to fire, but the man had surrendered. His gun was on the ground, and his hands were in the air.

'All clear,' shouted Dan.

Steve walked round the corner with the rest of the unit.

The spot had been well-chosen. The walls of ice secluded it from the worst of the storms, and it was hidden away: a fold in the endless expanse of glaciers into which a man could disappear. An inflatable dinghy had been placed on top of two thick blocks of ice to create a roof, and two big sheets of plastic were draped down the side to make a small, rough shelter. Next to it stood a big bear of a man, at least six foot three, wearing a shaggy coat and a woollen hat, and with a straggly beard covering his dirty face. When asked, he put down his hands and handed across his AK-74 to Henri, who promptly released its mag and slotted it into his webbing.

From the tent, another man emerged. Shorter. About five ten, with a stocky build, jet-black hair that was growing down the back of his neck, stubble that was turning into a beard, and a snow suit that looked as if it had been put through a cement mixer.

Steve recognised him at once.

Markov.

'Who the hell are you?' he demanded, striding forward so that he was standing directly in front of the unit. 'And what are you doing here?'

'Funny,' replied Steve crisply. 'I was about to ask you the same thing.'

Forty-One

NICK STEPPED UP TO FRISK Markov. The man offered no resistance. He stretched out his arms, and although it was hard work to check right through his thick snow suit, it was soon clear he wasn't armed. Henri checked the other man. A burly former Spetsnaz soldier called Gregor Tyutin, he was Markov's personal bodyguard, but the AK-74 was the only weapon he had on him apart from an eight-inch hunting knife that the Frenchman quickly removed.

They didn't appear to be a threat, thought Steve. But what the hell are they doing out here?

'Who sent you?' demanded Markov, as soon as the search was completed.

He was looking at Bruce, then Steve, then David, as if he was trying to work out who was in charge of this rough-looking group of men who'd stumbled across his hiding place. His face was dirty, and his eyes cold and tired, but he spoke with a natural authority. The voice of a man who was used to being obeyed.

'Alecsei Kolodin,' answered Steve quickly. 'He sent us out here to find the black box from your plane.'

Markov stared at Steve, examining him the way a butcher might examine a slab of meat on his carving block. Steve stood absolutely still. The oligarch was a born manipulator of men, he judged. Strength, mental as much as physical, was the only quality he would admire in a man, and he would identify any weakness immediately, and exploit it without mercy.

'If you're working for that bastard, then you might as well kill me right now and have done with it,' he said. He chuckled, but there was no humour in it.

'No one's getting killed, not yet anyway,' said Steve firmly. 'Just tell us what happened, and then we'll decide what to do.'

'Come inside then,' Markov said finally. 'And we'll talk.'

He turned round, and led them into the simple shack. It was surprisingly well-built. The dinghy provided a solid enough roof that kept the worst of the snow out, and the two side walls sheltered them from the wind. There were two beds made out of plastic sheets laid on the ground, and, at the back, a simple metal stove from the plane's cold-weather survival kit was running on aviation fuel retrieved from the wreck of the A319. The two men had been living here for almost a month now, reckoned Steve. They'd made themselves as comfortable as possible, but in these conditions it was still a tremendous feat of endurance.

'Who are you?' asked Markov.

It was a tight squeeze inside. Maksim and Nick were standing by the entrance, unable to fit inside. Steve could feel the flickers of warmth from the stove, and took a moment for the heat to warm him up before replying.

'Never mind who we are,' he said briskly.

'A man has a right to know who he is speaking to.'

Steve and Bruce glanced at one another.

'We're a British private military corporation called Dudley Emergency Forces,' said Bruce finally. 'Like Steve says, we were sent here by Kolodin to find the black box.'

'Mercenaries,' said Markov. There was a sardonic twist to his tone. 'So you really have been sent to kill me.'

'We're not killing anyone, and certainly not until we know what happened.'

'What did Kolodin tell you?'

'He thinks someone tried to murder you,' answered Steve. 'And from what we saw on that plane, I reckon he was right.'

Markov looked at his bodyguard Tyutin, smiled, then looked back at Bruce and Steve. 'There's no mystery about who wanted me dead. It was Kolodin.'

Steve looked straight into the man's eyes. They were blue, but dark, close to black. I wouldn't want to face you over a poker table, mate, he thought to himself. There's no way of telling what you're thinking.

'Kolodin?' said Maya. The shock was evident in the tone of her voice. 'But he sent us to investigate why the plane came down. He wants to find out who made an attempt on your life in case they come after him next.'

There was a murmur of agreement from the rest of the unit. Markov might believe it was Kolodin who'd bought down the plane, but there was no reason for the rest of them to.

Markov simply shrugged. 'I can prove it,' he growled.

'Go on then,' said Ollie. 'We're all ears.'

At the back of the shelter was a stack of kit. Blankets and food retrieved from the plane in the hours after it crash-landed.

Markov pulled aside a pair of blankets and retrieved a rectangular object measuring six inches by twelve, with what looked like a circular drum attached.

This was the object they'd risked their lives for. The black box.

'It's sodding orange,' said Nick.

Markov smiled. 'This is a cockpit voice recorder, made by the American electronics manufacturer Honeywell. As your friend has noticed, despite its name, it is indeed orange. You'll find one on every commercial aircraft. It records the audio from the cockpit and digital information for the entire plane, on a continuous loop, so that it always has the last thirty minutes of data stored on it.' He tapped the side of the device.

'These things are tough,' he continued. 'It can survive an impact of 3,400G. One G is the force exerted by the earth's gravity, so that is a hell of a bang. It will endure crushing by a 5,000-pound weight. It can survive a fire temperature of 1,100 degrees centigrade for thirty minutes, and you can chuck it 20,000 feet underwater without doing it any damage at all. You still have all the data safely stored.' He looked around the men in front of him. 'Would you like to hear what the pilots were saying when the plane came down?'

Steve nodded. 'Why not?' he replied. 'It might clear a few things up.'

'It certainly will,' answered Markov.

The box didn't have any speakers, but Tyutin had hooked it up to his iPod. One of the pilots was Russian, and the other Czech, but they talked in English, the universal language of the skies. Their pronunciation was crisp, and the recording quality was excellent. You could hear every word as clearly as if you were sitting in the cockpit.

There was silence as the playback started.

It's not every day you get to listen in on a plane crash, thought Steve. It's almost worth trekking through this hellhole for.

The recording opened with an innocent discussion about the weather. The pilots were examining reports of some possible turbulence up ahead, the way anyone in their trade might. There was indeed a bad storm raging that night, and the A319 was getting knocked about a bit, but it was nothing that experienced pilots wouldn't have seen a hundred times before. It was certainly nothing to worry them.

Markov fast-forwarded. It was on fifteen minutes that the conversation turned serious.

'Get ready to release the gas,' said Yuri Vasin, the pilot.

There was a shuffling noise as the co-pilot, a man called Karel Bilek, prepared some canisters. 'When shall I shall switch it on?' he asked.

'Wait until we've found somewhere to land,' answered Vasin.

There were a few minutes of silence, interspersed only by the background noise of the engines. Steve imagined the plane was dropping out of the sky. It would have been dark, and the A319 would have been swaying in the wind, but the headlamps would give the pilots an idea of the terrain they were flying over, and allow them to start searching for a strip of ice flat enough to land on.

'We're changing altitude to avoid some turbulence up ahead,' announced Yasin over the intercom.

A ruse, thought Steve. He doesn't want anyone asking questions about why the plane is dropping out of the sky.

'Release the gas,' said Yasin.

His voice was soft, as if he was nervous of being overheard. But the Honeywell had picked up the words with perfect clarity. 'On one minute, send out a regular signal,' continued Yasin. 'Make it appear that everything is fine with the flight. Then kill the radio.'

A minute ticked by.

There was complete silence as the men listened intently to the recording.

'It's done,' said Bilek. 'No one will ever hear from this plane again.'

There was another silence between the two men that ticked through a minute.

'I've found a place to land,' said Yasin. 'It's going to be rough, but it's nothing we haven't run through a hundred times on the simulators. We'll get this plane down and we'll take the black box with us so there isn't any evidence of what happened to it. The plane will be buried in snow soon enough. With a bit of luck, they'll never find it.'

'How far are we from Kolodin's yacht?' asked Bilek.

The killer question, thought Steve. By asking it, the co-pilot had revealed exactly who they were working for. It was all anyone would need to prosecute the man for at least twenty murders.

'No more than a five-mile walk,' said Yasin. 'We've got all the equipment we need.'

'This is the Arctic, it's going to be rough.'

'Kolodin is paying us ten million dollars each to bring this plane down,' answered Yasin. 'Think of it as two million a mile. That should make it easier.'

'It certainly will.'

'What are you going to do with the money?'

'I haven't decided.'

'I'm going to disappear to Brazil for a few years,' said Yasin, with a rough chuckle. 'I'll sit on the beach in the sunshine drinking beer and watch the girls walk past in their bikinis,'

'Are all Russians like that, Maksie?' said Steve.

'All the good ones.'

'We're coming down,' said Yasin on the tape. 'Brace yourself.'

There was a crashing sound, and a stream of swear words in Russian and Czech. It sounded as if the pilots were getting bounced around as the plane skidded across the ice. But they'd handle a few bruises for ten million.

The swearing on the tape was suddenly interrupted.

A door was opening.

There was a scuffle.

Then a pair of shots.

Markov leant across and switched off the box.

'And that was where I came in,' he said, looking up at the men in front of him. 'I guessed what was happening as soon as the gas started coming through. My guard here and I bludgeoned our way past the stewardesses and up to the cockpit. We had some gas masks in my private cabin and we used those to keep ourselves alive until the pilots had landed the plane . . . and then we shot them.'

All the men were silent. They were still trying to take in what they had just heard.

'So you see why Kolodin wants that black box so badly he sent you out here to find it, and no doubt paid you a fortune for your trouble,' said Markov finally. 'The pilots never showed up for the rendezvous at his yacht. He knew that I might well be out here somewhere, or I might be dead. But it doesn't make much difference. Because if the black box was ever discovered, it would prove conclusively that he was a murderer.' He stopped and looked straight into Steve's eyes. 'You've been sent out here to cover up a crime.'

Forty-Two

MAYA STEPPED FORWARD. SHE WAS looking straight at Markov, an expression of anger etched into the features of her face. But she wasn't angry with him, realised Steve. She was angry with herself. Kolodin had deceived all of them. But her most of all.

'One question,' she said. 'Why? A feud between Russian oligarchs? A business deal that went wrong?'

Markov shook his head.

'This,' he answered. He held up an eight mega-bit SanDisk memory stick.

'What the hell's on it?' demanded Steve.

'Data,' replied Markov. 'Probably the most valuable piece of data in the world right now.'

Tyutin had brewed up some water on the small stove, and mixed in some stock cubes. The two men had retrieved some cups from the plane when they fled. They were only five of them, but by sharing them, they could make them go round. Each one was made of delicate china, suitable for a luxury private jet, but completely out of place in the middle of the Arctic. Still, the beef stock tasted good, hot and salty. Each man drank it down gratefully and refilled their cups from the big pot the bodyguard had steaming away on the small fuel-powered stove.

'I don't know how much you know about the Arctic, and its resources,' continued Markov, taking a thoughtful sip of his own drink.

'We know there's a lot of oil under the polar ice cap,' said Ian.

'The last great reserve of oil to be exploited anywhere in the world,' chipped in Maksim.

Markov nodded. 'I'm an oilman myself, and it's all true, what they say. Nobody has done any more than test drilling so far, but . . .' He tapped his foot on the ice sheet underneath them. 'There's a lot of oil down there. Hundreds of billions of barrels of the stuff just waiting to be pumped up.'

'But who does it belong to?' said Ian. 'That's the question, isn't it?'

'Absolutely,' said Markov. 'The Russian government has been laying claim to the Arctic for years. It is still classified as neutral territory, however. The validity of the Russian claim depends on a piece of land called the Lomonosov Ridge.'

'What the hell is that?' asked Ollie.

'It's a stretch of land that rises up far enough from the seabed of the Arctic Ocean to be considered part of Russia,' said Markov. 'It's under the sea, where it stretches out into the Arctic Ocean. Under international law, Russia's claim depends on how high the ridge is.'

'What difference does that make?' questioned Nick.

'If the ridge is high enough, it counts as part of the Russian state. The height determines the border. If Russia can prove it

Matt Lynn

is high enough then it has a legal claim to half the Arctic, including where we are right now, and the North Pole itself. Billions and billions of barrels of oil will come under its direct control.'

'So why can't they just measure it?' asked Bruce.

'It's not that easy,' said Markov. 'It's underwater. And it stretches for eighteen hundred kilometres, all the way from the New Siberian islands in Russian territorial waters over to Ellesmere Island in Canadian waters. You need to spend months surveying with expensive submarines to establish precise average heights right along the ridge.

'In the last three months, the Russian government has claimed to have the proof they need. Their data has been submitted to the United Nations. It should be approved within the next few days. All that oil will fall under its control. And Kolodin's company will be awarded the concessions to exploit it. He's Moscow's man for the Arctic and always will be. Once this gets approved, he'll be the richest man in the world. Probably the richest man who ever lived.'

He paused, glancing from man to man, then holding up the memory stick.

'On this device is the data assembled by my own underwater surveying unit, at a cost of several million dollars to me personally,' he continued. 'It proves conclusively that the Lomonosov Ridge isn't as high as the Russians are claiming. They have systematically falsified all the data. I was flying to San Francisco to get my data independently verified by the world leaders in marine science at Berkeley University. And then I was planning to lodge it with the UN. Kolodin had to stop me. That's why he wanted the plane brought down. To kill me and destroy the data.'

Markov smiled softly to himself.

'You have to hand it to the bastard. It was the perfectly planned and executed crime. A plane crashes. Everyone dies. The plane itself is quickly buried in the ice, and so is the data. No one ever finds the black box, and so they never discover that it was anything other than mechanical failure.' His eyes were suddenly angry as he finished the sentence. 'But when the pilots didn't show up at the rendezvous point, he knew something had gone wrong. So he sent you men in to find the black box and cover up his crime.'

Forty-Three

MARKOV DRAINED THE REST OF the stock in his cup. The anger vanished from his eyes as quickly as it had erupted, and was replaced by a furrowed brow. This was a man up against formidable odds, thought Steve. A man with an enemy who'd downed a whole jet just to kill him, and then paid millions to cover up the evidence. An enemy who seemed to have the whole might of the Russian government on his side. But he wasn't discouraged or defeated. Instead, he'd spent a month up here in the most brutal climate in the world, fighting for survival.

It was impossible not to admire the strength of the man's character.

Markov looked at Steve sharply. 'What regiment were you?' he asked suddenly.

'SAS,' replied Steve.

'I know only a little of the British special forces,' said Markov. 'But I imagine it teaches its men a sense of right and wrong.' 'And you?' he said looking at Bruce.

'SAS.'

'And you?' he asked Ollie.

'Household Cavalry,' Ollie replied proudly.

'Ah, the Queen's own regiment.'

One by one, Markov went through the men in front of him. It was an impressive roll-call of military expertise. The Irish Guards. The Australian SASR. Commando Hubert. The Caracal Battalion. The Spetsnaz. Nick's time in the Territorials didn't count for much, and Ian's years as a bomb-maker for the IRA were hardly in the same league, but even so you'd be hard pushed to find so many fighting traditions in the same unit anywhere else in the world.

'The decision is yours, gentleman, but when you make it I ask only this,' said Markov finally. 'Make it with the traditions of your regiments in mind.'

Steve hadn't read up on the man's background, but if he'd been told that Markov had done a few years in the Russian Army before getting into the oil business, he wouldn't have been surprised. Markov seemed comfortable around soldiers. He knew how to talk to them, what tone to use, and what buttons to press, the same way Bruce did. And that only came with experience.

'You can work for that murderer Kolodin, and allow a Russian landgrab of the world's last great wilderness. Or you can fight along with me to keep the Arctic what it always was – a resource for the whole world to share.' He paused. 'So either shoot me right now or help me get this memory stick into the right hands. As I said, it's up to you. All I ask is that if you are going to shoot me, you do it now. I don't want to wait to die. And I don't want to be taken back to that bastard Kolodin alive.'

As he looked at the man's face, Steve could see a trace of

uncertainty in his eyes. He genuinely doesn't know whether we're going to kill him or not, he thought to himself. He's just delivered what might well be his last sentence, and no man can do that calmly.

Maya stepped forward. 'I'm with you,' she said, with a glance at the rest of the men.

The rest of unit remained steady, nobody moved.

'What's the matter with you?' she said, her tone suddenly furious. 'He's telling you the truth, can't you see that? Kolodin was using you to cover up a crime.'

'He used you for longer,' growled Henri.

'True enough,' snapped Maya. 'But at least I've got the guts to admit it and do something about it.'

'No one here is short of guts, thank you,' said Henri.

'Then show some,' said Maya defiantly.

'There's no need to argue,' said Bruce. 'Every man here has got a decision to make and he is entitled to do that on his own terms and in his own time.' He looked at Markov. 'If Kolodin was behind the crash, who's been out there for the last thirty hours trying to shoot our bollocks off?'

'The Spetsnaz,' interrupted Maksim. 'We already know that.'

'But why?' asked Bruce.

'Like I said, so long as this data doesn't get to the UN in the next few days, then Russia will get control of this territory. They've sent the soldiers up here to search for me, and to make sure no one else finds the wreck of the plane. They'll shoot at anyone who trespasses on to what they think is now their territory.' He looked at the men. 'So, are you men of honour or are you just mercenaries?'

'Actually, I'm just a mercenary,' said Ian. 'I come from a place where men fight for honour, and for religion as well, and I didn't think much of the results. I'll take the money, thank you very much.'

'All right,' said Markov. 'How much is Kolodin paying you?'

'Half a million a man,' said Ian.

Markov whistled to himself. 'I didn't realise I was so valuable dead. I might take that contract myself.'

He chuckled at his own joke, but no one else was laughing.

Ian held out his handgun, offering it to Markov. 'You can shoot yourself if you want to.'

The Russian shook his head.

'Once you delivered that black box, you'd have known too much. He couldn't take the chance you might have found some way of listening to what was on it. He'd have had you killed.'

'We're pretty useful in a scrap,' said Ollie.

'It doesn't make any difference. It might take a week, it might take a year. He'd have sent his assassins to pick you off one by one.' A sly smile suddenly creased the oligarch's face. 'But I'll tell you what. I'll match the bastard's fee. Get me out of here, and make sure this data gets to the UN on time, and there's half a million for each man. An instant transfer to any account you choose anywhere in the world.'

Another silence.

Finally Bruce stepped forward.

'Looks like the job just changed, lads,' he said firmly. 'We're switching horses. But at least the pay is the same.'

Steve took a step, joining him. 'Like I said in Kabul, boys, we're giving a bad bastard a malleting and we're getting well paid for it, and a man can't ask for much more out of a day's work than that.'

'I'm in,' said Ollie

'And so am I,' said Nick.

One by one, the men in the unit took a step across, a movement of less than a foot but one that indicated they were now working for Markov rather than Kolodin.

All except Maksim.

'Christ, mate, I've never known you miss out on a scrap,' said Steve.

The Russian remained mute, his eyes cast down.

'What's up, pal?' said Ollie.

'It's my own government and my own army I'm meant to be fighting against,' he said. 'The Spetsnaz. My own men.'

'I'm a Russian as well,' said Markov. 'What they're doing up here is murder and theft. A man's under no obligation to support that.'

Maksim remained silent, his eyes rooted to the ground.

Debate is not what Maksie does best, thought Steve. Shooting people and drinking vodka are his only real talents, and even those he takes too far. He's not the right man to engage in a political discussion.

'It's a fair point, mate,' said Steve, with a sideways glance at Markov. 'Whether the cause was right or wrong, I don't think I'd fancy getting into a fight with the Regiment; I don't think Ollie would want to start blasting away at the Blues and Royals, and I'm sure Dan wouldn't want to start turning his fire on the SASR. There are some things a man can't be expected to do, no matter what the circumstances. It would be like killing a part of yourself.'

'I can stay here,' said Maksim.

'You come along with us, pal,' said Ollie, 'and just leave the shooting to us. Nobody expects you to get into a scrap with your old pals.'

'Maksie sitting on the sidelines when there's a ruck going on?' said Dan. 'Now this I have to see.'

Forty-Four

'HOW MUCH KIT HAVE WE got?' said Bruce, quickly taking charge. 'And how much food and fuel?'

Gregor Tyutin ran through the materials they had salvaged from the plane. They'd brought the basic cold-weather survival kit stashed in the hold, but all it consisted of was four snow suits, a pack of flares, a portable stove, and a basic medical kit. Markov and his bodyguard had supplemented that by siphoning off three cans of jet fuel, and they'd managed to modify the stove to run on that, and they'd grabbed as much food as they could from the A319's in-flight supplies, but it was still a meagre haul. The two men had been out here for a month already and they'd run through most of what they'd managed to salvage from the plane. Two men might be able to survive on what they had for a couple more weeks. Twelve people would run through it in two days. Maybe even less.

'Remind me never to be on a plane that crash-lands in the Arctic,' said Steve, as he helped inspect the stash. 'This is sodding useless.'

'The survival kit on planes always is,' said Ian. 'It's just there for the health and safety monkeys. When a plane gets into trouble, either the pilot manages to make it to an airport, in which case everyone is OK, or else it crashes, and everyone is dead. No one ever actually uses the stuff.'

'We used it,' said Markov.

'Aye, but your plane was bought down deliberately,' said Bruce.

'The point is, we can't survive on this,' said Ollie. 'We won't last more than a couple of days. Not the way Nick eats.'

'Which reminds me, I'm starving,' said Nick. 'I feel like I haven't eaten for days.'

'Er, Nick, that's because you haven't,' said Dan.

'So what are we going to sodding do?' said Steve. 'We need to get back to civilisation, and as fast as possible.'

'We could go back to the plane and get more supplies,' said Henri.

'Like what?' said Maya. 'We didn't see any more food on board.'

'We could get some more jet fuel,' said Henri. 'There's food to catch out here. Seals. Polar bears . . .'

'I'm not taking on another sodding bear,' said Nick. 'I don't like them.'

'We have to get this data to the UN within the week,' said Markov. 'We couldn't move out by ourselves. But you can.'

'Then there's only one option,' said Ian.

All the men turned to look at him.

'We've still got four hours to get to Kolodin's yacht. It's an ice-breaker. It can take us anywhere we want to go.'

'It's heavily armed,' said Steve.

Ian just shrugged. 'So we take it,' he answered. 'What were

you expecting? A chopper to drop down out of the sky and whisk us off to the local Hilton?'

'I've worked on that yacht,' said Maya. 'There's more sophisticated defence equipment on it than a modern naval destroyer.'

'I think she's scared,' said Henri, a mocking tone in his voice.

'It's impregnable,' said Maya angrily.

'We're sodding Death Inc.,' said Nick. 'There's nothing we can't do.'

Steve admired the Welsh boy's spirits. No challenge ever daunted him. But there was a line between bravery and recklessness, and Nick hadn't figured out where it was yet. A real soldier kept himself on the right side of that divide, and Nick was still some way from learning that.

'How far are we from the yacht?' asked Steve, looking at Ian.

'Ten miles, and that's if we can walk in a straight line,' answered Ian. 'Which knowing what this sodding place is like isn't very likely.'

'We could be facing half the Spetsnaz on the way as well,' said David. 'We'll need to watch our backs every foot of the journey.'

'That means we have to cover two and half miles an hour while evading a far better equipped enemy,' said Henri. His face was drawn and his tone grim. 'In the Arctic, those kinds of speeds are unheard of for men on foot.' He glanced at Ollie. There was no hostility in the look. Merely an ugly reckoning of the odds. 'Particularly when one of them is an invalid.'

'You can leave me here, pal,' said Ollie, trying to sound cheerful. 'A bit of jet fuel and a couple of paperbacks to read and I'll be right as rain. Come and pick me up when the weather's improved.'

'No one is leaving anyone anywhere,' snapped David.

'Very heroic, old sausage,' said Ollie. 'But I know when I'm crocked. I'll just slow the whole unit down. Leave me here, and you've got a fighting chance of getting to the yacht and then coming back to collect me in a chopper in a couple of weeks when the storm has blown through.'

'He might be right,' said Ian. 'It could be the only way of giving everyone a fighting chance of getting out of here alive.' He looked at Ollie, and shrugged. 'Sorry, pal, but it's the truth.'

'We're not leaving anyone behind,' said Steve firmly. 'Think we can make it, Bruce?'

Bruce shook his head. 'I don't know,' he replied. He sounded worried, noted Steve. And that wasn't a tone he'd often heard in the man's voice before. 'I tell you what, though. If there were any other choices, I'd take them. Any at all. But I don't think there are. If we stay here, it's a just a question of whether we starve or freeze first, and anyway, we have to get our man back to civilisation. We can't radio for help, because we don't have the kit, and even if we could find it on the plane, it would bring the Russian Army straight on to us, and I don't think we can count on winning another scrap with those lads. So I reckon we should get our skates on and move out of here. The sooner we start, the sooner we'll get there.'

His eyes went from man to man. It was clear that none of them disagreed. They'd make a dash for the yacht. It was the only option left to them.

'I tell you what, lads,' said Dan. 'If we're going into a fight like that, we need some grub.'

'Fantastic,' said Nick. 'About time.'

'For Christ's sake, man,' interrupted Henri. 'We've only got four hours.'

'I thought you Frenchies liked your food,' said Nick.

'I've told you, we can't waste any time,' repeated Henri.

'No, Dan's right,' said Steve. 'We'll move faster if we have some energy inside us.' He looked at Tyutin. 'How quickly can you get that grub ready?'

'A few minutes,' answered the Russian bodyguard.

'Then crack on, mate,' said Steve. 'I've lost track of what time it is in this hellhole, but it's breakfast and lunch and supper all rolled into one.'

The man was fast, Steve had to grant him that. He was a big guy, six foot three, and weighed at least two hundred pounds, with a burly build, and thick working man's muscles around his forearms and legs, but he was nimble as well, with long fingers that worked quickly. He'd be formidable in a fight, reckoned Steve. It's lucky he's on our side.

Tyutin asked Maksim to help him, muttering a few words in Russian. The two men refilled the stove with jet fuel, stoking the machine so that it burned with a bright yellowy-blue flame. There was a pungent, diesel smell from the fire, but no one was going complain about that. It filled the shelter with a heat which, after the freezing temperatures they had grown used to, seemed unexpectedly fierce. Tyutin unpacked a row of pre-prepared meals, each one in an aluminium container, that they'd salvaged from the plane and buried in the snow to keep them frozen. He placed them on a metal frame and held one side while Maksim took the other, warming the food over the naked flame.

'We've got beef casserole or chicken pasta bake,' he said to the men, who were staring at him hungrily.

'Airline grub,' said Steve. 'Usually I'd pass, but right now I'm so sodding hungry, I reckon I might just eat it.'

'I can't decide,' said Nick. 'Maybe I'll take both.'

'I'll take three,' said Ian. 'And one of those little bottles of red wine, if you have any.'

'And some brandy from the duty-free as well, pal,' said Dan.

The smell of the food, a bubbling mix of chemicals and meat, made Steve painfully aware of just how hungry he was, and how much punishment his body had taken in the last thirty-six hours. Pounds had melted off him so fast, he reckoned he'd be able to find his bones through his skin, if only he dared open up his snow suit enough to take a look. As it was, he figured the polyester might be the only thing holding him together. There was dirty stubble across his face, grime in every fingernail, his socks were so sweaty they might well have stuck to his feet, and he had aches in places he didn't even know it was possible to feel pain. Some calories would be good, he reflected. Without them, I'm not sure we'd even make it across the ten miles that separate us from the yacht in a week, never mind four hours.

'Grub's up, boys,' said Maksim with a rough grin. He slapped down a tray of the ready-cooked meals.

Each man grabbed one, using either their fingers or tin spoons from their webbing to eat with. 'Nick can be the trolley dolly,' said Ollie, chuckling as he stuffed a huge portion of chicken pasta into his mouth. 'I reckon he'd look quite fetching in one of those tight blue uniforms. Almost as good as his mum.'

'Piss off,' muttered Nick.

'Maybe we could get an in-flight movie,' said Dan.

'Preferably with Keira Knightly and Angelina Jolie,' said Ollie.

'Or Catherine Zeta-Jones,' suggested David.

'And Alicia Silverstone,' said Dan.

'As well as Kristen Stewart,' said Ian. 'Even if she is a vampire.'

'Christ, lads, not this sodding larking around again,' snapped Steve. 'We've got ten miles to cover in less than four hours to get out of this crap hole.'

Dan and Ollie glanced at one another.

'What's with him?' said Dan.

'Seems to be losing his sense of priorities,' said Ollie. 'Maybe the cold's getting to him.'

Forty-Five

STEVE BOWED HIS HEAD, LETTING the snow blow straight past him. They had been walking for two hours now and the strain was starting to make itself felt in every muscle. His back ached, his legs hurt, his toes and fingers had lost just about all feeling and whether his face was still attached to his skull he neither knew nor cared. The ground had flattened out for the last few minutes, but for half an hour before that they'd been climbing up a steep incline, the sweat pouring off each man as they tried to keep up what in the Arctic amounted to a sprint.

'How much further?' asked Steve, turning back to look at Ian.

The Irishman was ten yards behind him. The entire convoy stretched for thirty yards, a bedraggled group of weary men, fighting through the snow and wind. The skies had darkened, threatening yet more heavy snow, and the visibility had dropped to just a few yards. Even with her torch on, it was impossible for Maya to see all the way up to Henri and Dan at the front of the procession.

'We've covered four miles,' said Ian.

Matt Lynn

'Christ,' muttered Steve. He checked his watch. It was just after two in the afternoon, local time. 'Less than two hours before that yacht leaves. Kolodin will have given us up for dead.'

'Aye, and he might well be feckin' right,' said Ian.

'Just keep your heads down and keep going,' shouted Bruce. 'We can make this.'

For the next few minutes, Steve could detect a quickening of the pace. The march was accelerating as each one dug deep into whatever reserves of strength remained within them. The whip had been cracked, and they were responding: each person knew that catching and overwhelming the yacht was their last hope of getting home alive, and there was nothing like the fear of death to make a man walk faster. But, like a knackered horse, there was only so much flogging you could do; if the strength wasn't there, you couldn't magic it out of nowhere. And as they faced yet another steep climb over rugged and broken ice, Steve could detect the pace starting to slow again.

From the hobbling man a few yards in front of him, a song suddenly started up.

'In the summer time,' started up Ollie in his wobbly, croaky baritone.

Steve joined in on the chorus, and both men sang together, completing the first section of the Mungo Jerry classic

Up front, Dan and Henri kicked off the second verse. Then, right from the back, Ian and Nick took up the next part of the song. And suddenly the whole unit was singing the final chorus, a riot of tired but determined voices breaking out through the snowstorm.

'I tell you what, sodding Mungo Jerry never sounded so

good,' said Ollie chuckling as he hobbled forward.

Even Markov was grinning. 'If we get out of here alive, I might see if I can hire the band to play it live for us,' he said.

'A couple more rounds of that, lads, and we'll practically be there,' shouted Steve.

And, right on cue, Ollie started up with the first verse again. Over the next half-hour, the unit completed the song five times, each pair of men taking a verse, before the whole unit joined in on the chorus.

'Little darlin',' kicked off Ollie, using a slightly strangulated Liverpool accent. 'Here comes the sun,' joined in the unit when that couplet had been completed.

Three renditions of the George Harrison number were followed by another couple of blasts of 'In the Summertime', and those two songs alone seemed to get them through another mile.

'Who can remember the words to "Summer Holiday"?' asked Dan when they had finished the third rendition.

'Or "Club Tropicana",' said David.

'Or "Summer Lovin' " from *Grease*,' said Henri.

'Or "Walking on Sunshine",' said Nick.

'I tell you what, the sodding Spetsnaz might shoot us just to shut us up if we start singing crap like that,' said Ian finally. 'And if they don't, I might finish you lot off myself.'

The unit marched on. The songs had got them through another three miles. There were three left to go. Steve checked his watch. There was less than an hour before the yacht left. Kolodin might stick around for an hour or so more. He wanted that black box; how badly they now knew precisely. He'd possibly give them a bit of leeway on the deadline. But they couldn't count on more than an hour. If they couldn't get there soon, their last chance of survival was gone.

Steve brushed some of the snow and ice out of his face. The ice forming on his stubble was scratchy and rough, and it felt like the skin had flaked straight off, exposing the bone itself to the biting winds hurling into them from the north. The ground was rising again, presenting them with yet another hill to climb. All around them, the oppressive darkness was closing in; as they got closer to the edge of the ice shelf, what little light struggled across the sky appeared to vanish, and at times Steve could hardly see more than a few feet ahead. Ollie had switched places, and was now resting on Steve and Bruce's shoulders, hobbling forward, a grimace on his face. This is rough enough for me, thought Steve bitterly, but it must be even worse for that poor sod. Nobody had more ox-like stamina than Ollie, but he could sense even his willpower was starting to be sapped by the brutal hostility of the land they were marching through.

'Another mile,' announced Ian from the back of the convoy as the clock ticked towards three forty. 'We're getting close.'

'When we get back to civilisation, lads, I'm taking everyone for the hottest curry I can find,' said Bruce.

'There's a place in Swansea called the Raj that does a sodding spicy madras,' said Nick. 'I've been there after a few beers, and I practically fell over, the food was so hot.'

'A vindaloo, that's what I feel like right now,' said David. 'With a big helping of that red-hot chutney on the side.'

'And a bottle of Cobra,' chortled Maksim. 'Don't forget about that.'

'What we really need to do is get up to Brick Lane and order a phall,' said Steve.

'What the hell's that?' asked Nick.

'The hottest curry ever made, that's what. It's made from the Habanero chilli, and that bastard is only a couple of notches down on the burn-your-throat scale than the stuff the American police use to make pepper spray. Any hotter and it would count as ammunition rather than food.'

'I want two,' said Henri.

'The place I went, the waiters give you a free beer and a certificate if you actually managed to finish the sod.'

'I'm already making a booking,' chortled Maksim.

Steve laughed to himself. The wind had changed direction and was sweeping in from the east, just about vertical with the ground, and picking up a blizzard of snow and ice that hurtled straight into them. They were less than a mile away. A thousand yards or so, assuming Ian's calculations were correct. But it was impossible to see any sign of the sea. It was too dark for that. Maybe when they got close enough they'd see the lights from the ship, thought Steve. Until then they had nothing except the compass and their determination to guide them forward.

Suddenly a noise shattered through the storm.

Henri and Dan had already dropped to the ground before Steve realised what it was.

Gunfire. The unmistakable rumble of a machine gun bursting into life.

Steve flung himself into the snow. A bullet had smashed into the ground just two feet to his left, kicking up a chunk of ice.

'Get your sodding torches off,' snapped Bruce. 'If they can't see you they can't hit you.'

In an instant, the entire unit was lying flat on the ground, formed into a circle with Markov and his bodyguard at its centre.

'Where the hell are they?' hissed Steve.

With his StG in his hand, he was scanning the territory ahead, but he couldn't see anything he could fire at. And until he could, there was no point in wasting bullets.

'Up on that glacier,' said Dan, pointing straight ahead. 'Looking straight down on us.'

Forty-Six

THE UNIT SHUFFLED FIFTEEN YARDS to their left, moving in a tight circle. They were heading towards a boulder of ice that rose eight feet out of the ground and was at least five feet wide. Another burst of machine-gun fire raked across the ground in front of them as they ran, narrowly missing its targets, and as Steve threw himself behind the frozen wall, his heart was thumping in his chest.

'Christ,' he muttered to himself. We're never getting out of this hellhole. Not now.

Shafts of green tracer fire suddenly lit up the sky. The rounds momentarily illuminated the ground in front of them, making it possible to get an idea of the enemy they were facing. Steve's eyes moved from left to right, using the light to scope out the challenge ahead of them.

Only one problem, he realised grimly. We're stuffed.

Fifty yards ahead of them was a high glacier, rising at least seventy feet into the air like a cliff, and stretching as far as the eye could see in each direction. The Spetsnaz had taken up a position on its summit, digging themselves in with machine guns. They might well have RPGs up there as well, thought

Steve. Maybe some armoured vehicles too. Enough to slaughter anyone who comes close.

'They've guessed we're heading for the yacht, and they're blocking us off,' said Bruce.

'Can we march round it?' asked Ian.

'No time,' said Steve. 'It could take hours.'

There was a silence. The men looked at one another, their expressions uncomfortable. 'We'll have to fight the bastards then,' said Steve finally.

There was hesitation in his voice. Each of them could see their enemy was well dug in on what amounted to a cliff top, with plenty of firepower. There was no more formidable military challenge. Castles had been built on cliffs for a couple of thousand years for good reason. They were virtually impregnable.

'So what do you reckon, lads?' said Bruce. 'Scale it?'

'We'll get sodding slaughtered,' growled Ollie.

'They'll see us coming, and fire straight into us,' said Ian.

'So?' Bruce left the question hanging in the silence.

'We could come round from behind,' said Nick.

'If we could get over that sodding glacier without getting shot, we could just make for the bloody yacht,' said Steve.

'All right, all right,' said Nick tetchily.

Another silence.

A burst of tracer fire arced across the sky, briefly lighting up the harsh landscape. The rounds landed a few feet short of their position. But they were getting closer. Once they had a precise range, figured Steve, they'd bring in the heavier guns. Cannons, RPGs, perhaps even an attack chopper if they had one. And then we'll all be saying goodnight. Forever.

'We can blow them up,' said Maya.

All the men turned to look at her.

'With what,' said Ian. 'Feckin' firecrackers?'

'It's ice,' snapped Maya. 'We picked up some TNT from the Nazi shelter. Crawl up to the base of that glacier, hack a hole into it, and plant the explosive inside. When you blow it, the ice will break up and collapse. Anyone on top of it will get killed when it comes down.'

'I think I preferred Nick's idea,' said David.

'No, she's on to something,' said Ian. 'Ice breaks up very easily. If you were a miner, you could blow open a cliff that way if you had enough explosive. Ice can handle much less force than rock. A few sticks might just do it.'

'OK, let's give it a go,' said Bruce. 'Steve, Maksim and Ian, you go up and lay the charges. The rest of us will cover you.'

'I thought Maksie wasn't doing any fighting,' said David.

'He's the strongest man here, and it's going to take muscle to dig into that ice,' said Bruce. He looked towards the Russian. 'You OK with that?'

Maksim nodded. 'So long as I'm not shooting at my old comrades, I've no complaints.'

'Good man.'

Steve hesitated for a second. The glacier was fifty yards in front of them, across flat ground. The snow was lying fresh across its surface, and the harsh wind blowing over the Arctic was piling up fresh drifts all the time. But the path was clear enough. So long as they weren't spotted, there was a chance it might work.

'Sodding go, man,' growled Bruce.

Steve glanced back at Ian and Maksim, then lay down on the

ground. He started to crawl forward, using his elbows and knees for leverage. The snow was bitterly cold. His suit was protecting him from the worst of the freezing temperatures, but when you were face down in the stuff, it was impossible to remain completely dry. His face was colder than he'd ever imagined possible, and the damp was starting to seep into his socks and mulaks. If he couldn't clean his feet soon, and get them dry again, he reckoned he'd lose a couple of toes to frostbite. And that was the best-case scenario. It would be easy to lose a whole foot, a concept Steve found hard to contemplate. Dying was one thing. It was quick and easy. But life as a cripple? Steve didn't reckon he could handle that.

He paused halfway. The glacier was looming straight ahead of them, and even in the near total darkness of the Arctic winter it cast a shadow over the ground as it blocked out what minimal light there was from the stars above the clouds. Steve looked back. Ian and Maksim were just a few yards behind, pushing forward with relentless energy. So far they didn't seem to have been heard or spotted. But one false sound, Steve reminded himself as he started crawling again, and a hailstorm of bullets will come flying into our backs.

'Here,' hissed Steve.

He'd completed the last twenty-five yards and was now close up against the glacier. All three men had snow shovels that could double up as rough pickaxes, and Ian had already prepped the TNT and a simple two-minute detonator. They started their work in silence, aware that it was too dangerous to speak. Even with the storm raging around them, in this wilderness a human voice could carry a long way, and the merest sound could alert the men above to their position.

Ian was no miner, but he knew plenty about explosives, and he'd figured out what they needed to do. They'd dig three tunnels into the ice, each six yards from each other. The deeper into the glacier they could get, the more impact the shock wave from the explosion would have, but they had to balance that against the amount of time available. Five minutes was the maximum Ian reckoned they could afford to risk. Once they blew the TNT, the three blasts should send a fissure right through the centre of the glacier, cracking it open.

'That's guaranteed, is it, mate?' asked Steve quietly. 'Do I get a refund if it doesn't work.'

'Nothing's guaranteed in warfare,' answered Ian curtly. 'You should know that by now.'

Steve started hacking into the ice. He drew back the shovel, and slammed it into the glacier, twisted it as hard as he could, then pulled it back. It might not have the strength of rock, he reflected bitterly, but it certainly felt like it. The first couple of times the shovel just bounced off it, but once Steve got the hang of the angle to attack it from, his rate of progress increased. He was soon swinging the shovel in regular strikes, cracking open the ice, then using his gloved hands to scramble away the broken chunks. It was harsh work, and his back was aching by the end of the first minute, but he was getting there.

'That'll do, pal,' whispered Ian behind him.

Steve jerked round. The soft, low voice coming out of the darkness sounded menacing and every instinct was telling him to swing out with the shovel before he realised it was Ian and steadied himself.

'It's deep enough,' continued Ian. 'We can't risk staying out here any longer.'

Steve remained silent while Ian crawled inside, cursed softly a couple of times, then slotted the sticks of TNT into place. 'It's set,' he said as he emerged from the tunnel. 'When I give the signal, flick the timer, then we've got two minutes to get our arses out of here before the whole glacier comes crashing down on our heads.'

Even before Ian had finished speaking, he'd started crawling back to his own tunnel, then to Maksim's. The explosives set, the Irishman waved down the line. One by one, each man set the timer on the fuse. As they did so, there was a sudden roar directly above them. Instinctively, Steve threw himself to the ground. Up above, he could hear rather than see an RPG whistling through the cold air. He covered his face, waiting for the inevitable explosion. It landed yards short of where the rest of the unit was taking shelter.

'Detonate, detonate,' yelled Ian.

With the din of the explosion still rattling across the plateau, Ian was confident that he wouldn't be heard by the soldiers stationed directly above them. Steve gritted his teeth, slipped inside the tunnel, switched the simple detonator, then scurried back on to the ice. Another RPG had landed straight ahead of them. A ball of flame burst into the air, and splinters of ice flew savagely in every direction. Steve could hear the rattle of gunfire as the men hiding behind the glacier retaliated with their StGs. But it was no more than token resistance, designed to remind the men confronting them there was a fight on rather than inflict any serious damage on the enemy.

At this distance, uphill, outgunned, there was nothing they could do except hunker down and hope something turned up.

Like us, thought Steve grimly. I hope to hell Maya's right about bringing down this sodding glacier. Because if this doesn't work, there's no way we're escaping this.

Steve ran towards Maksim and Ian. 'We're getting the fuck out of here,' he growled.

'Where?' said Ian desperately.

The fuses were already detonated. The clock was ticking down relentlessly. Steve reckoned they'd already used up twenty seconds, and that meant they had only a hundred left. He had no idea how much damage a collapsing glacier caused, or over how wide an area. He'd never seen one come down. But he reckoned it would be a hell of a thump and didn't want to be anywhere nearby when it kicked off.

'If we head back to the unit, those sodding RPGs are going to be falling on our head,' said Maksim.

'Head right, then steer back into the plateau to rejoin the rest of the lads,' said Steve.

The three men started to move out. They were running as hard as they could, first along the edge of the glacier, then out into the open ground fifty yards on from where they had planted their explosives. The snow was thick and fresh, with more falling all the time, and not for the first time Steve found himself cursing the impossibility of running through it. The seconds were ticking away, less than sixty remaining as they steered out into the plateau and away from the glacier. 'Shit,' muttered Steve to himself.

'*Ostanovit!*' barked a voice in the darkness.

Steve didn't know what the word meant but the thick, rough accent was Russian.

Three men were looming up out of the darkness. Big guys,

swathed in white snow suits, but with the unmistakable black gunmetal of an AK-74 strapped to their chests.

Maksim opened up on his StG.

Rival bursts of gunfire split through the snowstorm, munitions flying in every direction. Chaos, noted Steve, in one of the rare moments of calm reflection that sometimes descended upon him as a firefight kicked off. Brutal and dangerous, a ruck of uncoordinated crossfire in which a man could easily get himself killed. He slotted the Nazi rifle into his hands, and pressed his finger into the trigger. He was still getting used to the weight and feel of the antique weapon. He reckoned the soldiers were ten yards in front of them, firing hard into the darkness. Maksim and Ian had dropped to the ground, putting down a barrage of fire that would at least make the opposition pause for thought. Further ahead, another two RPGs had landed close to the rest of the unit, sending smoke and fire straight up into the black night sky. Steve squeezed the trigger.

Nothing.

A jam.

'Shit,' he muttered out loud.

There was a roar of anger a few yards ahead. Either Maksim or Ian had found their target, drawing first blood.

One scream, then another.

The bullets were thumping into the opposition, shredding their ranks.

Then Steve could feel a hand gripping his face. It clamped down hard on his throat, and even through his thick snow suit he could feel a handgun jabbing into his back. 'Drop your weapon, pig,' hissed a voice in Steve's ear.

Steve slammed the back of his elbow hard into the man's

chest. He was hoping to knock him off balance. Create a split-second of confusion, he told himself, and maybe he could turn the tables on his attacker. But the soldier had anticipated the move, readied himself for it, and absorbed the blow as easily as he withstood the snow and wind constantly hurtling through the Arctic.

'Do that again and you die, bastard.'

The soldier was spitting into Steve's ear. His accent was a rough Russian, something like Maksim's after a hard night's drinking. But there was no mistaking the brutal strength in it. Nor that the promise would be made good if Steve didn't do precisely what the man told him to.

The man's left hand slammed down on the StG, knocking it clean from Steve's hand. He yanked back hard, straining the muscles in Steve's throat, dragging him backwards.

Christ, thought Steve desperately. He's dragging me towards the glacier. He's got no idea it's about to blow.

Steve looked feverishly forward. Maksim and Ian were still laying down a murderous barrage of fire from their StGs. On automatic, the German weapon was still a match for any of its more modern imitators, and the bullets were flying across the ground with lethal ferocity.

Steve could see Ian start to stand up, and aim his weapon using the metal sights: a sure sign that the two men were no longer simply returning fire but had gained the upper hand in the firefight, and were concentrating on finishing off the men opposing them while they could.

But Steve was still being dragged backwards.

And there were only seconds remaining until the tubes of TNT they had planted at the base of the glacier detonated.

Forty-Seven

'JUST KEEP MOVING, PIG,' HISSED the Russian, still gripping Steve's throat.

The man smelt of sweat and gunpowder. He was dragging Steve backwards all the time, the gun pressed hard into his back. Up ahead, he could see Ian and Maksim start to run forward. He was losing sight of them through the darknes, and would have cried out for help if he could, but the man's hand was still clamped hard over his mouth, making it impossible to shout loudly enough to be heard over either the gunfire or the raging snowstorm.

'Shit,' muttered Steve silently. I'm losing them.

With a sinking feeling close to his heart, Steve realised he was done for. But then he saw Ian turning round, and even through the darkness he felt certain their eyes met.

Thirty yards ahead, Maksim loosed off the remaining bullets in his StG. He quickly snapped a fresh mag into the chamber, and prepared to fire. But there was no longer any need. The three men were already dead, the blood staining the snow around them crimson, and the falling snow already starting to conceal them.

He looked around. 'Where the fuck is Steve?'

Ian pointed behind him. 'They've caught him.'

Maksim immediately began marching out into the snow.

Ian caught his right arm. 'The TNT,' he started. 'It's going to blow.'

'He's our mate,' growled Maksim.

'Christ, man, the glacier's about to feckin' come down,' snapped Ian. 'A couple of million tons of ice are going to be collapsing on the bastard.'

Maksim shook Ian off his arm angrily. 'I said, he's our mate.'

Ian's eyes started to narrow. There was a coldness to his face, and it wasn't the result of the freezing temperature alone. 'That doesn't mean we throw our lives away for him. Those aren't the rules.'

Maksim ignored him, marching towards the soldier and Steve. 'They're *my* rules.'

Up ahead, Steve was struggling to breathe. The cord of his snow suit had snagged in the soldier's hand and was tugging tight into the skin just below his throat. Then he heard a sound. It was muffled, like an exhaust backfiring inside a garage. Tiny puffs of sound, nothing more. He felt the soldier hesitate as he looked around anxiously. Steve lashed out, hoping to use the moment to break free, but the man was as strong as an ox and as well-trained as anyone Steve had encountered in the Regiment, and it was going to take more than that to make him lose concentration.

'Behave, pig,' the Russian grunted, smashing the barrel of his gun hard into the side of Steve's head and making him wince with pain.

Then a silence.

Steve's heart sank.

Maybe it hasn't worked, he thought grimly. The TNT might detonate inside the ice with about as much impact as a piece of spit in a snowstorm. But before the thought had even finished rattling through his mind, he heard a creaking sound. It was gentle at first, like an old piece of furniture being pushed across a wooden floor. Then it grew louder, like the rumble of an approaching storm. Steve couldn't look round, not without risking getting shot in the back, so he couldn't see what was happening. But he could hear it all right: the ominous sound of thousands of tons of ice on the move.

'*Govno*,' shouted the soldier.

Steve didn't know much Russian but he'd picked up the word for 'shit' from Maksim's constant swearing.

'That about sums it up, pal,' he said sourly.

'What's happening?' asked the soldier.

The ground beneath them was starting to shake. Steve could feel the vibrations as the pressure within the ice plate built up. Behind him, he could hear a ripping noise, as splinters of ice started to break away from the main glacier.

'We're both about to die,' said Steve.

There was a chipper note in his voice that he calculated would rattle his opponent. He could sense that the man's grip on his neck was momentarily loosening as he glanced around him, trying to work out what the hell was happening. Steve could feel the nervousness in the man's fingers, but he was too well-trained to allow it to turn into an opportunity for his prisoner to escape. It's not just Maksie, thought Steve despairingly. It's the whole sodding Spetsnaz. None of the mad bastards care about what happens to their lives.

'You're the only pig who's dying,' grunted the soldier.

'You're entitled to your view, pal,' said Steve, his voice tightening. 'I reckon we'll be finishing this debate in hell.'

The soldier pushed Steve down on to his knees. He was yanking on his neck with his left hand, while pressing the barrel of his AK-74 into the back of his head. Steve knew at once what was happening. The Russian was planning to execute him, then make his escape.

'Christ,' he muttered to himself. I should never have set foot in this hellhole.

'Say your prayers, pig.'

'Say yours,' spat Steve.

Out of the swirling snow ahead of them, Maksim emerged holding his StG straight out in front of him. The man was covered in layers of snow, and there was ice hanging from the stubble on his face. For the first time Steve had a sense of how terrifying each man in the unit had become in the last forty-eight hours. Ghostly, ice-laden creatures, more like animals than men.

'Drop the weapon,' he barked.

Maksim glanced at Steve, then up into the eyes of the soldier. He realised at once the man was Spetsnaz, and repeated the command in Russian. The soldier was looking back at him coldly, his gun still tightly pressed to the back of Steve's head.

'You're a Russian?' he said in his own language.

Maksim ignored the question. It was no longer of any interest to him. 'Drop your weapon,' he snarled.

'You're Spetsnaz, aren't you?' continued the soldier. 'No one else could survive out here.'

Steve was struggling to follow the conversation. His Russian was virtually non-existent, Maksim's swear words aside, but he could pick up much of the gist just from the tone and facial expressions. And he knew the soldier had just questioned Maksim's loyalties. A judgement was about to be made, he sensed. One on which his life would depend.

'You're on the wrong side,' barked the soldier.

Maksim was thinking. Steve could see it in his eyes. Behind the frozen, steely mask, his brain was making a furious calculation. A soldier owed loyalties to his regiment, Steve was well aware of that. There were ties that neither time nor distance could sever. Your regiment made you who you were, and you could no more turn on it than you could your own parents. But there were also ties to the men you fought alongside; in combat, when lives were constantly in the balance, men learnt to rely on each other completely. That's the choice Maksim is wrestling with, reflected Steve. And if I'm being honest, it's one none of us would want to have to make. Except I know which way I want him to jump. I only get one life, and I'm not planning on finishing it here.

'You're breaching the trust that was placed in you as a soldier,' growled the Russian.

'For Christ's sake, man . . .' Steve hissed, looking straight up at Maksim.

The flicker of doubt that had flashed across his face suddenly disappeared. It was replaced by an expression of implacable fierceness.

'Drop the weapon,' Maksim barked.

'This pig dies first,' yelled the soldier.

Steve flinched. Maksim was already raising his gun, ready to shoot, but he was no marksman, not like Nick. Unstoppable aggression was his only real talent, and a battle like this required skill, not just force and anger.

Behind him, there was another crash. Steve's eyes swivelled round. Thirty yards behind them, the glacier had cracked, falling in on itself. There was suddenly a barrage of sound as the ice crashed downwards. The ground they were standing on bucked up, as if they were caught in the centre of an earthquake, throwing all three men off their balance. A wall of seawater rose up into the sky, then collapsed again, sending an avalanche of black, cold slush skidding out across the plateau. The Russian fired once, but the tremendous force of the ice plate splitting bucked him three feet into the air, knocking the gun away from Steve's head, and sending the shot harmlessly into the clouds above them. Maksim had already opened up on his StG. The ground he was standing on was shaking and breaking up, but the man had a rock-like, stubborn stability, and he kept firing, the bullets smashing into the body of his opponent as he flew upwards. Steve dived, and lunged forward, narrowly avoiding getting hit by the Russian as he fell back to the ground, blood pouring out of the multiple wounds that Maksim's gunfire had punched into his body.

'Run like fuck,' shouted Steve.

He picked himself up off the ground, ignoring the way the ice was splintering all around him. The two men started to sprint as hard as they could through the thick snow. And behind them, they could hear the screams of the men perched on top of the glacier, as it finally crashed to the ground, plunging them to an icy, painful death.

Forty-Eight

STEVE GLANCED ACROSS AT MAKSIM. He was kneeling over, panting for breath. The sea had already gobbled up the massive block of ice, drawing it down into its depths, and sending a wave of black water splashing out across the plateau. But the Arctic was a constantly changing landscape, Steve noted, moving and re-forming itself all the time, and within a few hours the freezing weather and relentlessly falling snow would have reshaped this area, and it would be as if nothing had happened. A dozen men could die and not leave the merest trace on this ground. The cold chews everything up, he noted grimly. And destroys it completely.

'Thanks, mate,' he said, patting Maksim hard on the back.

'It's OK,' grunted the Russian. He spat on the ground, taking huge gasps of the freezing cold air to refill his lungs.

'They were your own blokes,' said Steve.

Maksim just shrugged.

Steve sensed he didn't want to talk about it, and that was something he could understand. Maksim was a man of few words at the best of times. Whatever was rattling through his mind, it would stay there, at least until he was ready to talk to someone. Steve had been there plenty of times himself, and he knew what it was like. Some bloke intruding only made it worse. Even if he was a mate.

'I owe you a vodka.'

'The best,' said Maksim with a grin. 'Red Army vodka. First distilled in the nineteen twenties for the elite officers of the Russian Army . . .'

'It's yours.'

'And maybe some girls.'

'Blondes,' said Steve. 'Two of them, the best on the house. Maybe Swedish.'

'Then we're evens,' replied Maksim with a rough smile.

The two men started to walk forward. Behind them, the glacier was still shifting around, creaking as it did so, and the guns had fallen completely silent. Steve felt confident the Spetsnaz unit had been finished off. He felt sorry for the poor sods. Either they'd have been killed by a shard of collapsing ice, or else drowned in the frozen water. Neither was a pleasant death. But that was soldiering. They were all special forces guys. Not conscripts. They knew the risks they were taking when they signed the contract.

'What happened to Ian?' asked Steve, as the two men ploughed steadily forwards.

'He retreated,' said Maksim flatly. 'We could see you'd been captured but the glacier was about to collapse.'

'Bastard,' muttered Steve.

'Every man makes his own choices,' said Maksim. 'The odds didn't look good.'

'Even so . . .'

'Just leave it,' said Maksim. 'You're alive, aren't you?'

Up ahead, a torch was flashing through the gloomy darkness that had descended on the plateau after the firefight had abated.

'Here, here,' shouted Nick.

The Welsh boy was thirty yards ahead of them, guiding them home with his flashlight. The unit had retreated back a hundred yards, putting enough distance between themselves and the Spetsnaz unit to stay out of range of their RPG fire, and then the collapse of the glacier. Nick ran towards them, steering them back to where the rest of the unit was sheltering Markov behind a smaller glacier.

'Good work, boys,' said Bruce, slapping them both on the back.

'Sorry for the hold-up, lads,' said Steve. 'We had a bit of a run-in with some of Maksie's old muckers.' He described briefly what had happened, then shot an ugly glance towards Ian. 'It's sorted now,' he said. There was an unmistakable hint of menace in the tone of his voice.

Bruce glanced from man to man. He could tell at once what had happened. 'Drop it, lads,' he said. 'If there's any arguments to be had we can have them once we're back in civilisation.'

David looked around the rest of the unit. 'It's ten past four local time precisely,' he said. 'The yacht might already have buggered off. But if we're right in thinking our man might hang around for an hour or two to see if we found his black box then there's still a chance of catching the last bus out of this hellhole.' He grinned. 'So let's crack on, shall we?'

The unit reassembled itself, aware there wasn't a second to lose. Dan and Henri led the way, with the rest of the men following behind. Ollie was being helped to hobble forward by David and Nick. With the glacier down, the path was clear.

They took a smaller detour to get past the crevice that the explosion had opened up in the ice cap. But after that, it was a straight, flat run, mercifully free of any obstacles. Within minutes they could see the lights burning on the deck of the *Lizaveta*. 'Thank Christ for that,' said Dan, pointing to the yacht on the horizon. 'The bastard's still there. I tell you, I didn't fancy spending the winter out here eating seal-burgers. I'd miss the Ashes series, for one thing.'

'And the Champion's League,' said Steve.

'And the Six Nations,' said Nick.

'And the Ryder Cup,' said Bruce.

'Not to mention a new series of *Top Gear* on the telly,' said David.

'Looks like we're lucky to be getting home,' said Ollie. 'Tragedy averted.'

The unit stopped. They were still a couple of hundred yards short of the yacht, and in the darkness Steve didn't reckon anyone up on the deck would have seen them. The snow was still falling, and the wind still blowing, just as it had been when they'd stepped off the vessel forty long hours ago. But the script had changed, he reflected. They'd expected to be welcomed back as heroes if they found the black box. Now they were returning as enemies.

'There's just one problem,' said Bruce. 'We're going to have to take the boat by force.'

'Those security guards are first-rate,' said Maya.

There was no hint of nervousness in her voice, noted Steve. She was too brave for that. But there was a touch of wariness. She knew precisely what kind of men they were up against and she wasn't about to underestimate them. They'd fight fiercely, and to the death, and that would make them formidable opponents.

'It has a crew of twelve,' said David. 'And they're well-trained.'

'How many are military?' asked Ollie.

'All of them,' said Maya. 'At least six are former Spetsnaz. The rest are all former Russian Navy guys.'

'They any good, Maksie?' asked Steve.

'They drink like maniacs but they fight well enough.'

'We're a match for them,' said Nick defiantly.

'No question,' said Bruce. 'But that doesn't mean we don't approach the battle carefully.'

Steve glanced at Maya. 'You know it best. What are the weak points?'

Her brow creased. 'It has a radar shield all around it to detect any intruders. There are four machine guns inside the hull, two fore and two aft. You can't see them, but they'll emerge at the flick of a switch. All of the crew are armed, and have quick access to weapons if they need more. There are cameras in the hull to spot any underwater intruders. A safe room to hide in if you need to take shelter and call in reinforcements. A submarine for a fast escape. No expense has been spared to make that vessel as impregnable as possible.'

'Christ,' said David. 'Maybe we'd be better off walking home.'

'This is our only shot,' said Bruce. 'There must be a way.'

'Just don't suggest tunnelling in,' said Steve, glancing towards Nick.

'I wasn't sodding going to,' snapped Nick.

'Can we pick off some of the guards with sniper fire?' said Henri.

'It would take days,' said Ollie. 'And if we shoot anyone, the ship'll leave immediately.'

'Can we scale it?' asked Nick. 'Put some hooks up the side?'

'The radar will pick us up,' said Bruce. 'And those machine guns will open up straight on to us.'

For a moment, the unit fell silent. Maybe it is impregnable, thought Steve. Even for Death Inc., some tasks were impossible. Perhaps we'd be better off making a camp here, surviving as best we can, and waiting for the Arctic explorers to show up once the winter has ended. There's no point in throwing our lives away.

Then Markov stepped forward, glancing from man to man.

'Trojan horse,' he said, nodding towards Ollie.

'The bloke's from Dorset, actually, not ancient Greece,' said David. 'Though he does look a bit like a horse, I'll grant you that much.'

Bruce caught the Russian's logic and nodded. 'Ollie's too badly injured to take part in a fight. But Kolodin doesn't know that. And he doesn't know that we've got his pal Markov with us either.'

'Absolutely,' said Markov, a half-smile playing on his lips. 'I switch into Ollie's snow suit. He stays here, and my bodyguard Gregor will take care of him. With my face covered up, no one will be able to see me. The entire unit comes home, with the black box. Kolodin will welcome us aboard. Once we're inside, we can overpower the yacht, take control of it, and then come back and collect the two men left behind.'

'We're taking weapons?' asked Steve.

'Of course,' said Henri. 'Not the StGs. That would be too suspicious. We'll use the Walther PPs. We can tuck those inside our snow suits.'

'What if they search us?' asked Steve.

'No reason why they should,' said Henri.

'And if they do, we'll just kick off the scrap,' added Bruce. 'At least we'll be on board.'

Steve just nodded.

The plan was audacious and simple. It was dangerous, of course, with a slim chance of success, and a very large chance of getting killed. But they were used to those odds. And it certainly beat freezing to death during a long winter in the Artic.

'Then let's crack on,' he said simply.

'Looks like I'm sitting this one out,' said Ollie, getting uncertainly to his feet and starting to remove his snow suit. 'Best of luck, lads. And if anyone has a spare bottle of vodka on them, perhaps I could borrow it. It might be handy to while away the time.'

Forty-Nine

CE HAD THICKENED AROUND THE edges of the *Lizaveta* since they'd last seen it. There was some free flowing water around its prow, but it was going to take all the power of its ice-breaking equipment to smash its way back out to the open sea. Right now, the unit could walk to within a few yards of the yacht.

As they approached its side, Bruce, Henri and Dan all roared up at the top of their voices, and they were spotted quickly enough. A crewman waved from the deck, and seconds later a ramp had been laid down that would lead them straight up into the interior of the vessel.

'Everyone ready?' said Steve, glancing from man to man.

Each of them nodded in turn.

'Then let's do this,' he said crisply.

They started to walk. Maya led the way, with Bruce and Steve alongside her, and the rest of them following on behind in pairs. Like the animals heading into the ark, thought Steve with a wry smile. They'd slotted Markov right in the middle of the group where there was the least chance of him drawing any attention to himself. With the snow suit tied up around his neck and face, a balaclava pulled down tight, and with three weeks of stubble and grime covering his cheeks and mouth, he was hardly even recognisable as a human being, decided Steve. Identifying him as a specific individual was just about impossible.

Steve could feel a thump in his heart as he stepped across the ramp. They'd run through the possibilities, but they had no way of coming up with a precise plan for taking the yacht. All they could do was wait for the right opportunity, launch their strike, then pray that instinct and fighting spirit would somehow allow them to prevail.

But it was high-risk. No question about that. And we'll be lucky to come out of this alive, he thought.

'Welcome home,' said Kolodin.

The billionaire was standing right at the entrance, flanked by his chief bodyguard Igor Voytov and two other security men. He glanced down the line of men behind Maya, quickly counting their number, then nodding towards Voytov.

'All present and correct, sir,' said Maya crisply.

'And the . . .'

'The black box, sir?'

'Yes.'

Maya nodded towards Nick and David, who were holding a parcel wrapped up in a sheet of plastic between them.

'We've brought it home.'

There was just a hint of triumph in her voice, noted Steve. Enough to convince Kolodin she was pleased about her work, and to reassure him they hadn't listened to the recording.

'I knew it, I knew it,' said Kolodin. There was a broad grin across his face, and he was looking at Bruce and Steve. 'They told me you men were the best in the world, and I'm starting to believe it might be true.'

'We try,' said Steve modestly.

'Come upstairs,' said Kolodin. 'You must be tired and hungry and needing a hot bath, but first let me see the box, and hear about how you found the plane.'

Flanked by his security guards, he started to lead the unit up a single flight of stairs, towards the main conference room. Like the whole yacht, it was luxurious. There was a bank of computers at one side, a set of satellite TV screens at another, a long window with a magnificent view of the Arctic along the side wall, and a set of leather sofas in the centre of the room. The carpet was thick, the temperature was a pleasant twenty-two degrees, and there was fresh fruit in a bowl on the coffee table.

'We could be just in time for the late kick-off in the Liverpool–Everton game,' said Nick, walking towards the bank of TV screens. 'Have you got Sky?'

'You've been through enough, mate, without watching the forward fall over his own bootlaces,' chuckled Steve. 'Or a defender getting himself sent off.'

'It's better than watching sodding Chelsea,' growled Nick.

'Later, later,' said Kolodin impatiently. 'We'll get your rooms ready, and we'll get a meal cooked. There will be more food and drink than you've ever seen in your life.' He looked at Maya, then at Bruce and Steve. 'But first, tell me everything.'

Bruce gave a quick rundown of how they'd lost both the Toyotas, got themselves mixed up in a scrap with some special forces, but eventually found the plane buried in the snow and ice. It was a heavily edited account. It left out any details of what they'd found on the plane, and who'd they'd been fighting.

But Kolodin wasn't really interested anyway. He just wanted to know whether he'd covered up his crime.

'And the box?' he asked.

There was a hint of anxiety in his voice, noted Steve.

Maya gestured to Nick.

He placed the package down carefully on the table, and started to peel away the plastic wrapping. As he did so, Steve assessed the situation. They room measured twenty-five feet by twenty, a compact enough space. Voytov was certainly armed, and so probably were the two security guards alongside him. If they kicked off a scrap in here, they could be reasonably certain of taking the room without too much trouble. There were still another twelve soldiers on board, however. And they'd be a lot harder to deal with. But it might be the only chance we get, he thought, fingering the Walther PP inside his snow suit, and checking the mag was chambered. And we'll just have to take it.

Nick unwrapped the plastic. The box was clearly visible underneath. Kolodin walked swiftly towards it, his eyes hungry. He examined it briefly. From the look on his face, Steve judged he was clearly familiar with the kit.

Markov stepped forward. His face was so completely covered that no one recognised him. He plugged in the same iPod speakers he'd used earlier, and pressed play.

Suddenly, the voices of the two pilots filled the room, like ghosts drifting back from the dead. 'Get ready to release the gas,' said Yuri Vasin, the pilot. There was a shuffling noise as Karel Bilek prepared the canisters. 'When shall I switch it on?' asked Bilek. 'Wait until we've found somewhere to land,' answered Vasin.

Steve was watching closely as Kolodin listened to the

conversation. His brow was furrowing, and for the first time there was a smell of fear around the room.

'Details, details,' he said hurriedly, switching off the machine. 'We'll hand this over to the crash investigators and let them work out what happened to the plane.'

But Markov had already ripped off the hood on his snow suit. He glowered straight at Kolodin, his expression steely and determined. 'I already know what happened to the fucking plane,' he growled. 'I was on it.'

Fifty

STEVE KNEW THE SCRAP HAD kicked off the moment Markov moved forward to speak. It was a split-second advantage, but in a close fight between highly trained soldiers it was the narrowest of margins that made the difference between victory and defeat. Even before Markov had finished his sentence, Steve had slipped his right hand inside his snow suit and started to draw the Walther.

Kolodin was still staring at Markov. His eyes were shot with anxiety.

As well they might be, thought Steve. It's not often you're confronted by a man you'd assumed you'd already murdered. And found that he was surrounded by nine heavily armed accomplices, all of them set upon vengeance.

Kolodin started to back away.

Behind him, Voytov and the two guards flanking him were reaching into the chest holsters underneath their black sweatshirts.

But the split-second advantage was about to come into play.

The men facing them were fast, Steve didn't doubt that. Drawing their weapon, aiming and firing at a close target would have been a manoeuvre they would have practised a thousand times. But it didn't matter how well drilled you were. If your opponent was a step ahead of you, there was nothing you could do about it. You were already a dead man.

As Voytov's hand slipped into his shirt, Steve had already lined up the Walther, taken a careful, relaxed aim, and drilled a bullet into the side of the man's face. It wasn't a perfect shot, and he reckoned the handgun had lost some of its accuracy in the sixty years since it had last been used, but it was good enough to rip out a chunk of cheekbone and smash open a portion of the brain that lay behind. The man reeled backwards, blood dripping from the open wound. Steve fired again, then again, pumping the bullets into the man's head and chest, until he was confident the last embers of life had been punched out of him.

Across the tiny room, a hailstorm of gunfire opened up. Each man had drawn his gun the moment Markov revealed his identity. The two guards flanking Voytov had reached for their own weapons but it was too late for them as well, and they were cut to shreds in a sudden and murderous barrage of fire. The smell of cordite filled the room, and blood was splattered across the luxurious carpet as the men fell to the ground one after another.

But Kolodin had grabbed hold of Maya. He was surprisingly strong for a man of his age. He had bull-like muscles in his arms and shoulders, and he'd yanked her hair backwards with a merciless cruelty. Her body was being used as a shield, making it impossible to put a shot into him, and he was backing away towards the door.

Steve was standing closest to him, but he could see the look of terror on Maya's face.

'Feckin' shoot him,' yelled Ian angrily.

'Try it and the woman dies,' snapped Kolodin.

He was still backing towards the door. His eyes met Steve's, and he wondered if the man knew about the relationship that had grown up between him and Maya.

'I said feckin' shoot the bastard,' yelled Ian.

Steve remained rock steady, not moving.

Kolodin backed away through the exit, dragging Maya with him. Two burly soldiers grabbed him and hustled him away.

'Jesus, why didn't you put a bullet into him?' snarled Ian.

'You're a bit too keen on watching people die, Irishman,' snapped Steve.

'Leave it,' growled Bruce.

He glanced from man to man. The Trojan horse strategy had worked. They were inside the boat, and they'd taken the initiative. But there was still a long way to go before the battle was won and the yacht was theirs.

'We've dealt with three of them,' Bruce continued. 'There's still another nine soldiers at least left on this boat. We need to split up and search the vessel inch by inch. Shoot on sight. If they drop their weapons and surrender, fair enough, we don't have to kill them. But knock them out cold and tie them to a railing. We don't want to show mercy, then have one of the bastards comes back and kill one of us later.'

The men split into three units. Steve, Bruce and Nick headed down into the hold and the crew's quarters. Ian, David and Maksim took the main interior of the boat, which included the guest cabins, the conference room, and the cinema. Henri and Dan took the deck, including the bridge.

'Be careful, lads,' warned Bruce, as each unit set off. 'This is their territory, they are well-armed, and they know their stuff. I don't want anyone getting themselves killed. Not when we're this close to making it home.'

Dan led the way out on to the deck. A blast of cold air blew straight over his face as he slipped through the door. The snow was blowing hard across the yacht. The *Lizaveta* had been stationary here for nearly two days now, and snow had piled up in drifts along every exposed surface. They were being cleared with shovels every few hours, Dan reckoned, but there were still mounds four or five feet high, lying across their path like hillocks in a field.

'Head towards the bridge,' hissed Henri.

They'd come out near the back of the yacht, and the bridge was right up at the front, encased in toughened aluminium and glass, some two hundred feet away. Both men drew their weapons and advanced steadily in a crouch. A light shone out from the bridge, guiding them forward. Inside, they could see a solitary figure. 'The captain,' hissed Henri. 'Or else his first mate.'

Down below, they could hear the hum of the engines. In itself, that meant nothing. In weather this cold, the engines would be kept running twenty-four hours a day to keep the lighting and heating working. But there was also a shudder that ran up through the spine of the ship, shaking some of the mounds of snow.

'He's trying to move away from the ice,' said Henri, glancing across at Dan.

'We need to stop him,' hissed Dan. 'Ollie's still out there.'

Both men moved twenty feet closer. The captain was clearly visible at the wheel now, and so was the shadow of another man.

Henri lined up his Walther and steadied his right hand, readying himself to make a shot.

'For Christ's sake, man,' hissed Dan.

'We need to clear this boat,' growled Henri.

'That glass will be bullet-proof, and probably shock-proof as well,' said Dan. 'Your bullets are just going to bounce off the surface, and then they'll know we're here.'

Henri thought for a moment, then nodded curtly. 'OK,' he said flatly, 'We take the door. You go left, I go right.'

Dan would have preferred some other choice. The men they were fighting had modern weapons, and all the protective systems they needed. All they had was sixty-year-old handguns. The numbers were roughly level, but the difference in munitions meant it was hardly a fair fight. But right now, and with the time available, he couldn't see any other option. They'd have to confront the two men head on, and trust that willpower would be enough to pull them through.

Dan started to scuttle forward. The Walther had a seven-round magazine, and fired 9mm rounds. It had plenty of killing power, so long as you were within twenty feet of your opponent, but it had only limited accuracy. They'd have to make this close and personal. He could feel the boat starting to heave to life, and all around there was a crunching noise as it started to break up the ice and clear a path that would take it out into the ocean. Dan kept moving. He was crawling along the edge of the bridge now, keeping down low so that he was below the line of the window. He paused. The entrance was automatic, with a security lock. Maybe voice-activated. Or controlled by a numerical keypad. Either way, they wouldn't be able to just blast their way in.

Dan nodded to Henri, a few yards away on the other side of the doorway. The Frenchman was creeping forward, also under the window level. The engines were churning, and the big metal breakers at the front of the yacht were starting to crack the ice, creating a groaning sound that echoed up to its deck. Henri was scrabbling around on the edge of the bridge's exterior wall, until he found a metal plate, screwed down. He pulled a penknife from his webbing, then, using all his strength, unbolted it, ripping the box open. The noise bought one of the two men to the front of the window. He looked down and saw Henri. The man raised his Yarygin handgun, and pointed it towards the Frenchman but didn't fire. Behind, Dan rose to his feet, and released two bullets in short, sharp succession towards the soldier. As he suspected, the glass was bullet-proof, and the rounds simply bounced away, leaving only a scratch mark on the window. But it distracted the soldier for a moment, and gave Henri a moment to rip out the electrical wires and fuses in the box he had just opened.

The cabin was suddenly plunged into darkness. Dan rushed forward, and Henri leapt to his feet. With his massive, powerful shoulders, Dan crashed into the door. Without power to hold its electronic locks in place, it gave way easily enough. Henri was kneeling just behind Dan, releasing a rapid burst of fire from his Walther. The bullets spun into the darkness, hitting one man in the side of his chest, and the second in the top of his thigh. Dan crashed through the door and rolled across the floor, turning himself into a human cannonball, colliding into the legs of first one man, and then the second, sending them both tumbling to the floor. Henri had managed to get a clean pair of shots into one of the men, putting two perfectly placed bullets into the side of his head, ending his life in a second. Dan was tussling with the second man, wrestling with him as he fell on top of him, blood seeping out of the wound that had opened up in his thigh.

'*Mudak, mudak,*' he was cursing in Russian. Dan was momentarily pinned down, taken aback by the brutal fury of his attacker. But Henri swiftly grabbed him by the back of his neck, yanking him hard upwards into the air, and then flinging him against the back wall of the cabin. The man slumped forward on to the floor, blood escaping from the wound in his side, and a cut opening up in the back of his head where it had collided with the wall. He was still breathing but had lost consciousness. Henri stepped forward, and lined up the Walter to the side of his head, ready to finish him of with a single bullet through the brain.

'No,' said Dan. 'He's no threat. We'll tie him up.'

'Christ, man, we haven't time.'

Henri was looking up at Dan. He knew the guy had been wrongly accused of shooting a pair of Afghan kids when he was in the SASR and had spent a year in a military jail but he'd never realised it had made him so reluctant to take a life. The way Henri saw it, that was just soldiering. It was a brutal trade, close to butchery sometimes, but those were the terms of employment, and if you didn't like them then there was nothing to stop you finding some other way of making a living.

'There's another seven soldiers on this boat to deal with,' growled Henri. 'And we're steaming away from Ollie right now. We need to get this yacht under control.'

But Dan had already grabbed a rope used to secure a lifebelt to the yacht's railing, and was starting to bind the man's hands.

He'd checked the soldier's eyes to make sure he was still alive, and used a length of cloth torn from the man's own sweatshirt to create a rough bandage for his wound.

'Have it your way,' snapped Henri. 'I'm going to go help our comrades.'

Down in the hold of the boat, Steve, Bruce and Nick were advancing cautiously, their guns drawn, searching for the remaining sailors and guards. They were walking along a narrow corridor that ran down the central spine of the boat. Off it, there were storerooms, kitchens, the laundry, sleeping and living quarters for the crew, and up ahead the medical room and the armoury. They could hear the engine churning, and, from the sudden movement of the vessel, they could tell the yacht was starting to move away from the ice.

'We haven't much time,' hissed Steve. 'Ollie's still out there.'

'We could always pick the sod up in springtime,' smirked Nick.

'It's not a bad idea,' chuckled Bruce.

'Nah, he'll moan and moan and moan,' said Steve. 'I was cold, boys, sodding cold. Nobody can whinge like that bloke.'

Each man laughed, but the joke was interrupted by a sudden blast of gunfire. It was coming from the bend in the corridor, where it twisted off to the armoury. 'Take cover,' yelled Bruce.

Nick opened up with a blast of fire from his Walther. The bullets spat along the corridor, ricocheting off the walls to create a deadly assault of lead that temporarily forced their enemy into a retreat.

Steve pulled open the door directly to their right and slipped inside, motioning to Bruce and Nick to follow him. The cabin measured ten feet by five, had a single narrow bed made up with crisp white linen sheets, a TV and laptop, a desk, a basin and a small wardrobe. One of the crew rooms. It was a tight squeeze for three guys but it would provide some temporary cover until they could assess how many men were confronting them and figure out how to hit back.

The bullets were still spitting down the corridor as Nick and Bruce bundled inside.

A grenade rolled along the corridor.

'Shit,' muttered Steve. 'The bastards can't be using grenades on us, can they? They'll sink the ship, and then we're all dead.'

'Christ, man, don't you recognise it?' shouted Bruce. 'We need to get you back into training.'

Steve glanced again, then slammed the door shut. I'm getting out of practice, he thought. That's a sodding stun grenade. The SAS invented them, we trained with them plenty of times. I should know precisely how deadly a weapon that can be in the right hands.

'Cover your ears, lads,' he snapped. 'This is going to hurt.'

The device detonated with a brutal assault of light and noise. Stun grenades had first been developed in the early 1970s when the SAS asked Royal Ordnance researchers to come up with a weapon that would help them in their fight against the IRA. The result was the 'flash'n'bang', a grenade that mixed mercury and magnesium to produce a blinding flash – the equivalent of 300,000 candlepower – as well as a noise so deafening it was like standing under a couple of jumbo jets as they landed. The impact would confuse and disorientate the enemy, while the SAS boys wearing protective goggles and headgear could fight their way through the chaos. It was perfect for close-quarters fighting in confined spaces. Like here, thought Steve grimly.

The door protected them from the worst of the blinding white light that ripped along the corridor as the grenade exploded, but it was useless against the wall of screeching noise that shattered into them.

Nick was doubled up, screaming as the noise seemed to split open his eardrums. 'What the fuck was that?' he whimpered.

'It's called a thunderflash, lad,' said Bruce.

'They'll be coming for us, right?' said Steve, glancing towards Bruce.

The noise was starting to ebb, but it was still echoing through his brain, making it hard to concentrate.

'Bloody right,' Bruce answered tersely.

Steve nodded. If their opponents had stun grenades, they could be certain they had protective gear as well. They'd blow a pair of the devices, then while their opponents were still reeling from the detonation, they'd come and finish them with their guns.

'I guess they don't realise we're Regiment,' said Steve.

'We invented these sods, and we know how to deal with them.'

'Think you remember?'

'I spent enough days in the Killing House practising this drill. It never leaves a man.'

Steve flashed a rough grin. 'Then let's give the bastards the good news.'

He raised his Walther and fired four rounds, two into each hinge securing the door. It fell loose. Bruce grabbed the sheet from the bed, and tore it into three wide strips. He passed one to Nick, and another to Steve. 'Wrap this around your face and ears,' he snapped.

'I won't be able to sodding see anything,' complained Nick.

'Doesn't bloody matter,' said Bruce. 'Just shoot.'

'And pray,' added Steve with a rough grin.

Steve wrapped the cloth round his eyes and ears, tying it tight. When Bruce and Nick had done the same, the three men grabbed the metal cabin door and, using it as a shield, started to advance down the corridor. Another stun grenade detonated, filling the corridor with a noise so brutal it seemed to be sucking your brain clean out of your skull. But the cloth provided just enough protection to survive the aural assault, even though it took every ounce of self-discipline not to crumple and run. A volley of fire was directed towards them, but the door was made of reinforced steel – like everything else on the yacht, no expense had been spared – and was strong enough to deflect the bullets as they battered into it.

'Another few feet,' yelled Steve, struggling to make himself heard above the din. 'Then we'll level up the score.'

They advanced another three paces. The rate of fire was increasing, and there was smoke all around them, but the unit's nerve held. The door was taking a terrible beating as the bullets crashed into it, and the din of metal on metal mixed with the echoes of the stun grenade to create a barrage of noise so powerful it felt as if a man could hardly walk through it.

But they pushed on relentlessly, their teeth gritted to survive the attack.

'OK,' yelled Steve. 'Now . . .'

They dropped the door.

In unison, the three men opened up the Walthers. They had no idea where the enemy was. It was impossible to see anything through the blindfolds. But they could sense they were right in front of them. And as long as they laid down enough fire, the chances were they'd inflict some damage.

When all three mags were emptied, they stopped firing.

For a moment, all three of them remained silent, motionless.

Then Steve ripped aside his blindfold.

In front of them were three corpses, their bodies shot to pieces, lying in a heap outside the door to the armoury.

'Jesus,' muttered Nick. 'I never want to hear a stun grenade again.'

'You should have joined a proper army, lad,' said Bruce. 'Then you'd be used to it.'

Above them, they could hear the rattle of gunfire.

'Looks like the boys need some help,' said Steve.

Up above, Ian, David and Maksim were getting pinned down by a group of four soldiers who had taken the main conference room, the same spot where Kolodin had explained the original mission. They'd grabbed fifteen chairs and piled them up across one half of the room, making a barricade. The four men had strung themselves out along it, their AK-74s resting on top of it, putting round after round towards the three men facing them. David was crouching behind the door, attempting to put down some sniper fire in retaliation, but it was useless. He couldn't get a clean shot in; as soon as he put his gun round the door, a volley of intense fire blasted straight into him.

'Christ, we're getting nowhere,' he cursed.

Behind him, Ian had grabbed Markov. It was too dangerous to leave the man by himself. Enemy soldiers were rampaging across the yacht, and they had no idea where Kolodin or Maya had got to. The oligarch was squatting behind them, his beady eyes surveying the situation, while Maksim scouted the periphery of the conference room to see if they could find another way in. Markov had guts, noted David. He was crouching down, and he was shaking, but he was holding himself together. Not many civilians could do that. Usually they went to pieces at the first sign of gunfire.

'Pin them down,' growled Ian. 'I'm cooking something up for them.'

Maksim reported that there was no way into the conference room, not unless they tried to drill their way down from above. 'No time,' said David tersely. He looked towards Ian. 'What have you got?'

Ian held up a Thermos flask. It was a standard coffee warmer, from the store cupboard next to the conference room.

'I'd rather have a tea than coffee if you don't mind, pal,' said David. 'Two sugars, and milk in first.'

'A vacuum flask makes a fine grenade', snapped Ian. 'I've stuffed some of the TNT we had left over into it, and if you'll just help me break up some of these glasses here, we'll have ourselves a handy little shrapnel grenade in no time at all.'

'Good one,' said David with a rough grin, 'We don't call you the bomber for nothing.'

Maksim trod down heavily on the glasses Ian had taken from the cupboard, then knelt down to scoop the fragments into the flask. Ian screwed the lid down tight, then set the fuse.

'Cover me,' he said, glancing towards Maksim.

The Russian leant around the door, and opened up with his Walther. He blasted a full mag right into the barricade, sending the four men scurrying behind it for cover. There wasn't much accuracy to the fire, but there were enough bullets to force their opponents to keep their heads down for a moment. Ian counted to three, then hurled himself forward and lobbed the flask into the air. 'Take cover, lads,' he grunted. 'There's going to be a lot of red-hot glass flying through the air in the next few seconds and you don't want to be anywhere near it.'

The device exploded with a flash of vicious light, followed by an echoing roar as the crack of the explosion bounced off the walls of the enclosed space. David waited a fraction of a second for it to burn out, then allowed himself to peer round the door. The device had ignited just a few feet above the men crouching behind the barricade. The vacuum had split apart, its plastic outer layer melting, and the inner metal heating up and splintering in every direction. The compressed glass turned molten hot in the same instant, and flew in every direction, each shred capable of both burning and slicing open its victims. One man staggered backwards, his voice wailing in horror. A slice of glass had cut open his left eye, then drilled into the brain behind it, leaving him not dead, not even mortally wounded, but suffering from such excruciating pain that all he could do was lie on the floor whimpering, and wishing that he'd already passed on to some other world. Another man was shrieking as the shrapnel spilt open a wound in his right hand, forcing him to drop his weapon and start searching around for something that could staunch the bleeding.

But two of the soldiers had survived the attack unharmed. Both men jumped across the barricade, their fingers in the triggers of their AK-74s, firing the weapons on automatic. And they were running straight up towards the door, intent on regaining the initiative over their enemy.

David glanced across at Ian. 'I think you've really pissed them off, pal,' he said tersely.

The two soldiers were rampaging towards them. All military discipline had been abandoned, and they were simply charging them, like a pair of wounded bulls intent on death. Only thirty feet separated the barricade from the doorway, and they were closing that distance at alarming speed. Maksim leapt to his feet and turned his fire straight on to them. But they were moving too fast.

'Back, back,' yelled David.

Ian grabbed hold of Markov and started to run back along the corridor. The man had plenty of guts, but even if you'd spent half a lifetime on the battlefield, there was little scarier than two soldiers who appeared to have given up on life and were bent only on revenge charging straight into you. The oligarch was whimpering like a child, covering his face, tears of unembarrassed fear streaming down his cheeks as the bullets chipped into the walls all around them.

Maksim and David were laying down some more fire, but within a fraction of a second, their mags were empty, and there was no time to change them without getting shot to pieces. There was no choice but to make a fighting retreat.

Ian flung Markov back into the meeting room where they'd left the black box. He turned round, slotted a fresh mag into his Walther, and put down a few rounds of fire. It bought just enough time for him and Maksim to throw themselves to safety, taking cover behind the door.

But still the two men were advancing towards them, their guns spewing out a seemingly inexhaustible supply of ammunition. David took one glance at them, then retreated back behind the door as well. The intensity of the fire raining down on them was too great to make any form of response possible without taking an unacceptable risk with their own lives. He slammed the door shut behind him, and looked around for something he could barricade it with. But already the bullets were chipping away steadily at the metal frame, clattering into it relentlessly like hailstones on a windscreen. Any moment now the two men would be upon them.

'How many bullets left?' snapped David looking towards Ian, then Maksim.

'Six,' growled Ian.

'Four,' said Maksim, his voice strained.

David knew he had only two rounds left in his mag, and no spares left.

'Shit,' he muttered.

It might be enough to deal with the two men. After all, one bullet was all it took to kill a man. But you wouldn't want to count on it. He glanced back at the door. There was a brief respite in the attack. Then he heard the click of fresh mags being slotted into the rifles. The final, brutal attack on the door was about to begin.

'Steady yourself, lads,' said David, his expression grim. 'This is going to be rough.'

Suddenly there was a burst of gunfire from further back.

David flung the door open to see what was happening.

Behind him, Ian and Maksim had lined up their handguns, ready to pump their few remaining rounds into the men attacking them.

But both soldiers had tumbled to the ground, their backs punctured by multiple bullets wounds.

Steve and Dan were standing behind them, their faces grim; the look of men who'd been forced by circumstances to act as executioners, and who didn't much like the task. David could only sympathise. There was no job a soldier cared for less than shooting a man in the back, no matter how necessary it might be.

They kept walking steadily forward. Behind them, David could see Bruce, Nick and Henri. Steve stooped down, grabbed one of the AK-74s from a corpse, checked there were still rounds in its clip, then ran down to join David.

'I don't think those lads are going to be troubling you any more,' he said.

Fifty-One

BETWEEN THEM THEY MADE A quick tally of the dead.

Two men down upstairs, reported Henri and Dan. One dead, the other wounded and tied up. Three downstairs, reported Steve. All turned into corpses. Two men down in the conference room, and another two dead in the corridor, reported David.

'That makes nine,' said Steve. 'And three blokes in here brings the total up to twelve.'

'And they say educational standards are falling,' said Ian, with a smirk. 'The bloke did that without even using his fingers.'

'Sodding leave it,' snapped Steve, looking angrily at Ian.

'That's the lot then, isn't it?' said Bruce. 'Maya reckoned there was a crew of twelve.'

Steve nodded. 'Except for Kolodin. And Maya as well. There's no sign of the bastard.' He glanced from man to man. It looked as if they had control of the yacht. But they still had to find Kolodin. And they still had to rescue Maya.

'The submarine,' said Henri.

Steve could see at once the Frenchman was right. Kolodin's battle was lost. The oligarch had no choice but to try and make an escape or else see what kind of justice might be in store for him, either right here on this boat or else in a courtroom standing trial for murder. And the sub was the only way out of here. He'd be taking it for sure.

'Let's move,' said Steve.

Henri led the way. The submarine was located on the port side of the yacht. The Frenchman had noted its position on their first tour of the boat. It was down one flight of stairs, then through a sealed door. When they arrived, Kolodin was already inside the chamber. Maya was lying on the floor. And Kolodin was unscrewing the airtight door on the sub, after which he could flood the sealed chamber with water and make his escape.

Steve twisted the handle. His Walther was in hand as he did so.

But the door was locked shut.

He looked around for a key. The door was sealed electronically from the inside, and unless you knew the combination, it wasn't going to open. He raised his pistol so that it was pointing straight at the man on the other side, but Kolodin just looked back at Steve and smiled. He mouthed a couple of sentences. And although he couldn't be heard through the thick glass, the meaning was clear enough.

He's telling me to sod off, realised Steve. The glass is bullet-proof.

Steve glanced anxiously at Maya's body. Whether she was alive or dead it was impossible to tell from this angle. She was lying on her side, her face on the cold metal of the floor. There was no sign of movement. But she might just be unconscious, Steve told himself as he felt a stab of panic somewhere in the middle of his chest. We can still rescue her. If we can just get into this sodding room. Otherwise the bastard is about to flood the chamber with seawater. And then she'll be dead for sure.

'Can you blow the door?' asked Steve anxiously, looking towards Ian.

'I can blow anything,' answered Ian crisply. 'The question is whether I can bring it down without sinking the ship as well.'

'There's no need,' said Nick.

Ian turned to look at the Welsh boy.

'We're not going to tunnel in, Nick,' he said sourly.

'No sodding need,' said Nick. He rushed back to the armoury, and returned with an AK-74 and a set of cartridges. 'Here, SP6 BPs,' he said, holding out the rounds in the palm of his hand.

The SP6 BP was a Russian-made armour-piercing bullet, designed to drill through Kevlar or the steel plating of a vehicle. With a hardened steel core and a softer outer shell, it would literally shed its skin on impact, allowing the harder inner shell to drill its way through metal. It could penetrate up to ten millimetres of steel even at three hundred metres, and more when fired from close up.

'Will that break through armoured glass?' asked Steve.

'Easily,' said Dan.

'Everyone stand back,' said Bruce.

The men moved swiftly away from the door. Nick slotted the cartridges into the AK-74 and walked back fifteen paces. He raised the gun, aimed, then squeezed his finger on the trigger. 'Kill,' he muttered.

The door was made of thick steel, with a square window measuring fifteen inches by twenty. The bullet made a cracking sound on impact, then the glass splintered, falling with a crash to the floor. Kolodin looked round startled. The man didn't know much about guns, reckoned Steve as he glanced into his eyes through the broken window. He'd thought armoured glass could resist all bullets. Not just *some* of them.

Steve thrust his Walther through the window, pointing it straight at Kolodin. The man was shaking. Fear had suddenly taken hold of him. He reached down and grabbed Maya by the hair, and lifted her up so that she was shielding him from attack.

'Drop her,' barked Steve. 'Or I'll shoot you right now.'

The man looked at Steve, then at the submarine. He was weighing his options. If he surrendered, he'd face charges for murder, that much was certain. He could die right here today, if he wanted to, and maybe that wasn't such a bad option.

'I said drop her,' barked Steve, louder this time.

'Shoot me, and the woman dies,' he said.

There was a cruel sneer to his voice that got Steve riled up. He flicked the Walther slightly to the left, then squeezed the trigger. A bullet narrowly missed Kolodin's head, crashed into the metal wall, then ricocheted down to the floor. The man flinched but held himself steady, although a bead of sweat was running down the left side of his face.

'I said, the woman dies.'

'You've already pulled that sodding stunt once today,' growled Steve. 'And to be honest, I'm getting tired of it.'

A half-smile crossed Steve's face. The Russian's spirit was broken. He could see it in his eyes.

'The next bullet's yours. On the count of three . . .'

Kolodin wavered. He was looking around desperately.

'Two . . .' growled Steve.

Kolodin's brow creased, then relaxed. He put Maya back down on the ground.

Steve reached down and unlocked the door from the inside. It swung open with barely a sound. He kicked the broken glass away and stepped inside, swiftly followed by Bruce, David and Dan. Kolodin was backing away from them, his expression nervous. Steve rushed across to where Maya was lying on the floor. He checked her pulse. She was OK. There was a nasty bruise on the side of her head where she'd taken a bad knock, but with a few hours' rest and some painkillers she'd be fine.

Behind them, Markov stepped into the small room.

He walked up to Kolodin. Steve had no idea what the history was between the two men but he suspected it wasn't good. 'And now it's your turn to die,' Markov snapped, jabbing a finger straight into Kolodin's face. He turned towards Bruce. 'Get one of your men to finish him,' he snapped.

Bruce glanced at Steve and then back at the Russian billionaire. 'We're soldiers, not executioners,' he said. 'That wasn't part of the deal.'

Ian stepped between the two men. His Walther was in his hand, ready to fire.

'I don't know about the rest of you, but I've been a feckin' executioner in my time, and I don't mind doing it again if the rest of you are too squeamish.'

'Jesus, man . . .' hissed Steve.

'What the hell are you belly-aching about now?' snapped Ian. 'The man's a murderer, we've heard the tapes.'

He lowered his pistol so that it was level with Kolodin's face. There was sweat streaming down the man's face.

'We make our enemies pay,' continued Ian. 'It's the only way we know.'

Maksim stepped forward. He was holding his Walther in his

right hand, the tip of the steel barrel glinting in the neon light. 'He's right,' he said flatly. 'The man showed us no mercy. We owe him none.'

'I'm with Ian,' said Henri.

'And so am I,' said Dan.

Steve weighed the decision. It was killing a man in cold blood. No one liked doing that. Against that, the man had deceived them from the start. He'd have murdered them if he'd won the battle. They owed him nothing. Not even his life. 'OK,' he said flatly. 'Who wants to pull the trigger?'

Ian stepped across to Kolodin. 'Kneel,' he snapped. 'I'll put a bullet into the back of your head, Russian-style.'

The billionaire was trying to hold himself together. But his hands were shaking. He backed away further, clinging to the submarine as if it might yet provide some form of escape.

'I said kneel,' repeated Ian. He was pointing the Walther straight at him. 'Otherwise you'll get a bullet in the face right now.'

Kolodin looked at Steve.

'The address of the woman and the child,' he said. There was a hint of pleading in his voice. 'I still can give it to you.'

Sam, thought Steve. He knows her address. That was the reason I came on this sodding mission in the first place.

'If you'll let me live, it's yours.'

'Nobody gives a toss,' growled Ian.

'No,' said Steve. He stepped forward, pushing Ian's gun aside. 'I want to know.'

'Christ, man, you and your feckin' women,' snapped Ian. 'Skirt. That's all you ever think about.'

'She's the mother of my kid,' said Steve.

'It's nothing to do with the rest of us,' said Henri. 'Steve can sort out his own problems.'

There was a silence. Steve was looking angrily from man to man.

'Steve's right,' said David finally. 'We're mates. We help each other out.'

'It's a fair trade,' said Nick.

'It's family,' said Maksim. 'Sort of anyway. We can't interfere with that.'

'So let Steve get the address,' said Bruce.

'Have it your own feckin' way,' said Ian. He was scowling as he put the gun away.

'The address?' said Steve, looking at Kolodin.

The Russian had pulled a pen from his pocket and started to write on a scrap of paper. It only took a few seconds. He handed it across to Steve. An apartment block in Monaco. A phone number. And an email address.

'Here,' he said. 'I've seen her pictures. She's worth a man's life.'

Steve folded it away in his pocket. When he'd contact her he wasn't sure. Nor could he imagine what she'd say when he did. But at least he knew where she was. And the boy as well. That was something.

'Now, we kill him,' said Markov.

'No,' snapped Steve. 'We're men of our word.'

Fifty-Two

'HERE,' SAID STEVE, GRABBING KOLODIN roughly by the arm. 'You're coming with us, pal.'

Together with Bruce and Nick, Steve led the Russian back towards the main floor. Henri had already gone with Dan up to the bridge. The Frenchman was an expert sailor, and it didn't take him more than a few minutes to get the hang of the yacht's controls, and to start steering it back towards the ice.

As soon as it was in position, David lowered the ramp, and Steve, Bruce and Nick led Kolodin out on to the ice, heading back towards where they'd left Ollie and the bodyguard.

It was a walk of just a couple of hundred yards. They'd spent less than half an hour on the yacht, but even in that short time their bodies had warmed up, and they'd started to forget how miserably cold the Arctic was. The wind was blowing harshly across the empty, dark landscape, and the snow was piling up in drifts, making the ground harder to cross than when they'd been here just thirty minutes earlier. But they covered the ground quickly enough. All of them just wanted to get their mate back, get on to the yacht, and start the journey home.

'Take a good look around, boys,' said Steve. 'I reckon it will be a while before we come back again.'

'Not in my lifetime, if I have any say in it,' said Bruce. 'That's for sodding sure.'

When they found him, Ollie was shivering badly. Gregor Tyutin had created some ice blocks from the snow, making a rough shelter that was protecting them from the worst of the wind. But from Ollie's bloodshot eyes, and the way his shoulders were starting to sag, it looked as if his broken ankle was starting to get to him. The pain was grinding him down. He needs some treatment, thought Steve as he helped him to his feet. Some food, some warmth, and some rest. We all do.

'You missed all the fun, mate,' said Steve.

'I hope you saved a prisoner or two for me,' said Ollie, chuckling. 'I haven't shot anyone for hours. And make sure I'm first in the queue next time there's a scrap on. Only fair.'

He was starting to cheer up. Some food in his stomach, and a shot of decent brandy in his veins, and he'd be OK.

'There's not going to be another time. I'm through with this bollocks for good.'

'So you keep saying, pal,' answered Ollie. He rested one arm on Steve's shoulder, and another on Nick's. 'But not quite yet.'

'Just you wait and see,' said Steve.

Ollie looked up at Kolodin. 'What's that bastard doing here?'

Bruce pointed his gun at the Russian, digging it into his back.

'Taking your place,' he said firmly.

Kolodin looked at him anxiously. They had allowed him to put on a thick snow suit before they took him out on to the ice. There were some supplies of fuel and food they'd carried from the plane. But Tuytin had already removed all the ammo from the guns. He'd be taking that with him.

'You said you'd let me live,' said Kolodin angrily. 'We made a deal.'

'We are letting you live,' said Bruce. 'It's just that we didn't say we'd take you with us.'

'You'll be all right, pal,' said Steve. 'It's a bit chilly out here, I'll give you that. But another two or three months and the temperature will be getting up to minus twenty.'

'No . . .' started Kolodin.

Bruce raised his gun.

'Take the deal, mate,' he said. 'It's the best one you're going to get . . . and it's more than you deserve.'

For a second, Kolodin looked straight into the barrel of the gun.

'I can pay you,' he said desperately. 'Whatever you want . . .'

'Leave it,' growled Bruce. 'It won't do you any good. You've already deceived us once. You don't get another chance.'

The man was about to speak again. But Bruce had already turned round. Ollie was hobbling back towards the boat, supported by Steve and Nick. Bruce kept on walking, not looking back. Behind him, he could hear a whimpering sound, like a dog, but within a few paces the howling wind and the gusting snow had drowned it out, and it was only the wilderness he could hear.

By the time they got back to the boat, the rest of the unit had started to make themselves at home. David welcomed Ollie back on board, and Markov hugged his bodyguard. The ramp was pulled up behind them. Up on the bridge, Henri had control of the yacht and had charted a course that would take them out through the Arctic Ocean into the Barents Sea, and then down towards mainland Europe. Maya had come round while they'd been out on the ice, and David had patched up her head wound in the ship's medical room. She'd changed her clothes, washed, and had even found time to put on a bit of make-up. Just her presence was brightening up the room, noted Steve. And cheering all the men up.

'Let's get Ollie down to the medical room right away,' she said. 'We'll get that foot patched up as best we can.'

'So long as you're playing nurse, that sounds like a plan,' said Ollie with a rough grin.

'We'll give you a shower as well,' said Maya.

'Even better.'

'Maksim will be in charge of that.'

Ollie's face fell. 'Not so good.'

It took twenty minutes to get Ollie fixed up, with a proper bandage round his foot. He showered and washed, and cleaned away the mess of blood and grime where the ankle had snapped. By the time that was done, Nick and Dan had raided the kitchens. They'd found mountains of food stored in the deep freezer: steaks, lobsters, fish, rice and vegetables, and jars of caviar. Next to it was a wine cellar stocked with the finest French reds, and crates of champagne. Between them, the two men cooked up a dozen of the biggest steaks they could find, boiled up a heap of rice, several bowls of vegetables, and started to carry the whole feast upstairs.

In the main conference room, Steve and Maksim had cleared away the bodies. It was short, brutal work, but they'd tipped each of them over the side, adding a few weights from the yacht's small gym to the corpses to make sure they sank straight to the bottom of the ocean. By the time they'd done that, the food was ready. And the entire unit was gathering for what promised to be the meal of a lifetime.

We made it, thought Steve as Ollie hobbled into the room, his foot properly bandaged, and a pair of crutches under his arms so that he could walk without putting any weight on it. We're tired and dirty and a lot worse for wear. But we're alive. And that's not an outcome any of us would have put much money on just a few hours ago.

'I couldn't find any Stella, lads,' said Nick, holding up the bottle he had opened. 'So it looks like we'll have to settle for this . . .' He glanced at the label on the bottle. 'Chateau Lafitte Roths-whatsit. It's bit sodding ancient though. Says on the bottle it was brewed up in nineteen eighty-two. I don't know if we can still drink it.'

'I could handle a drop,' said Ollie. 'You might want to stick to the Stella though, Nick. Not sure this stuff will agree with you.'

Henri had joined them from the bridge. A bandage had been wrapped round his arm where the polar bear had cut him, and he'd taken a powerful shot of antibiotics in case it was infected. He grabbed a huge steak, and a plateful of rice, and started to eat hungrily, before knocking back a big glass of the wine and suggesting to Nick that he might want to think about opening a couple more bottles.

'This stuff is wasted on you lot,' Henri said, glancing around the room. Then he grinned. 'But what the hell? It was wasted on the Russian bastard who bought it as well.'

'Shouldn't someone be steering this boat?' said Steve, looking at the Frenchman.

'And preferably not someone who's been swigging back the Chateau Rothschild,' said Ian, as he refilled his own glass. 'At this rate, we'll wake up in the morning and find we've crashed into an iceberg somewhere off Greenland.'

'It's fine,' answered Henri calmly. 'There are more gadgets on this boat than a NASA space rocket. I've set the course, and put it on automatic pilot.'

'Then map a route for Scotland,' said Bruce. 'I know a cove where we can pull in without having to worry about customs or any of that nonsense.'

'Aye, aye, captain,' said Henri.

'How many days' sailing?' asked Markov.

'This vessel is fast,' said Henri. 'We can make it in four days.'

Markov raised his glass. 'That's plenty of time to get this data to the UN committee. I owe you all a big payday. But most of all I owe you a drink.'

Nick had opened another bottle of the Chateau Lafitte. He refilled everyone's glass.

'Get as much power out of this machine as you can,' said Bruce, looking across at Henri. 'There's a bloody good vintage single malt stored in the cellar at my place. And if ever a group of men deserved some real Scottish firewater to warm their bellies, I reckon it's us.'

Another toast was drunk.

But before they could finish, there was a sudden crashing sound from the bridge.

'Christ,' muttered Dan. 'It sounds like he's escaped.'

He slammed his glass down on the table and started to run upstairs.

'What the hell's got into Dan?' asked Ollie.

Matt Lynn

'He left one of the soldiers tied up on the bridge,' said Henri. 'I told him he should have shot the sod through the head. But the idiot wouldn't listen to me.'

Steve looked at him, stunned. 'You're letting him deal with it by himself?'

'The guy's tied up,' said Henri.

'It sounds like he's sodding escaped,' snapped Steve. He started to run.

He flung himself up the stairs that led to the deck. The wind was blowing harder now that the yacht was out in open water. It had turned into a gale that hurled into Steve as soon as he stepped out of the door, almost knocking him off his feet.

He looked towards the bridge. Dan was staggering out, clutching his chest. There was blood pouring down the side of his sweatshirt.

A bullet wound. Even in the darkness through thirty yards, Steve could see it clearly enough. The soldier lunged at him, pushing him to the ground, his fists pummelling into Dan's face.

Steve drew his Walther.

'Hold it right there,' he yelled.

The soldier stopped. He grabbed hold of Dan's hair, and stood up. A gun was lodged in his right hand, pressed hard into the side of Dan's jaw. The Australian looked to have lost consciousness. His eyes were closed, and his mouth hanging open.

'Drop him and put down your weapon,' yelled Steve.

He started to walk across the deck, ignoring the wind and the snow roaring across it.

Behind him, the rest of the unit had joined him. Bruce, Maksim, Ian, Nick, David, Henri and Maya were strung out in

446

a line behind Steve, their guns drawn. A wall of steel and fire.

The bastard didn't stand a chance. Except that he still had Dan.

'I said sodding well drop him,' snarled Steve.

The soldier just pressed his gun harder into Dan's cheek.

'Fuck off,' he shouted.

He spoke with a thick Russian accent.

'We'll shoot.'

'And I'll shoot your mate,' he said.

As he delivered the sentence, he shook Dan's head violently. Blood was pouring from the open wound.

'He's going to die in a few minutes,' hissed David. 'He's losing too much blood.'

'Drop him,' yelled Steve.

The man just yanked Dan up, holding him in front of him as a shield.

'Christ,' muttered Steve.

There was no time to play games with the sod. If they couldn't get Dan out of his hands in the next couple of minutes, the Australian was a goner.

'Nick, can you drop him?' he hissed.

Nick stepped forward. He still had the AK-74 on him, loaded with the SP6 BP rounds. 'I don't know.'

'Straight to the brain, Nick,' said Steve. 'You'll kill him before he can shoot Dan.'

Nick raised the gun. He levelled it to his shoulder, holding it as steady as he could despite the gusts of wind blowing straight through him. He lined the man up in his sights, the metal tip of the gun barrel precisely aligned with the soldier's head.

'You OK, pal?' said Ollie.

'I'm doing my sodding best,' snapped Nick.

'Just leave him,' said Steve. 'It's Nick. We never saw the lad miss a shot yet.'

Nick focused. He squinted his eye and concentrated.

'Kill,' he muttered.

And he squeezed the trigger.

Dan jerked backwards as the bullet collided with the side of his head, just below the right ear.

'Shit, fucking shit,' screamed Nick.

He flung the AK-74 on to the deck. A pair of bullets spat angrily from its barrel on impact, flying lethally through the air, but Nick was impervious to the danger.

The soldier dropped Dan to the ground. He turned round and started to run. Steve was hurtling across the deck, pumping bullets out of the Walther straight into the man's back. Not all of them hit home. But enough found their target to send the man tumbling over as round after round punctured his spine, and burst through to his lungs and heart. By the time Steve caught up with him, he was lying on the metal surface of the deck, his last breath already drawn.

Steve looked round.

Maya was already leaning over Dan.

'Get me some bandages,' she was screaming.

A few yards from him, Nick was kneeling, violently throwing up.

'I said, get some fucking bandages,' screamed Maya again.

David and Henri swung into action. There were medi-packs in the yacht's medical room. They rushed downstairs, and returned a few moments later with tourniquets, disinfectant, bandages, plasters and painkillers.

Maya stabbed a syringe into Dan's arm just below the shoulder joint, jabbing a shot of morphine straight into the vein. She grabbed some wipes, and started to clear away the blood that was streaming down the side of his face, then wrapped a bandage round it.

'Let's get him downstairs,' she said.

'Is he alive?' asked Steve anxiously.

'There's a bullet inside his head,' said Maya. 'He's a strong man, but not many people can survive that.'

'He's still breathing?'

'For now,' said Maya. 'Let's just get him out of this storm and into the warmth. There must be some blood plasma in the medical room. That will help.'

Maksim and Henri gently lifted Dan up, and, with Maya leading the way, carried him into the interior of the yacht. He was a big man, and even though like the rest of them he'd lost a lot of weight in the last thirty-six hours, he still weighed more than two hundred and thirty pounds. But the two men carried him as gently as a baby, while Maya held her hands across his face to keep him warm.

Bruce glanced at Steve and Ollie, and nodded towards Nick. 'Speak to the lad.'

The snow was blowing straight across him. He was still kneeling on the ground. He'd vomited up the food he'd just eaten, and he was staring straight down into it with tears running down his face.

Ollie rested his crutches on the deck, and knelt down. He turned Nick's face to his own. The boy's eyes were haggard, and his expression scared, as if he'd just looked into hell. Ollie wasn't sure he'd ever seen a man look so frightened.

'You did your best, pal,' he said.

Nick was shaking. He stood up, but looked away from Steve and Ollie.

'It's all right, mate,' said Steve. 'Dan would have wanted you to make the shot. He'd have known the risks. It was the only way of getting him out of that bastard's grip.'

'It's not fucking all right, is it?' said Nick angrily. 'It's never going to be all right.'

'None of us could have done any better.'

'I shot my mate, didn't I? How the fuck am I meant to live with that?'

Steve put his arm round Nick's shoulder. 'Come inside, and get some sleep, pal. We all need some rest.'

They started to steer Nick back inside the ship.

But as they walked, Nick's question was still preying on his mind.

How was he meant to live with that?

It was a sodding good question. And one Steve knew he didn't have the answer to.

Epilogue

OLLIE WAS SITTING WITH HIS leg in plaster, enjoying the football. 'You just rest yourself,' said Sandra. 'I'll get you another beer.'

'Thanks, babes,' said Ollie, a grin playing on his face.

'Some blokes have all the luck,' said Henri. 'You broke your foot early on, missed nearly all the fighting, sat on your arse while we did all the hard work but collected a big payday just like the rest of us. And now you've got Nick's mum playing nurse and lap-dancer all at the same time.'

'It's all well-deserved,' said Ollie. 'I've had my share of suffering.'

'You should have met his last bird,' said Ian. 'The woman made the Chelsea gaffer look frugal.'

Each man in the group laughed, and took another swig of their beer.

They were standing in an executive box at Barcelona's Nou Camp stadium, watching the second leg of the Champion's League game against Chelsea. The stadium was every bit as magnificent as they had expected. The vast sweeping curves that surrounded the pitch were filled to capacity, and the 99,350 spectators were waving flags, lighting torches and cheering wildly. The noise was deafening, and the match well-fought so far. Barca were sweeping forward with their lightning skills and silky passing. But the English team was digging deep, defending mightily, and causing Barca some problems on the break. The aggregate score was level. And no one wanted to predict how the game would play out.

Markov had flown them all out for the game, and no expense had been spared. The plan had been to sail back to Scotland, but after Dan got injured, they'd pulled into a secluded cove in Norway instead. Markov had paid enough bribes to the local officials to make sure not too many questions were asked. Dan had been taken straight to the best hospital the oligarch's money could buy. Ollie's foot had been re-set by a surgeon, and was expected to recover fully after six weeks in plaster. But Dan was still in a bad way. It had taken two days of surgery to get the bullet out of his brain, yet even after that none of the doctors could make any promises about a recovery. The man was still in a coma, and showed no sign of regaining consciousness yet.

The unit had hung around for a couple of days, but there wasn't much they could do for Dan in Norway, so one by one they'd flown home, their payment from Markov safely stashed away in the bank in Dubai where Death Inc.'s men always deposited the money from their missions. They'd been paid by Kolodin as well, but there wasn't a single one of them who wouldn't have exchanged the lot of it, and much more besides, for a single raised eyelid from Dan.

'Any word from the hospital?' asked Steve, looking across to Bruce.

Bruce had taken it on himself to place the daily call through to the senior nurse to check on their man's progress.

But although the woman was always polite, and spoke perfect English, the message was always the same. The patient hadn't changed over the last twenty-four hours. Alive. Breathing. But a vegetable.

'Enjoy the match, pal,' said Bruce with a shake of the head. 'That's what Dan would want us to do.'

It was true, reflected Steve. Markov had called each of them in turn a few days after they got back, explaining that he wanted to thank them personally for rescuing him from the ice, and suggesting a trip to the Nou Camp for the second leg of the game. Bruce had jumped at the plan. All the lads had their heads down over what had happened to Dan, and there was nothing like a jaunt, some football, and some drinks to lift men's spirits. A private jet had met them at Biggin Hill, flown them to Barcelona, and a pair of limousines had been waiting for them at the airport, taking them first to the luxurious Mandarin Oriental in the heart of the city, then on to the stadium.

Their spirits had certainly revived since they'd been here, reflected Steve as he winced at the blistering run one of the Spanish wingers was carving through the Chelsea defence before delivering an inch perfect cross that Chelsea's left back only just managed to head safely over the line for a corner. They'd been in bad shape when they got back from the Arctic. Thin, tired, and a man short. It was only ten days since then and some flesh was starting to return to their bones, and the tiredness was starting to ease. But Dan's injury had hit them all hard.

And no one more so than Nick.

The Welsh lad was standing by himself, with a bottle of

Spanish beer in his hands. There were a few girls in the executive box, part of Markov's retinue of hangers-on, and most of them were lookers, but he didn't seem to be able to talk to them. He wasn't even moaning about whether there was any Stella instead of the Spanish lager. He was just standing there, with a solemn, haunted look in his eye. He needs something to make him snap out of it, Steve reflected to himself. But what that might be, he had no idea.

'She was worth fighting for,' said Markov, standing next to Steve, pointing down to the front row.

'If you like rich blonde airheads,' said Maya sourly, a few inches away.

Steve caught her eye and grinned. 'She agreed to come along so I could meet the boy,' he said. 'I reckon there's more chance of our mate Kolodin walking out of the Arctic in one piece than the two of us getting back together again.'

Sam was sitting down at the front row, with Archie on her lap. Steve had called her a few days ago, on the number Kolodin had given him. The first few moments had been hard on the phone, but finally he'd persuaded her to come out and join the rest of the unit for the trip to Barcelona. She'd swapped a few jokes with the rest of the guys she'd been with in Africa a couple of years ago, then took Archie down to the front of the box where he could get a clear view of the match.

'Let me hold him for a bit,' said Steve, sitting down next to her.

Sam looked at him suspiciously. 'Think you know how?'

'Probably not,' said Steve with a shake of the head. 'But how hard can it be?'

Sam passed the boy across cautiously. He was a sturdy little fellow, just over one year old. He was wearing a blue romper suit, along with beige shorts and a black polo shirt. Steve reckoned he looked disturbingly like his own dad, but he wasn't about to mention that to Sam. She was prickly enough already, without making any remarks about family resemblances.

'My mum would love to meet you,' said Steve, looking down at the baby.

Archie just nodded happily, sat back on Steve's lap, and kept his eyes glued on the match. He felt warm and comforting, quite different from what Steve had expected. On the field, Chelsea were surging forward. Their captain was running on to a low cross and made a slight contact with his left boot but could only steer the ball wide for a goal kick.

'Sodding concentrate, fat boy,' yelled Steve.

Archie was chuckling and shaking his fist. 'Fa bo, fa bo,' he said.

'Not fabbo, mate, it was sodding rubbish. He missed a tap-in.'

'He's saying fat boy,' said Sam at his side. 'Although I would have hoped his earliest opinions would have had a bit more depth to them.'

'At least he likes the footie,' said Steve, wrapping his arms round the boy and rubbing his hands through his sandy-blond hair. 'And he knows which team he supports.'

'Actually, I think he's a Spurs supporter,' said Sam. 'My family always have been.'

'Ah, sodding hell,' muttered Steve. 'I can just about live with the poor little guy being called Archie. But supporting the bloody Yids . . .'

'I think they're having a domestic already,' said Ian, standing behind them.

'I'm the man to talk to, mate,' said David, swigging his beer, and patting Steve on the back. 'I know all the marriage guidance counsellors round our way. They reckon I'm a hopeless case, so they'd probably like someone new to talk to.'

Steve ignored him, looking back at Sam. 'He can be Spurs if he wants,' he said mildly. 'I might even take him up to the Lane occasionally, so long as they aren't playing our boys. All I want is to be able to see him once a week or so.'

'We'll see,' says Sam. 'If you behave yourself.'

'That'll be a miracle,' said Ian.

'He never has before,' said David.

'I might come up to the Lane with you,' said Nick, wandering across, a smile suddenly breaking out on to his face.

'Count me in for that jaunt, lads,' said Ollie, opening another beer. 'And when we're finished with that, we'll take him to the rugger. Get him used to some proper sport.'

'You see, what better influences could your boy have than a day out with Steve and Nick and Ollie?' chuckled Ian, looking down at Sam.

'Would you boys kindly mind sodding off?' growled Steve. 'I'm trying to make a good impression here.'

He lifted Archie up so that he could get a clearer view of the match. Chelsea's star playmaker had just kicked a magnificent through ball, and Luis Fessi was running on to it, muscling aside the Barcelona defender before smashing the ball decisively into the back of the net. Most of the stadium was silent, but the small group of travelling Chelsea fans were cheering wildly, and so were the boys in the executive box.

Archie shook his tiny fists in the air.

'He's a great kid,' said Steve with a broad grin. 'There's an

Austin Healey up in the garage I reckon he'd like.' He patted Archie on the head. 'It's yours already, mate. The best babe-mobile ever built . . .'

The first half ended, and Chelsea were a goal up on aggregate. Sam took Archie for a quick feed, and the rest of the guys retreated to the back of the box to refill their plates and their glasses. Markov had laid on a lavish spread. The table was groaning with plates of beef, whole hams and chickens, a steaming cauldron of paella, and as much beer, whisky and vodka as a man could drink in a month. Everyone was enjoying themselves, noted Steve with relief. Sam was softening up, Archie was a champ, and even Nick seemed to be getting back to his old self.

But Bruce was standing a few yards away from the rest of the group. His mobile was cupped to his ear, and he turned away from the rest of them for a few minutes.

'What's up?' said Ian, handing Bruce a beer when he rejoined them.

'Mike Royton,' Bruce replied crisply. He took a long hit on the beer. He had the look of a man who needed a drink.

'Royton?' said Ollie. 'Mad Mike?'

Bruce just nodded. All the men had heard of him. Mike Royton has been one of the most feared SAS soldiers of modern times. Twice decorated in the Falklands, he'd picked up more medals in the first Gulf War, and then become a legend among the mercenaries for his ferocity and discipline.

'What's he done?' asks David.

'He took a job up on the disputed border territory between Thailand and Cambodia and recruited some of the maddest, toughest bastards in the world for it. He's gone crazy, turned into a savage. The trouble is, we fixed him up with the job . . . If we don't sort him out, DEF is ruined.'

Everyone was silent.

'Enjoy the game, boys,' says Bruce, nodding towards the pitch. 'We'll talk about it later.'

'Be good to get into action,' said Nick. His face had suddenly brightened up.

And, as reluctant as Steve was to admit it, even to himself, a fight might be just what Nick needed.

The Weapons

The weapons, techniques, and military units described in this book are all accurate so far as possible.

Caracal Battalion: The Caracal Battalion is a mixed-sex combat unit in the legendarily ferocious Israeli Defence Forces. It is named after the Caracal, a type of small cat in which both sexes appear exactly the same. Women had always played an important role in the IDF, but they had largely been confined to non-combat roles, or else to intelligence work. The battalion was formed in 2000 to allow women to take a more active role in fighting. It was first assigned to patrol duties along the border between Israel and Egypt. Both men and women assigned to the Battalion are put through the same arduous physical training regimen at the Givati Brigade training base. The soldiers specialise in machine guns, advanced weaponry, grenades, and mortars. Both men and women are assigned to the Battalion for three years.

The 6th SS Mountain Division Nord: An elite unit of the Waffen SS, the 6th SS Mountain Division Nord was originally formed as the SS Kampfgruppe Nord, or SS Battle Group North, in 1941. It was created to specialise in mountain and cold-weather warfare, and was originally posted to defend the Norwegian border after the capitulation of that country to the Nazis. The Division was then committed to Operation Barbarrosa, the invasion of the Soviet Union. It spearheaded Operation Arctic Fox, in which German troops stormed through Finland, with the aim of capturing the key Soviet port of Murmansk. The port was not finally captured and the division suffered terrible casualties. It was then restaffed with high-quality Waffen SS soldiers, and although the whole division was never committed to the Arctic, individual patrols were tasked with pushing through the frozen wastelands of the Arctic Circle to fight Norwegian resistance forces, secure mineral supplies, and explore the possibility of a flanking attack on Russia from the north. By 1944, with Germany being pushed back along the Eastern Front, it was reassigned to the Western battlefields. The division suffered terrible losses to American forces in Trier and Moselle. It finally surrendered in Austria in May 1945.

AK-74: The AK-47 may be a far more famous assault rifle, but the AK-74 is a lot more modern. It was developed in the Soviet Union in the early 1970s, based on its legendary forerunner, and introduced into service in 1974 (Russian weapons are frequently named after their year of introduction – so the AK-47 came into service in 1947). The main difference to its predecessor was that it used a lower calibre round: 5.45x39mm bullets. The rifle first saw active service during the Soviet invasion of Afghanistan. When the Soviet Union introduced the rifle, it encouraged the other members of the Warsaw Pact to adopt it as well. It was manufactured in East Germany, Bulgaria and Romania, but has never been as widely copied as the AK-47.

Accuracy International Arctic Warfare rifle: The rifle is one of a family of bolt-action sniper rifles manufactured by the specialist British arms company Accuracy International. The Accuracy International PM, or Precision Marksman, was chosen by the British Army as a replacement for the Lee Enfield in the early 1980s. In the 1990s the Swedish Army commissioned an adapted version which was known as the Arctic Warfare. The rifle was reconfigured for use in extremely cold temperatures. It had a de-icing feature that allowed to it to operate at minus forty degrees centigrade, and it had an outsized trigger and magazine release that allowed it to be used by soldiers wearing mittens, vital in Arctic temperatures. The Arctic version of the weapon, which proved exceptionally durable and accurate, has since been adopted by many armies around the world, including the United States, Germany, Russia and Norway.

Yarygin PYa handgun: In the early 1980s, the Soviet Army started planning a replacement for the legendary Makarov PM, the handgun that had been the standard issue sidearm for Russian soldiers since the 1950s. The weapon eventually chosen was designed by Vladimir Yarygin, and, in accordance with Russian tradition, it was named after the man who conceived it. It is a sleek, functional semi-automatic pistol which fires a 9mm round from a 17-round magazine. It is made of metal although the handle is polymer, and it has a safety catch above the grip that can be released just as easily by soldiers who are either left- or right-handed. It came into full service in 2003, and is now the standard sidearm for all Russian soldiers and policemen, making it one of the most widely used handguns in the world.

StG 44 assault rifle: The Sturmgewehr 44, or the storm rifle of 1944, to give it its English name, is considered by military historians to be the first of the assault rifles that are now universally used by infantry troops around the world. Before the Second World War, most infantry units were armed with a mixture of bolt-action rifles and light machine guns. The problem was that the rifles were too large to be used in cramped conditions by mechanised forces, and the machine guns took too long to set up. What they needed, the German commanders realised, was a small, flexible weapon that could still achieve a rapid rate of fire – something between a traditional rifle and a machine gun. The result was the StG 44. Hitler was initially suspicious of the new weapon, but when he saw it in action on the Eastern Front he could see its effectiveness in the close quarters mobile combat that characterised WWII. He named it the Sturmgewehr, and almost half a million of the guns were manufactured and put into service before the war ended. The gun went on to inspire a more famous post-war generation of assault rifles, in particular the Russian AK-47 and the American M-16. The StG was literally a gun that reinvented the way that wars were fought.

MG 42 machine gun: The Maschinengewehr 42 was a simple, battlefield machine gun that entered service with the German army in 1942. The German MG 34 is widely considered the first of the modern battlefield machine guns. It was light, could be fed by a belt or a drum, and was carried into combat by infantry.

The MG 42 was a superior, updated version of that weapon. Its key characteristic was an incredibly intense burst of fire: 1,200 to 1,500 rounds a minute, depending on the barrel. It proved a lethal weapon, particularly on the Eastern Front where it was used to devastating effect on Russian cannon fodder thrown into its path by their commanders. By the end of the war, more than 400,000 of the machine guns had been manufactured. Like other Nazi weapons, the MG 42 provided the template for much of the post-war arms industry. Many of its design features were later incorporated into the American M-60 that was used from 1957 up until the present day, and was a key weapon in the Vietnam War, as well as the Belgium-manufactured FN MAG which was used by most of the NATO armies during the Cold War.

Model 24 Stielhandgranate: The Stielhandgranate was the standard-issue German hand grenade from the end of the First World War I until the end of the Second World War. It was first introduced in 1915, and was widely used to attack Allied trenches. Its distinctive design, with a wooden stick, with a metal warhead on top of it, set it apart from other grenades. The stick made it far easier to throw than British or French grenades of the same period. In the hands of a skilled soldier, the Stielhandgranate could be thrown thirty or forty yards, compared with ten to fifteen for a British grenade. But it also made it significantly more expensive to manufacture, and heavier to carry into battle. Cold weather could cause the grenade to fail, so a special powder was used for the fighting in Russia, along the Eastern Front and up in the Arctic. These grenades were marked with a K for *kalt*, or cold.

Flammenwerfer 35: The flame-thrower is one of the deadliest battlefield weapons ever invented. They were first used in the trench warfare of the First World War, but really came into their own during the Second World War. Both sides used them to clear trenches, and, in the street-by-street combat that characterised that conflict, particularly buildings, where snipers were often hiding. Its impact was as much physiological as physical: soldiers were terrified of being incinerated, or else just horribly injured, by a jet of liquid flame. The Flammenwerfer 35 was a standard-issue flame-thrower for German troops, produced from 1935 to 1945. It was a light, flexible weapon that could be operated by a soldier unaided. It weighed slightly under eight pounds, and consisted of a backpack to store the fuel, and a long nozzle to fire the flames through. It had a range of up to thirty metres, but could normally be fired twenty-five. Like all flame-throwers of the era, it was extremely dangerous to operate.

Walther PP: The Walther PP, and its derivatives, is one of the most durable handguns ever designed. It was first manufactured in 1929 by the German arms company Carl Walther and is still in production today, having been made under licence around the world (immediately after the Second World War, when the Allies suspended weapons manufacturing in Germany, it was made in France). A semi-automatic pistol, it owed its popularity to its extreme reliability, and the way its small size made it easy to conceal. It was issued to the German Army, the Luftwaffe, the police, and to senior Nazi Party officials. Ian Fleming chose the derivative Walther PPK as James Bond's standard sidearm for the James Bond novels, although the weapon doesn't make its first appearance until *Dr No*, the sixth book in the series. Because *Dr No* was the first of the Bond films, however, the gun featured in that story, and has since been seen in countless posters.

Now you can buy any of these other bestselling titles from your bookshop or *direct from the publisher.*

FREE P&P AND UK DELIVERY
(Overseas and Ireland £3.50 per book)

The Gods of Atlantis	David Gibbins	£6.99
The Legion	Simon Scarrow	£7.99
Buried Secrets	Joseph Finder	£6.99
Temple of the Gods	Andy McDermott	£6.99
Just Business	Geraint Anderson	£6.99
The Razor Gate	Sean Cregan	£6.99
The Blind Spy	Alex Dryden	£7.99

TO ORDER SIMPLY CALL THIS NUMBER

01235 400 414

or visit our website: www.headline.co.uk

Prices and availability subject to change without notice